r have been *momentarily* disappointed that Mandy ; lost myself, in sentimentality, the biggest part of hat I was alone and could avoid the questions that come as soon as Mandy looked at my face and saw anguish.

ırned about you, so
ıis, I turned to look at
ds anyway?" he added,

"Forget it," he said then changed the subje
anything tonight?" he asked. Was he serious? W
to 'do anything'?

"Uh...staying home sounds good. I really
explained. I w would get my mir

VIOLET'S GRAY

Adria Accomando

ISBN-13: 979-8-9887792-0-9

Cover design by: Art Painter
Library of Congress Control Number: 2018675309
Printed in the United States of America

For my mother who always told me I could be whatever I wanted and taught me to always keep moving forward.

PROLOGUE

As my mother's face materialized on the small screen in front of me, the ground beneath me disintegrated. My life was in free fall, and there was nothing I could do about it...

INTERVIEWER: Tell me about your experiences.

MANDY: Thirteen years ago, I was visited by extraterrestrials. I also think that they visited me before on several different occasions, but this particular visit stayed with me.

INTERVIEWER: Had you witnessed any of the mass sightings of the time?

MANDY: Oh yes, of course. The entire southern Hudson Valley had been a hotbed of sightings for years, and I'd been one of the first in Lake Hansen to report a sighting. Then, of course, there were the mass sightings of 2003, which so many people witnessed. Thousands saw what I saw.

INTERVIEWER: Didn't the government dismiss the sightings as experimental aircraft on a training mission?

MANDY: Of course they did. But, there were mass sightings all over the world over the course of six months. Are we really expected to believe their explanation?

INTERVIEWER: Did you report these *visitations* to anyone right away?

MANDY: No. I didn't remember what happened until a few years later when I was in therapy.

INTERVIEWER: So, what did you remember then?

MANDY: I remembered that on this particular occasion, small grays came into my bedroom and transported me to their ship. They performed some sort of medical procedure on me. I don't remember all of it, but I know that they immobilized me, so I couldn't feel what they were doing or resist.
INTERVIEWER: These 'grays' that you refer to, this is the common term for the small, humanoid figures with gray skin, small bodies, large, bulbous heads, and enormous black eyes?
MANDY: Yes.
INTERVIEWER: How were you 'transported', as you say, to their ship?
MANDY: I don't really know. It was some sort of teleportation, I assume. One moment we were in my room and then one of them picked me up. I was amazed by this because they were all so much smaller than I am and seemed almost frail. They had on metallic jumpsuits with a medallion in the center of the chest. The one who carried me pressed his and we were suddenly aboard the ship.

The interview went on like this for a few more minutes. The video would cut from Mandy's face to a cheap special effects scene of UFOs flying over a city, then to some overly-dramatized fictional footage of an alien hovering sinisterly over a woman who looked nothing like my mother. Then it would cut back to Mandy, sitting seriously in a comfortable armchair, emotionally reliving this supposed experience, then back to the dramatization. On the show there were also psychiatrists, professional skeptics, self-described experts on UFOs and extraterrestrials, and more people like my mother, *witnesses*.

That was five years ago. Life for me, Violet Arena, had instantaneously gone from bad to unbearably worse. "Socially awkward" is what the teachers and guidance counselors said. "Social Anxiety Disorder" is what the psychologist said. I never felt like either label really fit. They both implied that *I* was somehow to blame. That I could somehow *help* it. I was, and still am, isolated from the mainstream, this much is true, but while they viewed it as self-imposed isolation, I have always viewed it as rejection. And that rejection reached a fever pitch five years ago when my mother exposed us both. I had begged her not to do it when I found out.

***

Violet, you are never going to guess who is going to be on *The Truth* next month!" Mandy said excitedly.

"Who?" I asked, uninterested. *The Truth* was a really popular talk show that highlighted off-beat stories and featured people with *unique* interests. I had little interest in the show.

"ME!" Mandy shrieked. "I am...and my group! They are doing a feature on *the sightings* and UFOlogy groups and how they conduct research. Isn't that exciting?"

"WHAT!?" I screamed. "Are you insane!? Everybody watches that show Mandy! Everybody!"

"I know, Honey, that's kind of the point. We need the exposure to get more people interested and involved. There have been a lot of sightings again recently and our legitimacy is growing!" she added enthusiastically.

"Mandy...Mom..." I generally only called her "Mom" when I was trying to reason with her. "Couldn't the other people in your group do it? Why you?" I whined. Whining was not beneath me under these circumstances.

"Violet, this is very important to me. I am the founder of the group here. I can't just abandon them, Sweetheart."

"But...but, what about me? What about the problems this will cause *me*?" I asked.

"Violet, be reasonable. I *HAVE* to do this. Besides, if someone is that judgmental, why would you want to be friends with them anyway?" Mandy countered. I hated when she tried to get reasonable.

"No, Mom! No! I will not 'be reasonable.' I will be unreasonable and twelve. I am already a freak! I have no friends, besides Dexter!" I screeched. I was losing it now. I would stop at nothing to prevent this from happening.

"Oh, Violet, it's not my fault that you are so picky in choosing friends." She rolled her eyes. "No one is perfect. You take the good with the bad, and you just accept people for who they are." That was just like her, *friend to everyone*. She had no idea how difficult it was for me on a daily basis.

"Mom, please just promise me you will think about it. Please just try to see it from my point of view. Please," I pleaded, trying to sound calmer, hoping this approach would yield better results.

She let out the kind of sigh that said she thought I was being ridiculous, but she relented. "I promise I will *think* about it, okay?"

"Thank you," I said triumphantly, actually believing that my mother would never intentionally do anything that she knew would hurt me.

I was wrong.

The following month the feature aired. My mother was there, in full color, for the whole world, and more importantly, the entire population of Lake Hansen, NY, to see, with a caption that read "*Mandy Conrad: UFOlogy Group Founder*".

This was a betrayal, and it festered deep inside.

1

"You are so beautiful." I turned to see if I'd heard my best friend correctly.

"What did you just say?" I questioned accusingly

"I didn't say anything V," replied Dexter with a bewildered look.

I looked at his face, scrutinizing each line, and then decided that I believed him. I knew all too well that Dexter had *impure* thoughts about me. He was seventeen and his best friend—only friend—was a seventeen-year-old girl. But as a general rule, he kept these thoughts to himself. After all, we did live in the same house.

"Oh...forget it," I said aloud. "*I guess I'm just hearing things AGAIN,*" I thought to myself. This was not the first time this had happened since my senior year began. From time to time, I would hear these random phrases that sounded as if someone were saying them directly into my ear. Like it did every time, hearing the voice made me feel confused and uneasy. I generally chose to ignore it because of what acknowledging it might mean. I had enough deficits. I didn't need to add *insane* to the list.

Though I knew the words absolutely *could not have,* and *would not have* come from any one of the other students in the hall, I still instinctively moved my eyes back and forth, checking the periphery. I saw Stephanie Baker to my far left, laughing with her friends and tossing her bouncy bob around for the boys that flocked to her. I wondered how someone so vicious and mean could have so many friends. I was always led to believe, "what goes around comes around," but I decided that this belief was either completely false, made up by someone who had been ostracized as much as I have been, or it was something that would take a very long time—like an entire lifetime or several lifetimes—to come about...too long for my liking.

To my left, just past my only friend, was Luca Verone. I silently wished it had been him who had uttered those words. Maybe that's why I had imagined I heard them at all. Since he'd transferred in at the start of junior year, I had imagined many times that he would tell me I was beautiful, wished he'd say *anything* to me.

Well, that's not entirely true because if he had ever spoken to me at all, I probably would have just assumed it was a joke or a trick meant to embarrass me, like that time in eighth grade when Chris Fischer invited me to the winter dance. I was so excited that I made Mandy take me out that day to buy a dress and shoes. Then, the next day there was the teasing and the notes passed, not to mention the picture taped to my desk of a boy in a tuxedo being eaten by some alien-looking creature in a prom dress. So, of course, if Luca had ever spoken to me, I probably would have just ignored him.

As the bell rang, I shrugged off the voice and my Luca fantasies. Dwelling on either could bring no good. Fantasies give people false hope, and I had given up on hope a long time ago. Dexter and I scrambled to get our books out of our lockers and get to class. The last thing I wanted to do was be late...it wasn't worth the attention. "See you later," I mumbled to Dexter as I set off in the opposite direction.

"Later," he replied as he slowly strode away toward the gym.

As usual, my day drifted along anticlimactically. English was boring. American History couldn't hold my attention either, and math was excruciating. Then it was time for biology, a class I was remotely interested in from time to time.

I sat attentively, but invisibly, as an eager Mr. Collins spoke about a brief period in history when the earth went from being inhabited by apelike creatures, or primitive *cave people,* to being inhabited by a more advanced species, more closely related to modern-day humans. He explained several theories from the scientific community, and then added, with a slight grin and look of amusement, "Some people even believe that *aliens* may have interfered with human evolution, creating more evolved creatures." Muffled, but detectable giggles arose, and I knew why. "Perhaps we'll never know..." Mr. Collins trailed off, still chuckling softly to himself, swinging his head slowly from side to side as people do when they've witnessed something completely preposterous. I cringed in my seat and immediately tuned him out. How could my teacher betray me like this? Maybe he didn't know the story...though that was unlikely.

Now the no-longer-muffled snickers echoed in my brain, even with my head buried in my sweatshirt. *"Please let this class end!"* I thought, humiliation, coupled with the familiar anger toward my mother, welling up inside. Why did she have to be so vocal about her beliefs? Why did she have to make her obsession known to the world? The obsession that drove my father away. The obsession that gave her the *coveted* title of "eccentric," a label that ensured no kid would ever be able to spend time at my house and that I would always be a loner.

I could feel the eyes of my classmates on my back, especially those who knew the specifics of my mother's obsession, like Stephanie Baker and her friends. For years I had thought of Stephanie Baker as my nemesis. I didn't know if that was the way she thought of me, but I knew she didn't like me, that much was blatantly obvious. I thought it morosely ironic that we had once been good friends, back in elementary school. Obviously, things changed.

In fact, she was the most vicious since my mom did the interview, and had never let up even after five years. But I knew it didn't matter who knew the full story and who didn't; in high school, once you were labeled a freak, it stuck. This was the precise reason why I had spent most of my time at Lake Hansen High attempting to blend in—not fit in—but *blend* in, like camouflage—fade into the background—not attract any attention.

Mercifully, class ended shortly after Mr. Collins's inadvertent attack. Closing in on myself, head hung, eyes looking down, I ambled quickly out the door the second the bell chimed. I used my thick brown hair as a curtain—a shield between me and the rest of the world—as I walked to the art room.

I usually looked forward to art class, but I was a little disappointed when I walked in and the first thing I saw in the front of the room was an antique TV/DVD combo with the big screen lit up. A video. *"Great."* And a really, really old video. *"Even better."* I sat and rested my head on my folded arms, waiting for Mrs. Charmin's substitute to start the movie. It was called *Picasso's Vision*, and it actually wasn't terrible. Picasso was my favorite artist, so I actually didn't mind hearing, once again, how he had started out as a more traditional artist, but then, as he became more confident and was influenced by other artists of the time, gradually changed his style to the twisted, disfigured images and severe lines for which he's so well-known.

I liked how Picasso was able to find his own way, make a name for himself. I had my own Picasso-like dream of one day getting as far away from Lake Hansen as possible, and starting my own life where no one knew me, or my mother's story, and I was free. I might be a famous artist like Picasso, or I might work in a bookstore...it didn't really matter, as long as I could just be myself. And with graduation a few months away, my fantasy was closer to being a reality, even if it only meant the art program at the local college an hour away.

Just as I was immersing myself into my happy little daydream, Ibecame aware of a folded piece of notebook paper that had found its way directly in front of me. In the dim light of the classroom, I could see "Violet" scrawled carelessly on one side, so I knew it was intended for me. *"This can't be good,"* I thought. Whoever had spent the time to create whatever awaited me inside that folded paper, would get some sort of twisted satisfaction whether I opened it or not. The creator of it and I both knew that the mere act of passing it to me was an attempt to humiliate me. No one passed notes to Violet Arena. No one. Curiosity got the best of me, so while trying to stay hidden behind my hair, I slowly unfolded the paper. I didn't look around, though I knew whoever had passed it was watching my every move, probably elbowing his or her table mate and gesturing in my direction. I wouldn't dare look to confirm my suspicion.

Once unfolded, the paper revealed its ridiculous contents: a crudely drawn picture of what is commonly accepted as an alien: big head, large black eyes, two slits for a nose, one thin line for the mouth. Above the picture, in the same sloppy handwriting, were the words, "Self-Portrait." Just before the stinging tears began to build, a little piece of me wanted to laugh. Had it not been directed at me, it may have been funny. Juvenile, sure. But funny. However, it *was* directed at me. It was *always* directed at me. So, even after years and years of this kind of harassment, the tears still threatened to come. I pressed my forehead into my folded arms, but did not let a single one escape.

After allowing myself a minute to sulk, I composed myself, and picked my head up slightly, careful that my hair still strategically covered my face on both sides. I was grateful for the still-dark room. I didn't want my attackers to feel the satisfaction of knowing they'd gotten to me any more than usual, especially not in front of Luca, who was sitting a few seats away. Shortly after the movie ended, the lights went on, and I silently wished that if I sat completely still, I'd be invisible.

I was glad I sat close to the door so that the moment the bell rang, I came to life, slid from the stool, and burst through the door, making my second quick get-a-way of the day. As I left, I could swear I heard someone call after me, quite loudly, *You're better than them!* I knew it had to be my imagination because no one would ever stand up for me like that except for Dexter, and he wasn't in my art class.

As quickly as possible, almost running for the exit like the school was on fire, I fled. I didn't stop at my locker, and I didn't wait for Dexter. I didn't want to talk to anyone at all, not even the only person who'd ever really understood me. When I pushed through the exit door, I felt relief flood through me. I could leave Lake Hansen High School behind for at least forty-eight hours, and since my mother had to work all weekend—night shift— I could have space without her constant intrusions on my personal life.

It always started the same way: she would casually stride into the living room where I was relaxing—watching TV, listening to music, scrolling social media. She'd act like she was looking for something or watering the plants when she'd suddenly sigh too loudly and say something like, "So V, are you doing anything fun this weekend? Any big plans?"

I hated this game—and it was a *game*. My mother knew what the answer would be. She just wanted to hear me vocalize the word, "No," so that she could cheerfully berate me for being such a loner and explain to me how important it was to have friends and a social life. What she always failed to realize, and what I never had the heart to explain to her, was that it was mostly her fault that I only had one friend and was considered a freak at school.

Mandy would never understand. She too was a sort of outcast. But where I turned away from the world, she found a different path. She almost exclusively associated with other outcasts, namely her UFOlogy group and her *Fourth Kind* support group for people who believed they had been abducted or visited by aliens. And, no matter how bizarre she seemed to others, Mandy was completely at ease in her own skin. She accepted herself without condition, and in some small way, I envied, even resented, her for it.

Despite my mother's obvious flaws and eccentricities, I loved her, even if I didn't call her, "Mom." The story goes that I used to mimic my father by calling my mother, "Mandy," and it just stuck. After that it just always seemed more natural to call her by her name. She really was a good mother, a normal mother in *most* ways. She was loving, supportive of my interests, and as understanding a mother as any teenage girl could hope for. Sometimes I felt guilty for not having the typical teen problems, like self-image and boys, that Mandy was all too eager to help with. Well, I had those problems, but they had always seemed one-sided, and unworthy of discussion.

And Mandy couldn't help her nagging. She was a nurturer through and through. She was a nurse in the psych ward at Morgan Memorial Hospital. She was compassionate and kind and had a gift for working with the mentally ill. Of course, I would never tell her that. Most days I was usually pleasant enough to her, but there was anger and resentment just under the surface that often colored my words and thoughts. It was easier to give myself over to the bitterness I felt every time someone taunts me, and I was reminded of her obsession with UFOs and extraterrestrials.

It was her constant insistence that eighteen years ago, a little less than a year before I was born, she was visited by extraterrestrials. This all came to light when I was almost two years old, too young to remember, but not too young to suffer the consequences.

Apparently Mandy suffered debilitating post-partum depression and sought counseling when I was an infant. Somehow, through her therapy, which included a form of self-hypnosis for relaxation, she had supposedly *unlocked* memories of her apparent *visitation*. She snapped out of her depression almost instantaneously upon these realizations, and thus began her sometimes-manic quest to "uncover the truth," as she liked to say.

By the time I was three, my father, Jorge, had had enough. I vaguely remember this part. He pleaded with Mandy to just let it go, suggesting she take medication. This did not go over well, and the split was inevitable. Apparently, I chose my mother. And though my father questioned his wife's beliefs and newfound obsession, and could not continue to live with her, he knew her love for me was second to none, and taking me away from her would be the ultimate act of cruelty. I assume he still loved Mandy and hoped that his leaving would force her to leave the UFOs behind.

At first, he didn't go far. He rented an apartment nearby and would come over nearly every day. He tried very hard...for a while. But by the time I was four or five, he realized the aliens weren't going anywhere, and they'd become more important than him, than their marriage. Mandy had joined groups, gotten new friends who shared her enthusiasm, and seemed to have moved on. That's when he knew it was time to make a new start.

I didn't see my father for a while. He promised that once he was resettled somewhere, and stable, he would try to get me more often. *Somewhere* was Sacramento, California. And, by the time he was "resettled and stable," I was eleven and he was teaching history at a university and engaged to Claire, a very *normal* professor of British Literature with one young son of her own, Nate. I visited a few times in the beginning, and he and Claire came to New York to visit me. We'd all go out, they'd give me anything and everything, trying to force a bond to form between me and Claire and between me and Nate. But, he was younger than I was, and practically a stranger. It was awkward and unpleasant. I was either rude or withdrawn, making the visits anything but *quality family time*. Besides, I saw Claire as a thief who'd stolen my father and made Mandy seem even more bizarre by comparison. So the *happy family* thing didn't really work out.

Year after year, I talked to my father less and less until there was almost no contact, save for a visit every couple of years, a few cards each year for birthdays and holidays, emails every so often, and an occasional message on the social media site we both belonged to.

It's not that I don't love my father. I do very much. He is an interesting guy, and I know I am a lot like him. He too is shy, introspective and reserved, though not a recluse like me.

I'm built like him too, not tall, but definitely not short, slender but not slight like Mandy. I also have his thick, wavy brown hair, nothing like the silky, straight, dirty-blond mane of my mother. Unlike my pale skin, which is more like Mandy's than any other physical part of me, my dad's is tanned, reflecting the Mexican heritage of his father's family.

In retrospect, the split between my parents might have happened even if ET hadn't come between them. In so many ways, they had always been opposites. I think that like many "opposites attract" stories, they had fallen for the qualities in each other that they didn't possess themselves. While this might have been their initial attraction, it was also their fatal flaw. I have no real experience with love myself, but I imagine that two people should have *some* differences, but that similarities are necessary to sustain a meaningful relationship. So, I figured, aliens or no aliens, their marriage probably would have ended eventually anyway.

2

I was still thinking of my parents as I fumbled to get my house key from the front pocket of my backpack. Thinking of my mom and my dad *almost* made me feel disappointed that Mandy had already left for work. As often as she could, my mother went in early to take advantage of overtime pay. "It's never too early to start saving up for the holidays...or snow tires," she'd say. She always put me first... and Dexter, and Grandma, and her friends...

When I got into the house, the first thing I noticed was a note Mandy left on the little table by the front door:

> "V-
> Check your phone.
> Love,
> Mandy"

Mandy loves technology, and the irony of this situation did not escape me: Mandy wrote a note to tell me to read a text.

I had already looked at my phone on the way home and had no notifications, but now, the little box in the upper left corner told me I had a few. This was nothing new. My phone had been acting up on and off for weeks. I clicked the message box from Mandy:

> "Dinner in fridge. Dexter called. Call him. He seemed a little weird. Do you need to talk? If you are up when I get home, we'll have breakfast together. Try to have fun this weekend. I love you!"

Though I may have been *momentarily* disappointed that Mandy was gone, having lost myself, in sentimentality, the biggest part of me was relieved that I was alone and could avoid the questions that would inevitably come as soon as Mandy looked at my face and saw the remnants of the afternoon's anguish.

She read me so well, and I HATED it. She would try to get the details from me, and I would hold back as much as possible, conveniently leaving out the "alien" parts because I only used this against her when I was having an out-of-control tantrum (rare these days). Since I was one of the resident freak shows at Lake Hansen High, I learned a good deal of self-control and was a master at stifling my emotions.

When I was younger, these tantrums were intense releases of anger and resentment that usually ended with both me and Mandy in tears, and Mandy apologizing for embarrassing me, but explaining how she could not lie about who she is, and me telling her it was my problem for not being able to just accept her for who she is, and not to worry because I'd get over it. The worst, but also the last, tantrum had come after the talk show appearance.

I was twelve years old and already quite introverted, though I wasn't completely without a social life...yet. There were a couple of kids who still talked to me in school, whose parents hadn't heard about my mother's interests. However, Mandy's decision to do the interview put the final nail in the coffin of my social life. From that point forward, my armor grew thicker and thicker each year, creating a comfortable barrier between me and the rest of the world—a world that I believed didn't want me to be a part of it anyway.

The buzzing of my phone broke into my thoughts. There were only a few people who ever called me, and only two who called regularly: my mother and Dexter. Occasionally I'd get a call from my father, but it was highly unlikely. Since my mother was at work, I didn't even have to look at the phone to know who it was.

I seriously considered not answering it, but that would have just brought him crashing through the door in no time.

"Hey Dex," I said as casually as I could. I was already reclined on the couch, feet up, eyes closed.

"V—Why didn't you wait for me? Luca Verone said you left art class really upset. Are you okay?" Was it possible for him to sound both irritated and concerned at the same time? Dexter was very intense, so it definitely was. But I couldn't really focus on anything else...did he say Luca Verone? *"Luca Verone is aware of my existence?"* I asked myself in disbelief.

"V, are you there?" Dexter broke into my thoughts.

"Oh, yeah. I'm here. Sorry."

"So, are you okay?" he asked, sounding a little more worried than angry now.

"I'm fine," I lied. "I just had, and still have, a headache." I hoped this would keep him from pushing the issue and coming home right away. I really wanted to be alone more than anything. Especially now that I had this new piece of information involving Luca to chew on.

"Well, take some aspirin. Suck it up—I'll be there in twenty. I'm just leaving the library now," he said matter-of-factly.

"Dex...maybe you could wait a while. I really want to close my eyes," I said, tense with frustration at not being able to get my point across. Either I needed to work on my subtlety or Dexter was too dense to take a hint.

"You sleep. I'll come home—make dinner. Mandy home?" I decided it was option two.

"No, it's Friday, she went in early. I guess I'll see you in a little while," I sighed, defeated.

"See ya!" Dexter answered. I detected triumph in his voice.

As usual, my initial annoyance turned to guilt. He was, after all, my best friend. And when I looked at my phone again, I saw that he'd texted me three times already. The guilt intensified until

I decided to turn my lie into a partial truth and take a short nap. I knew Dexter would be there when I woke up. I closed my eyes, and not realizing just how mentally exhausting the day had been, drifted off easily.

I wasn't sure how long I'd been asleep, but I knew it was a while —at least a couple of hours— because the daylight was just about gone, and the light from the TV glowed in the otherwise darkening room. Groggily, I sat up and rubbed my eyes. I nearly jumped off the couch when I opened my eyes to Dexter, a few feet away, eating a plate of something and watching TV without sound. He turned as I sat up.

"Hey V. Man, you were OUT! I mean I made a hell of a lot of noise in the kitchen, and you didn't even move," he mused.

"You didn't break the kitchen did you? Mandy's still mad about the bathroom window," I mumbled sourly, still wiping the sleep from my eyes.

"Nah, I just dropped a pan on the floor... and then a glass..." He smiled timidly. "And besides, the bathroom window was so NOT my fault—I thought it was unlocked. Anyway, your food is in the microwave—spaghetti. Want me to heat it up for you?" Dexter's near-gushing generosity, while appreciated, was a bit overwhelming at this point.

"No thanks...I'm good for now, a little groggy. I—I'm gonna get up and move around, get some caffeine. Want anything?" I tried to return the generosity.

"Iced tea," he replied, and turned his attention back to the television.

But before I could get up and out of the room, Dexter got out the question he'd obviously been dying to ask all afternoon, "So what happened today in art. I don't buy the headache thing."

"UGGGHHH!" I screamed internally. I rolled my eyes with my back still turned to him. *"Can't he just humor me and give me a break?"* I thought to myself. "Dex, I don't want to talk about it,

okay?" I said harshly.

"Okay. It's just... Luca seemed...concerned about you, so naturally I would be too," he pressed. At this, I turned to look at him. "When did you and Luca become friends anyway?" he added, something new in his voice...jealousy?

"Um, we're not. Not that I'm aware of," I replied, confused, but also a little curious. I took a step toward Dexter. "You said Luca was concerned? About me? Are you sure?" I had to know.

"Yeah, I was surprised too...no offense," he said

"None taken."

"He came to my locker at the end of the day while I was *waiting for you*, and asked me if I'd seen you, and if you were okay," Dexter explained, obviously still annoyed at having been left behind.

Without commenting, I rolled my eyes, slowly turned, and dragged myself to the kitchen. Dexter started to say something but must have changed his mind because I heard the TV blaring by the time I was in the kitchen standing in front of the refrigerator. Once in there, I began to ponder what Dexter told me about Luca. I rarely allowed myself to even entertain the idea of a crush—it seemed pointless—no one would ever be interested in me. I didn't want to get caught up in some romantic fantasy that would always remain just that—a fantasy. But since Dexter had brought it up... *"Why in the hell would Luca Verone ask about* me?"

Luca was a quiet kid who, like me, was a loner. I had seen him speak to others occasionally, some skater kids at school, maybe they were even his friends, but most of the time, he was alone. The difference was that he was not socially ostracized. I'd never once known him to have been teased, taunted, or tormented. In fact, to me, he always seemed very cool and at ease with himself, like he had chosen this solo lifestyle. And, he had never teased me or even cracked a smile when others did. He seemed...*nice*, and therefore, he stood out.

He stood out for other reasons too. He had thick, dark, curly hair that hung over his eyebrows, skimming the tops of his eyes. His skin was sort of olive-tan, but with an almost ashen overtone, not unlike mine. His eyes were also like mine, almost black, like charcoal, though his were big and round and mine are exactly the shape of almonds. His features were neither too soft, nor too angular, just...pleasant. Yes, I had often thought about Luca Verone, but I was surprised that as I thought about him at that moment, my stomach fluttered a bit.

Standing in the kitchen, I decided I was hungry. Spaghetti didn't sound appetizing, but cereal did. Because my mind was now focused on Luca, I barely paid attention to what I was doing. But the act of making a bowl of cereal was as automatic as breathing. I absentmindedly rummaged through the small pantry closet until I found the box I was looking for. I got a bowl from the cabinet and opened the drawer to get a spoon when something bizarre happened—the spoon seemed to *jump* into my hand. That's the only way to explain it. I never reached for it, yet there it was, in my hand! I dropped it, didn't bother shutting the drawer, and abruptly left the kitchen. I found myself back in the living room in a bewildered daze.

Dexter must have seen me staring blankly, mouth hanging open dumbly.

"What's with you? You okay?" he asked.

I blinked and snapped back, realizing that there was *no way* I could ever even begin to explain something to Dexter that I wasn't even sure had really happened. So, I shook it off.

"Oh, nothing. I'm...I'm fine," I stuttered. "I just...zoned out... headache. I told you. I guess I'm not thirsty after all," I lied, hoping he couldn't see through me.

"Okay whatever," he said, then mumbled very quietly, "*I* was." I had forgotten his iced tea.

"Uh...sorry. I'll get your iced tea," I said as I turned to go back to the kitchen.

"Forget it," he said then changed the subject, "You wanna do anything tonight?" he asked. Was he serious? When did I ever want to 'do anything'?

"Uh...staying home sounds good. I really want to paint," I explained. I was hoping that would get my mind off of the strange *occurrence* that I had been trying, unsuccessfully, to shrug off since it happened. This got me thinking about everything that had been happening to me. *"Maybe I really am going crazy,"* was all I could think. The voice...the spoon...it all seemed too coincidental. Maybe it was inevitable.

Dexter eyed me suspiciously. I suddenly realized how I must look to him, so I decided I'd better put on a new face or the probing questions would ensue. It wouldn't be much different than being cross-examined by Mandy.

It was difficult to keep anything from him. We were so close. We'd been nearly inseparable since we were seven years old and *found* each other in second grade. Dexter never seemed to care about my social awkwardness or my crazy mother. In fact, he loved Mandy as if she were his own mother. His mother had committed suicide when Dexter was four. Mandy certainly treated Dexter better than his father, who was a tangled mess of alcoholism, drug addiction, and mental illness, which unfortunately left little time for child-rearing. So, once Dexter and I became friends, Mandy had encouraged Dexter to spend as much time as necessary with her and me. Sometimes that meant days or even weeks at a time, depending on whether or not his dad was taking his meds or *visiting* the psych ward. Eventually, my mother got legal guardianship of him after his dad left him in the parking lot of a liquor store in the middle of the night.

Dexter went on family vacations with us and attended family functions and holiday meals. He was, for all intents and purposes, a member of the family. And he was always grateful for his status. So, he never fully understood why I had such a problem with

Mandy. But, he respected my opinions, usually gave me space when I needed it, and just let me be myself. He also stood up for me and tried to protect me. However, like a good friend, he called me on my bad moods, harsh judgment of my mother, and even harsher judgment of myself. He was like the best friend and the best brother all in one.

Unfortunately, he wasn't my brother, and things had been changing between us. Since he had hit puberty a few years earlier, I had become increasingly aware of the fact that Dexter's *brotherly love* might be changing into something different, something that made me very uncomfortable. When we were fourteen, he had tried exactly once to act on his feelings, attempting an awkward kiss that left me angry and confused, and left him with a fat lip, painful regret, and burning humiliation, even though I simply pretended it never happened. I thought that seemed like the best thing for everyone involved.

He was hardly at home for nearly a week afterward, staying at the library until it closed each night and avoiding me as much as possible, forcing me to give Mandy an edited version of events. This is what caused Mandy to set up the "ground rules" for Dexter: he could only go into my room when Mandy was home, and he had to sleep on the couch until Mandy could figure out something else, not on my floor, or a cot in my room, where he had often slept before.

Shortly after, Mandy had a carpenter friend of hers close in our tiny dining room for him. To my relief, Dexter loved and respected Mandy too much and valued his family-member status too much to ever dream of breaking one of these rules. I just convinced myself that Dexter had just *confused* his feelings. I chalked it up to hormones and the fact that I was really the only girl of his age that he had any contact with. But in truth, I knew deep down that his feelings might be something different...something more. I kept this idea buried as far down in my brain as I possibly could. However, that night when he brought up Luca Verone, I knew I wasn't wrong when I thought I detected jealousy in his voice.

But as I stood there looking at Dexter, his unwavering loyalty made me feel so guilty for hiding anything from him. I briefly contemplated being honest with him. But, I love Dexter, and honesty might bring pain. I remembered how difficult it had been for him to deal with his father's mental illness, and I didn't want him to possibly have to deal with it in his surrogate family as well. I figured I would let him live in ignorance as long as I could, or at least until I knew for sure what was going on.

I decided to dedicate the night to hanging out with Dexter. I could paint any time. So, we played a few video games, watched television, and talked. Though Dexter tried to bring up questions about what may or may not have happened at school that day and about Luca, I was careful to steer the conversation away from any topic that could even hint at my *problems.*

When I went to bed, and was finally alone in my room, I thought about everything that was happening to me, Luca Verone, and Dexter's potential feelings for me. An all-encompassing fear gripped me every time I thought of the spoon...I was at a loss to even begin to understand why I was hearing a voice and imagining moving objects. I tried to convince myself that it was just a result of stress and fear over my probable insanity coupled with the rough day I had at school. But try as I might, I couldn't get it out of my head, nor could I wrap my head around it. My anxiety kept me awake for a long time. And when I did finally sleep, it was restless, so that I awoke on Saturday morning feeling tired and irritable.

Thankfully, the remainder of the weekend passed uneventfully. I read a little and did some homework, but mostly, I painted—my own form of therapy. Since Mandy and Dexter both noticed that I was distracted and edgy, it was easier for me to stay away from them as much as I could. I painted furiously, trying to deal with everything the best way I knew how, but even that didn't help much.

After a quiet Sunday dinner with Mandy and Dexter and a little more painting, I said my goodnights and went to bed. I dreaded Monday morning and whatever else was in store for me.

3

The week didn't start off too badly. I hadn't had another spoon episode, Mr. Collins had moved on to another aspect of human evolution, and we were watching *Pride and Prejudice* in English after having read the book. In art, there were a few giggles when I entered class, but nothing I couldn't handle. Then on Wednesday... things fell apart.

It started first thing in the morning. As Dexter and I approached the hall leading to our lockers, I swore I saw that mine had something on it...a piece of paper, maybe. I was at the far end of the hall when I first noticed it. I pulled out Dexter's earbud. "Dex, is something on my locker?" I whispered, craning my neck to see down the hall.

He squinted, "I can't even see your locker from here, Violet...you're imagining things," he said, shaking his head.

I looked again and I was sure I could clearly see our bank of lockers with something obviously attached to mine. "No, there's something there," I said, and I stopped us both. He squinted again.

"Violet, what the hell? I can barely make out the lockers...how can you see them?" he questioned, now looking at me strangely. "You've been acting weird since this weekend...are you okay?" He definitely looked concerned now, and I did *not* want to invite any questions. So, I decided that whether I could see the lockers or not (I definitely could), I had to drop it. The alternative was too much to even think about.

"I'm fine...I just...have a lot on my mind, that's all." I smiled tightly. We continued down the hall. Dexter was listening to music again, and I kept an eye on my locker. As we got closer, I could definitely see something stuck to the front of it. Then, the most bizarre thing of all happened—I saw Luca Verone move quickly past my locker, pausing for a fraction of a second in front of it, and when he was gone, the locker was clear.

Now I was sure I had imagined all of it...everything, from seeing the locker to thinking there was something on it, to Luca stopping in front of it. Of course I could not see a piece of paper on a locker that far away, and why would Luca ever remove such a paper if it had existed at all? What I had assumed to be the gradual onset of inevitable insanity seemed to be speeding up exponentially.

When we arrived at our lockers, I saw mine, free of any adornments, just as I had known it would be. Dexter didn't miss the opportunity to correct my error. "See, just a locker!" he said, mocking me. I shrugged and rolled my eyes. "You gotta lighten up, V—you are TENSE!" he observed. However, when I looked more closely, I saw a tiny piece of torn tape. Something *had* been taped to my locker, and Luca *had* removed it. But why? I decided Dexter didn't need to know this detail. It took every bit of strength I had not to glance at Luca.

"Yeah, whatever," I mumbled to Dexter. "See you later," I said, already walking to my class, not even going to my locker at all.

I was uneasy all through my morning classes. I couldn't focus on anything. My mind wandered through every detail, every time I had heard the voice, the spoon, my locker...I just kept trying to fit it all together, but it was like trying to assemble a puzzle that I'd lost the box to, and thus had no clue what the finished picture should be. I imagined myself, a few years in the future, neurotic and lonely, living in squalor, unable to do anything, not even paint, my mind a shell of itself. Maybe I'd even be in the psych ward where Mandy worked...lost inside myself.

This image frightened me most because of what I knew I'd be giving up...my plans, my dreams of escaping Lake Hansen, of becoming an artist, of being myself. And I saw how easily it could all disappear. I wouldn't even know it was happening. I knew all the horror stories from Mandy about the people who were brought in with no idea of what was real and what was a creation of their mind. People who had once been vibrant and healthy, now crippled by their own minds.

I was in biology when anxiety overtook me. I had to get out of there. I *never* asked to go anywhere, not even to the bathroom. In fact, I spoke as little as was *absolutely* necessary in my classes. Most teachers had stopped calling on me a long time ago, probably out of pity. But this was an emergency. My hand shot up, and when Mr. Collins called on me, the surprise in his voice unmistakable, "Violet?" Every head in the room turned my way, but I didn't care, I couldn't care.

"I don't feel well, can I please go..." I trailed off. I didn't give a destination, but I think either the desperation in my voice, or the fact that I was speaking at all, caused him to miss that, so he nodded, and I grabbed my bag and bolted for the door. I walked quickly to the nearest bathroom, praying that it would be empty.

I bounded through the door, moving with such force that the hinges creaked and groaned while the door itself ricocheted loudly against the wall. I was relieved to find myself alone. A whirlwind of emotion, with tears streaming down my face, I stopped in the middle of the bathroom. I was angry at myself for being weak and overcome by paranoia, but I was also frightened by what was happening to me. I wasn't thinking clearly. And as my emotions rose to a crescendo, something happened to stop them dead in their tracks.

In perfect synchronization, every door on every stall flew open, slamming against the wall of the stall next to it. The sound was deafening and sobering. Though I knew I could not have imagined it happening, I was dumbfounded as to what it might mean. I knew someone could come in at any time, so I locked myself in a stall, sat down with my head in my hands, and tried very hard to calm down. It was a difficult task, but I took several deep breaths, focusing on the sound of the air entering and exiting my lungs, and the rising and falling of my chest. After a few minutes, it began to work. I opened my eyes and sat up straighter. My emotions had ebbed for the time being, and I felt stable enough to stand.

I exited the stall and walked over to the bay of sinks. Above each sink was a piece of highly polished metal that was supposed to be used as a mirror, since apparently high school students could not be trusted with real glass. But these metal slabs produced inaccurate, disfigured images that could not be relied upon. I splashed cold water on my face and looked up. The image I saw looking back at me was startling. Reflected in this mirror was a large head, warped around the eyes, with an elongated neck and torso, completely out of proportion. I shuddered and looked away as the panic began to rise back into my chest.

Reaching into my bag, I grabbed my phone to check the time. In less than three minutes the bell would ring and the bathroom would be overrun by girls primping and chattering. I had to leave immediately. I knew I was not going to be able to endure art class. There were a few too many kids from my biology class in there to risk it. I glanced at the ghastly image in the metal one last time to be sure I could escape the bathroom without attracting attention. The red blotches on my face had faded, but my eyes were still bloodshot. No matter. My hair would shield me. Besides, I rarely looked up long enough for anyone to see my eyes. I decided to sneak out and make a dash for the bike rack. A few minutes after dismissal, Dexter would realize I left, see my bike gone, and head home.

I, on the other hand, would have to find somewhere to hide until school was over since Mandy would be home and probably awake. I decided to ride through the woods and then to Nature Park where I could stay hidden for a couple of hours. I quickly threw my bag over my shoulder and peeled the door open slowly, looking around for signs of other students in the hallway. I saw a boy walking in the opposite direction, but aside from him, the hall was clear. I sneaked out, almost tip-toeing like an art thief in mid-heist. I'm sure I looked ridiculous.

I finally settled into a normal pace and then sped up as I got closer to the exit. Just as I turned the corner to freedom, I heard my name. For a millisecond I thought maybe it was the voice again, it sounded so familiar. But then I heard it again, "Violet?" I turned and looked down the opposite hall and saw Luca Verone standing a few yards from me, looking at me expectantly. I stopped, unable to think or move.

He started to come toward me slowly. He probably would have made it to me if my momentary paralysis hadn't been cured by the bell ringing. Before I could comprehend what was happening, the hall between us filled with students. Instead of waiting to find out what he could have possibly wanted from me, I turned and rushed through the exit. I got away from the building as quickly as I could. Even as I fled, I felt an incomprehensible and inexplicable sensation, like Luca was *with* me. I imagined that I could somehow feel his presence. It wasn't eerie, like the feeling of being watched, but more intense, almost palpable. And oddly, it was...comforting.

When I was a safe distance away, I turned to look back at the exit door. There he was, leaning against the glass, looking at me again. I backed away then turned, still unable to shake the strange feeling. As I disappeared around the gym and neared the bike rack, I heard the voice, *"You're not alone."* I blocked it out. What I did know was that this time when I heard the voice, it was accompanied by some weird blue shimmery light that seemed to be behind my eyes, *in my brain*. Insanity was coming quickly.

When I reached my bike, I hopped on and pedaled furiously, my mind a jumbled mess of thoughts and emotions, not least of which was confusion over how, if at all, Luca Verone fit into this crazy puzzle my life had become. I stealthily got off the school grounds by following a decades old worn path in the woods off to the side of the gym. Since it was far from the student parking lot, there was no risk of running into Mr. Bradley, the janitor/self-appointed guard who made it his personal mission to prevent students from ditching school. His commitment was legendary. Even I had heard of his guard duty without ever having had any personal experience with the student parking lot.

After a short jaunt through the woods, I came out safely on the other side of Fremont Street. I rode south and crossed Moreland, trying to avoid main roads and concentrating on my destination above all else. A few more minutes and I would arrive at Nature Park, my favorite place in Lake Hansen. Nature Park was this beautiful slice of peacefulness that sat on the banks of Lake Hansen. Part of the grounds was the town commons, part of it was a wildlife-preserve, and a huge part was Nature Park, a sort of *people*-sanctuary with many little nooks to hide in.

I parked my bike at one of the many racks and walked to the area of the park that I hoped would bring me clarity and peace of mind, ignoring everything else. I didn't pay attention to the mothers, fathers and babysitters who pushed strollers, or the runners whose feet slapped the pavement. I just followed the gravel walking path until I reached the place I longed for...a little secluded Japanese garden that was the perfect place for reading or sketching —or hiding. It was walled-in by thick, green hedges, which made it very cozy. The ground was covered with tiny pebbles, and there was a small pond in the center that was rimmed with larger, flatter, smooth stones. Small potted trees and plants were placed in carefully chosen locations, and there were a few low, wooden benches scattered around. Rarely were there more than two or three people there, and most of the time when I went, I found myself alone. Thankfully today was one of those days.

I didn't feel instantly better, but I did feel that the potential was there. I walked more slowly now, having no farther to go but to the edge of the pond where I sat down on the ground with my knees pulled close to my chest.

Every thought in my head wanted to take center stage, but I knew I could only deal with one at a time, and I wasn't even sure I could do that. First, there were the bathroom doors...they had definitely flung open simultaneously. It happened. I saw it. I heard it. A part of me wanted it to be a figment of my imagination, a sign of my impending insanity, but I just couldn't accept that anymore.

Then, there was the voice again...this time it had felt different, like it was external. After that there was the locker from the morning. At the time, I had convinced myself that I was, once again, imagining things. But now...I wasn't so sure. Maybe I had. But I had seen Luca Verone in front of it. Luca. Twice in one day he was there when these strange things happened. It had to be a coincidence. But his very presence, and the fact that he had called my name. . .out loud.

I tried to look at the facts: Dexter said that Luca asked about me, that he was 'concerned' about me after art class the previous week; he may or may not have removed something from my locker that morning; and he was definitely in the hallway just before I left school, had said my name...that I was sure of (I think). Luca was looking at me through the door when I left. It was only now that I realized how far away I had been from the school when I saw Luca. It had to be twenty yards or more. What, did I have some kind of supervision now too!? And then there was that odd feeling of Luca being *with* me when he clearly was not. I shook my head trying to clear it. Insanity was beginning to sound like the lesser of two evils.

Although I would have liked to have stayed curled up by the water's edge for an eternity, and wasn't sure if even that would be enough time to take in all that was happening, I knew it was time to go. School would be over soon, so I got back on my bike and backtracked through the woods, waiting a safe distance from the gym until I saw Dexter coming out of the building. I was also hoping to get a glimpse of Luca. I thought that maybe if I saw him again, something would click and I would understand what he had to do with...anything.

I was growing increasingly aware of my eyesight, which seemed to be sharpening by the second. It was as if once I had realized that my eyesight was...improved, it just kept improving. Not unlike the voice or the apparent telekinesis. I shook at the thought. At this point, I still wasn't even sure if all of these things had even actually happened, other than in my own mind. And, if they had, whether they were connected to one another. But, I could definitely see Dexter from an abnormally far distance, of this I was sure.

And when I saw him, he was looking around in all directions, presumably for me. He looked irritated, and I couldn't blame him. This was the second time in a week I was a no-show. I should have gone right over to him, but there were so many people around, and I just couldn't have the confrontation that I knew was coming in front of them. So, I waited for him to angrily mount his bike and pedal off in the direction of home—not the library where he usually went when he was angry or upset, even when he wasn't working there. I was at least glad about that.

Once he was a good distance from other people, I hopped onto my bike and followed. It took me no time to catch up to him. I knew he was aware of me right behind him, but he chose to ignore me. Dexter often behaved immaturely at times like these. Knowing him as long as I had, I knew the best way to deal with him was to simply play along, let him get it out of his system, and wait for him to come to me, which he would—he always did. I was surprised when his silence lasted the entire ride home. When we pulled into the driveway, we silently parked our bikes side by side under the carport. His silence was starting to get to me, so I made an unprecedented move—I spoke first.

"Okay Dexter, let me have it," I said as he walked away from me. He stopped, but didn't turn, so I continued, "Aren't you going to say anything? Yell at me? Anything?" His immature silence coupled with my guilt was making me angry. "DEXTER!?" I finally shouted. He turned.

"What do you want me to say, Violet?" His tone was quiet, condescending...as if he was trying to prove that he could remain calm and levelheaded while I flew off the handle. I wouldn't give him the satisfaction, so I forced my tone to match his.

"Dexter, has it ever occurred to you that I just might need a little bit of alone time? I had a bad day, that's all...nothing personal," I tried to explain. By the end of my question, my quiet tone was honest and remorseful—no faking necessary. I did feel bad for my friend. It wasn't fair that I was keeping him in the dark and being so evasive with the only person I had ever trusted. But, I also wasn't about to divulge anything. I couldn't begin to say these things out loud. That would make them too real, and that's exactly the opposite of what I wanted. So, I hoped Dexter would be satisfied with my meager attempt at appeasing him.

Whether he was or not was difficult to say, but he did eventually talk to me again. After Mandy went to work, we made small talk...kept it light. We worked on our homework together in the living room then said our goodnights.

4

On Thursday and Friday I felt as if I were tiptoeing through my life, afraid that some new *occurrence* was going to sneak up behind me and tap me on the shoulder. I also tried to avoid Luca. It didn't matter that the thought of him twisted my stomach into knots or that my heart pounded uncontrollably when I passed him in the hall, or even that I still couldn't shake the feeling that he was near me even when he wasn't. Now more than ever was a time for me to deny what I wanted most. No good could come of it. Acknowledging any part of what was happening would only validate it. And that was the last thing I wanted.

Mercifully, nothing out of the ordinary happened. When I say, 'nothing out-of-the-ordinary,' I mean, I still got some of the usual giggles in the hall, even another adorable note in art class in the same poor handwriting. With everything that was already on my mind, these things seemed like nothing at all, almost welcome to make me believe everything was still normal—still the way it had always been.

Dexter and I rode home together, like usual. When we got home Friday, we spent a little time with Mandy, who was still home for an hour, and then I reluctantly agreed to go to the movies. I knew I owed it to Dexter for all that I had put him through that week, and I figured the dark theater would be safe. This made Mandy very happy—Dexter and I spending time together like "the good old days." But I could tell by the way she looked at the two of us that she knew something was up, and Mandy could not tolerate discontent.

***

Dexter and I went out into the night. We saw a bloody slasher film—not my usual fare—that left me wondering why I'd bothered to leave the house in the first place. After the movie ended, we were standing outside, discussing what to do next when a group of students from our school began to look in our direction. It only took a second for me to realize that one was Stephanie Baker. My stomach churned because I knew our night was not over.

Over the years, I had learned to ignore Stephanie, but Dexter approached his role as a social pariah much differently than I did. He took it on willingly. Embraced it, goading people to say something to him, look at him awkwardly. Anything to get into an altercation. And *he* definitely wasn't concerned about being camouflaged. I was growing anxious just thinking about his potential reaction to the current situation. The group, which included two other girls I recognized as some of Stephanie's drones and three nondescript jock-types that I was sure went to Lake Hansen High, began laughing and making loud, thinly-veiled comments about me and Dexter without actually saying our names.

"Anybody see the freak show?" someone yelled. "Yeah, it's more disgusting than that movie we just saw," added one of the boys.

Like with the note in art class, I might have laughed at their lack of creativity if I hadn't been the target of their cruelty. Instead, my face reddened, and I could sense Dexter tensing up next to me. I tugged at his sleeve as I tried to pull him in the other direction. He was unmovable stone.

"Let it go, Dex," I pleaded in a whisper.

"No, Violet, I'm sick of it! I'm sick of the way they treat you, and I'm sick of you not defending yourself!" he snapped more loudly than I would have liked because it made Stephanie's group howl.

"It's not worth it," I argued weakly, hoping it would keep his temper from flaring.

Stephanie, or one of her friends—it really didn't matter—called out, "Hey Arena, did you show your picture to your boyfriend?"

"Yeah, maybe your mom will put it up on the fridge?" One of the jocks moronically spouted. Stephanie was nearly doubled over at this point, though I didn't dare look directly at her. I remained turned slightly away, embarrassed, ashamed, and even a little nauseous. But I fought to maintain my composure.

Unfortunately Dexter was not so restrained, and he had no clue as to what Stephanie was referring to since I hadn't told him of the events that transpired in art class the week before. This probably made him even more frustrated. The fact that she had managed to insult him, Mandy, and me at the same time also ensured that this was not over.

"Shut the fuck up, Stephanie!" he yelled back to the ringleader standing in the center of the boisterous group. There was an edge to his voice that I recognized. I knew it meant that Dexter was not going to let this go. I stiffened beside him.

His bold words definitely had the intended effect. "What did you say, you little asshole?" Stephanie screeched, her smile now replaced with an angry snarl, revealing the truly ugly person she was.

"Why can't you just leave her alone?! Don't you and your cretins have a sewer to crawl back into?" Dexter replied. This stopped them momentarily.

"Leave it to Dexter to make them think about the insult that has just been hurled at them!" I thought, shaking my head. Again, I tried in vain to pull Dexter away, hoping he would be satisfied with having confronted Stephanie, but fearing that things were about to get even worse.

"Please let it go, Dex. Please!" I pleaded quietly. At the sound of my obvious torment, I felt Dexter's arm loosen a little. He looked at me and his fierce face seemed to calm. Unfortunately, by then Dexter's last comment had finally sunk in, and Stephanie's group was bloodthirsty.

"You FREAKS need to learn to keep your mouths SHUT! Don't you get it? You don't count. You don't matter! The sooner you figure that out, the better off you'll be!" she ranted and then cackled loudly. Even the onlookers in the courtyard who had been watching this exchange with enthusiasm, some laughing at times, cringed at the raw harshness of Stephanie's words.

Whatever had softened Dexter was now gone. He turned and stared down the angry mob, which seemed to be growing even angrier with his defiance.

"There are no little Martians to help you here. Or do they only visit your mom?" she directed to me in a sickeningly mocking tone. "How does that work exactly?"

That was it. Dexter could not, would not, tolerate Stephanie insulting Mandy twice. He took a few steps closer, closing the gap between them a little more as he screamed, "Why are you such a FUCKING BITCH? Rotting in Hell would be too good for you!"

Just then, a security guard came into the courtyard outside the movie theater and addressed both Dexter and me and Stephanie's group, looking back and forth as he spoke. "Is there a problem here?" he asked sternly.

"Nope," Dexter spit out through clenched teeth, and then added, "No problem here."

"No, sir," one of the boys in Stephanie's gang said with exaggerated politeness.

"Then let's move on. It's almost curfew," the security guard ordered as he tapped his watch.

Dexter narrowed his seething eyes at Stephanie for just a fraction of a second before angrily turning away.

I had an ominous premonition that this was not the end of the conflict, even if Stephanie and her cronies turned to leave, feigning obedience.

"Have a good night, sir," someone else with Stephanie called out smugly, sarcastically

"That was a bunch of bullshit!" Dexter said through his teeth as he joined me. I had already begun my retreat.

"Dex, it's no big deal. I'm used to it, and frankly, you should be too. I mean, I appreciate the whole 'knight in shining armor' bit, but it's not necessary," I said softly, holding back tears that were threatening. I quickly wiped my face and tried my best to appear strong. Dexter did not need to see me cry. It would only make things worse. My goal—my responsibility—was to calm and comfort my friend.

The altercation caused us to miss the last bus, so we'd have to walk home. Not a big deal, maybe two miles, well-lit for most of the way. Our silent walking was interrupted by my phone. It was Mandy. Though I had NO desire to talk, I had to answer it or she'd be frantic with worry. I took a deep breath and tried to sound casual.

"Hi, Mandy."

"Honey, it's after eleven, aren't you home yet?"

"We're on our—Mandy? Mandy?" The line went dead.

"These stupid lost calls are getting ridiculous!" I grumbled as I punched at my phone to call my mother back. "This has been going on for months now, and NO ONE can figure it out!?" I complained to Dexter, knowing full well that he and everyone else was aware of the recent worldwide cell phone disruptions. Satellite TV signals, as well as other satellite communication had been interrupted frequently too. The *scientists* were trying to figure out what was going on—they all agreed it was strange. But most of all, I just considered it annoying, especially at this moment, given my already frustrated state of mind.

"Mandy. Yeah, I'm fine. Just another stupid call drop. I know.

I hope they fix it too. NO MANDY. I DO NOT THINK *THEY* HAVE ANYTHING TO DO WITH IT! I'M NOT HAVING THIS CONVERSATION...AGAIN!" I yelled, louder and harsher than I'd intended. "Sorry," more calmly now, "You're right. We are all entitled to our own opinions," I said with an exasperated sigh. "Okay, yes. Goodnight. I love you too. Yes, I'll remind Dex. Bye." I was impatient now. I should have been used to my mother's "alien involvement" theory. It was basically her go-to reason for any *unexplainable* occurrence—missing people, strange lights in the sky, even some terrorist attacks! But after the day and night that I had endured, Mandy's words stung more than usual.

"You okay?" Dexter asked once I hung up. I assured him that I was. He was used to my reactions to Mandy's theories. He, on the other hand, was a little more willing to give Mandy the benefit of the doubt. Dexter thought it was possible that life existed outside our realm of understanding. In fact, it was sort of comforting for him to think that we humans were not alone in this vast universe. Of course he wasn't a total believer because he hadn't seen or experienced anything himself, which was an important criterion for him to believe in anything. "What are you supposed to remind me of?" he asked.

"Uh...not allowed in my room," I said sheepishly.

He rolled his eyes and gave me a half-hearted smile. I smiled back. We both knew the rule and neither of us was going to break it. That much we could be sure of.

We continued on our way back to the house, crossing over Washington Avenue and turning right onto Hamilton. The streetlights on this section of Hamilton were out, so it was darker than usual. This wasn't something that bothered me. I knew this street well and had never been afraid of the dark, even as a kid. In fact, I always thought of the dark as an equalizer—a place where I existed on a more level playing field.

All at once, however, I stopped and turned my head. To Dexter it probably appeared that I was straining to the left to hear something. But I wasn't actually straining, I had heard something clearly, and I was trying to focus and identify the sound. Dexter had apparently heard nothing because he looked at me curiously.

"What is i— ?"

"Shhhh!" I whispered inaudibly, holding a finger to my lips. "Do you hear that?" I mouthed.

He replied with a quick shake of his head.

"I think someone might be behind us," I whispered, my head still turned in the direction of the sound I knew I had heard. "I hear footsteps and laughing. You don't hear that?" I asked worriedly.

"No, Violet. I don't hear anything. Why don't we just get out of here. You're freaking me out." Dexter replied in a strained whisper.

I just nodded and we began moving in unison, quickening our pace, hoping we would soon emerge from the darkness, though I was somewhat grateful for the darkness that hid the fear and utter bewilderment that must have been emblazoned across my face. If Dexter hadn't heard the sounds that I was still hearing... *"I'm hearing things again, aren't I?"*

Then, from out of nowhere, a glass bottle hurtled past Dexter's head and shattered on the pavement about ten feet in front of us. Sounds of laughter erupted from the direction the bottle came from.

"I heard *that*!" Dexter said morosely. "Run!" he said louder and with more urgency, grabbing my sleeve and tugging me along. But the people who'd been laughing began to run too, their feet thudding quickly against the pavement. I turned back to see Stephanie and the two girls standing back while three athletic boys sprinted forward, easily overtaking Dexter and me.

One grabbed both of my hands with one of his hands, gripping them tightly behind my back. The other two held Dexter, each of them taking one of his arms. Stephanie and her friends strode over casually, smirking at us. Stephanie bent down and picked up a large shard of broken glass from the shattered bottle. With a vicious, humorless smile spread across her face, she walked directly in front of Dexter and me.

"Violet would be so sad if anything were to happen to her boyfriend," she said with the reserved calm of a diabolical villain. Then she looked me in the eyes, "And Violet, you are just so sad already," she added, sounding like she was talking to a toddler, complete with pouty lips and drooped eyes. Then she let out a burst of laughter.

I was briefly paralyzed with fear. I wasn't necessarily scared of my own physical pain, but I feared for Dexter's safety. Two against one is never a fair fight, and for all his talk, Dexter is not the warrior he pretends to be.

Stephanie took a step to the left so that she was directly in front of Dexter. She reached up with the jagged piece of glass she'd been holding and lay it against his cheek. At that moment, I felt a presence. There was no other way to describe it. I just felt as if someone else were there. I shifted my eyes around, taking in the dim surroundings that suddenly didn't seem so dim. In fact, I was surprised at how well I could see. Then, to my complete astonishment, I saw Luca Verone standing behind a dumpster to the back and right of Stephanie's friends.

"*What is he doing here?*" I wondered briefly. Luca held a finger to his lips, and I heard someone say, *I am here to help if you need it.* I looked around and realized I was the only one who'd heard it. It was *the* voice! Again it was accompanied by the silvery, shimmering blue that swam through my head as I heard the words.

I pushed away the infinite questions and the beautiful blue light and let the most important thought come to the surface—Dexter. I shot one more look to Luca who nodded, and a strange new feeling of strength coursed through my body. Instinctively, my muscles flexed. I didn't know the source of this strength, and I didn't have time to concern myself with it either. In that moment, I only knew that I had the ability to save Dexter. So, I did.

Without hesitation, and with surprisingly little effort, I broke free from the hands that had been restraining me. The startled boy tried to grab me again, but I simply reached out with my own smaller hand and shoved him in the middle of his chest. This action should have had little or no effect. But instead, this boy flew backward five yards into a grouping of trash cans. With a groan, he stayed put, wondering how a 120 pound girl had just knocked him to the ground. I actually wondered the same thing. I looked around at the awed faces that stared from me to the kid still flat on his back. Maybe they were afraid now, or maybe they were just done with their game—whatever the reason, Stephanie made a move.

"They're not worth the trouble. Let's go," she growled from her curled lips.

The two goons holding Dexter let go of him. The kid on the ground got up, wiped himself off, and walked to his group of friends, carefully avoiding me, but not taking his eyes from me either. Stephanie looked closely at me, the fear and confusion in her eyes betrayed the sneer on her face and the words she then spat. "We are NOT done Arena!" She then motioned to her minions to follow, and they slithered off together, not looking back, and not saying a word.

Dexter finally emerged from the shock he'd apparently been in after witnessing my astonishing actions. "I...what...what just happened?" he finally managed to get out. At that moment, I just couldn't pay attention to Dexter. I didn't acknowledge him. Instead, I took slow, measured steps toward the dumpster, wondering if the image of Luca had been a mirage. When I was within a few feet of it, I stopped. I couldn't name the feeling or sensation, but I knew Luca was there, I *sensed* his presence. Abruptly, I realized I wasn't sure if I wanted to face who or what was behind the dumpster. But, I didn't get to decide.

Luca quietly took two steps out from his hiding place, careful not to move any closer. I could tell by the perplexed look on Luca's face that even though he was there, and had been a silent witness to what had happened with Stephanie, he wasn't really sure what was going on either. Dexter must have seen him too, but he said nothing. We all seemed to be waiting for the others to say something.

The silence that shrouded the three of us was awkward and unbearable. Luca was the one to end it. "Umm...let's get out of here —then we can deal with all of this," he said quietly, his eyes never leaving me. His words reanimated me. I nodded my head, but my eyes didn't leave Luca's until he came completely out from behind the dumpster and joined Dexter and me.

Without discussion, the three of us began walking silently down Hamilton. The walk cleared my head enough to let me remember the difficult situation Dexter had just been in. "Dex, are you alright?" I turned to him, hoping I sounded apologetic.

Dexter seemed pleased that I had finally remembered his existence. "I'm fine," he said, still looking dazed. "How are you?" I knew that this question was layered with meaning, and a look came over him that begged for information.

"Dexter, I'm fine. Look, I know you've got a ton of questions, but now is not the time. Let's just do what Luca said and get out of here first. Then we'll talk. Promise. Okay?" I noticed that Dexter had winced the slightest bit at the mention of Luca's name. But, he nodded, looking a little defeated, and turned to face forward as we continued walking.

By the time we reached the other end of Hamilton, the streetlights were working. I looked at Luca first, then Dexter out of the corners of my eyes. I knew that each of them had a head full of questions—some the same, some *very* different. As we neared the corner of Washington, Luca spoke.

"My car is just over there. I can drive you home." I knew he meant Dexter and me, but he only looked at me, making me feel suddenly vulnerable and uncomfortable. No one had ever looked at me like that before, intensely and curiously, like I was interesting and important, and I wasn't sure what to make of it. So I did what I usually did when I was uncomfortable, I looked down, and said, "Sure. Thanks."

We all climbed into the car, Dexter carefully and slyly making sure that I was in the backseat and he was up front with Luca. I was exhausted, and I dreaded the inevitable conversation I would have to have with Dexter, if not tonight, eventually. But a part of me didn't want the night to end just yet...I had so many questions for Luca, and I knew he wanted to talk. So, in un-typical Violet fashion, I blurted out, "Why don't we go to our house since Mand—I mean, my mom is at work." It wasn't really a question, and I was surprised at my own boldness

"Okay," was all Luca said.

Can we talk alone? It was the voice. Luca's voice. This time I looked for the blue light, but I didn't have to. It was there. I figured it had probably been there all along, but since I'd been denying the voice, I'm sure I was blocking the color that came with it as well. It startled me, but I kept my composure. I had decided that until I was completely sure about what was going on, I was going to keep this from Dexter.

Instinctively, I looked to Luca's eyes in the rearview mirror, letting him know I had received what he thought to me. I opened my mouth to speak, but stopped myself. I knew I should *think* this to him, I just wasn't sure if I knew how it worked. I looked at Luca and just directed my thought to him—it was almost an involuntary act, not something I had to make an effort to do. It seemed to happen naturally and automatically. I thought about wanting to say something to him, and the thought directed itself.

Dexter is my best friend. He has the right to know what's going on. Besides, he lives with me—us. The thought seemed to reach him as I was thinking it. No time elapsed between me thinking it and him receiving it.

Alright, it's up to you, he replied silently, still looking at me in the mirror. I glanced at Dexter to be sure he couldn't hear what was being said.

"Turn here." Dexter pointed to our street, though Luca seemed to have begun the turn before Dexter had directed him. I was glad Dexter hadn't noticed that. "It's the yellow one on the right," Dexter said as he pointed up the hill.

We pulled into the driveway. The clock on Luca's dashboard read 12:12. It was late, which is why I was not surprised when my phone buzzed. A text from Mandy.

"R U home yet?"

I saw there were three messages on my phone. Probably all from Mandy. I quickly replied, not wanting to give my mother any reason to worry and come rushing home. "We are home and fine. Nite. Love you."

"Luv u 2"

"Everything okay?" Luca asked, seeing my furious texing.

"Yeah...just my mom making sure I—we're home. She left a bunch of messages," I explained.

We exited the car and walked up the illuminated path to the front door. I noticed that Luca paid close attention to the unique stepping stones that led to the porch stairs, each one different from the others, colorful tiles in abstract mosaics laid out on twelve-inch, round cement paving stones. I made them the summer I was fourteen. He looked up at me. I wanted to look up at him, but I couldn't, so I looked down at the tiles.

We were all crowded on the tiny porch while I fumbled with the lock, fingers shaking involuntarily. Dexter asked impatiently if I wanted him to do it, but I just ignored him. Once I got the door open, we all walked in and stood in the small, cramped foyer while Dexter flipped on the lights. Dexter, obviously wanting Luca to see just how comfortable he was in *our* house, strolled in casually and plopped down on the worn sofa, feet up on the coffee table (an act that would have drawn a reprimand from Mandy), remote in hand. I knew that inside Dexter was not the picture of relaxation he was trying to pull off. He might know me well, but that goes two ways. I knew he was seething, dying to know what happened.

In contrast, I was as uncomfortable in my own home as Luca, who stood stiffly by the door. But I felt the need to be hospitable, at least. "Luca, you can come in and sit down. Dex...you can move." I spoke to Dexter as if he were a toddler and then whacked his feet off the coffee table. He scowled at me then gave me a sarcastic smile. "Do either of you want something to drink?"

"Iced tea for me thanks," Dexter said, pretending to watch TV, but really watching Luca out of the corner of his eye.

"Luca?" I asked again.

"Water please," he said, barely above a whisper

I went into the kitchen, thankful to be alone, even if it was only for a few minutes. I needed to process everything that had happened. Facing the counter, I gripped the edge, feeling the need to steady myself. I slowly raised my head and took a deep breath with my eyes closed. I felt my mental equilibrium stabilizing just a little.

"Okay," I thought to myself, *"Okay. Luca Verone and I can communicate telepathically."* Then another thought occurred to me, *"Can he hear me now?! What if he can? Oh God!"* I began to panic and peeked out of the doorway, looking at Luca who sat nervously at the edge of the loveseat, looking around the room, but not at anything in particular. I could also see Dexter, still watching Luca. To my tentative relief, Luca didn't seem like he was aware of anything I was currently thinking about, but I couldn't be sure.

Anyway, I didn't see the blue light, and then I decided it didn't matter and continued to make a mental list of my *powers*. *"Besides the telepathic communication with Luca, there's the spoon thing—and the bathroom doors—so, telekinesis?"* Every thought that entered my head led to a thousand more questions. *"Does it have to be metal?"* I was tempted to try it again, but afraid of the outcome. *"...and I'm strong—although that* could *have been adrenaline... and I can see really well..."* my thoughts wandered now.

I knew that even though all of this was impossible to believe—the stuff of comic books and sci-fi movies, it *was* happening. To me! And Luca. But to what degree I wasn't sure. There was a piece of my brain that was actually glad that at least I wasn't going insane. Another part of my brain was also very aware that Luca Verone was in my house. *"Breathe, Violet!"* I said to myself.

I relaxed as much as I could, trying to distract myself by doing what I had come into the kitchen to do. After retrieving glasses from the cabinet, I filled two with water from the pitcher in the refrigerator. Then I got a bottle of Dexter's favorite iced tea that Mandy kept in the house just for him. With another deep breath, I turned the corner and headed purposefully back into the living room where Dexter and Luca sat in silence.

Though Dexter still reclined casually on the couch, attempting to give the impression of comfort and ease, I knew him better than that. I could see his muscles were rigid, his jaw tight, and his eyes fixed, still looking sideways at Luca. Luca was still propped at the very edge of the loveseat, elbows on spread knees, head bowed and resting on his hands— the picture of stress and unease.

Luca's head rose slowly as I entered the room—his eyes immediately going to mine. Dexter's eyes slid back and forth between me and Luca. His jaw tightened even more. Uncomfortable with the way Luca looked at me, I looked away quickly.

"So, let's talk," I said uneasily, placing the drinks on the coffee table and sitting down on the other end of the loveseat, just a few feet from Luca. I knew this move irritated Dexter; he sat up a little straighter, his muscles tensed even more, and the look on his face became a cross between defiance and confusion. I ignored his reaction, which I regarded as a temper tantrum, and began.

"Luca, what's going on? What do you know?" I blurted out, more forcefully than I had planned. Through my thoughts, only for Luca, I added, *Let's keep...* this *part to ourselves for now.* He nodded almost imperceptibly. I was shocked at how easy this communication was now that I had figured out how to do it.

"Well, what I know so far is that sometime in the last few months, strange things have been happening to me..." he said aloud. His voice was quiet and calm.

"What kinds of *things*?" Dexter jumped in. He was now very interested in the conversation. I assumed he was connecting my recent behavior with whatever Luca might be about to say. I imagine he was hoping to get the answers that I had not provided.

"Uh...well..." I could tell he was debating what to say without mentioning our new form of communication, "...a few weeks ago I was out skateboarding, and my board got away from me and rolled under my car. I bent down to see how far under the car it was, and I put my hand on the side of the car for balance. I was really annoyed because it had stopped right in the middle under the car, so I couldn't get to it from any angle." He was demonstrating this with his hands.

"Then, the car started to slide sideways. It took me a second to realize that I was pushing the car with the hand that was leaning on it." The way he spoke made me think he was almost afraid to say it too loudly, but his eyes were filled with excitement.

Dexter's face was a mask of awe and disbelief. He probably would've thought the whole story was ridiculous if he hadn't witnessed my display of strength earlier that night.

I sat still as ideas raced around my head. "*Then it wasn't adrenaline tonight? Could I move a car? Can I communicate with others telepathically, or is it just Luca?...What's happening to me...to us?"* That was the question I got hung up on. The idea seemed to settle like a massive weight. And then a single question wormed its way into my conscious thoughts, "*What* am *I?"* I looked at Luca's face. His eyes were still wide.

Dexter wheeled his head in my direction, his eyes wild with excitement, curiosity, wonder. "So it wasn't just an adrenaline rush?" he asked me, as if he were reading my mind.

"No. I don't…I mean...I don't know. At the time I thought it was, but now, I'm not so sure," I responded to Dexter as honestly as I could, my words tense, quiet.

Luca looked at me like he felt guilty for bringing on my anxiety. "Violet, I know this is a lot to take in. Believe me, I'm freaked out too." I can't explain why, but I didn't fully believe this part. He seemed so relaxed about the whole situation. Then he surprised me by reaching out and gently putting his hand on top of my hands, which I was wringing in my lap. I flinched slightly. My first instinct was to pull away, but I fought it and let his warm, soft hand linger on mine.

"I don't know exactly what's going on, but I do think we can figure it out together." Luca looked so deeply into my eyes that tears began to form in mine. I tried to keep them in, but one solitary tear bested me and rolled down my cheek, landing on the back of Luca's hand.

Everything—this exchange, the bond between us, the staring, his easy, gentle touch, his closeness—it all became too much for me. I was someone who let very few people in. And, no matter what feelings I had begun to allow myself to have for Luca, this was more than I could handle at that moment. I was overcome. "I can't do this right now," I said quietly, but forcefully. Pulling my hand from beneath Luca's, I stood and began pacing behind the love seat. I was frightened, this much was obvious. But, I suspect Luca understood that I needed time and space because he didn't get up.

I attempted to take a calming breath, but it came out shallow and ragged. "Luca, I think you should go. I need to think," I managed to get out.

"I'm sorry," he said solemnly, "I didn't mean to upset you."

When I didn't respond, he stood up and walked in front of me to add, "We can figure this out Violet. I know we can. I'm scared too, but we'll deal with it." This last part was almost a plea.

"No!" I nearly shouted. Then I composed myself, "I'm not ready. I don't want to *deal* with it right now. I think I liked it better when I thought I was going insane...at least that was an explanation!" I cried. "I just—I can't right now, I'm sorry," I added in a near whisper.

Dexter sprang to his feet and moved to my side, putting one hand on each of my shoulders. He had been silent for much longer than usual. "It's all right Violet, I'm here." His attempt to sound comforting came out more like gloating. He obviously thought, or hoped, that I was so upset by Luca that I needed him to rescue me. He couldn't begin to know what was in my head, and his doting just annoyed me. I shrugged him off.

Luca had taken a few steps away from me, but still watched me patiently. "I'll go, but please call me when you're ready to talk." He slowly turned and moved toward the door. Before he opened it, he turned to look back at me. I had finally stopped moving and looked at him. His face was full of meaning. It told me he didn't want to leave. But, I wasn't ready for anything else, and he knew it. As he lowered his eyes and turned to walk out the door, I said silently, *I'm sorry. Just give me some time. Please.*

He paused, but didn't turn around as he replied, *Take all the time you need, I'll wait for you.* Then he walked out into the early morning.

I felt a surge of some emotion I wasn't familiar with. Its heat pushed through every part of me. While I was confused by what was going on with me and frightened by what it all might mean, I was also comforted because Luca seemed to now have some part in my life, even if I had just told him to leave.

With Luca gone, I realized I was exhausted. I glanced at the clock that now read 3:33 am and then at Dexter, who looked more dejected than anything else, and I knew that the night would have to go on just a little bit longer. I owed him an explanation. "Dexter. Let's sit, okay?" I said sheepishly. I sat down on the couch and waited patiently for him to join me, which I knew he would do eventually. A minute later, he was a few feet away from me, occupying the same spot that Luca had only a short time earlier, studying his hands intently.

In the ten years we'd been friends, we had been through everything together. My mother's interview, my social demise, his father's multiple hospitalizations and drinking binges, my dad's rejection...everything. No conversation had ever been too personal or too awkward. I told Dexter everything, until now.

This was different somehow. This conversation was going to be the most difficult of any we had ever had. It wasn't just the fact that I could barely grasp what was happening to me, it was also the fact that there was an obvious *something* going on between me and Luca, and I knew Dexter could see that. I also knew that I could no longer continue to ignore Dexter's feelings for me. I never thought I'd have to deal with them because I never imagined anyone else would ever be interested in me.

"Dexter." I paused, trying to get my words right, "Uh, Dex. I don't know exactly what to say. Lately, all these weird things have started happening to me. I just thought I was going crazy, and I might be, but now I believe...there is something more to it. Luca..." I felt guilty just saying his name- "...as you obviously heard, he seems to be going through the same things as I am..." That was enough for now, I decided.

Dexter waited for what seemed like an eternity to respond. He spoke quietly and never looked at me. "I wish you would have told me what was going on before tonight. You've never lied to me before, have you?" his voice was shaky as he waited for my response. I shook my head. I couldn't think of a time when I had ever lied to my best friend.

"Well, I'm pissed off that you didn't tell me, but I also feel bad that you've been dealing with this by yourself. I'm your best friend...more than that, I thought." I wondered what he was implying, though I knew I had never led him to believe that we were *anything* more. He was my family.

"How do I explain something that I don't understand? Besides, this has only been going on for a few months that I am aware of. There may have been some other things that have happened that I just blew off or didn't realize...So, I wasn't lying to you, technically." I even managed a weak smile to try to help ease the tension. "I still don't know what's going on. I don't know what Luca has to do with this either, but I think I am going to have to find out. I hope you know that I want you with me on this...this journey...I guess that's what it is, or uh, will be." I hoped that these words would be enough to comfort him so that I could go to sleep. I meant what I said to Dexter, but I still felt guilty about trying to appease him.

"I'll always be here for you, Violet," he replied, and the similarities between his spoken words and Luca's unspoken ones did not go unnoticed. I looked through Dexter for a moment and recalled Luca's face before he'd turned to leave, the depth of his eyes as he'd stared at me. "Violet. Did you hear me?" Dexter asked, concern saturating his tone and his eyes.

"Oh, yeah. Yes. Sorry. I know you are." I smiled at him. "I'm just beat. I'm gonna go to bed. You okay?" I asked, knowing full well that Dexter was not alright. That he would stay out here watching TV until he passed out on the couch instead of going to his too-quiet room where he'd be forced to think.

I'm not sure if he just didn't have any fight left in him that night or if he could see that I didn't. Either way, I was grateful for what he said next, "I'm okay. Goodnight, V."

"Goodnight. Lock up," I replied and turned toward my bedroom. I was mentally and physically exhausted. I contemplated not even changing clothes, but knew I'd sleep better in my comfortable pajamas than jeans and a t-shirt. I shed my clothes and slipped on my worn-in blue plaid boxers, soft gray t-shirt, and fuzzy pink socks. When this ritual was complete, I stood, almost too tired to move, thinking only about being in my bed. And then it happened.

Without warning, I felt my feet come off the floor and I essentially *floated* to my bed, resting gently on the edge. I gasped loudly, but quickly covered my mouth before I let a scream escape.

"*WHAT WAS THAT?*" I whispered into my hand. My eyes were wide in the darkness of my room, pupils pushing their limits. "*Okay, okay, so I...I ...floated. I FLOATED? What the...What does that mean?*" I continued to whisper, though I wanted to shout. I sat frozen for several minutes, taking in the newest twist in my *metamorphosis.* I wished I could talk to Luca right then and ask him if anything like this had happened to him. Walking over to look out my window, I wondered if Luca was thinking of me too, and if I tried, could he *hear* me at his house.

I shook my head and realized I wasn't ready to try. After spending a long while staring out my window looking at the sky lightening as morning made her initial approach, I decided that I really would go insane if I didn't sleep soon. Like I told Luca, I would deal with all of this when I was ready. It was almost five in the morning, and I was definitely not ready! I lay down, pulled the covers up tightly around my neck, and to my surprise, fell asleep quickly.

5

My dreams were vivid and filled with all of the thoughts, fears, and anxieties that my awake-brain was not able to grasp yet. But not all of my dreams were unpleasant. I remembered that I dreamt of flying high above Lake Hansen and then New York City, looking down and feeling free. And I also dreamt of Luca.

Though I didn't remember exactly what the dream was about, I knew he was present in my mind throughout the night. When I finally opened my eyes, I had that disoriented feeling of not knowing what time it was or even what day. I could tell by the way the light streamed into my south-facing room that it was way past morning, though I didn't exactly feel well-rested.

I immediately wondered if it was time for Mandy to be up. Given the current situation and recent revelations, I felt that seeing my mother as little as possible would be ideal. Dexter was another problem. *"Is he up? Is he still here...of course he is,"* That thought brought up a frightening question, *"Will Dexter say anything to Mandy?"* Growing up, he had been devoutly loyal, but given some of the new circumstances, I wondered if his personal feelings might make him do something out of character. At this, I flew from my room, nearly ripping the door from its hinges in the process. I was really going to have to learn to get a handle on my new strength!

I was still sprinting when I reached the living room and saw Mandy and Dexter at the small dining table that sat at the far end of the kitchen. "Violet. Good...afternoon," my mother said with a wry smile.

"Morning," I mumbled, leaning against the door frame.

"I've rarely seen you sleep *this* late. Late night, or are you not feeling well?" There was some concern in Mandy's voice, but mostly amusement. I realized I must have looked as groggy and disoriented as I felt.

I decided to ignore her question and just change the subject. "I guess I didn't miss you." I tried to sound happy about that fact. "Uh, what time is it?"

"It's three...as in *PM*," Mandy answered.

"Oh well, yeah, I...we had a late night," I said, nodding in Dexter's direction. "Didn't Dexter tell you we stayed up late?" I asked, eyeing Dexter suspiciously.

"No...nothing I need to *worry* about, I hope," Mandy asked in an accusing tone, but the smile on her face made it clear that she was being facetious.

"No, definitely NOT!" Dexter answered, a little too quickly and with an edge that made me glare at him. Mandy seemed to be briefly aware of the conspiratorial look that was exchanged between us, but didn't press any further.

"Well, I don't have to leave until about six, so is there anything you want to do?" she asked, as always, trying very hard to bond with me.

"Oh. Um, I don't know," I responded. I felt a sudden and strange need to appease my mother. I racked my brain to find something we could do that would make her happy. "Why don't we cook an early dinner and eat together," I suggested. I knew she would love this idea.

"That sounds great. What should we make? Veggie burgers?...Oooh, how about Caesar salads?"

"Can we have pancakes? I know it's three, but my stomach thinks it's morning," I said with a sleepy smile. I stretched and yawned, trying to come to life.

"Dexter, pancakes okay with you?" Mandy asked, always sensitive to Dexter's feelings.

"Um, actually, I need to go to the library and do some research for World History," Dexter replied. I wasn't sure if this was true, but I was fairly certain that this was Dexter's subtle way of giving me some time with my mom. I wasn't sure how I felt about that. On the one hand, I always liked having a buffer, especially when Mandy got on her prying kick, but on the other hand, Dexter might not be the best buffer right now, and I could use a little space from him at the moment. He got up and headed for the door. "I'll see you ladies later." I followed him.

Quietly so Mandy couldn't hear, I questioned him in a strained whisper, "You didn't say anything, did you?"

"Give me some credit, V," he whispered back, obviously annoyed at my lack of trust. Then he turned and left, but I knew he'd be back in a few hours.

The afternoon passed pleasantly. Mandy and I made pancakes together, set the table together, and ate together. Mandy was in an exceptionally good mood, and didn't make a single comment or ask a single question to irritate me. This kept me feeling a little more at ease. For the first time in a long time, I was enjoying having my mother around.

I cleared the table as Mandy got ready for work. I was doing the dishes, and it occurred to me that this might be the perfect time to *test* one of my new abilities with some of the silverware. First, I looked around to make sure I was completely alone, then I tried to concentrate on moving a knife that was at the bottom of the sink, using my hand that hovered about twelve inches above it. "Come on," I whispered, "move." The knife trembled a little, but didn't come to my hand. "Hmm?" I wondered out loud. "Move," I said again. Just then, Mandy walked in, dressed in her nurse's scrubs, and looked at me strangely.

"What are you doing, Violet?" she questioned. I realized I must have looked ridiculous, standing there with soap-covered hands held out in front of me, eyes squinting, staring at a knife in the sink. I hoped Mandy hadn't heard me talking to myself.

"Uh...nothing. I'm just washing the dishes," I said, trying to sound casual. I turned back to the sink and kept scrubbing as if Mandy weren't there.

"Okay," Mandy said with her usual trusting smile that made me feel instantly guilty for lying. "Well, I'm leaving for work. Are you going out tonight?"

"No. I'm going to stay in and work on a new painting, maybe watch TV, or study... low-key."

"Sounds good. I'm sure Dexter will be home soon." Then she paused, "Are you two okay?"

"We're fine," I growled.

"All right...I just sensed a little...tension or something."

"Not on my part. I think he just needs to *reevaluate* some things," I said bitterly.

"Take it easy on him, Honey. He's just...*confused*. I'm sure his feelings for you are hard for him to deal with too."

"What feelings?!" I gasped. "What feelings?!" I repeated.

"Violet. You can pretend if you'd like, but you know as well as I do how Dexter feels about you," she said with a sweet smile.

There was a long, long pause. Then Mandy proceeded to tell me how she knew about it. Apparently Dexter confessed to her a couple of months before. So now she decided I needed to have a heart-to-heart. It was pure torture. After I had admitted to Mandy that I knew about his feelings, she frowned and looked at me with consoling eyes, and made me promise to be as sensitive as possible to Dexter. I agreed, not letting her know how angry I was that Dexter's feelings had changed everything and had begun taking my best friend away.

"I know, Mandy. I'll be nice," I promised when she'd finally finished.

Dexter was home by eight. He came in more quietly than usual and didn't say much to me. Instead, he just sat on the couch and flipped on the TV. He even kept the volume low. It seemed to me that he was trying to make as little noise as possible. Maybe he thought that by staying very quiet, he could avoid the awkwardness that we both knew existed between us now.

I decided to take Mandy's advice and give Dexter a break. No matter how frustrated I was with the situation that existed between us, I was going to be the better person.

"So Dex...wanna see my new painting?" I asked. I hadn't planned this, but when I saw him sitting pathetically on the couch, I just knew I needed to do something drastic.

Dexter's face lit up. "Really? You're gonna let me into the studio, *and* you're gonna let me see an *unfinished* painting?"

"Yeah. It's no big deal," I shrugged. Actually, it was a *huge* deal, and we both knew it. As a general rule, I didn't let *anyone* into my studio, and I rarely let Dexter or my mother or anybody see my paintings before they were completed. In fact, I often didn't even let anyone see the finished ones. Mandy had persuaded me to hang a few throughout the house, and I had reluctantly agreed. My grandmother had several in her room at the nursing home, but the largest collection of my work was stored in my locked closet.

I went to my room to put on my painting clothes. Not many of my clothes were non-painting clothes. Most had some evidence of the extended periods of time I spent in my studio. My *studio* doubled as the shed in the backyard. Years ago, when Mandy realized my talent, she had, in true Mandy-form, been kind enough to have electricity run and installed an air conditioner and lights into our old garden shed in the backyard. It is my refuge, the place where I can escape and be completely and unapologetically Violet.

I led Dexter out to the studio. Once inside, I walked over to my easel, which was covered with an old sheet. It may sound melodramatic, but I truly felt like I was about to undress in front of him. In fact, that might have been easier. My paintings were like little pieces of my soul slung onto canvases. "Okay. It's still *very rough*. So, don't judge," I warned.

"V, your work is always amazing." There was a hint of awe, worship even, in his voice. Dexter rarely brought the blush to my cheeks, but this comment and the reverent tone of his voice did it.

I took a deep breath. "Well, here it is..." and I pulled back the sheet to reveal the unfinished painting beneath it. It was something I had started working on recently, as the *imagined* voice had become more frequent. Like most of my work, it was very non-traditional. So far, it contained a solitary human-like black figure in the center, and around it were several multi-colored swirls, like small tornadoes, all beginning at the head and appearing as if they were spinning the central figure around while simultaneously taking little bits of the black away from it.

Dexter looked for several minutes before commenting. "Wow. That's really...interesting. What is it? Sorry, I mean, what does it represent?" Dexter asked, staring at the painting.

"Um...it's...it doesn't have a name yet, but it's about how life pulls you in many different directions," I lied. I couldn't explain to him that it was about the *voice,* knowing now it was Luca's voice, and it did have a name, *Mi Cabeza Loca, My Crazy Head.*

Dexter nodded his approval. "Well, you nailed it!" And for the rest of the night, his high was enough to keep him appeased in the house while I painted. I knew, however, that this calm was temporary and eventually reality would come raging back into our lives. But for now, we were both content. I had my painting and Dexter had his best friend.

When I finally came in, it was late, and I was ready for bed. Dexter was playing a video game, but he stopped when he heard me. "Hungry?" he asked

"No thanks," I replied.

"How's the painting coming?" he asked eagerly. I could tell he'd been dying to ask.

"It's good, nearly done. Just a few touches to add when this layer dries," I explained. I was glad I had been able to avoid any more questions about my powers or Luca and made Dexter happy at the same time. It gave me a sense of accomplishment. "I'm going in the shower and then to bed. Good night, Dex."

"Goodnight, Violet," he said, still smiling.

I went into the bathroom, turned on the water, and undressed. I looked at myself in the mirror, studied my features, and said to myself, "*What is happening to you?*" I was deeply in thought when it happened again. I began to lift off of the ground. I was two feet from the floor, and about to scream, when I realized that this was another power I would have to learn to accept and manipulate.

I tried to push aside the complete and total shock I was in and focus on getting down. I thought, "*I want to be back on the ground,*" and as easy as that, I was. Just like the thoughts, I guessed my powers were controlled by my mind, both consciously and subconsciously. That was the only way to explain the fact that I was hearing Luca's voice before I knew who or what it was, and that I had now floated twice, involuntarily. I was still completely on edge.

I hoped that the hot shower would help clear my thoughts and calm me for bed. Only one more day before I had to face a new week of high school hell. This thought abruptly put me in a panic. First, there was the situation with Stephanie Baker. What would happen at school? Surely there would be some kind of retaliation. I was confident that the revenge would not be physical, unless Stephanie and her friends were willing to test my strength again. It would be something brutally humiliating, probably on a whole new scale of evil. This made my stomach churn.

Then another thought came to mind: Luca. Things were obviously different between us now. Would he speak to me at school? I wouldn't be surprised if he didn't. After all, who'd want to be known to have befriended Violet Arena? Although, I had to admit, the word, "friend" didn't quite seem to fit. What were we, exactly, aside from a matching supernatural pair? Maybe...nothing. A fresh set of butterflies swarmed inside my stomach now. I wasn't sure how I'd react to him. I was not exactly known for my warmth and friendliness. I didn't know if I could let down my walls and allow him into my life. The results could be devastating...for me.

After my shower, which did not have the relaxing effect I'd hoped, I donned my old, soft, green robe and headed for my room. Once there, I put on my pajamas and was about to climb into bed when I decided I would try something. First, I double-checked the lock on my door, then I moved to the center of my small room. I closed my eyes and thought about rising from the ground, and like the other powers, it just happened. This time, instead of one or two feet, I was able to go even higher. I wasn't sure how high I could go, but I was able to control the height at which I stopped. I only had to raise my hand to touch the eight-foot ceiling.

Once I was airborne, I wanted to see if I could move from the spot I started in. I thought about turning my body horizontally, like Superman flying. As I thought it, it happened naturally. I was now hovering horizontally, about five feet off the ground, the front side of my body parallel to the floor. I couldn't stop to appreciate how amazing this power was because I felt the need to concentrate on exactly what I was doing, afraid that any break in my concentration would result in me crashing to the ground.

I continued to test my ability, now willing myself to move backward toward my bed so that I was now directly above it, in the direction that I slept in. I began to *think myself down.* At first it was a gentle descent, but then a knock on my door jolted my concentration, and I fell hard onto my bed. My foot hit the wall with a loud BANG! I was just thankful that I had been above my bed and not above the floor.

"Violet? Are you okay?" Dexter called from the other side of my door.

"Yes. What do you want?" My words echoed my frustration.

"Um...nothing, really... Are there any more batteries anywhere? Remote's dead and there aren't any in the drawer," he answered. "Are you...sure you're okay?"

"Yes, I'm fine!" I grumbled. "I don't know where the batteries are, try the little drawer in the table in the foyer," I replied, slightly calmer now.

"Okay...G'night," Dexter called.

"Goodnight, Dexter," I sighed.

More dreams of Luca and the changes I was dealing with flooded my mind as I slept. Again they were both exhilarating and frightening. I awoke in the morning still feeling unsettled.

The day passed easily enough. Mandy slept until early afternoon and then went out shopping. Dexter went to the library, stopped by to check in on his dad (he did this from time to time) and then came back and spent the rest of the day reading. I painted for most of the day and wrote a paper for English. Overall, it was a normal day in our household, although inside I was a completely different person. A person who wasn't "hearing things." I wasn't sure what I was, but I took an ounce of hope in knowing that at least I wasn't insane—not yet.

6

My alarm screamed at me to get up. I reached out and banged down on the snooze button. Not realizing my strength, my hand came down onto the clock harder than I intended, sending shards of pink plastic onto the floor next to my bedside table. I stared dumbly over the edge of my bed, trying to absorb what just happened. Looking down at the broken clock on the floor with wires and electronic components sticking out, I knew I was going to have to be very careful from now on since my powers seemed to be getting stronger by the day.

I climbed out of bed and got down on the floor to clean up the mess. As I began picking up the pieces, I mourned the loss of my alarm clock which had been a gift from my dad when I was nine. I hated it, but it had sentimental value. It was a basic digital alarm clock, but it was pink with little hearts and princesses all over it. Of course, even at nine, it was nothing that I would have ever picked out myself, and I knew that it was just another example of how little my dad knew about me, but it *was* from my dad, and that's why I kept it.

There were so many tiny pieces stuck in the carpet. Picking them up was tedious. Then I thought, "*I wonder...*" I knelt next to the mess and extended my hands out above it. I thought about each little pink shard lifting up from the carpet. I concentrated on finding each piece. Slowly, some began to move. At first they just trembled slightly, like they were being stirred by a gentle breeze, but as I pushed my mind further, they slowly lifted up. I raised my hands an inch or so, and the pieces rose further. I felt I must be guiding them with my hands, sending some kind of energy pulses from my mind, through my hands, and into the pieces themselves. I looked over at the wastebasket near my desk and moved my hands in that direction. A small cloud of jagged pink debris hovered inches below my hands, and moved as I did.

I got up, walked to the wastebasket, and centered the pieces above it. Deliberately, I lowered my hands, and in my mind I turned off the connection so that the pieces were no longer under my control. Gravity took over, and they fell into the small wire mesh basket. "*Well, that could come in handy,*" I thought to myself. I stared at my hands, turning them over and over, in awe of my own powers.

Then I remembered that I had to go to school unless I could fake an illness. But then I'd have to deal with Dexter's questions, and I wouldn't see Luca. I groaned and began to get dressed. There was a trip to the bathroom to make myself presentable. I pulled a brush through my thick, wavy locks, frustrated as usual by my hair's inability to do anything I wanted it to do.

After a few minutes, I gave up and settled for a pony tail at the base of my neck. I splashed water on my face and brushed my teeth. I was about to leave the bathroom when I saw the small make-up bag on the shelf above the toilet. The bag was a permanent fixture in its place on the shelf, dusty from not having moved in a very long time. I rarely wore makeup, and even more rarely did I wear it to school, but something made me grab the bag and explore its contents. I put on a light coat of dark brown mascara and a little plum-tinted lip-stain. I passed Dexter in the hall on my way to the kitchen. It was his turn in the bathroom. "Good morning," I said.

"G'morn..." he mumbled in reply without really opening his eyes.

Mandy hadn't gone to bed yet, having just gotten home. She was at the kitchen table having her usual cup of chamomile tea to help her unwind and reading the newspaper. She looked up when she saw me, and her eyes grew large.

"What?" I asked defensively, startled by her reaction. Was I floating or growing another head?

"Are you wearing *makeup?*" Mandy scrunched her face and looked very closely at me.

"No...maybe a little. Is it too much? I should go wash it off," I said quickly, feeling very uncomfortable.

"No, you look great! It's very *minimalist.* I just...I haven't seen you wear it in so long. Is there an occasion?" Mandy got that excited gleam in her eye.

"No, Mandy. There's nothing going on, I just felt like doing something...different. That's all," I replied, still defensive.

"Well, you look beautiful." Mandy smiled and went back to reading the paper.

"So...are you working tonight?" I asked, ignoring the compliment and making an effort to change the subject while pouring a bowl of cereal.

"Yes. I work tonight, tomorrow, Friday, and Saturday this week. I do have my UFOlogy group Wednesday night. We're meeting here. I just want to give you fair warning," she said as I sat down at the table to eat.

"Great." I rolled my eyes.

"Oh, stop...get over it. They are all perfectly nice people, and you know it." Mandy was the defensive one now.

"I know, I know," I said. "Well, except for one maybe," I mumbled. I was thinking about Marilyn, my *least* favorite of any of my mother's friends, and unfortunately my mother's best friend of many, many years. Mandy grimaced, knowing exactly who I was referring to.

Just then Dexter came out of the bathroom, much more awake than he had been earlier. He too went into the cabinet to get himself a bowl of cereal and joined Mandy and me at the table. He was about to start eating when he looked over at me. His reaction was similar to Mandy's. His spoonful of cereal dumped back into the bowl.

"Whoa...what the...? Violet, what's going on with your face?" he chuckled.

I cut my eyes and glared at him. Mandy looked at him and shook her head, warning him to shut his mouth. He didn't take the hint.

"I'm sorry, V. It's just...you look different. You don't look bad," he explained. "Just different," he quickly added.

"So I am wearing makeup! Can the two of you just drop it? Please!" I said loudly. "I'm going to wash it off!" I started to get up.

"No, no. We're sorry," Mandy spoke for herself and Dexter. "Please, Honey, just be...you." I grudgingly sat back down and sulked into my cereal.

We continued our breakfast in silence. When I was finished, I got up and put my bowl in the sink without a word to my mother or Dexter. I went to my room to gather up my things for school and put on my shoes. I avoided any reflective surface, so I wouldn't lose my nerve and run for the bathroom sink.

I was irritated now and wanted to ride to school alone. Dexter wasn't ready yet, and I could get a head start. As I passed the kitchen I said, "Bye" without turning to look at either of them. I didn't wait for a response or a reaction, I just headed for the door. Of course my new super-hearing allowed me to catch the rest of their conversation. I waited outside the front door, letting my ears tune in to Mandy and Dexter.

"Why do you think she's wearing makeup today?" Mandy pried. She knew that if anyone knew what was going on, it would be Dexter.

He hesitated. "I'm not sure...maybe she's just...I don't know," he didn't lie well, especially to Mandy.

"Hmmm," Mandy replied. "Have you noticed she's been acting a little weird lately?" she pried a little further.

"Uh no, not really." I could tell he was lying without seeing his face.

"Oh, well. Maybe she's interested in someone," Mandy said offhandedly. I imagined that about a second after saying those words, Mandy would have realized how hard it would be for Dexter to hear them. Her mouth would turn down at the corners, and a look of worry would come over her face. I knew I was right because of what Mandy said next.

"Sorry Dex. I just...you know it's going to happen someday. I know what you want and how you feel, but you know it's not the same for Violet." Her voice was soft and full of motherly love.

I knew that these words were going to hit Dexter harder than ever because of what had happened with Luca. It was hard for Dexter, and there was no easy way for any of it to happen. Of course, I wasn't even sure if anything would happen with Luca. But, I knew that whether it was Luca now or someone else five years from now, it was going to hurt him. I hated it, but it was inevitable. I didn't wait around to hear his response. I walked over to my bike that leaned against the carport wall, hopped on, and took off down the hill.

I pedaled quickly. Though I wasn't late, I knew that Dexter would catch up to me soon enough, and I was still a little angry with him. Sure enough, it was only a few minutes before he came huffing and puffing around the corner, pedaling faster than I was aware he could. Dexter was not exactly inclined toward exercise. "Violet!" he called, out of breath, "Violet, wait up! Please!" he called again desperately. I slowed, knowing that if this wasn't resolved before school started, I would have an even more miserable day than I already planned on having.

"What, Dex?" I snapped without looking at him.

"Why'd you take off?" he asked, regaining his natural breathing.

I could see the sweat beading on his head.

"I don't know, I just..."

"It's okay," he said quietly, not forcing me to say anymore. I slowed down as an act of forgiveness that he'd understand.

We rode the rest of the way without talking, but the tension had eased a bit. When we got to school, put our bikes in the rack, and walked in side by side, as usual. As we approached our lockers, we both saw Stephanie Baker and some of the same people who'd been with her Friday night, gathered in their usual circle, talking and laughing. I was about to put my head down, resorting to my usual position to avoid conflict and confrontation, when it occurred to me that given the events of Friday night, I could actually have the upper hand in this situation. So instead of hiding and looking at the ground, I did something I had never done before: I held my head high and defiantly looked Stephanie in the eyes.

Though inside I trembled, on the outside I appeared willful and strong. Stephanie momentarily stopped talking. For a split second, I noticed a strange look flash across her face. I thought it looked a lot like fear. Then, it was gone and Stephanie was sneering angrily, her face twisted and ugly. I could hear what she was saying even if no one outside of her group could.

"I don't know what that bitch's problem is! All of a sudden she thinks she can hold her head up. Thinks she's somebody? She's the same loser freak show that she was last week!" She laughed loudly enough that I didn't need my extraordinary hearing to listen.

Stephanie's words were like a physical blow. I knew she was right. Just because I had supernatural abilities didn't change anything. I was still Violet Arena: friendless, awkward, freak!

I was about to drop my eyes and shuffle off to my locker, defeated, when I turned and saw Luca. He was watching me intensely. He had obviously witnessed my small act of defiance and had also heard what Stephanie said. He simply and silently said, *She's wrong.* And then one corner of his mouth lifted into a half-smile. I couldn't help but give him a weak smile in return. *You look amazing,* he added. My cheeks reddened, and I turned away from him.

"I am never wearing makeup again!" I vowed to myself.

Dexter had also witnessed me defy Stephanie, but he had also seen my exchange with Luca. He sighed and yanked his books from his locker. I joined him at my own locker and gathered my books silently. We separated and walked on to our classes.

I skipped lunch and hid in the library, so I didn't see Luca again until art class. Today we were sketching, so I knew I would have a chance to talk to Luca...if I wanted to. When class started, I took my usual seat by the door. Then, unexpectedly, Luca came in and took the stool next to me without a word, and the butterflies returned. We were working on the initial sketches for a still life—easy—even boring. But, I was glad we weren't doing anything that took too much brain power because I wanted to focus on Luca.

I watched him in my periphery and noticed him taking peeks in my direction. Surprisingly, the silence between us was easy, not tense or weird like I'd expected. I was also surprised by how much I liked being near him. It felt... sort of natural, normal. We didn't speak at all, not aloud or telepathically, but I definitely felt something between us. He kept his promise and didn't try to force his presence on me, but his proximity was comforting. I had to admit to myself that I enjoyed having him near me even if it did cause others in class to stare, whisper, and even giggle. When the bell rang, we gathered our belongings and moved toward our lockers together, still not speaking, but walking in step with one another. Once at our lockers, we separated.

Dexter joined me where Luca had left off. "So, did anything *happen* today?" he asked.

"What do you mean?" I asked, glaring at him

"With Stephanie," he said, as if I should have known what he meant. "Why, what did you think I meant?" he asked with a sideways glance.

"I thought you were talking about—" I whispered now, "—my new... *abilities*." I widened my eyes to emphasize what I meant.

"No. Why, *did* something happen?" he asked, eyes wide.

"No," I answered curtly. I realized that he was unaware of most of what I could do. I was eventually going to have to let him in on the whole thing, but I just wasn't ready yet. We shut our lockers at the same time.

"Ready?" Dexter asked, either unaware of Luca or ignoring him. I assumed it was the latter.

"Um...yeah," I said. I glanced at Luca who was looking at me, and then I turned and walked away.

***

The next couple of days went on similarly. Luca seemed to be near me often, but at the same time, kept his distance. I struggled with the desire to talk to him. I wanted nothing more, but my past experiences had hardened me and made it nearly impossible to give in to my desires. Denying myself had become an integral part of who I was. By Wednesday afternoon I had a change of heart. I'm still not sure what led me to drill a tiny hole in my defensive wall, but I did. Maybe it was Luca's constant presence or my growing urge to be near him, but I cracked...slightly.

As Dexter and I were packing up to leave, and Luca was, as usual, at his locker a few over from Dexter's, I said, "Just give me a minute." Dexter had obviously noticed Luca leaning against his own locker each day, waiting for something. So when I said this, he looked at Luca and connected the dots. Clearly, Luca was waiting for me, as he had every day.

"Yeah," was all Dexter said as he turned and sulked toward the exit.

Luca seemed to understand. He took Dexter's leaving as his cue to approach me. Though we had just been sitting next to each other for an hour, we'd been in a crowded class. Now, the crowds were thinning and the hall was nearly empty. The pressure was on. I became instantly nervous, regretting my decision to stay.

As if he read my mind, or knew what I needed, Luca spoke first. “So, do you want a ride home? I can fit your bike in my trunk,” he asked in that quiet, sincere tone that he'd used at my house.

“Well, I usually ride home with Dexter. He's waiting for me,” I said reluctantly.

“Oh.”

“I just...” I froze. Why had I stayed back? What did I envision myself saying to him? Though Luca was patient, I still turned pink as I tried to find words...any words. “I...I just wanted...” Nothing.

“Was there something you wanted to talk to me about?” he asked.

I really wanted to ask him about the floating, but this just didn’t seem like the right place, and I couldn’t seem to get that many words out.

“Umm...not yet.” I sounded like an idiot. “Sorry,” I mumbled, turning my eyes down.

“It’s okay. I’m just glad you’re finally talking to me.” he smiled. I glanced up at him quickly without returning his smile.

“Okay well, I’ve gotta go...Dexter...” I made a slight gesture with my hand, barely indicating that Dexter was waiting for me outside.

“Okay,” he answered. Not once did he look at me like I was crazy, even though I felt exactly that.

“Bye,” I said.

“See you later,” he replied, then turned toward the exit at the opposite end of the hall that led to the student parking lot. I proceeded to my exit. Before he turned the corner, I called to him, *Luca?* It was easier to speak through my mind than to open my mouth and let the words escape.

He stopped and turned to look at me. *Yes?*

Before I could say anything, I was captivated by the silvery blue that filled my brain with his words. And it became more difficult to speak with his eyes focused on me. I tried to concentrate on what I wanted to say. *Thank you.*

For what? he asked, sounding confused, his face echoing the sound of his thoughts.

For being patient and giving me time.

No problem, he replied with a gentle, earnest smile. Then he turned and walked away.

I found Dexter at the bike rack, waiting impatiently. I was struck by the differences between him and Luca. Dexter's dirty-blonde hair, in need of a trim, hung limply over his fair skin and blue eyes. He was tall and lanky, with a permanent "the world sucks" scowl on his face. If I didn't think of him as my brother, I could admit that he was attractive, or could be if he cared at all.

Luca too was tall, at least six feet, but he was a bit more filled out than Dexter, not muscle-bound or overweight, but solid. His hair was also overgrown, but his dark, loose curls made it look tousled rather than unkempt. And Luca's face always seemed so serene and patient. "I'm ready," I called to Dexter, trying to sound bubbly, but feeling disappointed. I hoped this didn't show. We both mounted our bikes and were on our way.

We arrived home quickly. Mandy was home; *"Getting ready for her 'group' no doubt,"* I thought, annoyed. Dexter went in first, still not talking to me. He went immediately to the kitchen. I went to my room. Mandy was out back, getting the patio ready for her guests. This time of year, she liked to meet outside.

This group had been meeting for at least ten years, and at this point they didn't even focus on UFOs most of the time, unless some new "research" or "evidence" had emerged. They mostly just talked about their lives, their families, and whatever else people talk about when they are just catching up with one another. I was just grateful that I would have the solitude of the house. I had a ton of homework.

I went to the backyard to say hello to my mother. "Hi, Mandy," I said as I walked down the slate back steps. "Mandy? Where are you?" I called. I could hear her, but I couldn't see her anywhere.

"I'm back here!" she called breathlessly from behind the shed. I found her trying, in vain, to push, or pull a half-full rain barrel. It took everything in me to restrain a laugh. It was so typical of Mandy to be attempting to do something too difficult for one person to do.

"What are you doing?" I asked rhetorically.

"I need to move this over to the gutter by the house," she motioned.

"Why?"

"It's supposed to rain a lot this week, and I want to fill it up. Give me a hand."

I hesitated. I knew I could move it easily with one hand, but I could not let my mother know that. I bit my lip as I contemplated my choices.

"Violet, get over here and help me!" Mandy demanded, choosing for me.

"Oh. Sorry. I was daydreaming," I lied. I moved to the opposite side of the rain barrel, crouched down, and put my hands on the middle of its body. I wanted to keep my hands as out-of-sight as possible.

"And...push!" Mandy called.

I puckered my brow and feigned a strain. I tried very hard to moderate my strength. It took no effort on my part, and the barrel slid as easily as if it were on rollers. In no time, it was across the back yard and under the gutter.

"Well, we make a good team." Mandy said, as she put her arm around me and squeezed my shoulder. I smiled, but remained stiff.

Of course, Mandy was a hugger. Nearly everyone she met was greeted with a warm smile and a hug, or some sort of touch, to their hand, their shoulder, something. That's probably why she did so well with the psych patients. When someone met Mandy, they never forgot how welcoming she was.

I peeled myself from her and looked around the backyard. Mandy had outdone herself, as usual. She had pulled every chair, bench, and table she could find and assembled them in a grouping on the slate, mosaic patio. Off to the side she had placed our outdoor fireplace for warmth, if necessary, and to keep away the bugs that started to become a nuisance this time of the year

"Looks nice, Mandy," I complimented.

"Thanks. Will you help me with the food?"

"Sure," I said.

As we walked in, Mandy continued to question me. "Did you have a good day at school?"

"Yeah, it was good," I replied. I prayed that she would stop her questions right there. No such luck.

"Good. Oh, by the way, the other day...the makeup. Did it work?"

"Did what work?" I asked, confused.

"Whatever you wore that makeup for, did it work out?" Mandy pried, too deeply this time. I lost it.

"God! What is with you and Dexter? So I wore a little makeup to feel good about myself. Am I not allowed to do that?" I demanded, maybe a little too loudly.

"I'm sorry. I...forget it, okay?" Mandy said apologetically. "Forget I said anything. Let's just go get the food ready." She tried to recover as we walked into the house together. We passed the large mirror that hung in the living room and Mandy stopped and put her arm around my shoulder, holding me in place. "See how beautiful you are," she whispered as she looked at us in the mirror. "It helps that you have such a ravishing mother," she said with an exaggerated model pose. I smiled, but as I stared into the mirror, trying to find the similarities, it struck me, as it often did when we were next to one another, how different Mandy and I were in appearance and demeanor.

Mandy was petite in stature, almost waifish, with straight, silky, dark blonde hair that she wore long, and usually in a braid down her back. Her eyes were bright green, and they almost sparkled. And Mandy's skin had a bronze tint to it from all the time she'd spent outside over the years. She was open and friendly with a sunny personality and an optimistic disposition. I was her antithesis in every way.

I was several inches taller, slender, but definitely more filled-in and curvy than my mother. My unstyled brown hair fell in thick, loose waves to the sides of my face and several inches past my shoulders. My eyes were black as coal and had a certain quality that made it so that most people wouldn't look me in the eye for any extended period of time. Dexter said it was because they had an "infinite and mysterious depth to them," but he was biased.

I was pale, almost ashen, but when I was embarrassed or upset, or angry, the most horrible shades of pink and red flared in my cheeks. And of course, where Mandy took life in stride, always finding the silver lining, I was guarded and pessimistic, maintaining a secure barricade around myself.

When I looked away from the mirror, I caught Dexter staring at me. I was angry for a brief second, but then I remembered how he had once told me that it made him happy to see Mandy and me together, with me, "allowing her to be" my mother. So, I convinced myself that was the reason he was staring, and my anger faded even before he looked away. Mandy and I disconnected and she walked further into the living room toward Dexter.

"Dexter, you okay?" Mandy asked him over her shoulder. She'd obviously seen him in the mirror too.

"Yeah." He smiled. "What are you two up to?"

"We are going to get the snacks ready for my group. Tonight is bruschetta and brownies!"

"Sounds good. Need help?" he asked.

"Well, the brownies are already done," Mandy thought for a moment, "but you can chop tomatoes."

There was still a bit of a chill between Dexter and me, but it was beginning to thaw now that we were all in the kitchen having *family time*. For me, this was the way it was supposed to be with Dexter. In a moment like this, I could think of him as a brother again and forget the awkwardness.

I was on bread-slicing duty. I hesitantly opened the silverware drawer and reached in carefully to get a knife. I concentrated on reaching in and grabbing the knife before it grabbed me. Then I walked over to the wooden cutting board that sat on the counter permanently, and began to slice. We all talked and laughed. We were having a good time. I wasn't looking at what I was doing when the knife slipped. The blade slid across the side of my index finger. Instinctively, I yelled, "Ahh!" and dropped the knife. But when I looked down, there was nothing wrong with my finger. I blinked and stared at my hand in bewilderment. I knew that my finger should have a deep cut, but it didn't. In fact, I'd hardly felt the touch of the knife. I had reacted out of instinct and anticipation. Mandy turned to me.

"What happened?" she asked in alarm.

"Nothing, I just hit my hand on the edge of the counter," I quickly lied.

"Oh. Are you all right?"

"Yes, I'm fine," I smiled nervously.

But when I caught a glimpse of Dexter's face, his expression confirmed my worst fear: *"He saw!"* He continued to look between my face, my uninjured finger, and the knife. I panicked. Then I shook my head anxiously at him. "Later," I mouthed. He nodded, but his expression remained unchanged. I dreaded the eventual conversation I'd have to have with Dexter, so I stayed busy, helping Mandy more than usual.

Just as we were taking the bread out of the oven and cleaning up the kitchen, Mandy's friends began to arrive. Most of them were people that I had known for a good portion of my life. They were kind of like family, except I didn't want them to be. They were a varied and interesting lot, from all walks of life.

There were the stereotypical *weirdos*, like Tom and Evelyn, always bug-eyed and looking over their shoulders, people you'd expect to see on a street corner, holding a sign, warning about the coming of the end. But most of them were *normal* people who led *normal* lives, less vocal about their experiences outside of this tight circle of sympathizers. These were the ones who had "rules" about contact outside the group. Like Ed, a seventy-year-old retired dentist from Peekskill, who I was allowed to acknowledge but only if I pretended to be a former patient; or Sarah, a forty-something cashier who would act like a stranger if we happened to run into one another in the *real world.* Then there was Mandy's best friend, Marilyn, a single, childless shrew of a woman to whom I could never warm up, though I'd known her since I was six.

She seemed forever-angry and had always eyed me with what I regarded as either suspicion or contempt. Mandy said Marilyn had never "gotten over" what had been done to her by the Grays. Most of the people in the group regarded their supposed *experiences* as positive, or at least interesting. But Marilyn was different. Mandy said she was bitter and angry. She blamed *them* for ruining her life —causing her to lose her fiancé and rendering her sterile. I often asked Mandy how she could be friends with someone like her, but ever-compassionate Mandy reminded me that Marilyn was lonely and sad and needed her friendship more than anything. So, despite the loathing I felt for Marilyn, this was another reason I secretly admired my mother.

It wasn't that I didn't like these people, apart from Marilyn, of course. It was just that they represented a part of Mandy's life, and my life for that matter, that I didn't want any part of. I said my "Hellos" and even accepted a few hugs, but then I retreated to my room to work on my homework and wait for Dexter's knock at my door.

I could hear laughter and talking outside. I heard Marilyn's distinctly sardonic voice ask, "What's *her* problem?" to which Mandy replied without any negative overtones, "She doesn't have a problem, she's just not comfortable with all this, you know that, and that's her right." I could picture the sneer on Marilyn's face and the serene smile on Mandy's.

I knew I could listen to everything they talked about, but I decided they probably were saying very little that I wanted to hear, so I tried to tune out their conversations by sticking in my earbuds. "Come in," I said when I heard the knock I knew was coming.

"Hey, V. We *need* to talk." Dexter stood in the doorway like he wasn't welcome.

"Well, first come *into* my room and sit down. You're making me nervous just standing there," I commanded. He walked in and looked around as if he were seeing my room for the first time, though there had been a time when he had known my room almost as well as I did. Over the years, he spent a lot of time in here with me, playing board games, reading comics, and talking about absolutely everything. It was only in the last couple of years that I had essentially barred him from it.

My furniture was all basically in the same place it had always been in, but given the small size of the room and the limited wall space, that was expected. Two walls were mostly windows from about half-way up, almost to the ceiling. It made it very bright from early in the morning until late in the day, regardless of where the sun was. So, heavy, light-blocking curtains were a necessity. They were a deep crimson, lush and velvety with dark blue and gold accents. My bedspread was equally dark, blue like the midnight sky in the painting that hung above my same old, wrought iron bed.

Up until recently, it had always been my favorite painting, one I'd done the year before. It was enormous, at least three feet by five, horizontal. Against the deep blue midnight of the background there was a silvery-gray, elongated oval disc at the top. Below that were four elongated, gray, almost light bulb-shaped figures, all standing in a row, cut across the middle by a horizontal white figure with brilliant green eyes. The gray figures were standing on top of another lighter gray figure with black, pleading eyes, crushing it. This figure was becoming dismembered and disfigured by the stampede of gray figures above, its limbs stretched to their maximum at the places where the joints should be, and its head stretched unnaturally with vibrant colors leaking from it, pooling around it.

Dexter stopped looking around and pulled out the ancient wooden desk chair that I had painted with swirls of color and blocks of black and gray, still parked beneath my mismatched white, wooden desk with peeling paint and little girl stickers adorning some of the legs. He turned the chair to face me. I was sitting cross-legged on my bed, papers and books scattered around me, my laptop closed to my left. I thought it would be fair if I spoke first.

"I don't know what that was in the kitchen, but I am assuming that my skin is a little tougher than your average skin," I said casually. "I've been thinking...have you ever seen me with a cut, or have I ever needed a band-aid?"

"I...I don't know," he said, sounding bewildered.

"Well, I don't think I have, at least not since I was really little," I replied before he could think about it any further. I was now staring down at the bedspread, playing with a piece of loose thread.

"Now that I think of it, I really can't ever remember you getting hurt or anything." He looked at me intensely.

"So maybe that's been the case my whole life. No one ever noticed, I guess," I conceded, looking up.

"Is that all, or is there more?" His face begged for information.

"Well, I don't know how to explain this, so I'm just going to say it...I can float, or hover, or...maybe *fly*," I said the last word quietly and with an inflection that made it sound like a question.

"You can WHAT?" His face was wide with awe.

"SHHHH!" I scolded.

"Sorry." He looked as if he were having to force his mouth to stay shut.

"Well, I only just figured it out, but I floated, twice involuntarily, and then once on purpose," I explained. There was a very long pause.

"What the hell is going on, V?" Dexter finally asked, quiet now, unable to hide the worry in his voice.

"I honestly don't know," I said, barely above a whisper, and looked down into my lap again.

"And Luca...he can do this too?"

"I don't know, maybe. So far he seems to be able to do the same things I can." I was getting uncomfortable now, thinking about Luca with Dexter there looking so worried about me

"Is there anything else?" he pressed.

"Well, I seem to be able to...*sense* his presence and...he can sense mine," I said reluctantly, knowing how much this part would hurt him.

"Oh," was his only verbal response, but physically he seemed to falter slightly, like if he hadn't been sitting, he may have stumbled.

"Yeah. And you know about the strength, which is becoming hard to control if I don't concentrate. That's it. That's all I know about so far." I decided to continue to keep the telepathy to myself.

One of my reasons was selfless: to spare Dexter. My other reason was completely selfish: I liked the part that allowed me to have this communication that no one but Luca could hear, and I wasn't ready to share it yet, not even with Dexter— especially not with Dexter.

"Okay, so now what?" he asked, taking shallow breaths.

"I don't really know, Dex. I mean last week I assumed I was going insane, and now...I don't know. I'm still really overwhelmed, and scared, and like I told Luca the other night when I freaked out, I don't know if I'm ready to deal with it. But since I seem to continue to get more powers and they continue to get stronger, I don't think I'm going to have a choice," I explained.

"I understand, and I meant what I said, I'm always here for you," he said, adding, "Does that mean you'll be spending a lot of time with Luca?" I could tell this was the question he really wanted an answer to.

"Not sure. I guess that depends on what he wants from me, if anything," I confessed. I looked up to meet Dexter's sad eyes.

"It's getting late. I want to work on this paper for a little while longer...are we okay?" I asked, hoping the concern was evident in my tone.

"Yeah, we're okay," he said with a tight-lipped sort of smile and a quick head nod. But I didn't believe him. "'Night."

"Goodnight."

7

The remainder of the week was fairly uneventful. Stephanie glared at me daily, but never approached me. I hoped maybe she was done with me, but I assumed she was probably planning something diabolical. That thought made me shudder; I never did like surprises, and lately I had been inundated with them.

Things with Luca were strange— to me, at least. We didn't say much, though our proximity had changed. He was *around* more, and there was more eye contact. Of course, any eye contact would be *more* in my case. He did seem to be trying to live up to his promise and give me the time I needed. He sat next to me in art class every day now, and I actually liked it. I was beginning to loosen up. I thought maybe I'd even be ready to talk about *it* soon. Luca didn't seem to come around as much when I was with Dexter, though. I wondered if it was some male-ego-jealousy thing or if he was being sensitive to mine and Dexter's friendship.

However, Friday at lunch, Dexter and I were sitting together, as usual, when Luca walked over to us. It was harder for me to *sense* his presence at school. I wasn't sure if it had something to do with concentration or the fact that he was always there, so his nearness was constant.

"Would you guys mind if I sat with you today?" he asked quietly.

We both looked up, surprised. I was about to open my mouth to say, "Yes," when I realized that Dexter might not be too happy about it. So, I looked to him, my eyes asking what he thought. It was

Dexter who answered, "Sure." He looked up at Luca and even smiled a little. I felt relieved.

None of us said anything for a minute, but then Dexter asked me, "Is Mandy working this weekend?" I wondered why he'd asked this particular question, but then assumed it was his way of letting Luca know, again, how much a part of my life he actually was.

"Yes, tonight and tomorrow night, as usual. Why?"

"Just wondering," he mumbled through a mouthful of pizza.

Luca didn't seem affected by Dexter's question at all. He just ate, seeming completely at ease.

I had to say something. Sitting there mute was even beginning to annoy me. "Is that peanut butter and jelly?" I asked, looking at what Luca was eating and trying to start some kind of conversation. I felt stupid the minute the words came out.

"Yeah. It's my favorite," he replied.

"Me too," I said quietly, showing my own sandwich to him.

"I'm a vegetarian," he added.

"You're kidding?" Dexter asked wryly. I knew he wanted to roll his eyes.

"No, why?" Luca asked, confused.

"Tell him, V," Dexter said, motioning to me.

"Tell me what?" Luca asked.

"It's just, I don't eat meat either." I didn't know why this revelation was so difficult, it just all seemed so odd...how much we had in common.

"Well, it's not for the reasons you might think, I just *can't* eat meat," Luca stated. I thought he almost sounded like he was apologizing for something.

"Really? Me either. I've never been able to digest it well," I said, more enthusiastically than anything I usually said. "But, I probably wouldn't even if I could...just don't like the idea." *"Okay Violet, don't babble!"* I told myself. I was just having a difficult time controlling my emotions these days, particularly around Luca. We stared at each other for a moment.

"Me either," Luca replied.

"You either what? Can't digest it, or wouldn't eat it even if you could?" Dexter asked.

"I get sick to my stomach when I eat it. I'm sorry to tell you that I would probably have no problem with it otherwise." He shrugged his shoulders and grinned

"Hmm," was my only response.

Dexter was squirming in his seat with a look that was a cross between revulsion and fear. I knew he couldn't stand to hear one more thing we might discover that Luca and I had in common.

"So...what are your weekend plans?" Dexter asked Luca. This brought all my attention to Dexter. I could not believe he was asking Luca a question! Knowing Dexter, he could care less about Luca's weekend plans but was actually just jealous and wanted my conversation with Luca to end.

"Uh...I have to go to my grandparents' house for a big dinner. It's their fiftieth anniversary," Luca replied.

"Wow, fifty years? That's amazing," I said. I was interested in everything…anything he said.

"Yeah, it really is. My parents have been together for, like, twenty years, and that seems like forever."

"How about your family, Violet?" Luca asked me. I wasn't prepared for this question, but I decided that I might as well be honest.

"My mom and dad split up when I was around four."

"Sorry," he replied sincerely.

"Don't be. I think for them it was for the best; they are so different. To be honest, I don't know how they ever got married to begin with," I said, thinking of the seemingly polar opposites who were, somehow, my parents.

"That must've been hard for you," he said.

"Oh, it's no big deal. They've been apart so long, I've never really thought of them any other way," I shrugged.

"Where's your dad, if you don't mind me asking?" he continued. No one had ever taken this much interest in me, and to my surprise, I liked it.

"California. He's remarried...whole *new life* scenario," I explained, trying to sound indifferent, and hoping the resentment, anger, and hurt didn't leak into my words.

Luca nodded. I guessed I'd convinced him. "What about you, Dexter?" I knew how uncomfortable Dexter would be with this question, and I wanted to protect him from having to open up. I was about to say something, when Dexter jumped in.

"My dad is insane, and my mom…is dead," he answered directly, face emotionless. I was in shock. "I gotta get to class. See ya later," he said and got up quickly without looking at either of us. Then he took off. I thought it would be better if I didn't go after him. I'd see him after school, and we could talk then if he wanted to. But Luca felt terrible.

"I'm sorry, I didn't know... Should I go talk to him?" he asked, his face pained.

"No. He'll be okay. Besides, you didn't know any better. He's had it rough, that's why my mom sort-of unofficially adopted him when we were kids and then became his legal guardian," I explained. I was satisfied that I hadn't revealed too much. I knew it wasn't my place to tell Dexter's story.

"Are you sure?" he asked again.

"Yes."

After a quiet moment, I thought about asking him about the floating, but then I looked at the clock. "We'd better get to class," I said.

We walked slowly out of the cafeteria, until it was time to go our separate ways.

"See you in art. And please tell Dexter that I'm sorry," Luca said with a hopeful smile.

"I will. See ya," I replied, shyly returning his smile.

Art class went on as it had all week. However, Luca and I started to talk a little more than usual...just music and other light subjects. And as usual, after class, he walked me to my locker then let Dexter have his time with me. Also, like he had all week, he walked me out to my bike. Every day he offered to give me a ride home, and every day I chose to spare Dexter's feelings. Today being Friday, I said before leaving, "Have fun at your grandparents'. Wish them a happy anniversary."

"I will, thanks." Then he paused, "Can I call you?" he asked shyly, but tapped on his temple.

"Yes," I said simply, smiling. Then I hopped on my bike and rode off to join Dexter.

The afternoon and evening were peaceful. Mandy was gone when Dexter and I got home, and of course there was dinner in the refrigerator. We stayed in. I painted for a while, then joined Dexter for some TV before bed. We didn't talk about my powers or about Luca, or about the awkward exchange at lunch. We stuck to less controversial topics. It seemed to me that we had both had a long week and needed to forget—for a night, at least.

***

I could hear Mandy on the back patio when I woke up. When I looked at the clock, I was surprised she wasn't asleep yet. She did have to work again that night. We usually passed each other a few times on Saturdays between her getting home and going to bed, then later when she was getting ready for work.

"Hey, Mandy, what are you doing up? Hey, Dex," I said when I found the two of them on the back patio cleaning and moving furniture.

"Hey." Dexter stopped what he was doing briefly to greet me and then returned to his sweeping.

"I don't know. I just couldn't stay asleep. I think it's this nice weather," Mandy explained. I saw that she looked very content, but also tired.

"Spring is great. I hope your patients enjoy it as much as you do. Shouldn't you sleep for their sake?" I asked sarcastically.

"*They* will be fine, and so will I." She dragged a huge planter across the patio. "So, I have a few extra hours to kill. Wanna do something together?" Mandy asked excitedly. She loved when "the stars aligned" as she liked to say, and she and I could spend mother-daughter time together. She loved Dexter like he was her own son, but I knew she craved time alone with me. I saw the look on her face and could not deny her.

"Okay. What do you want to do?" I tried not to sound put-upon.

"Want to go grocery shopping? We haven't done that in a while, and we do need some stuff. What do you think?"

"Sure. That'll be...fun," I said, trying to convince myself.

"Dexter, you're welcome to join us, you know," Mandy added.

"Um, I'm good. I just got a new book I want to start," Dexter replied. I wasn't sure if this was true, but I was fairly certain that this was Dexter's subtle way of giving me some time with Mandy. He finished sweeping and walked into the house. I followed him.

"Bye, Dex. See you in the morning," Mandy called after him.

Quietly, so Mandy couldn't hear, I questioned him in a strained whisper, "You didn't say anything about Luca, did you? She seems abnormally happy...even for Mandy."

"No, Violet!" he whispered back, obviously annoyed. Then, he turned away and went into his room, leaving me feeling terrible.

8

For most of the short ride we talked very little, and when we did it was small talk. Then Mandy did the one thing she is really good at, brought up something to annoy me. Thankfully, it wasn't aliens or UFOs, but Dexter.

"Dexter seemed pretty down today. Is everything okay between you two?"

"Yes. We are fine. He's just being Dexter," I answered, looking out the window. I didn't like lying to my mother. Before now, the only times I had ever lied to her was to protect her feelings when kids picked on me *because* of her.

"I don't know. He seemed more glum than usual. Did you have a fight or something?"

"No. Same old stuff. He's still just...he's having a hard time with the fact that I don't feel the same way about him as he does for me. That's all," I said this more confidently. It wasn't a total lie. That definitely was *part* of the problem.

"He just doesn't know anything else, Violet. That's why he thinks you would be great together..." Mandy trailed off. I winced and turned so that Mandy could fully see the disgusted expression on my face.

"Sorry...I know, I said I would never push that issue with you. I just feel bad for Dex, that's all. I won't bring it up again. Promise," she said in earnest.

The rest of the drive was spent in uncomfortable silence.

It was Saturday afternoon, so the store was a bit more crowded than I preferred. We parked toward the back of the lot and had a long walk in. The grocery store was in a shopping center with a variety of other stores that dot suburban America, making one shopping mall indistinguishable from another. As we approached the store, I felt him. And then, I saw, to my surprise and joy and discomfort, Luca. He was outside the skate shop next to the grocery store, sitting on a bench, listening to music. He looked like he was waiting for something. Then it hit me like a brick, *"He is waiting for me! How did he know I was here?"*

He looked up as I got closer, probably sensing my presence. His stare was so intense, I had to look away. I was brimming with a sudden surge of emotions. So many that I couldn't even identify them all in that moment. I felt the heat begin in my cheeks and spread through me. At the same time, I felt a little annoyed. He knew I needed space, but there he was. Above all else, I was confused. I thought to him, *What are you doing here?*

He replied, *I was just...skating.* I wasn't sure I believed his explanation. Though Lake Hansen isn't that big, it still seemed too coincidental.

Mandy noticed me looking in Luca's direction and asked, "Do you know that boy, Violet? He was staring at you when we walked up." Mandy could hardly contain the excitement in her voice; the tone of her implication was anything but subtle. She arched her eyebrows and smiled, "He's cute, Honey," she added, too enthusiastically.

"Huh?" I responded.

"I said that boy was staring at you. Do you know him?" She lifted her chin toward Luca, and I could hear the smile in her voice.

I blushed when I realized she had caught me staring at Luca. "Yeah, I know him a little," I admitted.

"He's so cute!" she repeated.

Before I even realized what I was saying, I answered, "Yeah, he is." *Damn!* I looked shyly in Luca's direction. At my words, his head picked up and there was a small smile across his face and a surprised look in his eyes. Instantly, I realized that he had heard me. I had forgotten about the exceptional hearing that we were both developing. My face turned a deep shade of crimson as I realized that the power had just shifted slightly in Luca's favor. *Damn again!*

"Come on Mandy, don't you need to work tonight?" I grabbed my mother's arm gently and guided her into the store.

"Do I sense a little avoidance here? Is there more to that boy than you are telling me?" she asked playfully.

"No. I don't know. I don't want to talk about this right now. Okay?" I pleaded. I could see the questions swarming inside of my mother's head. This was a moment Mandy had waited for my entire life. I felt terrible for not being able to tell her how interested I actually was in Luca. Partly because I had barely come to terms with the feelings myself, and partly because there was so much going on between us that I just couldn't grasp, and Mandy was the *last* person I wanted to discuss that part with. She'd have to be happy with that little bit of information for now.

"Whatever you say Violet," and then she just dropped it.

When we left the store, Luca was gone. Or at least, I didn't see or hear or *feel* him anywhere. I decided that he was probably lurking about somewhere, keeping an eye on me. The ride home began uneventfully. Mandy and I made small talk. To my relief, it seemed she had taken the hint and let the Luca thing go. We were behind an open flatbed truck that was hauling large, cement pipes like the ones they use beneath roads. Traffic was tight, but moving steadily.

I never liked Mandy's driving, and as usual, I was holding the door handle tightly for leverage and comfort while Mandy followed too closely behind the truck. When the truck came to a sudden stop, Mandy stopped abruptly too, causing a chain reaction. I felt a hit from behind, jolting me forward in my seat. And then, I watched as a strap that had been holding the pipes down on the truck's bed, detached.

With the momentum of the stop, several of the pipes were airborne, deadly projectiles headed for our windshield. I acted instinctively. I perceived the imminent threat, reached my hands out and then swung them to the right. At that exact moment, the pipes stopped their forward motion, and rolled to the left of the truck, crashing to the ground with a thundering, clinking sound, and rolling over the sidewalk before coming to a stop.

It all happened instantaneously, yet I saw the entire situation as if it had happened in still frames. "Violet, are you okay?" was all Mandy pressed, surveying me.

I sat perfectly still, jaw clenched, shallow breaths coming quickly through my nose as I tried desperately to grasp what had happened and gather my thoughts. Unable to do anything more, I nodded. "How did...What just happened?" Mandy stammered.

"I don't...I'm not sure," I uttered almost inaudibly after a moment. But, I knew exactly what had happened. I had recognized the threat, and I had used some power, like what happened with the spoon, the bathroom stalls, my clock, and I moved the pipes. I moved the pipes with my mind!

"Are you sure you're okay?" she asked again.

"I'm fine, really. Are you okay? Did you get hurt?"

She swiveled her neck, moved her shoulders up and down and stretched out her legs. "I think I'm fine," she assured me. "We should get out and see if everyone is all right," Mandy said after another long moment had passed. I simply nodded in agreement.

I willed myself to undue my seatbelt and open the car door. I quickly surveyed the scene and realized that Mandy and I had gotten off very lucky. I immediately heard screaming two cars behind ours. This car had certainly bore the brunt of the accident, having been rammed from behind by a monster SUV that hardly had a scratch. The car in front of it, which was the one behind ours, was damaged, but the people inside were fine. In the crushed vehicle, I could see a woman in the driver's seat who was bleeding from her forehead. Mandy had already rushed to the woman, her nursing skills kicking in like second nature.

I felt helpless as a crowd began to gather around the woman's car. I could hear pieces of a quiet conversation my mother was having. It sounded like a 911 call, "I think she's trapped behind the steering wheel...can't open her door. twelfth and..." she paused to look at the cross-streets. "...Lysander...I'm a nurse...If they don't get her out...possibly some internal injuries...loss of circulation..." In that moment, I knew what I had to do.

I took a deep breath, ran over to the small crowd outside the woman's car, looking as frantic as I could, stood beside my mother and yelled, "I think there's someone under those pipes, on the sidewalk. They need help!" Everyone looked at one another, and then at me. Mandy eyed me strangely. "Hurry! They could die! Those pipes were big! Come on!"

"What about Carol here?" I assumed that was the woman in the car. "She needs someone with her until the ambulance comes. I didn't see anyone on the sidewalk," someone in the crowd said.

"I saw someone! And I heard someone crying. You guys go, please. I'll stay here with her!" I pleaded. I met my mother's eyes. I had always been a terrible liar, but Mandy must have seen something in my face that made her react.

"If someone is trapped under those pipes, they must be hurt badly. Come on, we'll all need to help!" Mandy called. I gave my mother a conspiratorial look, but then lowered my eyes as Mandy got the crowd moving.

I got to work immediately, knowing how little time I had. "Carol? Hi, my name is Violet. I'm going to try to get you out of there okay?" I looked at the woman in the driver's seat. I was suddenly very scared. I had gambled this woman's life with some potential power I might have. What if it had all been my imagination? What if I was really just insane? Then, I looked into the car and saw Carol. She was fading in and out of consciousness, slipping away. I shook off my doubts, knowing I had to act fast, before the crowd realized there was no one under the pipes or Carol slipped too far away for anyone to help her, superpowers or none.

I looked for a spot on the door to get a good grip. I grabbed hold of a wrinkle in the metal and heaved toward my body. It was almost too easy. The door pried back like the lid on a tuna can. When I saw the steering wheel bent unnaturally into her abdomen, I realized the gravity of the situation. I reached over Carol and grasped each side of the steering wheel, but instead of pulling like I had with the door, fearing further injury, I pushed. To my astonishment, the entire steering column pushed back into the engine compartment a few inches

By this time, the crowd was coming back, and no one looked happy. Mandy looked confused as she studied my expression, which was guarded and anxious, adrenaline pumping through me. Everyone seemed to forget about my wild goose chase, though, when they saw that Carol's door was open. Then the questions began.

"How the..."

"How did you do that?"

"Violet, what's going on here?" Mandy questioned quietly as she pulled me apart from the crowd that had begun inspecting the scene of my handiwork.

I reached for words to appease her. "Um...Uh...the door was not as bad as everyone thought." It came out almost sounding like a question. "I just grabbed onto a spot and pulled. It opened easily." I said, looking down at the ground. "Guess it was just the right spot."

Even I didn't believe my last lie. Fortunately, everyone was so overjoyed that Carol was free that they seemed to forget all about me. All except for Mandy who gave me a look that said, "We aren't done talking about this."

By now, the rescue team had come and Carol was on a stretcher, being assisted by paramedics. I wished I could run, get away, hide. Mandy had been looking at me strangely for a while now, and I knew that no matter how much I lied, she would know I was being evasive. Most people tended to believe the simplest, most logical explanation for things—not Mandy. For her, the bizarre, off-the-wall, out of this world explanations *were* the simplest and most logical. I knew I'd have to think of one of those kinds of excuses quickly.

The paramedics checked Mandy for injuries. Not a scratch, though they warned her that she might be sore the next day. Next, it was my turn. I assured the paramedics that I was fine, but everyone, especially Mandy, insisted that I get fully checked. I was at least thankful that I had talked them out of a precautionary trip to the ER.

Once everyone was sure that I was okay, and I had given my account of the accident, I sat on the curb, waiting for my mother to work out the messy details of the accident. Fortunately, given the rules of traffic accidents, the SUV had been the last one in the chain of events, and that driver would be cited with negligence.

I overheard another conversation between the witnesses and the police officers. I was amused by the officer's frustration when each of the witnesses seemed to differ in their view of what happened with the pipes on the truck, "...yes, that's what I said, they just stopped and then rolled to the side!" one man said. "I don't know, they were flyin' off the back of the truck, headed for that car." another said, motioning to our little car. I also listened to my mother's view of things. "My daughter and I were behind the truck when it stopped short. Then I saw those big pipes fall off to the side, and I felt a jolt from behind. It all happened so fast." I was starting to enjoy this super-hearing ability. It was a very convenient way of eavesdropping.

I sat there, elbows on bent knees, chin resting sideways in my hands, mind wandering. As I stared at the pile of pipes that looked like pick-up sticks dropped from some giant hand in the sky, I felt a little tingle...Luca? I instantly began to look around. Finally, I saw him coming around the side of the pile looking anxious, wringing his hands. I should have known he would be nearby. He stopped short. I met his eyes and thought he looked like he was deciding whether or not he should approach me. I thought to him, *It's okay.* He continued forward until he was sitting down next to me.

"How long have you been here?" I asked him, speaking to him and looking directly at him for the first time.

"I saw the whole thing. I thought..." he broke off. I was pretty sure I knew what he had been thinking...that the pipes were going to come through the windshield and that Mandy and I would most likely be dead or seriously injured.

"I'm...we're, me and Man...my mom, are fine." I assured him as a strange warmth began to grow inside of me at the thought of someone besides Dexter caring whether I lived or died.

We sat there without talking for a minute until I was compelled to get it out of me. *I moved those pipes! I mean, I saw it all happening like slow motion. They were coming at us, and I put my hands out like this...* I demonstrated the act*...and just sort of pushed them to the side...* I could hardly believe what I was saying, what I was allowing myself to admit. It felt good. Better than good, it felt like a relief. Even thinking the thoughts was as cathartic as saying them aloud.

I know. I think I might have helped you. When I saw it all happen, I raised my hands and did pretty much the same thing, he said silently. "It seems like our powers are getting stronger and easier to use. I've been thinking...and I think our powers are stronger when we are in danger. Like a defense mechanism or something," Luca said out loud. I nodded.

Silence again. I didn't necessarily feel uncomfortable about the fact that we weren't talking. This was really the first time we had spent more than a few seconds alone. It seemed very natural. All these years I had shied away from any kind of contact like this, only allowing myself to maintain a safe friendship with Dexter, never believing that something more could exist for me. I was so happy in that moment that I didn't even care that Mandy was grinning hugely in my direction, my conversation suddenly overshadowing the horrible events of the last thirty minutes.

Mandy walked over to us. We both stood. Now I felt awkward, like I was naked and on display. I didn't like feeling vulnerable, so I fidgeted—wiped imaginary dirt from the back of my jeans, pushed my hair behind my ear, twisted the end of my hair with my fingers. Luca was calm and still. He spoke first.

"Hi, I'm Luca Verone," he said easily, then stuck out his hand to greet Mandy.

"Nice to meet you! I'm Mandy Conrad, Violet's mom," she said, smiling too hard and shaking Luca's hand too vigorously. It was embarrassing.

"Mandy, Luca was just..." I wasn't sure how to finish this sentence.

"I live around the corner, and I came out when I heard the accident. I'm glad you two are okay," he said. I stared at him. *Nice save.*

"Thanks. So, how do you know Violet?" Mandy pried.

"We go to school together. We have the same art class," he explained.

"Oh. That's great. So you know how talented my girl is," Mandy beamed. I gradually turned every shade of red that exists.

"Yeah, I do." Luca smiled and looked at me. He seemed as enthusiastic as Mandy.

"Um, Mandy, how's…Carol?" I asked in an effort to end this awkward exchange before I exploded, which I was sure was going to happen soon.

"I think she's going to be okay. She has a concussion and probably a few broken ribs, but she'll heal."

"Good...Um, don't you have to work in a couple of hours? Unless you're not feeling well enough to go in," I asked.

"Oh, no, I'm fine. Of course I'm going in. I guess we'd better get going."

"Ms. Conrad—" Luca began unexpectedly.

"*What could he possibly have to say now?!*" I thought.

"Mandy, please."

"Mandy, could I drive Violet home? My car is just over at my house. I was hoping she and I could hang out for a while. If you'd like to...?" He turned to me, asking me now, not Mandy. "Maybe we could go get some pizza or something?"

"That's okay with me." Mandy replied, ready to bust. "V?"

"Um...yeah. Okay. Pizza sounds good. But, how are you getting home and to work? Your car is a little…squished," I asked my mother. "*What was happening here? Was I really about to go out with Luca?*"

"Oh, I called Marilyn. She's on her way. She's going to help me get the groceries home then drive me to work and pick me up. She owes me a favor. So, you go have fun, okay? But please wear your seatbelt. Oh, and I'll tell Dex you'll be home later." Mandy rambled. "Luca, it was so nice to meet you. I hope I see you again," she added with a hint of optimism.

"Thanks Ms.—Mandy. It was nice to meet you too," Luca replied.

Mandy smiled at me, then turned and walked toward a woman who was waving at her. Marilyn. My least favorite person in the world…well, except maybe for Stephanie Baker. As Mandy left, I felt relieved to be separated from her questions and suspicions surrounding the afternoon's strange events and Luca. But now I had another situation to deal with. Pizza with Luca.

"We don't have to get pizza if you don't want to," Luca said, looking down at the ground, "We can just go somewhere and talk..."

"Pizza is fine. I haven't eaten all day. We can talk and eat." I said, feeling somewhat optimistic. Luca looked up, smiling, obviously pleased by my response.

"My car is just over there." He pointed to a compact, blue, four-door parked on the curb in front of a large, ranch-style house with a neatly landscaped front yard. It was much different than our small, yellow bungalow adorned with brightly colored flowers and eclectic lawn furniture in the front and back yards.

"Nice house," I said, feeling the need to say something

"Uh...thanks," Luca replied with a smirk, "I like yours. From what I've seen, your yard is really cool."

I stopped briefly. Had he read my mind? I shook my head and continued walking.

"What is it?" he asked, looking a little concerned by my reaction to the compliment.

"Nothing...I just...I was just thinking about my yard, and then you made that comment...Did you *hear* me?" I asked, a bit frightened, analyzing the implications if he had.

"No. I don't think I can read your mind. I think you have to direct thoughts my way. But, that's just a theory," he replied with a teasing smile. "Just a coincidence, I guess."

"Oh. Yeah, I kind of thought the same thing actually," I recovered.

9

As we approached the car, I walked over to the passenger side and was surprised when Luca followed me over and opened the door for me. I blushed once again, said, "Thank you," in a whisper, and got in without meeting his eyes. Luca closed the door after me and walked in front of the car to get into the driver's seat.

"So, is Mama Bella's okay?"

"The one by school?" I asked, dreading potentially running into kids from school.

"No, the one out by the baseball fields. The one by school will be loaded with people. I hope you don't mind?" he explained.

"No. I prefer that one." I said, relieved.

For a while, we drove in silence, but then Luca thought, *I'm glad you came.*

I replied, *Me too.* And then looked up to see that he was looking at me. He smiled a half-smile, and my stomach flipped.

We arrived at the restaurant quickly. Like before, Luca got out and came to my door before I could even get my seatbelt off. He opened it, and I stepped out, thanking him again quietly.

Like I had hoped, the place was nearly empty. There were a couple of families with young kids, but no Lake Hansen High students. I breathed a sigh of relief.

Luca and I sat in a booth at the far end of the front window. It was quieter there, so we would be able to talk. The server came over and took our order, brought our drinks shortly after, and then left us alone. I was finding it difficult to stop looking at Luca. The girl who never looked anyone in the eye because she felt unattractive or unworthy, or because she wanted to remain hidden from the brutal world that rejected her, couldn't tear her eyes away from Luca Verone.

I knew he was attractive, but I had never realized just how attractive he was, and the depth of his eyes made me feel like I could see into his mind even if we didn't have this strange connection. And though I could hardly believe it, Luca stared at me with the same wonder that I imagined must be on my face. I attempted some small talk...something I'd never been good at. "So, how was your grandparents' anniversary dinner?"

"Nice. Their three kids each made a speech...so my dad spoke. It got boring after a while. I'm the oldest cousin, so I didn't really have anyone to talk to, just a bunch of little kids. But, my grandparents were really happy, so it was worth it."

"Oh, good."

More silence.

It was Luca's turn to break it, and he wasted no time getting to the heart of the matter. "So, what do you think is going on?" he asked me casually, as if he were asking what my favorite color was. I would have preferred that.

I hesitated before offering my attempt at humor, "I really don't know. Um...maybe we're like mutants...you've seen *X-Men*, right?" I said with a humorless chuckle.

Luca didn't laugh. Instead he answered in such a way that made me realize he had actually entertained that idea. "I thought about that actually. But, I think there's more to it," he said with a smirk.

I knew we were both nervous. Luca looked relaxed, but his foot hadn't stopped tapping since we'd sat down. I was nervous for so many reasons, but I wondered what exactly Luca was nervous about. I was sitting there in a perfectly normal pizza place, discussing my supernatural, potentially mutant powers with a boy who apparently shared my afflictions. But there was more.

I was also out with a boy, other than Dexter, for the first time EVER! I stopped short of calling it a date, even in my own mind. I knew that Luca and I shared some strange connection, and there were hints that there might be more, but I didn't want to assume that he felt anything more than friendship or just plain curiosity toward me. So, I tried to think of nothing else except for our shared powers and getting to the bottom of what was happening.

It was easiest to believe Luca's nervousness came from having to discuss our given situation. But, I couldn't get over how at ease he seemed to be with the whole *supernatural powers thing.* If that *was* the case, then maybe there was more to this than I would allow myself to believe. I cut that thought off abruptly, not allowing it to fully form.

I didn't *really* want to ask this question, but I did anyway. It just seemed like the right question. I was sort of curious about his ideas. "So, what do you think then?"

"Well, I'm not really sure. We could be some new step in the evolutionary process, maybe even a kind of mutation. But, that wouldn't really explain a lot of it. Which leads me to think it's something else." He paused, took a deep breath, then added, "Violet, I know you are going to freak out, but please just hear me out, okay?"

I shifted in my seat. Here it was. The theory he was about to propose was a theory I had pushed far back into the darkness of my mind. It could not be true. It would not be true. I would not allow it to be spoken because if it escaped from his lips, it couldn't be taken back. So, I reacted swiftly. Irrationally.

"Luca, don't say it. Please. If you care at all about my sanity, you will keep that theory to yourself," I said in a carefully controlled tone.

"But Violet, it all makes sense! I've done research...there are a lot of reputable people now who believe in the possibility of—"

I cut him off again before he could finish. "Please. Don't. Say.

It. You have NO idea what the implications of your words could be. You have no idea how those ideas and beliefs have altered the course of my life, and I am NOT going to even *entertain* them. Not now, not ever!" I was almost hysterical, and definitely speaking loud enough to get a few backward glances from the other diners. My eyes were filled with hot tears that I was trying desperately to keep inside. Luca backed off.

"Okay. Let's just forget the how and why part," his tone changed and he seemed to be trying to comfort me. "Let's deal with the *what*. As in, what exactly are we capable of? I have experimented a little on my own, but I am dying to see what we can do together."

I looked up. He was excited now and I could see his eyes grow wide and light up, obviously enjoying his newfound capabilities much more than I was. I had only just begun to realize the usefulness of a few of them. I also liked hearing him say, "together." It poked and prodded at that little idea I had hidden away earlier.

"So, what have you found out?" I asked, not merely feigning interest, but genuinely wanting to know. I could handle the *what*.

"Well, obviously we can communicate with one another. Like I said before, it seems like we have to direct our thoughts; I don't think we can just intrude on each other's minds." He looked down. I was very glad that I could control what he could and couldn't hear and see in my mind. At that thought, I blushed slightly. I was fairly certain that he picked up on the pink that colored my cheeks so suddenly. However, he didn't say anything, and I was grateful. He just continued with his list.

"Of course there's the strength thing, which I think might be amplified by need…not really sure. And I don't know about you, but I...I don't know how to put this...I can sort of fly..." I was the one whose eyes grew wide now as I remembered my own floating incidents, one involuntary, one a deliberate test.

"Has that ever happened to you?" he asked eagerly. I just nodded, unable to articulate my experience.

"When it happened to me, I didn't know what the hell was going on," he continued, nearly bouncing out of his seat.

"Me either. I...I was really tired, and it just happened."

"Yeah. That's kind of like what happened with me. What d'you think's up with that?"

I shrugged. Then sighed. "I don't know. I don't know anything anymore." I felt defeated all of a sudden. With my head hung, I could see his hand start to reach toward mine, but then pull away. Instead, he quietly said, "Violet, don't worry, we'll figure it all out." Though I wasn't sure I believed him, I enjoyed hearing him use "we" again. I nodded.

After a long silence, I swallowed hard and said, "I was slicing bread. I missed the bread, and I got my hand instead." I held it up as if I were going to show him an injury. He looked baffled.

"There's nothing there," he said blankly.

"Exactly. There should be a huge gash or no finger at all, but...nothing," I explained. Then I added, "And I don't feel anything from the accident. I'm not sore, no bruises, nothing."

"Whoa...that's cool," he said with more enthusiasm than I could bear. How could he be so upbeat about all of this? It took him a second, but he eventually caught on that I did not share his enthusiasm about this, and his demeanor changed. "Well, it is *interesting*."

"I realized after I talked to Dex about it—he saw it happen—that I've never really been injured...I can't remember anything when I was little, and nothing in the last several years, never broke any bones—" I told him.

"You know, I can remember minor injuries, when I was a kid, but they always healed so fast, it was like they never happened," he said, looking introspective now. "Never broke anything either."

Just then, the pizza came, and we ate in silence for a few

minutes until I worked up the courage to ask another question, "So, um...why do you think our abilities are so strong now, why not before...what do you think *that* means?"

"I don't know. I assume it has something to do with the *how* and *why*..." he trailed off. He obviously didn't want to upset me again.

"Do you think we're the only ones?" I asked. This question had been festering in my mind from the moment I knew that Luca was going through what I was going through.

"I can't believe that we are. I mean, it seems too coincidental that we have *found* each other." More silence. More eating. "Logically, there have to be more..." he stopped, as if he were lacking the right word to define what we are.

We were full, having polished off the better part of a medium pizza between the two of us. Luca paid even after I insisted on giving him money, but he finally agreed to let me leave a tip. Even after we paid, neither of us moved. I knew that I was unsure of our next move, and I wondered if Luca was too. Where did we go from here? I was relieved when Mandy texted me. It gave me a purpose...something to do.

> "I'm at work. Hope u r having fun:) Dex is home.
> Please be nice. Spare his feelings. Luv u. Be careful."
>
> "Still having pizza. Be home soon. Dex will be OK.
> Love you too"

"That was my mom. She's just checking up on me," I said.

"Do you want me to take you home? Or do you want to hang out a little longer?" he asked.

"DON'T TAKE ME HOME!!!" I wanted to scream. Even if the reason that brought us together was awkward, I was out with Luca Verone, and I was actually enjoying myself. "I wouldn't mind staying out a little while longer," I said shyly and without meeting his eyes.

"Good. I was hoping you'd say that." I looked up at him and he smiled. "Do you need to let your mom know?"

"No, she's at work now. She's a nurse at County. She's on the night shift."

"So...do you wanna go to Nature Park?" he asked.

***

It was dusk by the time we reached the park. We found a parking spot easily, and this time I just waited for Luca to open my door, knowing it was coming. The usual Saturday park crowd had thinned. There were only a few scattered individuals and couples meandering down the park's lighted footpaths. Luca and I took our place among them. We walked for a few minutes until we came to a particular garden that I'd seen but never visited before. The wooden sign at its entrance read, "The Maze". Luca took the lead and I followed. I was amazed when I found myself immersed in eight-foot tall hedges on either side of me. They were dense and impenetrable. We continued walking to a bend that led to more hedges. I was instantly intrigued by this place. There were soft orange lights, like the ones that lit the footpaths, shining down on us from posts high above the hedges.

Luca just stood back and seemed to be enjoying me enjoying the maze. I kept a step ahead of him, looking for the next bend, wondering where it would lead, all the while wondering how I had ever missed such a magical part of the park. After a little while, I slowed down and let Luca catch up to me.

"So, do you like it?" he asked, though I knew that he knew the answer.

"It's amazing. How did I ever miss it? I've come here for years, and I thought I'd seen every part of this park."

"You can see why I like to come here?" he asked. "It's the perfect place to let my mind just wander."

"It really is. Thanks for showing it to me," I said, still smiling and looking around in wonder.

"I didn't just bring you here to show you the maze. I wanted to try something," he admitted, now more serious, but also enthusiastic.

"Okay." I became reluctant.

"I was hoping we could test our telepathy when we are not in sight of one another. Would you mind?" He sounded childlike and eager.

He was so excited, and he'd been so forthcoming with me about everything, I felt as if I couldn't disappoint him. So I said, "Sure. What do you want me to do?"

"'I'll go a little further into the maze and try to lead you to me. What do you think?" he asked.

"Sounds good," I replied, a little apprehensive.

"Alright, so just *listen* for me." Luca said with a smile as he darted around a bend ahead of me.

I waited for his directions, nervous excitement building in my stomach. Luca's enthusiasm was infectious. As I waited, I thought about him and how he seemed so positive about our abilities, almost like they were a gift, while I had viewed them as a curse.

But, just for this moment, I allowed myself to see things from Luca's point of view. I *did* save my mother's life and my own. I may have also saved Carol. I had been able to diffuse a situation with Stephanie Baker that could have resulted in Dexter getting beaten up, and maybe me too. And, to top it all off, I *may* even be developing a relationship with a boy I had liked from a distance for a very long time. In this light, in this place, I felt almost happy about my potential...*our* potential.

Just then, I heard Luca. At first, I instinctively looked around, not realizing right away that the voice was inside my head. Silently, I asked him to repeat what he'd said. *Walk around the bend and take the first right. Tell me what you see,* Luca's disembodied voice beckoned.

I did what he said. *I am directly in front of a sign with a squirrel on it,* I replied.

Okay, I'm going further away now, Luca said.

Okay.

I waited again. I was enjoying this game.

Can you hear me? Came his voice, as loud and clear as ever, accompanied by the shimmering blue light.

No problem. Where are you? I questioned.

I can't tell you, we're still play-- I mean testing. I smiled. One thing was becoming very clear: Luca made me happy.

So, where do I go now?

I want to try something else. Are you okay with that? Luca asked.

O...kay. I responded, now with less hesitation than I'd shown earlier.

Trust me, okay?

A simple question. But I had a difficult time responding. Trust meant letting my guard down even more than I had already, and I already felt as if I had laid myself bare. But then I remembered that Luca had not given me any reason not to trust him, so I nodded, then realized that I had to respond with a thought. *Okay. I guess I trust you.* Those words were difficult to get out, even if they weren't out loud.

Good. Now, close your eyes and listen, and see if you can find me.

Close my eyes? I couldn't imagine where he was going with this. *What? I...I don't understand.*

Violet. I want you to just think about me, try to visualize where I am and find me.

Can I do that?

I think so. Just try, please.

Okay.

I closed my eyes tightly and brought an image of Luca into my mind. It wasn't difficult. This last week had given me plenty of time to see his face more clearly than ever before. Abruptly, the image in my mind began to take shape. Then, something amazing began to happen--while I couldn't actually see *him,* it was almost as if I *were* him. I could see what he saw, but it was fuzzy, and difficult to grasp at first. I felt as if I wasn't focusing hard enough. So, I concentrated my thoughts on the *need* to find him, rather than on just him. This seemed to work better. The image cleared slightly, and I could see pebbles below me and a little pond next to me. He was in the Japanese garden! Now, I just had to figure out how to get out of the maze.

I know where you are, I thought to Luca. I knew he could hear the excitement in my voice.

Can you get here? he asked.

With my eyes closed, focusing only on his thoughts, I began to move slowly. *I'm still in the maze. You think I could get a little help?* I asked.

I think you can get to me without it. If you do the same thing you've been doing, you'll just find *me. Will you try?* he asked apprehensively. It seemed he wasn't sure if he should push me any further.

I was a little frustrated. This was difficult, but I played along. *I'll try. If I'm not there in a few minutes, I'll call you,* I answered, suddenly a little more willing to take risks.

I had not opened my eyes yet, so I let myself fall back into a deep concentration, thinking only of getting to Luca. Then, I felt a pull. It was difficult to describe, but it was as if there were some invisible, yet strong thread that connected me to Luca and was suddenly guiding—or pulling—me to him.

I began to think about how interesting this new ability was, and as my mind began to analyze this, my concentration on the task diminished, and with it, the pull seemed to subside. So, I pushed the new thoughts away and brought back Luca, and my need to get to him. I just moved, almost by instinct, making sure now to keep my concentration unwavering. Within a minute or two, I felt a gentle breeze ruffle my hair, and I knew I was out. Though I was tempted to open my eyes, I decided to have faith.

I listened carefully to hear if there was anyone around me. This was another one of my newly discovered powers that I was learning to manipulate. I heard nothing but the night sounds of chirping crickets and buzzing mosquitoes. In the process of listening, I had almost lost my pull toward Luca again. I found it was easier to get it back this time, now that I knew what to do. I regained my connection and let it pull me along until I noticed the ground beneath my feet changed—it began to crunch...*pebbles!* I'd made it. Exhilaration rushed through me.

Before I even opened my eyes, I heard his movement, as, I guessed, he was rising from where he sat.

You did it! You can open your eyes now, he thought to me. He didn't try to mask his excitement.

I opened my eyes, and just as I'd suspected, he was standing only a few feet from me, wearing a triumphant grin. I couldn't help but return it. He moved to the edge of the pond and sat on the pebbled ground. His face changed. A softer look replaced his smile. One that made the warmth spread throughout me again. He looked at me and said aloud, "Why don't you come sit down. Something interesting happened that I want to tell you about."

We had communicated telepathically so much in the last hour, that I had to do a double take to realize he was actually speaking out loud. I sat down beside him and stared out into the water. This garden was lit differently than the rest of the park. Instead of orange lights, there were soft, glowing white ones staked into the ground along the pale, pebbled path, and twinkling fairy lights hung from the tightly packed trees and shrubbery that created the perimeter of the garden itself. By now, the sun was almost completely done for the day, and a few stars shone faintly in the darkening indigo sky. The air had turned cooler and the breeze slackened. I hugged my curled knees to my chest, closed my eyes gently, and enjoyed the stillness for a moment.

"Remember before, when I said that we couldn't intrude on each other's thoughts? Well, I don't think that's entirely true," he said looking down, but then looked up to see my frightened eyes staring at him. "Don't worry," he said, noticing that my body language matched my eyes. "I don't think that we can just, you know, like...trespass on each other's minds. I think that when our minds are *connected* like we were just now, that they are sort of open..." he trailed off, allowing me to soak it in.

"So, could you see what was in my mind when I was looking for you?" I asked, embarrassed.

"Yes," he admitted directly. I looked away, trying to remember what I had been thinking. Nothing came to mind, but I had no way of knowing what he saw in my subconscious.

"So, it worked I guess—" I was trying to ignore what it all meant and change the subject. "I found you.

"Yes, you did." Luca looked much more serious now.

"You knew it was going to work, didn't you?" I asked when it hit me that Luca had done this already. I realized it was how he had found me that night after the movie and this afternoon. "Have there been any other times?" I asked quietly.

He shrugged. "Like I said, I think it's only when the connection is open. I saw you save that woman today. You were amazing." I looked down, embarrassed by the compliment. "I was looking for you at the time, and I guess your mind was distracted, so it was...*open.*" He understood that what he was telling me was going to upset me. So, he didn't give me time to react, he just continued.

"I think if you hadn't been distracted, you would have *felt* me there and I wouldn't have been able to see in." He paused briefly. "Although, I wonder if we can *choose* to open our minds other times." I was frozen at the thought of him having potentially seen what was in my mind the times he'd been searching for me. As if he could read my mind at that moment, he responded.

He sighed, nodded, and thought, *Sorry.*

"I thought it would be better for you if you experienced it yourself," he explained out loud, guilt and remorse flashing across his face.

"You're right. If I hadn't experienced it, I probably wouldn't have allowed myself to accept it," I admitted. I was in awe of how well Luca seemed to understand me already. It was like he knew the exact right words to say to me, to question me, but not push me too far and also to soothe me when this all got to be too much. Maybe it was this supernatural bond that we shared, maybe it was something more, or maybe it was a combination of the two.

Whatever it was, it made me feel vulnerable and afraid and comforted all at the same time. It was difficult to reconcile all of these conflicting emotions. The feelings of fear and vulnerability were not new to me...I knew them well, but the feelings I had for Luca were frightening and stronger than I would've ever believed possible.

There was an extended silence, but here didn't seem to be any tension in the air around us now. It was the kind of silence that was necessary when so much has happened so fast. It was Luca who gently broke it. "I think you've probably had enough for one day, you look—," he didn't finish his sentence, but I knew it could've ended many different ways: "tired," "overwhelmed." I was exhausted, but I also felt a little self-conscious. He quickly amended his statement, "I just meant that it's getting late and the park is about to close."

"You're right. I probably should get home. But this has been...helpful and interesting...and nice," I admitted. It was strange, but I actually hated the thought of leaving him. I wanted to draw the night out, make it last as long as possible.

We both got up and reluctantly left my favorite Japanese garden behind. As we walked past *The Maze*, I looked back and smiled. Though the circumstances that began this *date* were strange at best, I knew that this had been one of the best days of my life.

When we reached Luca's car, I dutifully waited for him to open my door. We drove to my house, making small talk, discussing music. He liked my favorite band, Max. I didn't even know anyone besides me even knew who they were. At least for a few minutes, there was no talk of our powers or anything else *abnormal*. To a fly on the window, we would have seemed like two ordinary teenagers enjoying one another's company. And, in many ways, we were.

As we turned up my dark street, Luca commented casually, "Besides being able to hear really well, I've noticed that my eyesight is amazing now. What about you?" I looked out the window, paying closer attention.

"Yeah, I noticed it a few weeks ago, but it's gotten better. I can see eerily well right now. It doesn't seem like nighttime at all," I explained. Then we arrived at my house faster than I would have liked.

When I saw Dexter's bike leaning against the corner of the house, under the carport, my stomach immediately twisted into a knot. I dreaded facing Dexter. I didn't want to cause him pain. I stared at the house but didn't move. Luca saw the bike and seemed to read my mind again.

"Dexter's?" Luca motioned to the bike. I nodded, still looking at the bike.

"He seems like a really good friend. Cares a lot about you," Luca commented.

"He's more than my friend," I answered.

And before I could realize what Luca may have heard in my words, he replied, "Oh, oh yeah, I... of cou—"

"NO!" I interrupted when I finally understood what he was thinking. "No. He's not my *friend*; he's more like my *brother*," I explained.

Luca looked very relieved, but then asked, "I take it he doesn't quite think of you as a sister?"

"Are you *sure* you aren't a mind-reader?" I laughed.

He shrugged. "I saw the way he looked at you last night, and how he looks at you at school. I've also noticed how protective he is of you. It's not hard to see," he explained.

"I hate it! Ever since he decided he…I don't know…*liked* me, things have been weird and different," I confessed. It felt good to get this out of my system, so I continued, "I have tried very hard to ignore it, and hoped it would just fade on its own, or that he'd meet some other girl, but..."

Luca waited a second, making sure I was finished ranting, "So, did you and he ever...you know, try to be more than friends?" Luca seemed very interested. Too interested.

"Ewww. NO! I told you, to me, he's like my brother. He lives in the same house with me, which makes everything that much harder, of course. And to make matters worse, he's one of those suffer in silence types who pretends he doesn't care, 'as long as we can still be friends,'" I said this last quote in a deep voice, attempting to mimic Dexter.

Luca hadn't taken his eyes off of me while I talked. I thought he looked as if he were trying to hide how pleased he was by my reaction to his question about Dexter and me.

"I mean, I couldn't even contemplate it..." I said, continuing to talk about Dexter. I hadn't realized how much this had been bothering me until Luca brought it up. "I just…it just makes me so angry…I mean, sure, it would have been easier if I had felt what he felt…I even tried to convince myself. I figured, 'no one else wants me,' but it just isn't there. He's my best friend. Or, he *was*. Now, I don't know." I stopped.

This complaining wouldn't help anyone, and now I was getting upset. I looked down into my hands and swallowed hard. Luca was already sitting nearly sideways in the driver's seat when he reached over and gently took my hands in his. My initial reaction was to pull away, not used to someone touching me. But I fought it.

"I'm sorry, Violet." he whispered. "And, as far as there being 'no one else' interested in you...well, I don't know about anybody else, but I have been interested since the first day of sophomore English." He stared at me intensely, exhibiting no signs of embarrassment with this confession.

I was speechless. I looked away from Luca, and stared out the windshield when I saw Dexter peering out through the curtain of the big front window, trying to look inconspicuous. Luca apparently saw him too.

"Do you want me to go?"

"No, I don't want that." It was my turn for a confession, "But I think it would be easier if you did...for Dexter," I clarified quickly. I thought of how Dexter must be feeling. It was enough to find out that the girl you loved was, for all intents and purposes, a superhero, let alone that she was also in a... budding romance with her supertwin. I felt as if the world that I thought I knew so well had just turned upside down. It wasn't just Dexter. It was everything. How could it all change so quickly? My face must have given away my mental anguish because Luca gripped my hands a little more firmly.

I can stay if you think it will help, he thought to me.

I know. I just think I need to do this the right way. I owe it to Dexter.

Are you going to tell him everything? Luca asked, but he didn't sound like he was pressing me.

I've told him some, but I'll tell him whatever he hasn't figured out for himself already whenever he asks.

Will you tell him about this part? Luca said as he leaned closer. I knew he was referring to our telepathy.

I shook my head slowly as I answered, *Not yet.*

Then, he did something that surprised me, even though the night had been truly perfect, and this next step seemed inevitable. He leaned forward and kissed my lips softly. This was my first *real* kiss, save for the one Dexter had attempted that ended with him flat on his back with a fat lip. Though I enjoyed the feeling of Luca's lips on mine, I had always shied away from contact, and now I pulled back. I just couldn't let myself go, no matter how much I wanted to. I didn't know how. Luca cleared his throat. "Sorry," he said softly.

"Don't apologize. You didn't do anything wrong. I'm just not...used to this...this...closeness."

"I'm not either, you know. I just feel really...comfortable with you," he confessed. We sat unmoving for a moment before I remembered the window.

"Oh no," I whispered, mainly to myself. I looked to the front of my house and saw the curtain moving back into place. My heart dropped into my stomach. Luca's eyes followed mine, and he sat back in his seat, taking a deep breath.

"I think I should go in now," I said, still looking to the spot where Dexter had just been standing.

"I understand." Luca replied with a forced smile.

"You can call me later if you want to. I don't know how far our telepathy goes, but try it out. If it doesn't work, there's always the old-fashioned way." I grabbed my phone and held it up with a weak smile.

"I will. Goodnight," he said as he leaned forward and gave me another quick kiss that made me regret my decision to send him away.

I was about to say, "Goodnight" in reply when he got out and walked to my door. I got out slowly, straightened myself, and looked at Luca before walking toward the house. I turned back when I realized that he was waiting for me to go inside. I smiled to myself, realizing how much I enjoyed being treated like I was somebody. Then I turned the doorknob to face the inevitable.

Dexter sat slumped on the couch, no TV, no music, just him and the silence. I knew I hadn't really done anything *wrong,* but I was brimming over with guilt anyway. He was turned so that I could see his profile. I knew that he knew that I was standing there. Obviously he had heard me come in. I saw his shaggy blonde hair hanging over his closed eyes. His forehead was resting in one of his big hands, long fingers threaded through his hair.

Dexter was attractive, and other girls would probably be interested if he wasn't so wrapped up in me or so angry with the world. I wondered why I couldn't just feel something *more* or different for him, but I just couldn't. He was family.

I walked slowly over and sat close beside him on the couch. Though I didn't want to give him the wrong idea, I needed to comfort him, so I put my arm around his shoulders, and he flinched slightly. I had to say something, but the right words were slow in coming. "Dexter. I know you are really angry with me right now, and I am so sorry."

"Why are *you* sorry? I'm the one with the problem," he said so softly that I knew he'd been crying. When he cried, his voice became soft, and he sounded like his nose was stuffed. Over the years I'd heard him cry many times—skinned knees and other injuries were the main culprits, but there were the times when he was younger and trying to cope with his family situation. He would curl up in a ball in his sleeping bag on my bedroom floor and let the tears come, thinking the dark of night would shroud him and drown out the sound, but it didn't. On these occasions, I would go to him and silently help him up and lead him to my bed where I would wrap my arms around him and let him cry until he fell asleep.

We were eight or nine then, and it was okay. As we got older, even before Mandy's rules, I got a sense that it was not acceptable for him to be in my bed at night anymore, and eventually, my room. And Dexter had learned to accept his life for what it was, content in knowing he had another family that loved him. But, our closeness had not ever diminished. Not until recently. To my surprise, my own eyes filled with tears.

"Dexter, you haven't done anything wrong. I should have been more sensitive to your feelings...been more discreet," I cried.

He looked at me and saw the tears on the verge of spilling over. "No, Violet. You can't help your feelings. I just have to learn to deal with it." His voice was still hardly a whisper and it cracked a bit. "I guess we just aren't the same anymore. I've known it for a while now."

"Dex, please don't be upset, you and I will always be *us,* no matter what *changes* I seem to be going through."

"We haven't really been the same since *I* changed. This is just a further complication," he added flatly.

"Dexter, I don't know what you want me to say. You are like my brother. I know it hurts you to hear that, but...it's the truth."

"I know. It does sort of hurt, but I'd rather be that than nothing," he said. There was a long period where neither of us said anything. Then Dexter spoke again, this time a little louder, and more composed, "I'm tired. I'm going to go to bed. See you in the morning."

"You don't have to leave, Dex. This is your home as much as it's mine," I pleaded.

"I know that, Violet, I just need a little *time and space* that's all." I was struck by how his words felt. They were the same words I'd said to Luca when I had reached my limit. I wondered if Dexter had reached his and if he had chosen those words purposely.

"Okay. Will you be around tomorrow?" I asked. "Mandy is going to ask when you're not, you know that."

"I'll see you at some point."

"What about dinner?"

"Yeah, okay. I'll be here."

"Okay, if you are sure you are okay and not just running away."

"I'm sure. See you tomorrow." He managed a weak smile and got up to leave. I got up too and gave him an awkward hug, which he returned.

"Night," I said.

"See ya," he replied. And he was gone.

It was several minutes before I was able to move. I was worried about Dexter, but there was a part of me that was admittedly, glad to be home alone. It happened so rarely. Dexter wasn't intrusive, but I could never fully relax with another person in the house...even Dexter. I thought about calling Luca, testing the distance of our telepathy, but I decided to wait and paint for a while. It was late, but I had a lot of emotions to work through, and painting would help. I looked at sketching and painting as the equivalent of keeping a diary, and tonight I had a lot to say.

I went out to my studio, flipped the lights on and got ready to work. Usually, if I were going to begin something new, I would sketch it out first, create a mental plan of attack. But tonight I knew that would not be necessary. I got out my brushes and palette and began to squeeze out thick piles of oil paint. I usually used bright colors sparingly, as accents in my darker works, but tonight I prepared sunny yellow, rich crimson, blue, pure titanium white, green, and vibrant orange. I wanted my colors to match my mood. I was painting about Luca. As I looked at the palette of colors, I felt as if I were seeing each one for the first time, especially now that I was tuned in to my new eyesight.

I removed the finished *Mi Cabeza Loca* from the large easel in the middle of the room and set it against the wall. I placed a new canvas on the easel and began painting furiously. It was like a stream of consciousness; as if the brush were connected directly to my brain and I didn't even have to think about what I was doing.

My brushstrokes were wide and I lay the paint on thick so that the finished piece would have texture, depth. The painting depicted two small images, one a black, messy, erratic swirl, the other the same size, but bright yellow, smooth around the edges. The objects were close together and connected by a thread where the black and yellow blended into one. Right at the point where one color became indistinguishable from the other, they exploded above into a shower of bright colors, shooting upward and outward like fireworks, and falling onto the two solid-colored objects. Of course I wouldn't finish it that night, but I knew it represented my newfound optimism in what Luca and I meant to one another, and what we might become.

I worked for several hours, fueled by adrenaline and raw emotion. But like all highs, I came crashing down, exhaustion overtaking me. It was time for bed. I didn't even bother cleaning up properly, knowing I'd be angry with myself the next day, but not caring. I went into the house, washed up, and went to bed. Just before I fell asleep, I said, *Goodnight, Luca.*

As I drifted off, I heard him say, *Goodnight, Violet.* Eyes closed, I smiled to myself. The long, life-changing day took its toll, and I slept soundly, dreaming of Luca.

10

I stretched as I rolled over and slowly opened my eyes, feeling well rested for the first time in a week. The last week had been mentally draining with each day bringing new powers or new facets of the ones I already knew about. I lay in my bed for a few minutes, letting myself fully wake up. I wondered if Mandy was up and if Dexter was home, but the largest part of my thoughts were taken up with Luca. *"What is he doing right now? Is he thinking about me? Will I talk to him today?"* These questions brought a smile to my face. Then I nearly jumped out of bed when I heard a loud, crashing sound coming from somewhere else; it sounded like it was outside the house. I bounded from my bed and ran to see what it was.

I rushed through the backdoors and stopped abruptly, shocked and amused. I began to laugh uncontrollably. I was doubled-over when Mandy finally spoke, "Violet, instead of standing there laughing, maybe you could help me!" she fumed.

I tried to control my laughter long enough to help my mother who was pinned to the ground under a very large alien mannequin. From what I could see, it was about eight feet tall, green, with an enormous head and large black eyes. Normally a reminder like this of Mandy's "other-worldly" obsession, particularly one in my backyard, would have sent me into a rage, but seeing my mom being crushed beneath it was so ironic that I couldn't find anger anywhere inside of me. I bent down and easily moved the creature aside. I didn't need my super strength; it was much lighter than it looked. Mandy stood up and dusted herself off.

"Thanks," she said, still a little annoyed. I bit my lip to restrain a smile.

I sat in one of the chairs on the patio and Mandy went inside and got us both a cup of tea and fresh scones. Mandy's mother was from Ireland and had taught her how to make the best scones I had ever tasted. We sat eating scones and listening to the sounds of the lazy Sunday afternoon: a few lawn mowers were buzzing and I could hear kids playing down the street. Spring had finally arrived in full bloom.

To me, nothing was better than spring in New York. The warm air, the endless shades of green, the fragrant flowers, the new life everywhere. Though I was enjoying the peace and quiet of the late morning, I finally had to ask.

"So, what's with the giant alien?" I figured I basically knew the answer. Throughout the years, Mandy had, on more than one occasion, *altered* displays and advertisements that she felt belittled her beliefs and insulted the people whose lives had been "affected" by extraterrestrials. To her it was the equivalent of mocking someone's religion, like using Jesus to sell cars or something. Blasphemy!

"You know the used car lot over by the hospital?" She didn't wait for my reply. "Well, that...*abomination* was out there with a big sign that said, 'Our Prices Are—"

"Let me guess," I interrupted, "out of this world.

"YES!" Mandy cried.

These were the moments when I was reminded of her mother's "eccentricities." Most of the time I could at least pretend my mother was normal, but when something like this happened, there was no denying the truth. Anger began to flare in the pit of my stomach. To suppress it, I quickly spoke, my tone less playful than before. "So, how did you get it?" I was still curious.

"Well, I saw it on Thursday, and it just irked me, you know."

No, I did not know how someone could be irked by an eight foot plastic and foam alien.

"So, since Marilyn was driving me to work and picking me up in her big SUV, I figured it was *a sign*." I rolled my eyes. "I knew the dealership wouldn't be open on Sunday, so no one would miss it until Monday..." Mandy had an excited gleam in her eyes, as if she'd just pulled off some great bank heist.

She took a breath and continued, "Anyway, I told Caroline, my boss, that I had to leave a little early this morning because you weren't feeling well— sorry—I walked across the street, Marilyn met me, and we cut the tethers that held it to the posts, dragged it to her waiting car, threw it on the roof, covered it with a sheet, tied it down, and voila."

I was dumbfounded by Mandy's description of her antics. I didn't know what to say. Then I became the parent. "So, you *stole* the giant alien?" Another rhetorical question. "What if someone saw you? Those places have cameras, you know!"

"They'll probably think it was some prank...bunch of kids. Besides, we tried to stay hidden behind it as much as we could, and...we wore old Halloween masks." She bit her lip and winced as she said the last part. She looked as if she were gearing up for a blow to the face.

Maybe it was my euphoria from the previous night, maybe I just realized how funny it must have looked for my mother, in a nurse's uniform and a Frankenstein mask, to be dragging a giant alien onto the top of a car, but my anger faded and I laughed again. I laughed harder than I had intended until tears began to stream down my face as I continued to try to recreate the scene in my mind.

Mandy, who was used to my negative reactions to her beliefs, stared at me in disbelief. Then, she made the connection. I was still howling when Mandy interrupted. "Violet Arena, you had a DATE!"

Instantly, I stopped, like someone had pressed an "off" button.

My eyes grew wide and begged Mandy not to pry. Not a chance!

"Tell me! The cute boy from the grocery store and then the accident! That was a strange coincidence, wasn't it?" Her mind wandered slightly. I didn't want her thinking about that particular coincidence, so I decided I had to say something.

"Yes. We went for pizza and then a walk in Nature Park." I looked away, embarrassed, my cheeks glowing pink.

"Oh, Honey, I am so happy for you. Did you have fun?" She was on the edge of her seat now, waiting for more information.

"We had a lot of fun. He's...." I didn't complete the sentence. I was already bothered by the fact that I had given Mandy more information than I had intended. It also bothered me that my emotions were right there, hanging on my sleeve again. I wondered what was happening to the carefully cautious image I'd crafted over so many years. Was it Luca?

"He's what? Details!" Mandy was *not* giving up. She had been waiting for this since I was thirteen.

"Mandy!" I whined.

"Come on, just a few...PLEASE!" Now Mandy whined like a five-year-old begging, which I guessed was similar to what was going on.

"Well...he's very courteous, he opened my door for me every time I got into the car. He loves Nature Park too and showed me this beautiful maze that I'd never seen before, and he is so patient and understanding." *"Oh god, why did I say that? Mandy doesn't know why he'd need to be patient and understanding...now she'll just ask more questions."*

"What does he have to be patient and understanding about? You're amazing!" She was being defensive now. I thought it would be rather sweet if it didn't have to lead to me lying even more.

"No Mandy, he is...I think...Well, I just meant, you know how I am...quiet, not very...open. I don't get close to people." I was spitting back words that the psychologists had used years ago. Words I had never agreed with. I hated it, and it made me squirm in my seat. But it seemed to have worked. She no longer had the fierce look of a mother lion protecting her cub. She now wore a look of understanding.

"Oh, I see. Well Violet, you're worth it. I've always tried to tell you that." Mandy said.

"I know, er- thanks." I replied, feeling guilty for lying to my mother once again.

"So, did he kiss you?" Mandy was full of eagerness again.

"Uh...yeah," I admitted sheepishly, looking at the ground, remembering the quick, but meaningful kiss. As I sat, head bent, the kiss came back in full detail. I allowed myself to get lost in it for a moment. I hadn't been able to fully appreciate it at the time because of Dexter. As I remembered Luca's hands on my face and that feeling that I was beginning to become familiar with: warmth began to spread from my tingling scalp through my entire being. Mandy was quiet. She seemed to be giving me time to reflect, or she was lost in her own thoughts. Whatever the reason, I was thankful. Then, Mandy set fire to my happy place.

"So, is Dexter okay? He's not here." she said, concern saturating her voice.

"I think he will be. We had a good talk last night. He saw us kissing from the window..." I answered honestly.

"Oh no, that must have crushed him!" Mandy cried.

"I don't know...maybe, but I think it was for the best. He had to know something like this would happen one day. I just hoped he'd meet someone first and forget he ever felt *that way* about me." I replied. I was getting uncomfortable now, shifting even more in my chair. I was going to need to end this conversation soon.

"I think you're right. It's for the best. Maybe this is what he needed to get on with his life."

I racked my brain, looking for a way to change the subject. I looked around aimlessly, and it came to me. "So, what are you going to do with *your friend?*" I asked, motioning in the direction of the alien.

"I don't know. I've got to hide it or destroy it, which I am more partial to. I think Edgar wants it. He said he'd probably stop over later today or tomorrow and get it." Mandy answered.

"You really outdid yourself this time," I said. We ate some more, and Mandy began to rub her neck and shoulders.

"I'm sore from the accident, and now an alien on top of me! Don't your muscles feel sore today?" Mandy asked. I knew I should be at least sore from the impact of the crash, but I wasn't. I rolled my shoulders and swiveled my neck, but I felt perfectly normal. "*Weird.*" I thought. I didn't want Mandy to be suspicious, so I lied...again.

"Oh yeah, I'm a little sore too."

I got up to go into the house. I grabbed Mandy's empty plate and stacked it on top of my own then hooked both of our empty tea cups in two of my fingers.

"Thanks." Mandy smiled as I turned to walk toward the house. "Oh, by the way," I stopped. "The woman, Carol—it's Carol Hunter —she's going to be okay. I checked on her last night and she's doing well. She'll be in the hospital for a few days, but she'll be okay. Just thought you'd want to know." She looked at me suspiciously, obviously fishing for more information about what happened with the car door. She wasn't going to get any.

"Thanks, Mandy, I'm really glad." I continued in the house, "I'm happy she's going to be alright," I quickly slid into the house so that Mandy couldn't ask any follow up questions.

11

Can you hear me? Violet? I heard Luca's unmistakable voice.

Yes! Where are you? I was surprised and automatically looked around the studio.

At my house. I guess our connection is getting stronger.

I guess so. What are you doing? My mind suddenly filled with the same silvery blue that colored Luca's thoughts last night. In fact, my new favorite color was this mystical sky blue tinged with a silver shimmer, like the very top of the ocean on a bright, clear day.

Thinking about last night. Even though Luca was miles away, I instinctively blushed at his declaration. *How did things go with Dexter last night?* Luca asked.

I guess as well as they could. He went out this morning, though, and I haven't seen him since.

Sorry. I'm sure he'll be back; he cares too much to stay away.

I hope so.

So, what are you doing? Luca asked in return.

Painting. I started something new last night.

Will I get to see it?

Maybe. This piece was very personal, but I was sure that I would want Luca to see it eventually. It was strange that I didn't feel the need to hide myself from him.

So, do you want to do something later? I've got an idea about testing our powers again.

Another test?

I think this will be even better than last night, he said playfully. Of course I didn't know if it was possible for something to be better than the night before.

Okay. What do you have in mind?

You'll see. He was being purposely evasive now. It made me smile at the thrill of what his little surprise might be.

Hesitantly, I asked, *Uh...what should I wear?* Though I rarely thought twice about what I wore, I also didn't want to embarrass myself.

We'll be outside, if that helps.

It does. It didn't! Where was he taking me? I was intrigued and nervous.

I'll pick you up in half an hour. Is that all right?

Can you give me an hour? I've got paint all over.

Sure.

See you then.

I scrambled around the studio hastily cleaning up, soaking my brushes. I was sure to turn the painting around, an indication to any snoopers that I did NOT want anyone looking at it. Then I bolted for the house. I ran through the back door quickly and slammed into Dexter. He flew back several feet and landed hard against the kitchen wall.

"Oh. Sorry, Dex!" I moved quickly to try to help him up.

"I'm okay." He groaned but with a smile on his face. "This super strength is dangerous."

"Yeah, I keep forgetting. I have to learn to control it. I'm so sorry," I continued.

"I said I'm fine." He slowly got up, and I could tell he was in some pain. I held his arm, though he protested, and helped him to a chair in the dining area. "Where were you going anyway?" he asked once he was settled into the chair. I went into the kitchen to get him some water.

"I'm going in the shower." I hesitated. "I'm going out." I said quietly, avoiding his eyes.

"Hmm. With Luca?" His voice sounded a little annoyed, and I knew he was not waiting for a response to his question. "What are you doing?" he asked.

"I don't know. He said he wants to test our powers. That's what we were doing last night." I still couldn't look at him.

"Looked like you were doing something else to me," he said. This time there was joking sarcasm in his tone. Either way, he was irritating me. I scowled and rolled my eyes. "Sorry," he said flatly. "Too soon?" He smirked.

"A little." I looked at him now and realized he was trying to lighten things up, so I smiled weakly back at him.

"Thanks," I said. He smiled and nodded slightly. This was one of those moments where I was glad that Dexter knew me so well, because he knew why I was thanking him, even without me saying it.

"So, can I see you *in action* one of these days when I'm not about to get my face pounded by some testosterone-fueled jock?" Dexter asked, obviously referring to the events of the previous weekend when Stephanie's goons were all too ready to do the pounding.

"Just give me a little more time to see what I'm...*we're* capable of. I told you that our abilities seem to be getting more powerful, so...I don't really know exactly what to expect. I wouldn't want you to get hurt." This last line had a double meaning, and Dexter knew it.

"Okay. Just let me know."

"I will. I promise." I felt so much better now that the tension seemed to be eased a bit between my best friend and me.

"Where's Mandy? She was here when I went into the studio," I asked.

"Marilyn came to pick her up. I'm sure you're sorry you missed her." He bristled as he said her name. He despised her as much as I did.

"Oh, yeah, but I'm sure I'll be lucky enough to see her at dinner," I answered sarcastically.

"Mandy said she was going to get her rental car but she'd be home soon and she'd make dinner," he added. But then he changed his tone, "Hey, that sucks about the accident. Are you okay?"

"Yes. Not even sore." *Oops! I* debated telling him about moving the pipes, but I decided against it for now.

"Good." He seemed like he was stalling, like he wanted to keep talking. Maybe he thought he could stop me from leaving. "Did you see the alien?" he asked with a laugh.

"Yeah. It's not out there. Where did it go?" It occurred to me that I hadn't seen it when I left the studio. It was kind of hard to miss a giant alien in your backyard.

"I helped Mandy drag it behind the studio while you were painting. It's hilarious. I can't believe Mandy took it!" He paused and said, "Yes I can!" We both laughed, then I glanced at the clock. I only had fifteen minutes to get ready!

"Dex. I gotta get ready," I said, firmly but apologetically.

"Oh. Okay." He seemed to tense slightly.

I dashed into the bathroom, stripped, and got into the not-yet-hot shower. Our house had a well, and well water in New York was generally cold most of the year, and it was only April. Our hot water heater was old too, and it took a while for the water to come out of the tap hot. So, I anticipated the cold water and held my breath for a second like I always did as I climbed in. But, the water didn't seem to be cold. I opened my mouth and let a few drops enter. They felt cool on my tongue, but my skin seemed unaffected by the temperature. "*Interesting,*" I thought. The surprises were becoming less-surprising.

I ran to my room and turned my music on loud. I threw on my favorite jeans, faded and worn-in, and a T-shirt I'd gotten when

Mandy and I went to the MET to see a Picasso exhibit a few years earlier. Although I didn't get to the city that much, I hoped that would change. While debating whether or not to bring a sweater, my whole body tingled, and I knew Luca had arrived! I was enjoying the sense of knowing when he was close by. *I'll be out in five minutes,* I thought to him.

He answered quickly, *Take your time. Your mom and I are having a nice conversation.*

No! I wasn't sure if I had sent that thought or not, but had to get out there! I rushed to finish getting dressed, still pulling on my shoes as I ran out of my bedroom. I sprinted down the short hallway and skidded to a stop when I entered the living room where my mother, Dexter, and Luca sat talking.

From what I paid attention to, it was still all small talk, so I had gotten there in time. Luca was on the larger couch with my mother, and Dexter sat deep in the loveseat. Mandy's smile couldn't get any wider, Luca looked as cool and relaxed as ever, and Dexter was trying very hard to equal Luca's relaxed demeanor. I tried to appear calm as I slowed my pace and strolled into the room. "Um...Hi, everybody."

"Violet, Honey, come sit down." said Mandy, patting the cushion beside her. I reluctantly sat next to my mother. Luca stole a glance in my direction behind Mandy's back. He smiled, looking quite amused. I just rolled my eyes and nervously chewed my bottom lip. "So, we were just talking about the accident and how coincidental it was that Luca lived around the corner," Mandy explained with a hint of, "Why don't you two tell me what really happened," in her voice.

"Yeah. That's weird," I agreed, desperate for a subject change. "So, are you ready?" I bent my head in front of Mandy and asked Luca impatiently.

"Sure, if you are," Luca replied.

"Luca said you are going on a little hike by the lake?" Mandy asked, apparently wanting me to corroborate his story.

"Uh, yeah...I guess," I responded, trying not to sound surprised. *Hiking?* I asked Luca silently. Somehow my brain was now capable of being part of two conversations simultaneously.

Well, sort of, replied Luca, while he continued to tell Mandy about how much he enjoyed hiking, especially on the trails around Lake Morgan.

"Just be careful." Mandy said, sounding concerned.

"We'll be staying on the lower trails, close to the water, and near the road. We'll be fine. I go there alone all the time," Luca reassured her.

"Oh, okay. Have fun," she said, seeming convinced by Luca's answer. "Will you be home for dinner? It's Sunday..." Mandy reminded me, "Luca, you are welcome to join us." Sunday was a night that Mandy rarely worked, so it was almost always family dinner night. Sometimes Mandy invited a friend or two.

To my dismay, Marilyn came most Sundays. Mandy made her only vegetarian specialty, eggplant parm with spaghetti. There was also salad and bread and always some kind of rich, decadent dessert. I knew Mandy looked forward to Sunday dinner all week.

"Will we?" I looked at Luca, clueless as to what his plans were.

"I was going to ask you if you wanted to get something to eat later, but I'd love to eat here. What are you having?" He looked at Mandy.

"Eggplant parm. You're not a vegetarian too?" asked Mandy. There was a strange look on her face as if she could not believe that Luca and I had found one another. I couldn't believe it either.

"I am. I love eggplant," Luca replied.

"Hmmm, what another *interesting coincidence,*" Dexter said with a sarcastic edge. He'd been so quiet that I had almost forgotten he was in the room.

"Yeah, it is!" I glared at Dexter. I turned from him to Mandy, "So, I guess we'll be back for dinner."

"See you later," Luca called as he and I finally made it to the door.

"Bye," they said in unison, one voice bright and cheery, the other flat and sad.

As we walked down the stairs into the breezy, warm spring day, Luca grabbed my hand and held it tightly. I smiled over to him and let him lead me to the car where he let go of it and, of course, opened the door for me. I slid in and buckled my seatbelt, confident that I was ready for whatever Luca had in store for me.

12

We drove for some time, leaving town and heading southwest on the twisting, hilly roads that led to Lake Morgan. This was one of my favorite drives. Over the years, Mandy and I had made it so many times, even when we had nowhere in particular to go. Mandy always liked to go for long drives, "exploring" the areas around where we lived, and "discovering" new places. She was originally from a bigger town just outside of New York City, but had gone to college in upstate New York where she met my dad. After graduation, he had gotten a job in Lake Hansen, at the community college, and so they settled there. After the "incident," and the consequent split, Mandy said she felt "tied" to Lake Hansen and the area in general, so she and I stayed.

Part of the drive consisted of densely packed trees on either side of the road continuing back until they rose up gradually to the lower parts of the mountains, leaving a smattering of boulders scattered throughout the landscape. The trees' thick canopy allowed only streaks of sunlight to reach the forest floor, so that while driving past there was a shimmering effect that could be dizzying. The road itself had been carved right out of the woods, and it hugged tightly to the forest. I couldn't imagine a more picturesque landscape.

I looked at Luca and wondered what he was thinking. At the same time, he glanced at me and smiled. "Are you wondering where I'm taking you?" he asked.

"Not *where*...unless of course, we aren't going to Lake Morgan.

I was just wondering *what* we are going to do," I replied, blushing as I realized that he might have read more into my question than I intended. I wasn't very good at this yet.

He didn't seem to think my question implied anything but curiosity based on his answer. "We are going to Lake Morgan—sort of—and, like I said, I think we should *test* some of our abilities," he answered.

"What do you have in mind?" I inquired.

"Well, the levitation thing, for one. I mean, how high can we go? How far? How fast?" His face lit up as he rapidly asked these questions. "And then there's our strength. Like, what can we do? And the telekinesis!" His excitement was infectious. I had to smile. "There are some open areas where we can try levitating, and then there are plenty of boulders for testing out mental and physical strength..." He had obviously thought this through. I still couldn't understand how he could be so accepting of all of this. And even though his enthusiasm was contagious, it was also a bit unnerving. He must have seen the smile on my face become strained and forced. "I'm sorry if I'm moving too quickly...too much, too soon. I'm just so glad that...you're *here* and that you're willing to try." He sounded sincerely apologetic.

"It's okay. I just keep wondering how you're so comfortable with all of these changes." I finally admitted.

"Violet, I wasn't 'so comfortable with this' at first. I was terrified. Like you, I thought I was going crazy. But, gradually I began to see the positive aspects of my new powers. I could help people if I wanted to. I could protect myself if I needed to. And, these powers...well, they brought me to you, and once I...*we* made our connection, my powers...*our powers*...seemed so much more natural and part of me," he explained. I was far from being an expert on emotions, having only really ever been an observer rather than a participant, but I knew that people usually didn't speak with such unfiltered candor. I found it overwhelming, but I also felt bad for forcing him to explain himself.

"You're right. I mean, I was afraid because I didn't want this to make me more of a fre—"

Luca interrupted, "Please don't say that. You are not now, nor were you ever, a freak." His words came out with an edge of fury that I didn't know he was capable of.

"Sorry. I just didn't want there to be something else wro—*different* about me," I corrected. "People find enough *fault* with me as it is," I said. I wasn't wallowing in self-pity, I was simply speaking truthfully.

"Someday you're going to have to stop worrying about everyone else. You are fine exactly how you are. Hopefully, one day, you'll see it too." His words were softer now, they'd lost their edge.

My cheeks began to feel warm and I knew they were getting pink. "Okay, okay, enough about how great I am. You sound like Dexter." I rolled my eyes. He smiled.

"I guess he and I have a lot more in common than I thought." He laughed, then continued, "We're almost there. The trailhead is just up ahead." He pointed to an opening in the trees just up ahead of us. We passed the *official* park entrance and parked in a pull-off close to the trailhead.

"Are we really hiking?" I asked. I wasn't opposed to the outdoors, and I loved nature...in theory. I just didn't have a lot of experience with it aside from Nature Park, and that was tame and controlled.

"Just a short distance to a clearing. It's usually empty. That's why I chose this trailhead instead of using one inside the park," he explained.

"Oh," I said, more apprehensively than I would have liked.

"Don't worry. I know where we are going. I come here a lot," he reassured me. "Are you ready?"

"Let's go!" I said as enthusiastically as I possibly could. As usual,

Luca was at my door before I had unlatched my seatbelt. He held his hand out in a very old-fashioned gesture. I willingly gave him my hand and stepped out of the car. I felt a little bit like Cinderella being helped out of the enchanted coach by Prince Charming. I smiled to myself as I thought of this very odd comparison.

"What?" asked Luca in response to my smile.

"Nothing." I said quickly, not able to erase all of the smile from my face.

We entered the trailhead together. I saw that if we were going to walk side by side, we would need to stay very close because the trail was so narrow, and that would take longer. I thought Luca would prefer me following him since he knew where we were going. I was wrong. He reached down, without saying a word, and took my hand. His hand was cool, and his palm felt a little clammy. It made me feel better to know that maybe he was nervous too, even if he wasn't acting like it. I interlocked my fingers in his, and we walked the rest of the way up.

The first twenty minutes of the hike were easy and flat. The air within the woods itself was damp and cool with the smell of rotting trees becoming part of the moist earth. I listened as Luca pointed out trail markers, trees, and birds. I was impressed by how knowledgeable he was. Underneath the canopy, the birds created a cacophony of sound, like a collage of different pitches and whistles going back and forth, echoing from the trees and rocks. I was intensely aware of other sounds too—water gently spilling into more water—probably a small waterfall—they were common in this area, though it must have been some distance away because I looked around and couldn't see it nearby.

My ears registered the WHOOSH of cars racing by on the road that we'd left behind. I heard the wind blowing freely over the tops of the trees, but I also heard it fighting its way through the thick underbrush. It occurred to me that though there were many sounds, I was able to separate them and hear each one individually.

"Luca, have you noticed how, even though your mind is doing all of these new things—the telepathy, the unbelievable hearing—it's like you can somehow focus on all of it at once without it being difficult or distracting?"

"Yeah, I know what you mean. That's kind of what I wanted to test. Remember at Nature Park when you said you'd had trouble finding me when your concentration was disrupted? I wonder if that's how it always is for *that* power or if, as we get better at using all of our powers, they become second nature."

"Hmmm," was the only answer I could come up with. I began to wonder how much farther we were going. The land began to rise sharply, with the trees thinning slightly and the ground becoming somewhat rockier. I was surprised when it occurred to me that I didn't really require any extra effort to hike the steep incline. "Are you tired at all?" I asked Luca.

"No, are you? Do you need a rest?" he asked, concerned.

"No, I mean, I'm not tired at *all*. I don't feel like I just hiked all the way up here. I'm not winded, we haven't slowed our pace, my legs aren't cramped. And I NEVER hike," I clarified.

"I didn't even think about it. You're right, though. Cool," he replied casually.

"*Another Benefit,*" I thought with a sigh. It was getting harder to see the downside to my powers.

We reached the precipice when Luca told me we were going to be leaving the trail. I was a bit taken aback and my face must have shown it. "It's okay, Violet, we are just going to follow that ridge a little bit to a clearing not far from here." He pointed to another part of the land that continued in the same, seemingly endless, world of trees.

Instead of responding with spoken words that could betray me, I chose to send Luca a thought in response, *I trust you.* He obviously liked that because we hadn't been holding hands for some time, but he grabbed my hand now and squeezed it. I felt he wasn't going to let go willingly this time. He had let go earlier when we needed our hands to help us with the climbing, but now the walk, though no longer following the trail, was flat, the land soft and squishy beneath our feet, carpeted with decaying leaves, new spring moss, and spongy earth left damp from the heavy snows of the previous winter. I understood why Luca liked this place. It was beautiful and peaceful.

After several more minutes of walking, I noticed the trees thinning as more of the sunlight reached us. Then the trees disappeared altogether, and we were in a clearing, vast and open, ringed by the woods like some natural arena.

I couldn't believe it, but it was even more beautiful than the rest of the hike had been. Small tufts of crocuses and even a few daffodils stood out, dressed in deep purple and vibrant yellow against the long green and golden grass that was nearly knee high. Here the wind blew unencumbered, and I relished in my ability to hear it rolling over and through the grass and breaking against the edge of the woods like small waves breaking against a willing shore. I was lost in the beauty of the place when Luca reminded me of why we were there. *Are you ready?* he thought to me.

I was glad he used telepathy. It seemed to ease me out of my daydreams instead of disturbing the perfect quiet. "So, what power should we test first?" I asked, surprised by my own enthusiasm.

"The flying! Definitely!" he replied without hesitation. I was glad he'd chosen that. I was eager to test it out too.

"So, tell me how it happened for you at first," Luca asked.

"The first time it just happened on its own. It was last weekend, after you left my house, and I was exhausted and getting ready for bed. I was putting on my pajamas and thinking about how I just wanted to be in bed, and suddenly I was *floating* into my bed." Saying it out loud made it sound so unbelievable and strange, but at the same time, it felt like a relief to tell someone, especially someone who could empathize.

"But, the next time, I wanted to...try it...so I thought about rising up and then I thought about making my body horizontal, and then I thought about moving, and it all seemed to happen simultaneously, like there wasn't any time between thinking about it and it happening," I explained.

"It's pretty much the same for me. Like I said, it seems like our powers came when we *needed* them or when our minds were really distracted. Then, once we acknowledged them, they grew. And...that's why we're here."

"Come here and stand next to me." It was a request, not a command. I willingly walked the few feet that separated me from him, until we were side by side. He held my hand again. I was still astounded at how natural it felt to just put my hand in his, interlock my fingers with his. Like I'd done it a thousand times before.

"Do you think holding hands will make it more effective?" I asked curiously.

"No." He smiled. This made me smile and turn a dark shade of pink.

"Okay, so just think about lifting into the air, and we'll see what happens," he said.

We both closed our eyes, as if by instinct. Within seconds we began to lift, and my eyes sprang open in shock. As we moved further and further from the ground, I thought to Luca, *I don't think I'll ever get used to this.*

And it will never not *be awesome!* he responded.

It really is amazing! I responded with enthusiasm that nearly equaled Luca's. *Let's try going higher.* And, like before, we rose as quickly as the thought occurred to both of us.

We looked down to see how high off the ground we had lifted. "Wow," I said with a nervous laugh. "We must be fifty feet up. I can see the lake!" I was astonished. From where I hovered, a huge section of the lake was visible. I realized no other human, besides Luca, had probably ever seen what I was seeing. The sun glinted off the lake and turned the top a shimmering silver that took my breath away.

"It's amazing," Luca said. "Okay, let's turn horizontally and *really* fly."

Still holding hands, our bodies turned horizontally, and stayed there. We must have looked like we were lying on an invisible table, hovering, but staying still.

"I feel kind of like Superman and Lois Lane in that old movie where he takes her flying, but of course, she couldn't fly on her own, he had to carry her," I said. I was giddy with the thrill that flying created. While I was distracted, Luca let go of my hand, swung around, grabbed me, and cradled me like a small child. Like Lois Lane in the movie.

"Did you mean like this, Lois?" He grinned. It took me a moment to get over my shock, but when I did, I giggled the kind of giggle that hadn't come out of me since I was a little girl.

"Okay, enough, we're here to practice, remember?" I struggled weakly to free myself.

"I am practicing. I'm practicing swooping in and saving a damsel in distress," he joked.

"I'm not a damsel, and I am hardly in distress," I replied with an eye roll. Then Luca's face turned serious, and he looked so deep into my eyes that I almost looked away, unable to bear the intensity.

I disagree with both, he thought to me. I was going to respond, argue, but I knew he wasn't finished, and I did want to hear the rest of what he had to say. *Damsels are beautiful maidens, like you. And I think in some ways, even though you are strong and amazing, you are in distress, and I* do *want to rescue you—more than anything.* His thoughts paused, *If you'll let me.*

I had to hold back tears that wanted to pour out. This was the second time Luca said I was beautiful. I remembered the thought that reached me a few weeks earlier when I was at my locker. I had accused Dexter of saying it, but then assumed I'd imagined it. The heat spread through my body and my eyes burned into Luca's. I wasn't sure how I felt about the second part of his statement.

I didn't know if I'd describe my situation as *distress*, and I wasn't sure I needed rescuing. What I did know is that never, ever, in my entire life, had I ever felt so...right...around another person as I did when I was with Luca. All of my life I felt left out, awkward. I assumed I'd feel that way forever. But with Luca, I felt that anything was possible. I was staring at him unapologetically, and I wasn't embarrassed or ashamed. I liked having him know how I felt. *I'll let you,* I finally answered.

Thanks, he thought to me. I blushed for what seemed like the hundredth time that day. In fact, I seemed to be permanently scarlet when Luca was around. Just then, he released me from the cradle-hold I'd been in so I could fly beside him. We had been moving slowly through the sky, but staying in the clearing. We had not seen anyone else, so we felt safe to explore.

"Why don't we see if we can get above the trees," I suggested.

"Okay, I'll race you!" Luca seemed to will himself forward, and he propelled ahead of me. I matched his speed almost instantly, and was once again by his side. We pushed each other further, faster, and higher. I was surprised by my own eagerness to try new things. I was bold and daring. I felt so powerful.

We found that we could go forward, backward, straight up, straight down, or we could simply stop, in mid-air. We raced over treetops and all the way to where the rocky, gray mountain began to climb to its highest peaks, leaving trees and greenery behind. After what could have been hours, but felt like minutes, we flew back toward the clearing. We flew past it and were circling back around when I caught a glimpse of where we'd parked. I thought about how incredibly good my vision must be in order to see from how high I was. Then something frightening caught my eye. "Luca!" I yelled. He wasn't far from me and raced over.

"What is it?"

"There's another car parked near ours." I wasn't sure why I whispered; no one would hear us way up there.

"Relax. A lot of people use that pull off. Let's get on the ground and take it from there." He took my hand again to reassure me, and we descended together. The flying was almost automatic now. I didn't need to pay much attention to what my body was doing. We landed gently, on our feet, just at the edge of the clearing where we could duck into the woods quickly, if necessary, and be concealed by the trees.

As I looked around carefully, I tuned into my senses, letting them intensify what I could see and hear. My head snapped to the left when I heard what sounded like feet crunching on dried branches and leaves. Luca whipped his head around to see what had gotten my attention. I could have sworn I saw a figure peek from behind a tree, look in our direction, then turn back into the woods. I knew Luca saw it too.

"Do you think they saw us?" I whispered, though I knew that no one except someone with our abilities would be able to hear or even see us all the way across the clearing. I estimated the distance had to be the width of two football fields.

"I doubt it. I mean, who could see us from way over there...except for *us*?" he asked. Once again I was sure he must be reading my mind.

"Yeah, but do you think they saw us up there?" I motioned upward with my eyes and a nod of my head

"Probably not. Even if they did, they probably thought they were seeing a big bird from a distance or that they were just...seeing things." I couldn't tell if Luca was trying to be reassuring or if he was being sincere. I decided that if he wasn't worried, I would try not to be either. *"It was just some hiker,"* I assured myself.

"Well, that's probably enough for today anyway, right? We did get *a little* carried away," I said.

"Carried away!? That was the most incredible experience I have ever had!" He almost screamed. We were both now reliving the *flight training,* the figure across the meadow all but forgotten. I couldn't help but smile because he was right. It had been amazing.

"It really was," I admitted.

Luca, always taking me by surprise, grabbed my arm and pulled me toward him. "Come here," he said. He let go of my arm and wrapped his own two around my waist. *You are amazing,* he thought to me, staring into my eyes. I was overwhelmed by my feelings for him at that moment. All the barriers I had constructed to keep the world out came crashing down around me, taking my inhibitions with them. I didn't wait for him to do what I knew he was going to do. Instead, I took myself by surprise and stepped, nearly lunged, at him, grabbed his shoulders, and pushed my lips onto his. Startled, he staggered back a half-step, but quickly regained his balance.

Our kiss was passionate. I never thought I'd use the word "passionate" in referring to a kiss *I* was involved in, but there was no other word to describe it. It was full of an eagerness and a longing that could be described no other way. My hands settled in his hair. I loved how soft the thick curls felt as I combed my fingers through them roughly. Luca seemed to lose himself in the kiss too, his hands cupping my face, then moving to my shoulders and down my back until they once again enclosed me tightly, and I dropped my arms to his neck. I briefly realized that I had never done this before, but kissing Luca was so natural, no practice necessary.

When we finally stopped to breathe, we locked eyes but said nothing. Neither of us wanted to let the other one go. My eyes closed, and I was attempting to breathe slowly and deeply in order to clear my head. Luca had frozen. "Violet..." he whispered with ragged breaths. I opened my eyes, and felt the weight of his stare.

"I..." I began. I didn't know what I wanted to say. I was not sure what my face was saying. Whatever it was made Luca feel the need to apologize.

"I'm sorry, Violet," he said. Now I was confused. "If I went too far or..." he trailed off.

I began to laugh softly. "I wasn't exactly fighting you off," I said. "As I recall, I was sort of the one who attacked *you*."

"Yeah, you're right. I'm just an innocent victim," he mused. This made me smile and refueled the fire I was trying to control inside of myself. I struggled with the want to touch him again and the need to practice self-control. I breathed deeply again, swallowed hard, and said, "So, are you ready to go?"

"No. But, I know we should," he said, disappointment leaking through his playful words.

We joined hands again and walked. I had an idea. "We'd get to the car a lot faster if we... you know..." I raised an eyebrow and looked up, daring him.

"Do you think the hiker is gone?" he asked and then looked around in all directions. I wasn't used to him being the apprehensive one.

"We can be *somewhat* discreet," I said. "Come on!" I begged, so that "on" had two syllables.

"All right!" he relented. "But let's stay close to the treetops so we can hide if we need to."

We began to lift off the ground together and moved straight up until we were above the tree line, then turned horizontally and flew. We sped up, but stayed close to the treetops, keeping a close eye on the forest floor below. Thankfully, we saw no one. In a break in the trees, just before we reached the end of the trail below us, we descended carefully. From where we landed, we walked to the trail's exit.

Once in the car, I turned to ask Luca a question that had bothered me from the moment he had joined me in the air. "Luca, do you think we are only attracted to each other because of our powers?" I knew Luca could hear the concern in my voice. I sort of expected him to cry out, "No, of course not!" But he didn't. Instead, he asked me his own question.

"When did you first have feelings for me?" I hadn't expected such a direct question, but I needed to be honest.

"From the first day I saw you two years ago," I said slowly, turning my face down toward my hands in my lap. It was still so difficult to admit things like that out loud.

"Me too," he answered. I turned back to face him, still stunned that he'd liked me since all the way back then. "I didn't know about any powers. I just saw you that first day in English, and I thought, 'I want to know her,'" he paused, scanning the road. "Then, I saw how you were always with Dexter, so I assumed you two were *together*." I made a sour face at him.

"Well, I know that *now*," he insisted. "But *then*...anyway, I figured you just didn't like anyone because you always stayed by yourself...and then..." he stopped.

"And then what?" I asked.

"Then I heard the rumors...I saw how some people treated you, and I couldn't understand how they could be that way to you. As far as I had seen, you'd never been mean to anyone. I wanted to be your friend, but I didn't think you'd let me, so I just decided to...wait. And, I'm glad I did."

My eyes widened and filled with anxiety. He had just said all of these amazing things to me, but the only part I could focus on was, *"He knows about me, about Mandy!"*

"What's wrong?" Luca asked.

"Don't you care about all the stuff people say about me and my mom?" I asked.

"Of course not. Your mother seems like a really nice person. And you are the most interesting person I've ever met. And, now I know, you're just like me...*a freak*!" He laughed out the last word. Normally, I would be offended if someone called me a freak, but when Luca said it, and included himself, it gave me a new feeling of pride; it empowered me. I looked at him and smiled at the irony of his words, unable to say more at the moment.

The drive back to my house was pleasant. I wanted to hear about Luca and his family. I learned that he was born in Westchester only two weeks after me. He liked skateboarding, soccer, and playing bass guitar. He liked to write, but claimed he was a terrible artist, which is why he admired my talents so much, and his favorite color was green.

"What do you write?" I asked.

"Well, I write short stories and I started a novel once, but mainly..." he paused, "don't laugh, okay?"

"Why would I laugh?" I asked, mystified. I would never laugh at anything Luca wrote.

"I write poetry"

"I love poetry. Can I read some of yours sometime?" I worried I was overstepping.

"I'd really like that," he said with a smile. I felt relieved, and our conversation continued.

According to Luca, his parents were pretty average and pretty boring, but he conceded that they were also nice, open-minded, and had always allowed him to be himself. His dad was a detective and had worked in New York City, but then decided he was sick of living in the city and didn't want to commute, so they moved upstate when Luca was fourteen. His mom ran a no-kill, dog rescue shelter. "Your mom must be a really kind person," I said.

"I think so," Luca said. I had a theory about people who took care of animals. I always felt that it took a special kindness and compassion to see animals as important and worthy. I could never have a pet because Mandy had severe allergies. The irony was that Mandy loved animals. I explained all of this to Luca and he promised that I could come to the shelter anytime, that they always needed volunteers. I was thrilled at the prospect.

"So, no brothers or sisters?" I asked.

"No. After me, my mom couldn't have any more kids," he told me.

"Strange," I mumbled, though I knew he would hear.

"What is?" he asked curiously.

"Well, it's just that...Mandy wasn't able to have any more kids after I was born, either."

"That is weird," he said and then looked straight ahead. I thought he looked as if he were trying to solve a puzzle, his brow furrowed and his lips pulled back tight in a straight line. I was afraid to ask what he was thinking. Though I wasn't exactly sure why, I was aware that the mood in the car had changed. It wasn't tension exactly, just something there, an obstruction. From that point on, we barely even made small talk.

When we arrived at my house, I wasn't sure what to say to Luca who still seemed to be putting something together in his head. I couldn't quite decipher his mood either. It worried me a little. I bit my bottom lip, waiting for him to say something. He must have sensed my unease or was finished with what he was thinking because he turned to me and said, "I'm sorry. I was just thinking of the *how*, and I didn't want to upset you."

I turned away. "Oh," I said quietly. Though a little piece of me wondered what theory he had concocted, I pushed it aside, unwilling to allow myself to think of it.

"Just forget it, okay," he pleaded gently.

"It's just...I...I know eventually we're going to have to deal with *that* part, but I'm not ready. I'm barely used to the idea of having these powers...I mean, I feel like we've hardly scratched the surface of what we can do. I understand if you can't hold back thinking about that part of it all, but..." I was rambling, bordering on sounding irrational.

"Violet, I told you I would be patient and wait until you're ready, and I will be. I...it's just something you said really made me think, and I was...lost in that thought. I'm really sorry."

I knew I needed to say something to make him stop feeling so guilty. "Please don't apologize anymore. You didn't do anything wrong. Let's just forget this whole conversation. And *I* promise that I will try very hard to open my mind and try to think about the *how* soon. Okay?"

"Whenever," he replied earnestly.

"Are you sure you're ready for this dinner?" I asked him.

"Of course. As long as it means we get to spend more time together. Besides, like I said before, your mom seems great."

"All right, let's go inside. Oh, and I have a painting I started that I'd like to show you," I said.

"Really? I'm honored," he seemed truly excited. I couldn't believe I was willing, even looking forward to, showing someone my work.

He opened my door and we headed toward the house together. I wondered if Mandy had been looking out the window. I saw Marilyn's car, Dexter's bike, and, to my surprise, a car I hadn't seen in a while, Gerry's black Mercedes. I knew this evening would be interesting.

I stopped abruptly before opening the door. "I have to warn you before we go in."

"What?" He laughed at my seriousness.

"Well, first of all, my mother's best friend is here. She's the one who picked my mom up after the accident the other day. She is a horrible, miserable woman who has never liked me."

"Will I have to defend your honor?" he asked with another

laugh.

"I'm serious," I said, though he had succeeded in making me smile a little. "She's usually at least somewhat courteous to me when Mandy and Dexter are around, but when I was a kid, she watched me a few times..." I trailed off, remembering with stark clarity the time Marilyn had put me out in the rain in my socks because I would not eat the lunch she'd made for me. She told Mandy that I had sneaked away and she found me a half hour later outside in the rain. I didn't tell my mother the truth because I assumed that Mandy would believe a grown up and not me. I briefly explained this to Luca and then added, "And Dexter has been...*protective*... of me with her as well. So, she should be on her best behavior."

"She sounds great," Luca replied sarcastically. "Will Dexter be there?" For the first time, I heard a note of unease in his tone. It actually made me feel a bit of relief—Luca wasn't perfect.

"Don't worry about Dexter...he should be good tonight; we had a nice *talk*. I think he understands...but don't be surprised if he acts a *little* weird. This is all really hard for him."

"I got it. It's going to be fine. I like Dexter. I just hope he can get past *us* and give me a chance," Luca admitted.

My heart leapt at the word "us," and I realized that befriending Dexter was important to Luca. I smiled because it only seemed to confirm how much Luca cared about me.

"Anyway, are you sure you don't want to reconsider walking through this door?" I asked.

"Are you kidding me? I have superpowers, what do I have to be afraid of?" he said in a mock-macho tone.

"You're about to find out!" I smiled and opened the door. Then I thought to him, *Remember, act like you've never been here before.*

Got it!

13

Luca and I paused in the foyer. "Ready?" he asked, taking my hand.

"Not for this yet. Not in front of them." I let go of his hand. I had said "them" but I had meant Dexter, and Luca knew it. "Sorry. It's just another thing to deal with. Soon though, I promise." I noticed the brightness in Luca's eyes diminish slightly. It made me feel sad and guilty. I had to hurt one person in order to not hurt another.

"I hope so because I'm not planning on going anywhere," he said in a way that sent a shudder through me. I looked at him, bewildered. This was all so new to me, and even a little frightening. I turned and walked into the living room with Luca close behind. "Hi. Mandy?" I called loudly.

"Hi, Honey. I'm in here," she directed me, though I knew exactly where she was, because I heard the banging of pots and clanking of dishes in the kitchen. Mandy rarely did anything quietly. We went to the kitchen and found her finishing dinner.

"Can we help?" Luca asked instead of starting with any kind of formal greeting. Once again his easy demeanor threw me.

"Hi. Thanks." Mandy looked up and quickly appraised Luca before throwing him a genuine smile and returning to what she was doing. "Yeah, can you get the salad together? I washed everything. It's in the sink. Bowl's up there..." she pointed, using her chin, to the cabinet next to the refrigerator, "...and the knives are right there on the counter."

"Sure," Luca said. Mandy smiled, and when Luca turned to get the knife, Mandy smiled and winked at me, causing me to flush pink and roll my eyes. Mandy mouthed, "Sorry." But I knew she really wasn't. Mandy was nearly bursting with excitement over my new *relationship*. I wondered what my mother would say and do if she knew the whole story. The thought made me glad I was keeping it to myself. "Violet, could you cut the bread and make some iced tea? I'll open a bottle of wine." She moved over to the smaller counter beside the refrigerator.

"Oh, and Dexter, Marilyn and Gerry are out on the patio if you want to go say hello."

"Um...I'll finish in here first." I was in no rush to either parade Luca in front of Dexter or spend *quality time* with Marilyn. I liked Gerry though. He had only been in the group for about three years. He was a quiet, reserved man from England with an accent that I thought sounded elegant. He apparently had an *experience* about five years earlier and had struggled for a couple of years with what happened to him until he met Mandy in a coffee shop and they *bonded*. I knew that they had an on-again, off-again relationship.

Though I wasn't happy about Mandy being involved with someone who had the same *beliefs* as her, I had to admit that Mandy and Gerry were great together. He treated her like a queen and was very kind to me, never pushing the alien-thing in my face like some of the group members who couldn't understand my avoidance. In fact, knowing I wasn't thrilled about it being part of my life, he didn't ever bring it up. Instead, he always asked about my painting or about school. He remembered my birthday and even got me small gifts. I definitely liked him. But, I could wait to say, "Hello".

"Are you and Gerry *together* again?" I asked Mandy. I knew that Mandy had put her love life virtually on hold while raising me, and I felt guilty about that. I just wanted my mom to be happy. Maybe now that I was *involved* with someone, Mandy would allow herself to be happy as well. I hoped this was the case.

"No, I don't know...he's here, okay? And it's not for group. That's all I can say for sure. We'll take it one day at a time." Having to define things between her and Gerry made Mandy flustered. It was odd, but I completely understood.

"Okay."

Luca thought to me, *I really like your mother.*

Yeah, she's great, I agreed. I hadn't been looking at him, but I turned and smiled at him then. He returned my smile, and as usual, when our eyes connected, warmth spread through me. Mandy caught sight of this and absentmindedly dropped a bowl on the floor.

"Sorry. I'm so clumsy," she apologized, frantically trying to cover up the fact that she had seen the look that passed between Luca and me. I glanced around the kitchen and realized how ironic it was that only a few days before, a scene eerily similar to this one had played out but with Dexter in Luca's place. It struck me as interesting that I was just as comfortable with Luca there as I was with Dexter, but in an entirely different, inexplicable way. Dexter and I had always been as close as I thought two people could be, but what Luca and I shared was something entirely different.

Ever the observer, the fly on the wall, for years I had seen girls at school act brainless in front of boys they liked. I'd seen them lose their identities in order to become who or what they thought a certain boy might want. I'd overheard countless conversations between friends trying to determine the exact right words to say to a boy or discussing and painstakingly analyzing every inflection of even the briefest conversations they'd had with the object of their affection. Even I had once imagined that if Luca had ever spoken to me, I'd stumble over my words or go mute altogether, leaving him with the impression that I was a moron. But there was none of that.

Yes, there was the heat that coursed through me at every glance and even the slightest touch, making me wish I could hide my blush. Yes, there were silences, but they were never awkward. Luca and I seemed to just *fit.*

At the moment that I was thinking all of this, a voice startled me. "Can I hel...Oh, hey, V." It was Dexter. "Luca," he added with a nod to Luca. It was hardly a friendly "hello," but civil, at least.

"Hey, Dex," I said a little too cheerfully.

"Hi," Luca said quietly, only looking up from the salad for a second.

"Okay, I'll start carrying the food out? Is the table set, Dexter?" Mandy asked. She seemed to be trying to ease the tension that had seeped into the room with Dexter's arrival.

"Yes."

Mandy scooted quickly out of the kitchen carrying the eggplant and glided out the back door, giving Dexter her best, "Be nice!" warning look.

"So what did you do today?" Dexter asked me.

"We went to Lake Morgan to hike." I wasn't sure why I was lying, and I knew Dexter would see right through it.

I was right. "Hiking?" he asked with a smirk. "It's me, Violet. Either you've taken up a new hobby or you're lying to me for some reason," Luca looked up smiling when he said this.

He's good, thought Luca.

Like my brother, remember? I replied.

"Fine. We were testing some of our powers," I snapped in a whisper, not knowing who else might walk in unexpectedly.

For a second Dexter looked a little sorry that he'd pushed me. "Oh. Like what?" He perked up and sounded genuinely interested.

"We flew." Luca surprised me by answering Dexter's question. Luca didn't look up, and there was no boast in his words. He said it as he might state any other mundane fact.

"*Flew?!*" Dexter gasped in a loud, excited whisper directed at me.

"Yes. Now SHHHHH!" I spat at him. "Later," I promised. I was annoyed now. I wasn't exactly annoyed with Dexter; I couldn't blame him for wanting to know more. I wasn't annoyed at Luca for telling him. I decided I was annoyed because the moment Dexter had walked into the kitchen, everything changed. Rather, reality had made a sudden and crashing reappearance, and I didn't like it.

There were too many uncontrollable elements in reality. The comfortable world of ten minutes before when Luca and I had been working in the kitchen with Mandy, recalling our magical afternoon was now gone, replaced with unwanted interrogations and whispered replies. It was more than I wanted to deal with. "Let's just get this food out and get this meal over with, okay?" I said to Dexter, attempting to sound more pleasant, but failing miserably.

"All right, relax," he replied, sounding annoyed himself. We each grabbed armfuls of food and marched in silence from the house to the back patio. Both Dexter and I composed our faces into forced smiles and walked purposefully to the table while Luca followed behind.

"Thanks, guys," Mandy said as she stood to help get everything situated on the table. Once our arms were free, the introductions began. "Violet, why don't you introduce Luca," Mandy commanded.

"Um... Gerry, Marilyn, this is my...uh...this is Luca." I finally managed to get out. I realized that I wasn't sure what to call him. I guessed he was my boyfriend...or was he? Was he more? And then I thought that saying the word *boyfriend* would sound juvenile, and it might hurt Dexter. I also didn't want to be presumptuous. I wasn't in the mood to define it and decided I didn't need to. Gerry stood and stuck out his hand.

"Luca, it's good to meet you." They shook hands, and Luca nodded.

"You too."

"Violet. Look at you. You have grown so much. You are absolutely beautiful, as always," Gerry beamed. My face did its usual reddening.

"Er...thanks, Gerry. It's good to see you too," I said as I accepted a big hug from him.

"Luca, this is Marilyn." This was all the courtesy I could muster for this introduction.

"Marilyn, it's nice to meet you," Luca said politely, and put out his hand.

"Mm hmm," Marilyn replied flatly as she limply shook his hand and eyed him suspiciously, probably wondering what kind of person would ever be interested in me besides Dexter who she thought even less of than me. I clenched my jaw and tensed up. "Hello, Violet" was all Marilyn said to me. I didn't respond.

"So, let's eat," Mandy interjected, again attempting to keep things positive and light.

Dinner was underway.

"So, Luca, how long have you and Violet known each other?" Gerry asked.

"Um...we've had classes together for a couple of years, but we've only really *known* each other for a few weeks," Luca answered then glanced at me with a look I couldn't quite place…playful?

"Violet, anything new with you? Still painting?" Gerry now asked me.

"No, yes...sorry. No, nothing's new," I explained. Just then Dexter let out a cough to try to cover a laugh. I shot him the death look, which stopped him abruptly. I hoped no one else noticed. "Yes, I'm still painting," I added.

"Anything we could see?" Gerry inquired further.

"N—," I began, but was cut off.

"Violet has this really great new painting, it's not done, but she..." Dexter blurted out, but stopped when he saw my face. I was furious. How could he? I only showed him that painting to make him realize that he was still important to me. Now I regretted that I had ever shown him anything.

"Oh, will we be able to see it tonight?" Gerry asked.

"NO! Absolutely not," I said quickly. "Sorry, I...just don't show my work until it's complete," I continued, trying to soften my tone.

"And even then, we don't always get to see the finished product," Mandy added. I heard the disappointment in her voice.

I was quiet for a few minutes. I simply listened while Gerry and Mandy and Marilyn talked about their jobs, Mandy's car, auto repair prices, and other boring miscellaneous topics. Occasionally Dexter or Luca would comment or answer a question asked of them. As I sat, still fuming, Luca thought to me, *Are you alright?*

I'm fine. Sorry. Dexter just made me angry. I don't ever show my work before it's done, but the other night he just seemed so...sad and I wanted to make him feel better, so I showed him something I had started, I explained silently without looking up. I loved being able to have conversations like this.

Oh.

Don't worry, I planned to show it to you too if you wanted to see it, I thought when I realized that Luca might be disappointed that Dexter had seen the painting that was about Luca. But I had every intention of showing it to Luca even before I had decided to show Dexter.

Of course, he replied.

"So, Violet, Mandy tells me you were quite a hero at that car accident." I looked up to be sure I'd heard correctly. Marilyn was directing a question at me? And it was a topic I had hoped Mandy had forgotten. I finished chewing and swallowed before answering.

"Um...no, I just opened the door," I replied shyly, trying to keep the subject from becoming one we would discuss. *"Damn!"*

"It *was* weird. I mean we had all tried to get Carol out, and then Violet just...opened the door," Mandy added. I knew this was her not-so-subtle way of letting me know she eventually wanted an answer.

"I think I just found the right spot to pull on, that's all," I explained softly, looking at the food I was pushing around on my plate. "I was there and I felt helpless, so I just did what anyone would do...I tried to get her out."

"Hmmm. And Mandy tells me you were there too, Luca?" Marilyn now spoke to Luca.

"Yes. Well, not at first. I live just around the corner. I was outside washing my car and heard the accident. When I got out there, I was surprised to see Violet and her mother there," Luca explained as cool as can be, looking Marilyn right in the eye.

"What a coincidence," Marilyn said. "Mandy said something about metal pipes that fell off a truck. You're lucky they didn't come through the car's windshield."

"Yeah, we were lucky," I said. I knew I had to change the subject. Marilyn's sudden interest in me and Luca was unsettling, though I couldn't quite place why.

"Uh...Mandy, Luca's mom runs a no-kill dog shelter," I said, abruptly changing the subject. So abruptly that everyone at the table snapped their heads up to look at me. I ignored them. "Isn't that cool?" I added.

"Yes, it is," Mandy replied, giving me a strange look. For the next ten minutes Luca was on the hot seat, answering questions about himself and his family. Thanks to Dexter, even his grandparents' anniversary was a topic of conversation. I was impressed, but not surprised that Luca took it all in stride, answering every question they threw at him. I just sat back and listened, admiring Luca. Then, once again, the conversation went in a direction that I couldn't handle.

"So, have you all known each other for a long time?" Luca made the mistake of asking this to Mandy, Marilyn, and Gerry.

"We've been friends for over thirteen years, since I started the group," Mandy explained, pointing between herself and Marilyn. "We've known Gerry for about three years or so, right Ger?" Gerry nodded.

"Group?" Luca asked. Mandy looked at me to determine whether or not she could or should speak freely. I tried to shake my head to tell her, "No!" without Luca seeing. Unfortunately, he'd seen. "I'm sorry, that was rude. I didn't mean to pry," Luca said apologetically.

"We all belong to a group of people who have been visited by or abducted by extraterrestrials," Marilyn stated matter-of-factly.

"Oh," Luca replied, no surprise or disbelief on his face or in his voice. I sank in my seat and covered my face with my hands. Dexter reached over and put his hand on my shoulder. I shrugged it off. Luca reached under the table and put his hand on my thigh. I let it stay there. I knew Dexter noticed because I heard him force air through his nose, and when I peeked at him from the corner of my eye, he wore a scowl and his eyes were angry slits.

"Let's talk about something else," Mandy suggested.

"Why? What's wrong with talking about our experiences? I'm not ashamed. It was an experience that's defined...*ruined*...my life," Marilyn said loudly, defiantly. "Are you ashamed?" she asked Mandy.

"No, of course not, Marilyn. I just don't think this is the time." Mandy said sternly, looking at me with concern.

"I quite agree," Gerry joined in. "Violet's never been comfortable with this topic, and I think we should respect that."

"Thanks," I said, but didn't lift my head.

"Of course. Poor Violet," Marilyn said with mock compassion.

"Leave her alone!" Dexter said angrily to Marilyn. I looked up at him fully now, shocked that he was still defending me even though he was angry with me.

"Enough. Enough!" Mandy stood now. "Marilyn, you are my best friend, but if you cannot respect Violet, you are not welcome," she said firmly. The words themselves were harsh, but her tone, like her face, was pleading. I knew Mandy hated confrontations.

"I'm sorry Mandy, I'm sorry Violet, and I'm sorry everyone,"

Marilyn said almost as if she were running out of breath, forcing her face into some look that could pass as apologetic, though she couldn't fool me.

"Thank you Marilyn," Mandy said as she took her seat. Luca had been watching and listening. I had nearly shut down completely, head down, not eating.

Are you okay? What the hell is wrong with that woman? Luca asked me.

I told you, she hates me...always has.

I'm sorry you had to go through that, he said.

Thanks. I'm sorry you had to be here to hear it.

Nowhere else I'd rather be, he answered. This made me look at him out of the corner of my eye. He was looking at me too with a secret smile in his eyes.

The remainder of dinner went on awkwardly and rather quietly. However, Luca's comforting words gave me some fresh courage and tolerance. I picked up my head, ate a little more, and even talked a little to everyone except Marilyn, of course, who was also keeping quiet. Some of the other people sitting at the table may have believed she was embarrassed, or humbled, but I knew better.

After dinner, Luca and I cleaned up while Mandy and Dexter got dessert ready. Mandy seemed to be making an effort to be extra nice to Dexter, knowing he was going through a tough time. While Dexter was occupied, it gave me a chance to do something I had wanted to do all night. When the others were talking on the patio, I grabbed Luca's arm. "I want to show you something," I said as I led him toward my studio.

It was a short walk from the patio and around one of the giant oak trees that supported the hammock. "It's just in here." I rushed for the door, still holding Luca's arm. He willingly allowed himself to be dragged into the shed. We walked in and I flipped on the lights, revealing my second home, my studio, a place I seldom shared with anyone.

"Violet. This is your studio?" he asked, though it was obvious where we were. I nodded. Knowing me as well as he already seemed to, he understood what a big deal it was for me to let him into this very private part of my world. I surprised myself by how badly I wanted him to see this part of me. After all, we'd only really known each other for just a couple of weeks, even if it felt like we had known each other for...forever.

Luca looked around at the place where I produced my paintings. The room was small, only about twelve feet by ten feet. The walls were bare wood, and like every visible surface in the room, they were spattered in every shade of paint imaginable. There was a bare plywood floor covered almost completely with an old Persian-style rug in a pattern of burgundy and gold flowers and scrolling, looping lines. This too was covered in drips and splotches of color. Two small windows were set in the side walls, one of which held a small air conditioner, the other covered in a thick curtain. The room was lit by one bare bulb in the center of the ceiling and an ancient floor lamp in the corner opposite the door. There was an old armchair with worn, faded green upholstery, situated next to the lamp.

A table sat in the middle of the room, adorned with an assortment of painting supplies—glass jars, brushes, tubes of paint. Right next to it was my easel covered in a sheet. The rest of the supplies were in the wooden cabinet against the wall just next to the door. Luca smiled as he ran his hands over the colorful handprints that decorated the doors.

"Not Picasso's studio, I'm sure, but it works..." I said in reaction to his inspection.

"No, it's great. It's so...I don't know. It's very...you," he said, still craning his neck all around to see every corner.

"I...I just wanted you to see this part of me. And more specifically, I wanted you to see two paintings. One I started last night, and one I started a couple of weeks ago, right before we...met," I explained. I could not believe how excited I was to be showing Luca my paintings. It was scary and made me feel vulnerable because I put so much of myself into every painting, but it was also kind of liberating.

I walked over to the sheet-covered canvas that stood facing the wall. I pulled off the sheet and turned it around. "This is how I felt a few weeks ago, before...before everything," I said shyly, and I revealed the painting that I had shown Dexter the previous weekend. He walked forward a few steps, pacing back and forth, head tilted slightly like a true art critic.

Is this really how you felt? he asked silently. When he looked at me, there was sadness in his eyes. A knot formed in my stomach, and I regretted showing it to him.

Yes. I answered honestly. He put his hand to his forehead and stood unmoving like a sad statue. I didn't know exactly what to say or do. So I did something completely uncharacteristic of me. I went over to him and touched his arm. *I'm okay now,* I assured him. He moved his hand from his face to mine.

Are you? he asked, searching my eyes for proof.

Yes, I promise. Then I reached up and kissed him. It was not like our previous kisses. It was brief, but gentle and reassuring. I backed away. *I'll show you.* I took his hand and walked him back to the easel. "This is what I started last night. It's what I feel now." When I pulled back the sheet, Luca stared at the painting for a minute. Then a soft smile appeared on his face. His smile spread to my face.

"I still think you're too hard on yourself," he said, motioning to the black figure that obviously represented me, "but I like it. It's...it's a lot like how I feel about us," he said.

Once again, I was shocked by his raw honesty. It overwhelmed me. I knew people didn't just say exactly what they felt and thought. Except for Luca, who always seemed to do just that. I was also filled with satisfaction in knowing how well he understood me. No one had ever understood my work that quickly. Sometimes they *never* understood it. Maybe it was because it was about our shared experiences. But, it didn't matter why he got it, I was just happy that he did.

"Is something wrong?" he asked after I had remained quiet for a few minutes.

"No, nothing is wrong. Nothing at all." I hugged him tightly. He responded by leaning into the embrace. "So, what now?" I asked. My question was deeper than it sounded, and Luca knew it.

"I don't know. We do research. We learn what we can. We test ourselves and learn to control and use our powers..." he replied. He quickly realized that I wasn't asking about *that*. "Oh, you didn't mean that, did you?" he smiled.

"Not exactly, although those are things I guess we really need to do..." I said, but thought to myself only, *"Even if I don't want to face what we might find."* "I'm not ready for the research part yet... flying is good, though!" I joked. He laughed with me. Then he got quiet.

"What exactly happened at dinner?" he asked. I knew he'd wanted to ask since it had happened.

"It's a long story that I promise I will explain, just not right now, okay?"

"Okay. When you're ready, I'm ready to hear it," he said. "So, the other answer to your question...I'm here. We're...together. I guess you're my...I'm your...?" It was a question, not a statement. Did he really have to ask?

"I know it doesn't sound like it fits exactly, but...I don't know what else to call us. Of course, if you're *okay* with all of that?" he added.

"You know I am. I feel like we're...I don't know...*right*," I said honestly but with hesitation. I was afraid it might be too strong for our new, very complicated relationship...it might frighten him. *"Has it really only been a couple of weeks?"* I thought to myself.

"I can't think of a better word," he said seriously as he embraced me one more time, then pressed his lips gently onto my forehead. I knew I could stay that way forever, but it occurred to me that we'd been in the studio for a while, and someone would be in there shortly if we didn't come out. "Aren't you glad we got that conversation out of the way?" he asked.

"Oh yeah," I said with a relieved sigh. "Do you want some carrot cake?" I asked into his chest.

"Of course." He released me reluctantly.

"You know it means going back out *there,*" I teased.

"I can handle it if you can. Besides, I'm sure everyone's wondering what we're up to," he said with a hint of mischief in his voice. For the second time, I initiated a kiss. It wasn't quite gentle, but I also restrained myself because I knew he was right about someone coming in. I ended the kiss and backed away. We wordlessly joined hands and exited the studio.

When we walked around the tree, we saw our four dinner companions at the table turn their heads to us simultaneously, each face wearing a different expression. Dexter looked pained. Mandy was overjoyed with a smile that matched my own happiness and stared at our joined hands. Gerry simply smiled, and Marilyn looked something like annoyed or indifferent, maybe even angry. I fought my reddening cheeks.

"You almost missed dessert," Mandy said, but she was hardly scolding us.

"Yeah, I was nice enough to save you some," Dexter mumbled through a mouth stuffed with cake.

"Your favorite," I said, letting him know I hadn't forgotten that friends know a lot about one another. Luca and I joined the table and were each handed enormous slabs of carrot cake. We all ate and talked some more about non-controversial topics. The conversation turned to music and movies, even books, and

I learned that Luca, and I, not surprisingly, shared similar tastes in movies. Where we differed was in our interest in books. We both liked to read, but while I was passionate about historical fiction, Luca liked contemporary fiction, and especially enjoyed science fiction because he said he liked reading about what *could* be.

The dishes had been cleared and the conversation began to wind down as everyone grew tired and aware that it was Sunday night. Work and school awaited most of us in the morning. Gerry was the first to leave, promising he'd be back soon, and not just for group. I wondered again if this was the time Mandy would finally get serious with him. Gerry's exit was followed by Marilyn, who hardly acknowledged me, which suited me just fine. It was just me, Mandy, Luca, and Dexter.

Mandy put on her mom hat and subtly told Luca it was time to go. "Okay, well it's getting late. Violet, you and Dexter need to get to bed; you've got school in the morning." She stood and stretched. "Luca, it was great to see you again. I hope we'll be seeing more of one another." Another hint, this time not so subtle.

"I'd like that," Luca replied as he stood. "I should definitely be going," he said in an effort to let Mandy know that he understood what she'd been saying.

"I'll walk you out," I said.

"Dexter, it was good to see you again. See you tomorrow." He put out his hand and to my pleasant surprise, Dexter shook it!

"Yeah. Goodnight, Luca," Dexter said wearily. I couldn't tell if he was tired because it was late or because this whole situation was exhausting for everyone involved. Either way, I appreciated his effort and smiled a genuine smile at him.

"Mandy, thank you so much for dinner. It was delicious," Luca said. Mandy beamed at everything he said, which made me do the same. I had to admit, I was glad to see everyone getting along so well. Luca fit perfectly into every other aspect of my life, it only seemed natural that he'd fit into my family.

"My pleasure," Mandy answered. "Dex, can you help me stack these chairs, it's supposed to storm later," she added.

"Sure." Dexter replied as Luca and I walked around the side of the house to his car. We meandered hand-in-hand down the graveled path that curved around the side of the house to the little white gate that squeaked and groaned when it was open no matter how many times it had been greased. As we passed through the gate, I overheard Dexter and Mandy talking in the backyard.

"...did great tonight. I'm proud of you," Mandy was finishing a sentence.

"Thanks. It was okay. Luca *is* nice, and he seems to really care about her," Dexter replied to Mandy.

"Yeah, but it is strange...I mean, they've only really known each other a couple of weeks, right?" I realized Mandy was comforting Dexter and fishing for information. I was counting on Dexter to come through for me. Luca paid closer attention now too. It struck me, *"Of course he can hear it all too."*

"Um...well, they've had a couple of classes together this year and last, so...but I think they've been talking more seriously the last couple of weeks, yeah. Why?" Dexter didn't like lying to Mandy. He had once told me that it felt like betrayal.

"It's just...I don't know. I mean...I'd never even heard of him before yesterday, and now it seems like he and Violet have been *an item* for years," she said curiously.

"*'An item!' Ugghh!"* I thought in disgust.

"Don't get me wrong, I think Luca is just adorable, and I agree, he obviously cares. It's just...well, Violet doesn't have a lot of *experience,* I just don't want her to rush into her first relationship and get hurt. Ya know?" she explained. I squirmed, knowing Luca was hearing all this too.

"Yeah, I do." Dexter replied sadly. "But, I really think she'll be okay. And, to be honest, Luca seems like a good guy," he added, and at that moment, I remembered why I loved Dexter so much. He really did care about my happiness and he was nothing if not loyal.

"Well, I trust your judgment, and I do like Luca," Mandy sighed. "Thanks for being the best friend and big brother a girl ever had," she said in her best motherly tone. I imagined that Mandy was giving Dexter a huge, smothering hug at that moment.

See, everything will be fine, Luca thought to me. I looked up to meet his reassuring smile.

I know, I answered. Luca searched my eyes for something, maybe a sign that I was uncomfortable with the conversation that we both overheard. He found none. We had made our feelings clear to one another. I realized that to everyone else, our relationship probably did seem strange. One day we hardly acknowledged one another, and the next we were inseparable. Luca and I didn't need to explain it to one another. There really was no explanation; we both simply knew that we belonged together. It was almost like one of our powers; once we'd connected, we just *were.*

Hand in hand, we continued on to Luca's car. I had felt weighed down by my new powers and by Dexter's feelings, and now suddenly I felt just a little bit lighter. Luca took my other hand and intertwined his fingers through mine. He sighed deeply and looked at me. I wasn't sure if I would ever get used to just how intensely he looked at me, or *into* me was more accurate. "I...this night, this weekend...it's been..." He didn't finish. I thought maybe he couldn't finish.

"I know. Me too," I finished for him.

"I guess I'll see you tomorrow." He paused. "Can I please drive you? Dexter can come too. It doesn't have to be weird." He was almost pleading."Yeah...And you're right, it doesn't have to be weird...it'll be fine." At the same time, we reached toward one another, and our lips met. "I like this." I said after a brief kiss. "A little too much I think," I added, my eyes still closed, and my head pressed into Luca's shirt. Luca laughed quietly, and responded wordlessly,

Not too much...just the right amount, I think.

"See you in the morning," I said as I reluctantly tore myself from him.

"Pick you up at 7:15?" Luca asked, still holding my hands.

"7:15." I let go of him. I went into the house and Luca pulled out of the driveway.

There were no words to define what I felt at that moment. Every cliché that existed about romance popped into my head. I was "walking on air," my head was "in the clouds." If I hadn't been so happy, I'd have made myself sick. Mandy and Dexter obviously noticed my swooning as I came into the living room because I heard them giggling from behind the kitchen wall.

"Okay, YOU TWO CAN JUST STOP NOW!" I yelled, feigning annoyance.

"Oh, Violet, I'm just so...happy!" Mandy said as she came out of the kitchen. I was getting a hug whether I liked it or not, so I braced myself and accepted it.

"Thanks, Mandy," I mumbled into my mother's crushing embrace. "But, please stop being all gushy," I begged. I could see Dexter peeking around the corner with a crooked smile on his face.

"HELP!" I mouthed to him, but his smile just got bigger and he threw his hands up as if to say "I'm not getting involved in this," and disappeared back into the kitchen. "By the way Dex, we're riding with Luca tomorrow!" I called after him. He popped his head around the corner again and scowled. "*That should teach him!*" I thought. It was good to be joking again with my best friend.

"You and Dexter are riding to school with Luca, huh?" Mandy asked as she finally released me. "That's nice. I'm glad the three of you are being mature about all of this." She paused and I knew more was coming. I wished I could hear Mandy's thoughts at that moment so I could prepare myself for what was coming.

"Speaking of mature...you and Luca seem...very *close.*" I backed away and did the typical teenage rolling of the eyes. "Don't misunderstand me, I really like Luca, and I can see that you do too. And I can also see how much he cares about you...It's just that it's all very *new* to you, Honey."

I had turned away now, breathing slowly and deeply so that I didn't react emotionally. After all, I had anticipated this reaction from Mandy and others. I just wasn't in the mood to defend my relationship or define it, or make up a lie. I felt like all of that would detract from the elation I felt knowing that Luca and I were together. But, realistically I knew I had to say something.

"Mandy, I don't want you to worry. Okay? I know he's the first boy I've dated, but it just all feels right. Ya know? We just...clicked. I can't explain it. We *get* each other. And I'm really happy." I paused, composing the rest of my thoughts. I wanted to reassure Mandy without slipping and saying too much. "I know it seems like Luca and I are rushing things, but I can assure you that we are not. I'm not stupid, and I'm not going to *do* anything stupid, if that's what you're worried about. I mean if I was trying to hide something from you I wouldn't bring him here, would I?" I said a little too defensively.

"Okay. I trust you. And I *am* very happy for you," Mandy said. Her tone told me that she meant it.

"Thanks," I said.

"And, I love you." Another hug. I cringed again just before it came.

"Love you too," I responded.

"All right, you and Dex should get to bed, it's getting late, and you don't want to miss *your ride!*" she teased.

"Goodnight Mandy," I said. "Goodnight Dex," I called out.

"Night," his voice called back.

"Oh and by the way, he'll be here at 7:15!" I called out again, just to annoy him.

"Great," Dexter grumbled. Mandy, who'd been listening to our exchange, just shook her head and left the room.

14

The week started off as smooth as the previous one had. Luca picked us up promptly at 7:15. I knew it was crazy, but I had actually missed him in the nine hours since I'd seen him last. We piled into his small car and drove sleepily to school. Luca and I talked a little, but Dexter remained silent. "Don't be offended, it's not you. Dexter is just NOT a morning person," I said aloud to Luca so that I knew Dexter heard me too. "He hardly talks to me before noon." Luca nodded with a smile, clearly not offended.

We arrived at school and exited the car in the student parking lot. This was a new experience for Dexter and me. Though I had my license and drove Mandy's car occasionally, we never could afford a second car, and I had never really minded. Everything I liked to do was within walking or biking distance, and if it wasn't, there was the meager bus system.

Just like the scene inside the school, there were distinct groups of people hanging out around select cars. But when Dexter and I got out of Luca's car, every group turned its collective attention toward us. To make matters worse, after Luca opened my door for me, he took my hand and refused to let go, even though I weakly protested. I was thrust into the throes of reality. Over the two previous days, Luca and I had existed in a world of our own. We'd been able to forget the bullies and rumors that stalked the halls of Lake Hansen High. But walking through the student parking lot brought all of it back, and I realized that my years of attempting to camouflage myself were about to be completely undone.

My first instinct was to let go of Luca's hand, lower my head, and get as far away from the limelight as possible. But the feel of Luca's firm grip, and the way he gently stroked my hand with his thumb, was comforting and momentarily empowering. With a deep breath, I kept my head up and gripped his hand tightly in response. Dexter walked alongside us, completely unaware of, or unconcerned by, the onlookers.

You're doing great! Luca thought to me. I should have known that he would understand the awkwardness.

I feel like the ground is turning into jelly, I admitted.

I'll keep you on firm ground, he said. *And besides, if anyone messes with you, just put them in their place with your powers. You know, hurl a trash can at them with your mind...* I looked at him sideways, and he was smiling.

Yeah right! I thought back. *That definitely wouldn't draw any attention!* Then I smiled. It was hard for me not to smile when Luca was there. Of course I could never use my powers in front of people, but the memory of the look on the boy's face who had held me back that night in the alley, only to wind up on his back in a pile of trash cans, made the thought tempting. I pushed it aside.

We got to our lockers and the usual groups were assembled in their usual spots. Everyone and everything seemed exactly as it had always been, yet I felt like the entire universe had changed in just a few days, but Luca and I, and maybe Dexter, were the only ones who were in on the secret.

The stares continued all day. Many students spoke in hushed whispers as I passed them, unaware that I could hear every word loud and clear. "I can't believe *she* has a boyfriend!" I heard. "I didn't even know she talked to anybody," said others. "I didn't know she *could* talk."

Earlier in the day, fresh from having seen Luca, I was able to shrug off their comments, but as the day wore on, and my time away from Luca increased, it became harder to hear the comments and not internalize them. Each one was like a little needle jabbing into me.

Then, as I turned the corner on my way to art, and only a few steps from where Luca stood waiting for me, I heard a comment, spoken loud and clear, no superpowers required to hear it. "Oh, I guess she broke up with her other boyfriend...you know, the one with the big mouth. I wonder what she did to get her new one." Of course this came from Stephanie Baker, standing against the wall amongst her lemmings. Her friends were in hysterics over that one. "I mean, why else would anyone go out with that...*freak?* He's either insane or stupid!"

"Or desperate," one of her friends spat out.

"I thought he might have some taste. He's kinda hot, so what's he doing with *her?*" asked another.

No longer the painful pinpricks of the earlier comments, these were daggers, and their blades ran a searing pain into my heart. I wanted so desperately to say something, to shove Stephanie against a wall and make her tremble, but I didn't. I lost my nerve and instinctively put my head down and walked past Stephanie as my face became red hot. I then walked past Luca without looking up at him, went inside the art room, and sunk into my seat. I heard their obnoxious, howling laughter slowly recede down the hall with them, leaving a lingering echo in their wake.

Though I had believed I had the power to defy Stephanie again, like I had the week before, my confidence failed. I couldn't even look at Luca. I was a supernatural wonder capable of reducing Stephanie to a broken mess, the girlfriend of maybe the best person I'd ever met, who seemed to see me as flawless, but I still allowed Stephanie to control how I felt about myself. Now it was my shame in allowing that to happen that kept my head down when Luca came to sit beside me.

He was kind enough to give me a few minutes before he communicated with me. When he did, his angry tone surprised me. *Don't you* dare *let* HER *get to you!* YOU *are awesome. SHE is a monster who feeds on your misery!* My head lifted up at his words.

Thank you, and I know I shouldn't let her get to me, but for so many years, she's been the ringleader...it's hard to not think that she's right when she calls me a fre—" he interrupted me.

Please don't say that word unless you plan on including Dexter and me in your definition. Even in my head, his words were like a painful whisper. It was a complete departure from his usual calm nature, and it made me regret hurting him. But, it did have the intended effect. It sobered me and made me realize that it was more important to me to make Luca happy than to give in to Stephanie's attacks. I resolved to myself from that moment on not to allow Stephanie Baker to break me. I had Luca now, and that's what was most important.

I'm sorry. You're right. I just...old habits die hard? I shrugged slightly. Luca's eyes changed instantaneously. They were once again the deep, soft and serene place of comfort I had come to know. I smiled in relief. The thought of Luca being angry with me was difficult, but knowing that he was angry because of my own treatment of myself, something I could control, was unbearable.

You don't have to apologize. Sorry I was so angry...it just hurts me to see you back down to someone who isn't half the person you are. Stop beating yourself up. You are going through a lot.

Okay, if you're any nicer to me, I'm going to vomit, I teased. Luca laughed silently. It was only discernible by the slight shaking of his head and shoulders.

Sitting in class waiting for Mrs. Charmin to get started, it occurred to me that to the other students, Luca and I would have appeared to be two students sitting idly in class occasionally stealing glances at one another. Of course, the fact that he had chosen to sit next to me for the past week, and we'd been seen holding hands around school, did explain the more frequent glances in our direction.

Class proceeded. I was thrilled when Mrs. Charmin brought out the clay. I needed it today. Working with clay was very therapeutic, and by the end of class, I felt much more at peace.

After school the parking lot emptied quickly. Luca and I waited for Dexter to meet us at the car. I was just about to go inside to get him when I saw him jogging toward us. Immediately I knew something was wrong. Dexter's hair was a mess, and I could see a raised red mark under his left eye. I ran to him. When I got closer, I was able to better survey the damage. His top lip was swollen with already congealed blood sealing where it had been split. He blew past me and proceeded to the car where he paused briefly and turned away from me. I caught up to him and was about to grab his shoulder when Luca reached over and touched my trembling hand, lowering it.

Calm down, Violet, Luca said gently. *Just give him a minute.* Tears already streaked down my reddened face, but Luca's hands on mine kept me from losing all control.

"What the hell happened to you?" I asked Dexter quietly, but he flung the back door open and launched himself into the car's back seat. I nearly pulled the car door off its hinges and jumped into my seat with as much ferocity as Dexter had. Luca stayed outside the car, politely giving us time and space to talk. Of course I knew he'd be able to hear every word.

"Dexter!" I yelled. When he didn't respond, I continued. "Answer me, damn it!" I was getting increasingly more angry, though my anger came from fear, loyalty, and most of all, guilt because I had a fairly good idea of what had probably happened. "They did this to you, didn't they?" I asked in a hushed voice, suddenly sedate. I didn't have to say who "they" were; Dexter and I both knew who I meant.

I did this! This is my fault. My words trembled even in their silent form. As I thought the words to Luca, fresh tears welled up and overflowed freely. My shoulders shook and muffled whimpers escaped from my mouth as I struggled to breathe and cry simultaneously.

"Violet," Dexter groaned from the backseat, trying to sit himself up to get closer to me. I instantly swiveled around in my seat to look at him. One look at my tear-stained face made Dexter groan again and throw himself back into the seat with a short, violent exhale.

"What Dex?" I asked through sniffles.

"Please, stop crying. I can't take it," he begged, turning his head toward the window so he didn't have to look at me. I reached my arm up and quickly wiped my eyes and nose. I didn't want to upset Dexter any more.

"Okay, I'm good," I managed to get out, sniffling and clearing my throat. Neither Dexter nor Luca believed me. In fact, they both smiled a little at my effort. This annoyed me. "I'm FINE!" I commanded. "Now please tell me what happened!"

Dexter let out another breath, this time long and full of stalling. "I went to my locker after class, as usual, and I saw that bi—...HER in the hall with her little army. They were doing their usual talking shit about people, laughing, you know... Anyway, she starts calling me...'Dexter, right?'...So I look over at her and she starts saying stuff about you and him..." He nodded toward Luca. "It pissed me off. I...she...what gives her the right, you know? Anyway, I told her to fuck off, and I guess she didn't appreciate it, so when I stopped in the bathroom on my way out, those two assholes from the movies came in behind me, and well..." He threw out his hands and made an expression indicating the results of their brutality.

"God, Dex, I am SO sorry. When are you going to learn to ignore her?" I asked, my voice sounding defeated.

"Well, from what I hear, you aren't doing such a good job of ignoring her either. I just have the balls to tell her off," he spat at me.

"What are you talking about?"

"I heard she really got to you before art today. I thought Mr.

Wonderful would've stood up for you, and since he didn't, and you won't stand up for yourself, I guess it's up to me."

"I have never asked you to fight my battles for me!" I growled.

"Whatever Violet. Can we just go home now?" he said quietly, looking away again.

"Whatever," I repeated.

Luca, who had already gotten into the car but remained quiet, took this as his cue to start the engine. He looked at me. *Are you okay?*

I'm fine, I lied. He knew I wasn't and took my hand in his. I thought about pulling away. I was so angry with myself because I knew Dexter was right. I felt like I didn't deserve Luca's kindness, but I decided I was also selfish enough to want to be comforted by him, so I gripped his hand in response.

He's right, you know. Luca's words confused me at first.

About what? I asked.

I should've stood up for you.

Not you too! Please stop. You didn't do anything wrong. In fact, I'd be happier if you'd just be mad at me like he is! I thought.

No chance. And he's not really mad at you. I know exactly how he feels, and trust me, anger is way down on the list. There was a pause in his communication, and then, *But, I should've said something.*

It wouldn't have mattered. She'd find some way to twist it and use it against me. So, it's better that you didn't. Dexter shouldn't have either, I insisted.

At least he was brave.

No, he was stupid.

I was just hoping that you'd say something or at least ignore her completely, you know, really get to her.

I know. It was just a long day, I had no strength left...figuratively speaking, of course. Then I looked up at him and smiled weakly.

Sorry, Luca said.

No more apologies. Please, I pleaded silently.

Okay, Luca agreed.

The ride home was longer than usual. No one quite knew what to say. I wanted to talk to Dexter, comfort him, but I knew him well enough to know he needed time. Nevertheless, I squirmed uncomfortably in my seat, still clutching Luca's hand. Dexter sat still and quiet throughout the entire ride.

When we reached my house, Luca put the car in park, but didn't turn it off. I wanted him to stay, but thought it might be better if I went in and spent some time with Dexter alone.

"So, will I hear from you later?" I asked Luca. I knew that he knew what I meant.

"Of course," he said.

"Thanks for the ride." Dexter said as he got out of the car, without really acknowledging Luca.

"Yeah, no probl—" Luca didn't finish because Dexter was already halfway across the lawn.

"He's just...Dexter. Ignore him."

"It's fine. He's had a rough afternoon. I don't blame him for not wanting to *play nice* with me. If I were him, I probably wouldn't like me either," he admitted.

"Why is that?" I asked. I figured I knew the answer, but wanted to hear Luca say it.

"Well, for one, if I were Dexter, I would be very jealous that someone else got to spend so much time with you."

"But he gets to spend lots of time with me," I corrected.

"Not the *same,*" he reminded me as he moved a strand of hair from my face.

"Hmmm," I responded as my eyes closed, allowing myself to become absorbed in his adoration. "I see what you mean." He brushed my cheek where the dried tears still left their streaks.

"I don't like to see you cry," he admitted in a voice that was barely above a whisper. "I only want you to be happy. I want to make you happy." He then unexpectedly reached for his phone and clicked something. Almost instantly, my phone buzzed. Curiously, I clicked the message.

If I could be your superman
I'd swoop in
When your world turned against you
And save you.
Lift you into my arms,
Take you away
—If you'd let me

I would rescue you
A thousand times—a million
If it meant that
I could shelter you
If it meant that
I could save you from the pain
If it meant that
I could hold you—

If only for a second.

I looked up and Luca was inches from me. "Did you write this?" I asked, knowing full well that he must have.

"Yeah. That day after you ran out of the bathroom." I remembered that day vividly. I had to respond the right way, so I thought before I opened my mouth.

"You do make me happy. Happier than I ever thought I could be," I explained.

"Good," his staring continued. I swallowed hard and my breath quickened.

"What is it?" he whispered.

"It's...it's the way you look at me," I stammered.

"Sorry, do you want me to stop?" he asked with a mischievous grin.

"Uh...no. I never want you to stop looking at me that way, that's the problem."

"Why is it a problem?" he laughed.

"Because, it makes me...insane...makes my mind swim. It makes me feel like I am the only person in the world," I said.

"You are. To me."

"And there's *that*," I said.

"What?"

"You always say these...things that people don't say. Most people have a filter that they use even with the people they care about, to...I don't know, protect themselves. But not you. It's disarming and makes me feel...amazing and vulnerable. It's a little scary."

"I don't mean to scare you, Violet. I don't know how else to be with you. I want you to know exactly what I feel. I'm sorry if it's uncomfortable. If you want me to stop--"

Exasperated, I said, "No. I don't. I didn't say I didn't like it. I can get used to it. The vulnerability thing is my problem. I said I also feel 'amazing', remember?" I smiled.

"Good, *that's* how I want you to feel all the time."

"I do when I'm with you." Though our hands were entwined and we were only inches apart, we both shifted in our seats to get even closer. Then we shared another long, passionate kiss that I lost myself in just like I had in the woods. I threw out all inhibitions, gripping his hair, and sliding my hands down the muscles of his back. Luca reciprocated my enthusiasm, his hands finding their way to my waist, gripping me firmly. When we finally broke to breathe, I caught sight of the clock on the dashboard.

"I really need to go in," I said reluctantly, "We've been sitting here a long time."

"Wow, it's late. Yeah, I should go." He took a deep breath. "You really are incredible, you know.

"You're pretty great too," I said. One more, quick kiss and Luca was at my door.

"Talk to you later," I said.

"Bye." He let go of my hand and I went into the house.

Dexter was on the couch already with an ice pack on his eye. Mandy was sitting next to him stroking his hair and saying, "Are you sure you don't want me to call the school, Dex?" To which he replied emphatically, "No, Mandy, please, no!" They both looked up at me when I came into the room.

"Hi, Honey," Mandy said with little enthusiasm. I wondered what Dexter had said to her. It seemed as if Mandy was already blaming me for Dexter's injuries. *"What else is new?"* I thought to myself. But, I needed to know Dexter's story so I could corroborate and not give Mandy any reason to doubt the story I'd been told.

"Hi," I said to Mandy. "How's your face?" I asked Dexter.

"Great," he growled.

"Violet, I cannot believe you weren't there when those boys started with Dexter," she said, scolding me.

"Where? The boys' bathroom?" I snapped, though I knew that this was my fault, however indirectly.

"Ugghh!" Mandy growled impatiently. "Fine! I know it wasn't your fault," she exclaimed, but then softened, "Sorry. I just hate seeing Dexter this way," Then she looked at Dexter, "Of course, he should have *kept his mouth shut.* But, that doesn't give them the right to hit him."

"Can we just drop it? Please?" Dexter pleaded.

"Alright," Mandy said, but I wasn't sure she would.

I sat on the loveseat and looked at the muted TV. I grabbed the remote, and as I turned the sound back on I asked, "So, what are you guys watching?" Then I was sorry I hadn't simply said, "Hello," and headed to my room.

"It's called *Our Alien Past.* It's very interesting. It talks about evidence that aliens interfered with human development...you know, sort of helped man become more evolved by altering our genes and creating hybrids. There are art experts and anthropologists... It's kind of like what the grays told—" She stopped. My facial expression and body language told her that I didn't want to hear about it. I wanted to keep it as far from me as possible. There was no way I was going to allow my mother to speak about this for one more second. So, I got up without a word and left the room.

I went directly to my studio and decided to work on my Luca painting to completely clear my mind of Mandy's words that seemed to creep under my skin and gravitate to my brain where they were festering and trying very hard to form an idea that I was working equally hard to undo.

The act of painting helped. The feel of the brush in my hand as I guided it to create what I wanted was as energizing as ever. I loved the control I had over the brush, the paint, and the images that appeared on *my* canvas.

15

Luca picked us up again the next morning. Dexter was silent the entire way, giving Luca only a head nod when he got into the back seat. But, Dexter wasn't the only one who was quiet. I was nervous about any potential confrontations with Stephanie so I said very little as I played out uncomfortable scenarios in my head. I was committed to not letting her win today, and I laughed to myself as I thought that I felt like I was in a video game. I was the heroine, of course, and Stephanie was the evil creature that must be defeated. Dexter was my sidekick, and Luca was my energy source. For every second I spent with him, it was as if I were being given more power. I just hoped it was enough to sustain me throughout the day.

"What's so funny?" Luca asked when my daydream caused a silent snicker.

"Uh...nothing...I just...nothing," I said. It seemed way too silly to repeat.

We pulled into the student parking lot and were again greeted with the same stares and awed expressions as the day before. This time there were also added comments about Dexter and the circumstances that led to his obvious facial injuries. Most of them were quiet, but Luca and I could hear everyone. I was just grateful that at least Dexter was ignorant.

When we got to our lockers, I scanned the hall for Stephanie and quickly found her standing in a semicircle of her usual gang. My intention was to simply keep my chin up, focus on Luca, and get through the day. But then I overheard Stephanie talking about

Dexter and how he couldn't keep his "fucking mouth shut," so she'd had someone "shut it for him."

Without taking even a moment to compose my words, and with no thought to the fifty or so other students in the hall, I found myself moving purposefully in Stephanie's direction. Luca looked up just in time to see me make a move. He didn't say anything to me, but as I strode down the hall, I could hear him behind me. "Look!" he whispered.

"What is she *doing*?" Dexter asked, his voice full of shock.

I could hear the pride in Luca's voice. "I think she's finally had enough."

"Should we...I mean..." Dexter was at a loss for words.

"She's fine. We *know* she can take her if it gets physical. She needs this," Luca said.

"You're right," Dexter agreed, then reminded Luca, "I can't hear as well as you can."

"Right," I heard Luca move with him. They walked slowly, and stopped when I stopped, but gave me plenty of room.

As I approached, Stephanie first appeared to be amused, but as I continued without slowing down, her bravery faltered. I saw it, and in that moment I knew that the only power Stephanie ever had was the power I had given her. And I intended to take all of that power back right then and there. When I stopped less than a foot from her, everyone in the hallway stopped with me. Students froze where they were and held their collective breath, waiting. Every head was turned in our direction, and almost in unison, the phones came out. Stephanie tried very hard to get back an expression of indifference, but it didn't work. Even her friends, shock and confusion on their faces, inched back ever-so-slightly. I knew I was in charge of this conversation.

"Stephanie," I said in a tone that was almost cordial, as if I were greeting her.

"What do you want?" Stephanie again tried to sound annoyed,

but the words came out a little too shaky to be believable.

"What I want is for you and your friends to leave Dexter and Luca *alone,"* I said calmly, looking at each of her friends one by one when I spoke. The eyes of every student in that hallway widened. For most, I guessed this was the first time they had *ever* even heard me speak.

"What are you talking about?" she replied like a snotty child.

I moved a hair closer to Stephanie, and I could see her jaw clench and unclench. I could hear her breath coming in quick, shallow bursts through her nose. I wanted to laugh at her reaction, but I knew I had to keep up the intimidation angle. So, I lowered my voice to a whisper and answered, "You know *exactly* what I am talking about." I wasn't sure if anyone besides Luca would be able to hear my words, but it didn't matter. Stephanie's reaction was enough to let everyone know that I had gotten my point across.

"I...you..." she stammered, red-faced, and then turned and ran down the hall. Not a single one of her friends went after her. I stood my ground, narrowed my eyes slightly, and allowed the tiniest of grins to escape. A very long minute went by before anyone moved, including me. The first signs of movement in the hall came from Luca and Dexter who snapped out of their astonished hazes and rushed to me. Luca grabbed me and pulled me into a crushing hug, and Dexter squeezed my shoulder. I looked up from Luca's chest and smiled. In that moment, the enormity of what I'd done hit me. Then I felt wobbly and needed Luca's embrace for support. I gripped him tighter.

You were...I am so proud of you, he gushed.

"Violet, you are my hero," Dexter laughed.

For another moment, I hid my face in Luca's chest, embarrassed by their unfailing adoration. I might have stood up for myself, but I still wasn't good with compliments.

The other students in the hall came to life shortly after Luca and Dexter's initial reaction. They said nothing, but I noticed them looking at me in a new way. What was it that I saw on their faces—respect, fear, reverence? I wasn't sure, but all of those were preferable to disgust. I held my head up as I let go of Luca. "We'd better get to class," I said.

"Uh...yeah," Luca answered. His was definitely a look of reverence. He kept his hand on the small of my back as we proceeded to our classes with Dexter in tow. He didn't remove it until we had to separate.

"Bye, V. And thanks," Dexter smiled as he peeled off in the direction of the gym.

"You don't have to thank me. Bye, Dex," I responded. Then I turned my attention to Luca. "I couldn't have done any of that without you," I admitted, trying to equal the intensity of his eyes with my own.

"No way am I getting credit for the coolest thing I have ever seen," he said, shaking his head.

"That was all you, Violet. YOU!" he insisted.

"I know, but without you there with me, knowing you support me, I don't think I ever would have found the strength to stand up to her," I clarified.

"Okay, fine. We are both amazing. Alright?" he smiled. "Now let's get to class, because the sooner we get this day over with, the sooner I get you to myself." There was that look again.

"You are making it hard for me to justify *not* skipping school, you know?" I said.

"What, skip and miss all the attention?" I rolled my eyes but then leaned into him for one last embrace and a not-so-quick kiss. The kiss ended when we heard Mr. Wagner clearing his throat loudly in our direction. We separated and looked at him as he tapped his wrist to let us know that we were going to be late for class.

"I'll see you at lunch," Luca said.

"Bye," I said, not wanting to walk away, but Mr. Wagner was not going anywhere until we did. He glowered at us to make sure we knew who would win a stand-off if we chose to have one. As I turned away from Luca and walked to English, I thought to him, *The coolest thing* ever?

I could hear the laughter in his voice as he responded, *Without a doubt!*

***

That night, during dinner, Mandy made an observation, "Violet, you seem different today. What is it?" She studied me with extra scrutiny while I squirmed in my seat. One thing that hadn't changed was that I still hated being the center of my mother's attention. Mandy's attention was razor sharp and her need to find out information was relentless. She would never give up until she got answers. Dexter smiled a huge, toothy smile at me. I knew he wasn't going to keep his mouth shut. And before I could make something up to appease Mandy, Dexter jumped in.

"Violet kicked *ass* today, that's what!" he blurted out. He didn't usually talk like that in front of Mandy. It wasn't that Mandy minded so much, it was more a show of respect on Dexter's part. But he was obviously excited and busting to relay the story with his own twists and embellishments.

"What?" Mandy asked, surprise evident on her face.

"Mandy, she walked right up to that Stephanie bit—uh—girl and told her what's up...and that was it..." Dexter explained.

"That was what?" Mandy asked again.

"Stephanie backed off and hasn't been seen since," he said matter-of-factly. "You should have seen all the kids. They stopped moving. Stopped *breathing.* Everyone was in awe of V." It was apparent by his tone that he included himself in his definition of "everyone."

"Stop being so dramatic, Dexter, and, 'hasn't been seen since?' Please! You make it sound like she's missing, and now I'm a prime suspect or something," I barked. I was not enjoying this.

"Violet, is this true? Did you really stand up to that girl who has picked on you all these years?" Mandy asked, her face glowing with pride now.

"Yes," I said, exasperated.

"But isn't that the girl you used to be friends with before—" she stopped abruptly.

"Yes, Mandy, before the interview," I sighed wearily.

"Oh," Mandy responded. Her face was serious and all the previous excitement had vanished, but her eyes still showed traces of pride.

"Can we please talk about anything else now?" I asked, looking from Mandy to Dexter.

"Okay, Honey," Mandy said, but then added, "I am so proud of you." Then she got up and kissed me on the top of my head.

"Thanks," I mumbled. "And you...can you drop this?" I asked Dexter.

"Yeah, yeah, yeah," he sighed, but I knew he was not going to stop.

Later that night, after I had painted, while I was sitting on my bed, working on my biology homework, there was a light rapping on my bedroom door.

I had my headphones on, but my ears were able to pick up the sound anyway.

"Yeah?" I called out. Out of habit, I removed one of my headphones, but it wasn't necessary.

"Can I come in for a second?" Dexter asked quietly, though he'd already opened the door a crack.

"Yeah, what's up Dex?" I asked without looking up from my homework.

"I just...want to talk to you," he said. There was a seriousness to his voice that made me look up. The look on his face matched his tone.

"What is it? Is something wrong?" I asked, alarmed. "Your...dad?"

"No...nothing like that," he clarified, sitting down on the edge of my bed.

"Then why do you look like that?" I asked, confused.

"Like what?"

"Like you just lost your best friend." I realized what I had said and joked, "That was a bad comparison, sorry."

"It was actually kind of funny. And I haven't lost anything. That's what I came to talk to you about," he explained "I...it's just...I've spent all these years, you know, trying to protect you, sticking up for you—"

I interrupted, "I know, and I have always appreciated it, even if I have thought you were insane." I gestured toward his still-swollen eye.

"No, I'm not looking for a thank you. What I am saying...if you'd please stop interrupting..." he said with feigned annoyance.

"Sorry," I mouthed silently, putting my hands, palms-up, in front of me.

"What I'm *trying* to say is...thank you. Not just for sticking up for me, which was truly awesome, and I do appreciate it, even though I know you did it for you too, which is precisely the reason you should have done it anyway..." he was babbling, clearly nervous about whatever else he was trying to say. So, I did what I had always done, tried to ease his stress. I put my hand on top of his. For a second, I thought he might read more into the gesture than I intended, but I decided that I just didn't care. He was my best friend, had been forever, and he needed me. He paused for a second and looked at our hands, mine lying gently on top of his before he continued. "And you know, I feel immensely proud of you. But what I really want to say is...I'm sorry."

"Sorry? For what?" I was confused.

"I'm sorry for all the awkwardness over the last couple of years. I'm sorry for having the wrong kinds of feelings for you. I'm sorry for not keeping those feelings to myself. But mostly, I'm sorry for giving you such a hard time about Luca and for not being very...*nice* to him. He's really a good guy, and I know he cares about you. That's obvious. It hurts to admit it, but I think he cares about you as much as I do. So, no more feeling guilty, like I know you have been about Luca. You deserve to be happy. And I promise to give him a chance," he finally stopped.

My mouth hung open. Words were there but couldn't seem to find their way out of my mouth yet. A full minute went by with me looking dumbfounded at Dexter, before those words materialized.

"Thank you, Dexter. You really are the best friend I could ever, ever ask for." I pushed my books to the side and threw my arms around him in the biggest hug I'd given him since before he had made his true feelings known. Tears of pure joy streamed out of my eyes as I realized that things might actually go back to the way they had been before. Hearing the sniffling, Dexter groaned.

"Oh no, are you crying again? Is that one of your new powers?" he teased.

"Shut up, Dexter," I slurred through my tears, and I hugged him tighter.

"Owww!" he yelled. "You have super-strength, remember?" he laughed. I gasped.

"Sorry!" I whined.

"It's okay, just try to be gentle with my puny human body will you?" I didn't even let a comment that implied I might not be human dissolve my happiness. I shrugged it off and continued hugging my best friend. I hugged him like I was seeing him for the first time in years.

My heroics were the talk of the school and social media for the rest of the week, though the talk was hushed and never directed at me. Most of the student body continued looking at me in this new way that I'd first noticed just after the confrontation. A few students, very few, even acknowledged my presence. One boy in my biology class gave me a head nod in greeting as I entered class, and I gave him a strained smile in return.

Then a quiet, loner of a girl from my sophomore English class, who had also been a victim of Stephanie's wrath and suffered the plague of unpopularity, smiled at me as I walked to my locker after math class. But it was Dexter and Luca who made me blush endlessly with their relentless praise and admiration. Dexter continued to treat me as if I were some kind of goddess. Luca showered me with an unapologetic, endless stream of, "I told you so." I rolled my eyes and playfully elbowed him in the ribs each time.

Stephanie returned to school after being out for two days. She tried to keep up a defiant exterior, but she said nothing to or about me, and I was listening carefully. Dexter wasn't harassed either. I thought he almost seemed disappointed not to have anyone to glare at or complain about. All in all, it was a very pleasant week for me, Luca, and Dexter.

Luca drove us to and from school each day and ate dinner with us one night that week. Like the previous time, he charmed Mandy and won her over even more. Dexter even had a few awkward conversations with him. While I painted each night or did my homework, I spoke to Luca. We talked about *almost* everything. I couldn't believe how easy it was to tell him about my life. I spilled my guts about my dad and how hard it had been for me when he got remarried. I talked about mine and Mandy's sometimes-strained relationship, though I never went into detail as to why; I knew Luca was aware of the basics, but I wasn't ready to talk specifics yet. I knew I would be eventually. Likewise, I wanted to know every detail of who Luca was.

I learned that while his parents were supportive of him, they worried because he didn't have many friends. I also found out that he'd told his parents about me, and they wanted to meet me. The butterflies instantly came to my stomach. I wasn't sure if I had the courage to meet his parents. What if they knew something about Mandy? What if they didn't like me? What if they knew other parents and found out I was not the most popular girl in school? Luca must have felt the anxiety in my thoughts because he tried to assure me that his parents were not only excited that he had a girlfriend but didn't know a thing about Mandy, and if they had, they were not judgmental people. This didn't really make me feel better. Nonetheless, Luca and I agreed that I'd come over for dinner on the following Tuesday.

Mandy had to work on Friday night, so Thursday came *the talk*. I groaned the moment Mandy patted the couch next to her, indicating that she wanted me to sit down. I grudgingly hurled myself onto the couch, as if I were in actual physical pain rather than just being mentally tortured. "Violet, you know I have to work tomorrow night and Saturday."

"Yes," I mumbled. This was not news to me.

"And you and Dexter have had rules for a while now..." she had her motherly voice in full swing now.

"Uh...yeah, why?" I groaned when I realized that this conversation was leading a direction that I wanted no part of.

"We haven't had to deal with this situation before. I mean, you and Dexter...well, that's never been an issue. But now, there's Luca," she paused. "I trust you, Violet. And I trust Luca, but we have to set some basics...okay?" Mandy wasn't really asking.

"Okay, so no sex on the couch then?" I hissed sarcastically.

"Oh, fun-ny!" Mandy glowered. "Violet, I know you are seventeen, but you *are* my daughter and you aren't very...*experienced*."

I squirmed in my seat and made a sour face. "Please,

Mandy...just tell me your rules before I die right here."

"Okay. Okay. No spending the night! No in your room with the door shut... No, no in your room at all," she clarified after she thought about it a little more. "And, try to include Dex. He's been so great with this, but I know he's still hurting, and you know he doesn't really have any other friends."

"Ah...the real purpose of our talk," I thought to myself. "Mandy, Dex is fine, really. In fact, we're better than ever, and I am not going to be making out on the couch with Luca while Dexter sits and watches from the other end. Give me some credit please," I scoffed.

"*Alright*, sorry. I just love you both so much," she said. She sat silently for a few minutes. Then, "Do you have any plans for tomorrow night?"

"You mean besides the making out thing?" I smiled. Mandy rolled her eyes. "No, not as of yet. I'll let you know, though, I promise." Then I did something that I rarely did without provocation: I hugged my mother. Mandy nearly fell off the couch. She hugged me back tightly and didn't hold back a few happy tears. "I'm not going to do anything stupid. I'm not ready," I whispered in her ear and then let go quickly.

I'm not sure if I was saying this to convince her or me. When I was around Luca, it was hard for me to think straight and make rational decisions. But, at least I was sure that he'd never try to force me into anything I wasn't ready for. I caught sight of Mandy's face and was glad I had given her that hug. Mandy got up without saying anything and went into the kitchen. She returned with two cupcakes and two glasses of milk.

"I baked these today. They're your favorite, chocolate with vanilla frosting."

"Thanks Mom," I said. We ate our cupcakes quietly, enjoying the rare bonding experience.

16

"So, what do you want to do this weekend?" Luca asked on the way to school the next morning while Dexter slumped in the backseat with his ever-present earbuds popped into his ears. "Sorry, that was presumptuous...Uh, do you have any plans this weekend?" he corrected himself.

"Oh, huge plans," I answered sarcastically. "I've got to paint, study for finals, and let's not forget laundry...I'm swamped. Why, do you have any ideas?"

"Actually, I do. I want to take you on a real date...no tests, supernatural stuff, just two *normal* teenagers on a *normal* date. What do you think?" He sounded so eager. I thought it was adorable. I still couldn't believe he wanted to be with me.

"So are we inviting these *normal* teenagers on a double-date with us?" I asked sarcastically.

"Ha, ha," he answered dryly. But he wanted an answer. "So?"

"Yeah, that sounds great. Where to?"

"Ahhh, *that* is a surprise," he teased.

"Oh, so you've been planning this? What if I'd said, 'no, I'm busy...planting trees?'" I asked, grasping for something.

"Then I guess I'd be spending the weekend in dirt," he answered without missing a beat. I couldn't help but smile.

"So, tomorrow at three?"

"Three? That's a little early for a date, isn't it?"

"Not this date," he said mysteriously.

"Okay." I answered nonchalantly, though inside the curiosity was killing me. I couldn't fathom what he had planned. I only hoped he didn't plan anything that would require me to be in the vicinity of large numbers of my classmates. I may have stood up to Stephanie within the walls of the school, but I wasn't sure if I had faith in myself to do it anywhere else. "*He knows me well enough...*" I thought to myself, content in the undeniable truth of my own thoughts, "*He won't plan anything that will make me feel uncomfortable.*"

***

Friday dragged on. Luca hadn't mentioned anything about the upcoming night, and I wondered if I should just come out and ask. With all that we shared, it seemed silly to be so evasive now. So, in art, when the school day was drawing to a close, I asked him. *Are we at the point where it is understood that we will be hanging out on a Friday night?* I thought it so that I wouldn't lose my nerve. The question seemed to startle Luca who had been concentrating on the sculpture he was working on. It was a small tree with a thick trunk and spindly limbs. I thought it looked kind of sad.

Luca was silent for a moment, and for the first time I was worried that I had presumed too much about our relationship and his feelings for me. A sudden and gripping fear flooded through me and colored my cheeks. Tears even welled up in my eyes. Maybe Dexter was right, and crying was one of my powers! I had never cried so much before. I moved my hair in front of my face as inconspicuously as possible. I hoped he didn't notice. But he did.

Violet. Please don't get upset. I...just...class is over in three minutes, then I promise I will explain everything. Okay? Even his thoughts were pleading. I nodded my head, unable to meet his eyes.

Those next three minutes were like an eternity. As soon as the bell rang, I got up to leave, but Luca grabbed my arm. He wasn't rough, but he let me know that he was going to say his piece. I stopped my departure and fell into step with him. I owed him the chance to explain, which he began to do once we were in the hallway. He pulled me behind a wall where we could talk privately.

"Violet, please look at me," he said, pushing my hair back behind my ear. His touch made me shiver and momentarily forget why we were having this conversation. Then Luca did something to refuel my anger. He laughed. That got my attention. At that moment, there was nothing that I could construe as funny. I looked at him through hard, squinted eyes.

"Okay, listen...it's not what you think. You know...or you should know that there is not a second of my life that has passed in the last few weeks that I have not wanted to spend with you. In fact, sometimes it scares me how much I want to be with you." My eyes softened slightly.

"I just...I've been looking into some *stuff* that I know you don't want to know about...the how and why stuff...doing a little research...very preliminary," Luca confessed. "But, I want to follow-up on some of the information I've found," he paused, checking my face for any sign of understanding. He must not have been sure what he saw there because he continued. "I can't help wanting to know...and there are some things I found out, and I want to check them out. You are more than welcome to come with me," he urged, but his voice was still apologetic.

I now felt conflicted. On the one hand, I felt terrible for making him explain himself. He was right, I knew better than to question his feelings. But, on the other hand, there was a piece of me that was upset by his need to know more. I took a quick breath to allow myself to think clearly through what he'd just said. After all, I reasoned with myself, I couldn't be angry with him for wanting to know. In fact, that was normal. It was my complete avoidance of the issue that was abnormal. More than anything, I just wanted to apologize and get this behind us.

"Violet, please. I'm sorry, I won't bother if it hurts you that much," he pleaded. He sounded pathetic. And the tone in his voice tortured me until I finally found my own.

"Stop." I held up my hand. "Please stop apologizing. I'm the one who is sorry," I said forcefully. "You're right. I know you are. And I know I shouldn't have reacted that way. It's just that, well...rejection feels more natural to me, and so I reverted back to what I know." Now it was my turn to sound pathetic. "And...you know *basically* why I don't care to explore the how and why of our abilities, at least not now...*I* don't even fully understand my objections, I just know that they are strong and knowing scares me...can you understand that?" I asked.

"I can't say that I fully understand, but I support you. And like I said before, I'll wait as long as necessary, and if you ask me right now to stop exploring this until you're ready, I will. I promise. I don't want to do anything to hurt you, ever." I almost couldn't stand how kind he was. Surely I did not deserve his selflessness.

"I won't ask that of you. I know I can be selfish, but I won't be *that* selfish," I said quietly. "I only ask that, *for now,* you keep what you learn to yourself until I'm ready. Is that okay?" It was a sincere question because I didn't want to hurt him either, and if learning this information hurt him and he couldn't share it with me and count on me to be there for him, I couldn't live with myself.

"That sounds fair," Luca said. Then he grabbed me and held me tightly to his chest. I wasn't sure why, but the tears from earlier came back and spilled now. I tried to hold them back, but my shaking shoulders and muffled sniffles gave me away. Luca kissed the top of my head and stroked my hair gently until my body relaxed. I held onto him so tightly that if he didn't have extra-durable skin, I would've hurt him.

Then I thought to him, *Thank you.*

For what?

For everything...for letting me be irrational and ridiculous, and for making me feel like the most important person in the world, I explained.

He looked at me more intensely than ever before. It was so powerful that I almost turned away. *Violet, I have told you already, you* are *the most important person in the world.*

Then we shared a kiss that could've set off the fire alarms.

***

By the time we reached the parking lot, there were only ten cars left, and Dexter was the only person out there. I had forgotten all about him. Now I felt terrible, all the warmth and happiness I'd had when I left the buildings was sapped in that second. "Oh crap!" I said under my breath. Luca looked at me, and followed my eyes to his car.

"Oh," he said quietly.

"Yeah," I looked at my phone. "He's been out here for like, a half hour." I looked down at my phone and saw three messages from him. "He's never going to let me live this one down. And, you're not gonna be around tonight...he's going to torture me!" I whined.

"I could come over," he offered. It was tempting, but our previous conversation had convinced me that I needed to let him do whatever it was he had planned.

"Tempting, but no. I couldn't ask you to do that. I've got to deal with this," I told him.

I hung my head as I approached Dexter. He was sitting on the hood of Luca's car, leaning on the windshield, listening to music, as usual, eyes closed. He might have been sleeping, but I knew better; he was waiting to spring on me. I walked over to him, yanked one of his earbuds out. He didn't react.

"Dexter. I am soooooo sorry! I suck. I am the worst friend ever. Please forgive me. I'll do anything!" I pleaded. He opened his eyes, but didn't look at me. He just slid off the car. Luca opened the doors and we all piled in. We were silent.

About halfway home, Dexter finally spoke. "So, you'll do *anything?*" he questioned. I spun around to see him sitting back with a mischievous grin on his face. I was glad he was speaking to me but apprehensive about his demeanor.

"Oh God, what did I *do*?" I groaned under my breath. "Within reason!" I corrected Dexter. "So, watch it!" I warned, though I tried to keep my tone light and playful. I couldn't really be mad at Dexter. After all, he was the one who had been waiting in the parking lot for a long time. "What do you say tonight we get a pizza and make fun of crappy movies, a la *Mystery Science Theater*?" I asked him. I was fairly sure that this would ensure my forgiveness.

"Does *he* even know what *Mystery Science Theater* is?" Dexter asked in an arrogant voice. *Mystery Science Theater* was an old TV show that Dexter and I had once watched religiously. We'd begun mimicking it years ago, but hadn't done so in a while.

It was Luca who answered Dexter before I could. "I do. I love it. But, I won't be joining the two of you. I have...something I need to do." He said the last part hesitantly, like he didn't want to remind me again. He looked at me cautiously. I answered his look silently.

It's okay. Really. Don't torture yourself. This time when I said it, I meant it.

Dexter's face lit up. "So," he swallowed, "it'll be just me...and you?" he asked, looking more hopeful every second. I turned to face the front of the car and rolled my eyes.

"Yes, Dex. Just us," I confirmed with a sigh, hoping he didn't read too much into it.

Dexter cleared his throat. "That's cool," he said, trying to sound casual, but Luca and I both could hear the undercurrent of excitement in his voice. I hadn't realized until that moment how my relationship with Luca had so completely affected my relationship with Dexter. New waves of guilt and remorse peaked inside of me. I winced at the thought of his pain. It wasn't just that he loved me and now I was with someone else, it was also the fact that until a few weeks ago, Dexter had been my best friend, and now Luca had taken over that designation. I knew that even if I told Dexter he was still my best friend, it wouldn't be the complete truth.

He would always be special and important, my brother, but Luca was my world now. *He* was the one who comforted me when I was down. *He* was the one I felt compelled to share my experiences with. *He* was my best friend now. Suddenly I was actually glad that I was giving Dexter this time, even if I wasn't thrilled about the circumstances that were taking Luca away from me. It was the least I could do. Apparently Luca agreed.

You're a good friend, he thought to me.

I don't think I have been, but I'm going to try harder now, I replied. Luca smiled at me and held my hand. Dexter beamed smugly for the duration of the trip.

When we arrived at home, Mandy was already gone.

"Can you come in for a little while?" I asked Luca.

Surely his research could wait an hour.

"Of course..." he said. As was the new, usual routine, I waited for him to come around and open my door. It was a lot later than we usually got home, which would explain Mandy's frantic text message.

> "VIOLET WHERE ARE YOU???? I LEFT 3 MESSAGES! CALL ME!"

"Uh oh! I better call Mandy right now before she freaks. She's a bit...overdramatic," I explained before I left the room.

"Hi, Mandy," I said when my mother answered. I rarely called my mother at work, opting for the easier text message, but this situation warranted actual speaking.

"Violet! Where have you been?" Mandy demanded in a loud whisper.

"Sorry. We got held up at school," I explained.

"Oh, okay. Well, next time, please just text me or turn on your location. You know how I feel about communication" She was calmer now.

"I know, Mandy. Again, I am *really* sorry," I said in my best apologetic voice. Mandy had a strict policy. She trusted me completely, but the rule was a call or text whenever I was somewhere other than where I had planned to be, or if I was going to be late.

"It's all right. You're safe, and that's all that matters," she said. Then, "So, the three of you watching a movie tonight?" She was prying slightly. "Don't forget our talk..."

"Actually, it's just me and Dex tonight. Luca has something else he has to do," I told her.

"Oh. Well, that's nice...for Dexter. It will make him very happy to spend some time with you." She sounded overjoyed. I didn't take offense. I knew that Mandy's joy had nothing to do with not liking Luca, and everything to do with loving Dexter. "So, I'll see you in the morning. Have a good night. Call me if you need me. I love you."

"Love you too. Bye."

I returned to the living room and found Dexter half-lying on the couch, feet up, and Luca sitting in the beat-up recliner. They were watching some videos on their phones. "Mandy's okay now," I announced to the room.

"Good. I hope she wasn't too worried," Luca commented.

"No, just normal Mandy-freaked-out," I explained. Luca smiled.

"So, Dexter is going to borrow my car and go pick up the pizza. When he gets back, I'll go. Sound okay?" Luca asked. It sounded great to me. It would take Dexter at least a half-hour to get to the pizza place and back. He might even take his time since he rarely had the opportunity to drive. However, I was a little worried about Luca's car.

"Uh...Dexter hardly ever drives. Aren't you worried about your car?" I asked.

"Oh, please, Violet. I drive brilliantly. Who does Mandy always give the keys to? Huh?" Dexter teased.

"Fine. You're right. Be careful," I said as Dexter grabbed the keys Luca offered and headed out the door. "Do you have money?" I called after him.

"Yeah, the pizza jar is pretty full," he explained, and he was out the door.

"Mandy keeps a money jar specifically for pizza. It's a staple food in this house," I explained to Luca.

He walked up behind me and put his arms around my waist, resting his head on my shoulder. "So, we've got some time alone..." he whispered in my ear. My heart began to beat so hard that it hurt. "Great idea I had for Dexter to get the pizza, huh?" he said smugly. I whipped my head around to look at him in mock surprise.

I smiled brightly at him then, "So, what did you have in mind to pass the time?" I asked, in the same playful tone he'd been using. He didn't answer me in words, but in action. He twirled me around to face him and gently kissed my forehead. Then, he began to nuzzle my hair and neck. I could hear his uneven breath hot on my ear, then my neck. My eyes closed on their own, and I sighed.

"Wait!" I cried suddenly. Luca froze.

"What's wrong? Did I do—sorry."

"No, I just remembered something I wanted to show you," I explained, grateful to have come to my senses with my bedroom only a few feet away. "My painting—the one I showed you—I'm almost done. Do you want to see it?" I asked expectantly. I had never painted with anyone else's approval in mind, but it was very important to me that he liked this painting.

"Violet, just for future reference, you *never* have to ask," he clarified with a smile.

"Okay. Let's go." I grabbed his hand and practically dragged him out the back door. Along the way, he was looking all around, exploring each little piece of the yard. As we were about to enter the studio, something caught his eye. Something I did *not* want him to notice.

"What *is* that?" He pointed to something sticking out from behind the studio. He began to walk toward it. I realized what he saw and ran in front of him to block it.

"It's nothing. Please don't go back there," I pleaded, but he was well on his way, overcome by curiosity. He turned the corner behind the shed and immediately let out a boom of laughter.

"Why is there a giant alien behind your studio?" he asked, still laughing.

"Uh...it's a long story..." I trailed off, hiding my face in my hands.

"You know I *have to* hear it, don't you?" I knew there was no way out of this situation, so I told him the story of how the alien came to be part of our backyard landscape.

"And so now, some guy from Mandy's group is supposed to come get it," I added.

"Okay, but please tell me, in case I missed it, *why* exactly did Mandy feel compelled to steal this?" he inquired. I knew this was going to get even more uncomfortable for me.

I sighed and continued. "Okay, Mandy and some of her *friends* don't like the exploitation of the alien image. They think it's disrespectful to make light of something that has been 'life-altering' and, in some cases, 'traumatic' to people." I had lived with this philosophy for a very long time, and could quote the beliefs of my mother and my mother's friends in my sleep. I couldn't look at Luca. I imagined a wide-eyed expression of disbelief, maybe even ridicule. My own face was scarlet.

"Look at me, Violet." I heard no humor in his voice, so I reluctantly turned my reddened face to his. His face was serious, determined. "Why are you so upset?"

"I...I've been fighting this for as long as I can remember, Luca. Mandy's beliefs– Mandy's *obsession*– has been the focal point of my life." I was ashamed now. Not because of my confession, but because I hadn't had enough faith in Luca to take this in stride. "Before you say something nice to make me feel better, or even worse, let me apologize. I know I should've known you wouldn't judge me or Mandy. So, I'm sorry," I said in a small voice. Luca didn't respond verbally. He just put his arms around me and held me close. It took me a moment, but I tightened my grasp on him and let myself relax.

Then Luca asked, "So, don't you have a painting to show me?" I knew that he was purposely changing the subject to let me know that he was shutting the door on the unpleasantness of a few moments ago. My relief and gratitude were immeasurable.

"Uh, yeah. Let's go." I took his hand and led him into the studio.

After I opened the door, I flipped on the lights to my little world, a world I was so willingly letting Luca be a part of. I was eager to show him the additions to my painting, his painting.

"So, I've made some changes to the painting. I thought about what you said and then made some additions here and there." The painting was on the easel covered in a sheet. I pulled the corner of the sheet down and revealed the new and improved painting.

Impatiently, I studied Luca's face, waiting for even the subtlest reaction. His face registered the changes immediately. His eyes grew slightly wider, and his mouth had the faint beginnings of a smile. Then he took a step back and continued to survey every square inch of the canvas. I couldn't wait any longer.

"So...?" I asked expectantly. He didn't answer right away, and I burned with anticipation.

"I don't know what to say," he responded. I wasn't sure how to take this comment. I tried to stop my mind from jumping to conclusion after conclusion.

"Do you...like the changes?" I pried.

"It's indescribable. I mean, of course I like what you've done. I just...I'm overwhelmed." His voice gave evidence to that. "It's so...powerful." He finally tore his eyes from the painting, only to burn them into me. The power of his stare made me turn away, now overwhelmed myself. He walked over to me and took my chin in his thumb and forefinger, forcing me to look up at him.

"Tell me," he said.

"It's just, I don't know if I will ever get used to the way you look at me, like you're looking...into me," I admitted, this time keeping my eyes locked onto his.

"You'd better get used to it," he said with no trace of sarcasm.

Now I was really angry with myself for making him have to explain himself...again! "It's just nothing I'm used to," I admitted again, trying to make him feel better.

"Violet, like I've told you, this is new for me too."

Truthfully, even though it made me squirm, the last thing I wanted was for him to *ever* stop looking at me like that. "I guess I just have to get used to it, that's all," I smiled.

"Thanks," he said, putting his hands on either side of my face.

"For what?" I couldn't imagine what he could possibly be thanking me for. I felt like I was the one who should be thanking him over and over again for being so kind and patient and understanding, and accepting me, a social pariah with an eight-foot alien statue in her backyard.

"For letting me into your life. For *letting* me look at you like that. For accepting *me*. I know this whole thing has been difficult for you, but you've been so open-minded and generous."

"You're right about this being hard for me...it *was* at first, but being with you has helped me to be more accepting of my powers and changed my perspective, making me think that maybe they aren't the *worst* thing that's ever happened to me," I explained. Without warning, he leaned in and swept his lips gently across mine. The quickest of kisses, like a whisper. My eyes closed and my breath caught.

"So, what made you make the changes?" Luca asked suddenly,

changing the subject and the mood. I tried to hide my disappointment. I had been enjoying the mood.

"Uh...um...well..." I began to say as I walked over to the painting, trying to focus. "I realized, after the thing with Stephanie, that maybe you were right about me seeing myself in a negative light, and suddenly the black didn't seem...*right* anymore," I shrugged.

"So, you thought I was right, huh?" He smiled smugly.

"Don't get too full of yourself. It's not *that* big a deal," I teased. It was actually a huge deal.

"I love it. You've definitely captured your…essence—is that a good *art* word—more accurately this time."

I knew he was right. In the first version of the painting, I had been a black figure, while Luca had been yellow, bright and sunny, and our colors had leaked out and fused together in the center. But now, my image was shimmering purple and Luca's was shimmering blue. I had tried to capture the color that I saw in my mind when I heard Luca's thoughts, then the color he had described to me when explaining what my thoughts *looked like* in his mind. Also, before, mine and Luca's images were just heads, but now they were two bodies, fused by hands pressed together at the palms and by a kiss. These two points of contact exploded into swirls of every conceivable color, filling the entire canvas, laid on thick so that there was texture and depth.

"It's not completely finished. I have some *little* touches I want to add," I said with a smile. It was a private joke because my plan was to embed tiny pictures that represented our powers within the folds of the color swirls.

"I don't think it can get more perfect, but if anyone can do it, you can," he said with a respect and reverence in his voice that made me smile and blush. We both jumped a little when we heard a car door slam.

"I guess Dexter's back," Luca said.

"And I guess your car made it back in one piece." I smiled. "So, does that mean you've got to go?" I asked. I couldn't hide the disappointment in my voice.

"I don't *have* to." Luca pressed as he moved closer to me. His voice was hypnotic, seductive. I almost forgot why he should go until I heard the reason.

"V?" Dexter called from the back door.

"In...in here!" I called back. "I...we'll be right out," I added, not wanting Dexter to ruin this moment.

"'Kay," he answered and then I heard the backdoor close again.

"So...should I...?" Luca asked, searching my eyes.

"No. You should go," I said reluctantly. "You have...stuff to do," I reminded him.

"The how and why can wait," he said, seduction saturating his tone again.

"But Dexter can't," I reminded him. "Or rather, he has been for a while. Besides, we have our big date tomorrow, right?"

"You're right," he conceded. "I guess I should go so you and Dex can get movie night under way," he said. "But next time, I get to stay."

"Of course," I agreed.

"Well, we should go in so I can get my keys." He said this, but he didn't move. Instead he bent down and kissed me. It was a kiss I had to force myself to end so that Dexter and I would actually have our movie night, or else I might not let Luca leave the studio.

I pushed him away, gently "...movie night, remember?"

"Not until you just reminded me," he said with a smile. At this we disengaged. I smoothed out my t-shirt and Luca ran his hand through his silky hair. Just watching him do that made me tremble. I looked away and decided we needed to get out of there quickly.

"So, should we go in then?" I asked.

"We'd better. If you don't escape now, I might lock us in here," he warned wickedly.

"I might let you," I replied honestly. We joined hands and left the studio, walking a little more quickly than necessary into the house.

"Where have you been?!" Dexter asked. Then he looked at the flushed faces of both of us and connected the dots. "Oh," was his response. He didn't sound angry, but he looked at us in a way that let me know he was wondering whether or not Luca was actually going to leave.

"I'll see you tomorrow, Violet," Luca said. "Call me tonight before you go to bed?" Dexter's eyes brightened a little.

"Of course," I answered. "Bye, er...I hope you find what you're looking for," I said awkwardly.

He looked at me curiously and then said, "I already have." He let go of my hand and proceeded to the door. "Bye, Dexter," he called out behind him, remembering to be polite.

"Later," Dexter said from the kitchen.

Dexter returned to the living room carrying two plates with several slices of pizza draping over the sides of each. "Mushroom?" he asked.

"Yeah, thanks," I said as I took one of the plates from him. I settled myself on the couch and put my feet up. Dexter and I ate quietly for a few minutes.

"So, how's the world of the supernatural?" he asked off-handedly.

"It is just fantastic," I replied sarcastically, my mouth full of pizza. As much as I disliked the topic, this was the normal comfort level Dexter and I needed to get back to.

"So, what did you mean when you told Luca, 'I hope you find what you're looking for?'" he asked. Dexter *never* beat around the bush.

I let out a long, irritated sigh. If I hadn't wanted to talk about it with Luca, I definitely didn't want to talk about it with Dexter. But, I knew I'd have to say something or his inquisition would be brutal.

I took another breath, this time to settle myself and decide what I should say. Dexter was being patient, but I also knew his nature and that his patience would not last long either. I had to tell him enough to satisfy him, but try not to leave any openings for further discussion.

"Well, Luca has...Luca *is* interested in finding out why or how we are this way," I began slowly.

"Naturally."

"And so he is doing some research tonight," I continued.

"What kind of research?"

It occurred to me that I had no idea what his *research* entailed. "I don't really know," I said, trying to sound casual and indifferent.

"You don't *know?*" he asked.

"Uh-oh." I thought.

"If he's researching your...*situation*, then he must have a starting place...a hypothesis, or at least a hunch, right?" It wasn't a question. It was a statement of fact. "So, what's he think?" he pressed.

My stomach lurched. I was *not* having this conversation. "I don't know!" I said, too forcefully. I knew this would draw even more questions.

"Why aren't you with him? Don't you *want* to know?" he asked, now looking confused.

I didn't answer. I just let out another deep sigh that sounded like I'd been holding my breath. I had been.

"How could you not want to know? Not at least be curious?" He was almost angry at this point. I realized that this question of *what* I was had been plaguing him as well. I almost laughed when I thought that maybe he and Luca should be the ones spending the evening together. But, my discomfort and agitation overshadowed any humor I may have briefly seen in the situation.

I shot Dexter a furious look, a warning not to push this issue any further if he wanted the night to proceed pleasantly. He finally caught on. "*Whatever*. I...forget it," he pouted. Maybe he just decided to give up for the time being, or maybe he had some inkling of what Luca's theory might be. Either way, he dropped the subject, but he wore a scowl for quite some time afterwards.

"Do you want some iced tea?" I asked when I got up a few minutes later. I had to leave the room for a minute to try to regain some kind of composure and remember why I was spending this *quality time* with Dexter.

"Sure. Thanks," he answered without looking at me.

I stayed in the kitchen longer than it should take to get a couple of drinks, trying to clear my head. Gradually I calmed down and was able to push the subject of the unpleasant conversation back into the recesses of my brain. I knew it wasn't gone for good and would rear its head again at some point. But for now, I was just glad to have it gone. Eventually I returned to the living room.

"Here you go," I said as I handed the glass to Dexter.

"Thanks," he replied, still not looking at me, but then changed the subject. "So, are you ready to watch the movie?"

"Yeah, let me get the remote." I crossed the room and handed Dexter the remote, knowing he was much more decisive than I was at choosing a movie. He didn't disappoint, choosing something terrible from one of our more obscure streaming channels.

I returned to my seat on the couch, and as the movie began, I hoped Dexter and I would be able to get past the tension that had blossomed between us and be able to enjoy the movie. I knew that this night was extremely important, perhaps even pivotal, if our friendship was going to survive. So, at first, I forced myself to make the first few sarcastic comments. I knew they sounded contrived, but I didn't care. Neither did Dexter. In fact, he seemed to appreciate my effort, and in no time, he had joined in, and we were both genuinely enjoying ourselves.

After the movie, we flipped through channels, talked about

some new songs we both liked, and just had a normal, easy conversation. I was glad the atmosphere had relaxed, but it was late, and it had been a long day. I was ready for bed. I could see by Dexter's body language and nearly closed eyes that he was too. "I am exhausted. I'll see you in the morning. Goodnight." I stood up and stretched.

"Goodnight," he answered, eyes still closed. "I'll lock up."

"You sure? You look asleep already."

"No, I'm good. See you in the morning."

I was almost in the bathroom when I turned and said, "Dex, I had a great time tonight." I meant it too. I missed Luca, but it had been nice to spend time with Dexter.

"Me too." He opened his eyes and flashed me a genuine smile. "Goodnight, Violet."

I got ready for bed and settled myself under the covers, snuggling into my soft pillow. Just as my eyes closed, a disembodied voice spoke to me in the darkness. *Are you awake?* The familiar silvery blue light filled my mind.

Barely, I answered. My stomach did its usual flips and turns at the sound of his voice.

Did you have fun tonight?

Yeah, actually it was kind of nice.

Good.

You?

I wouldn't call it fun, but...interesting. He knew better than to elaborate. *Well, I just wanted to say goodnight. Actually, I want to say more, but it's late. Sleep well, Violet.*

I smiled at his usual candidness. *You too. Goodnight.*

Goodnight.

I was content to fall asleep with Luca filling my thoughts, playing back the scene in my studio from earlier in the evening. Just the memory was enough to send the heat pulsing through me again. I thought about how far things had gone and wondered what would happen the next time we were alone together. The thought frightened me a little. I wasn't sure if I had the power or the desire to resist him. It was this question that stayed with me as I drifted into sleep.

17

Luca sent me a thought before my eyes even opened. I wondered if he was actually able to direct thoughts while I was sleeping.

Good morning, he said.

Hi. Even my thoughts sounded groggy.

Did I wake you? Actually, can I wake you this way? he asked.

You know, I was just wondering the same exact thing. This time I was semi-awake, but we'll have to try it out some time. Now I was definitely awake.

So, are you ready for tonight? he asked playfully.

Well, I'm ready for the date, but I'm not ready to have to wait to see you until this afternoon. I couldn't believe how bold I was becoming.

It's ten now, and I was hoping to leave by three, so you don't have that long too wait.

It's ten!!?? I said this both out loud and in my thoughts. *I really need to get up and see my mother...if she's up...Okay, I'll see you at three. Bye.*

Bye. I could hear the laughter in his thoughts. His shimmering blue light shook and contorted. I was getting used to the accompanying movement of the light with his moods and words.

Wait! I searched my mind for the connection, trying to retrieve it so I could ask him something that had occurred to me.

I'm here.

What should I wear? I was not vain, I just didn't want to look ridiculous!

Hmmm? Jeans are good, maybe something nicer than a t-shirt...

Well, that's a BIG *help!* I said sarcastically.

Violet, you will look perfect no matter what you wear. We're not doing anything too elaborate, *so jeans are fine, don't wear a t-shirt, but bring one. I hope that helps you out a little more.*

I suppose. See you at three.

Bye.

I closed my eyes again, mulling over Luca's vague instructions. "'*Bring a t-shirt'? What does that mean?*" I tried to think of what we could possibly be doing that might entail a costume change. I groaned and rolled out of bed.

After a visit to the bathroom to wake up, I glided into the kitchen, hoping to catch Mandy before she was off to bed. I was in luck; she was up. I could hear the pages of the newspaper being crumpled on the edges. I paused briefly to listen to the crispness of this sound—which should have been inaudible—in my ears. My powers were still so new, and there were still many, many times a day where I would stop and marvel at some of my abilities. Or occasionally something would catch me off guard, like the sound of the newspaper's pages being handled, and I would feel momentarily overwhelmed, like I felt at this moment. I shook off my brief uneasiness and went to join Mandy at the table.

"How was work?" I asked.

Mandy moved the paper from in front of her face. I could see how tired she was despite her warm smile, and I had one of those moments where I appreciated Mandy's dedication not only to her patients, but also to providing for Dexter and me.

I had never really been filled in on the particulars of my parents' divorce settlement and how much child support my father paid. In the early years, my father wasn't making much money anyway, but what I did know is that never, in the thirteen years since they had split, did I ever feel the financial struggle that I knew Mandy dealt with. Of course, growing up, I knew I couldn't have everything

I wanted, and then Dexter came along. I'm not sure if Mandy received anything for him. But Dexter and I were never without the necessities, and never felt deprived of any material possession.

"Good morning, Sweetheart," Mandy said.

"You look really tired, Mandy, why don't you just go to bed?"

"I wanted to see you, and besides, I'm a little wound up; we had a rough night in the ward."

"Sorry."

"So, you have a date tonight, huh?" Mandy changed the subject. She didn't like talking about work. It wasn't that she didn't like her job, but I had always suspected that it also made Mandy a little sad to talk about her patients. I couldn't think about all that though, I was too busy wondering how Mandy knew about my date. I hadn't even told Dexter about it.

"Ummm...how did...how did you know?" I stammered.

"Why, is it a secret?" Mandy teased. "I thought you and Luca were out in the open about your relationship?" I couldn't tell if this was a statement or a question, but decided to answer it.

"We are. I just...Luca is apparently surprising me," I said. "And I didn't say anything about our date to anyone...not that I wasn't going to...I mean it isn't a secret or anything." I tried to recover. "I was just wondering how you knew, that's all," I explained. I felt a little guilty. I didn't want Mandy to think I was purposely trying to exclude her from my life.

Mandy put the newspaper back up. "Luca told me all about it. You are going to have so much fun!" she said, a little smugly. I pushed down the top of the paper, careful to control the amount of force I used. I was grateful that I had the foresight to remember my strength before exploding.

"What? When?" The thought of my mother having some private conversation with Luca both frightened and annoyed me. *"What else could they be talking about?"* I cringed at the thought.

What if Mandy spouted about her beliefs? No, she wouldn't.

"Don't worry, Violet!" Mandy said, almost reading my mind. "He asked me the other night at dinner if I 'approved' of the date he had planned," she explained. "He is sweet. And so thoughtful. He's gone through a lot of trouble to plan something special that suits you perfectly." She was smiling and gushing. I couldn't take it anymore.

"What could it be that he needed to ask Mandy's approval about?" I was completely stumped and extremely excited. No one had ever gone through any kind of trouble to plan something so special just for me. I couldn't begin to guess what it could be.

"A hint?" I asked hopefully.

"Not on your life!" Mandy scoffed.

"Okay, well if I try some stuff on, will you tell me if it'll be okay?" I pleaded. I knew Mandy wouldn't be able to resist a mother-daughter moment like that.

"I guess that'll be all right...doesn't seem like cheating," she agreed. "But, I've got to get to bed very soon, so let the fashion show begin," she instructed.

I went to my room, still groggy with sleep and grabbed a few of my favorite items out of my drawers and closets. I donned a pair of baggy, heavily faded jeans, only slightly spattered with paint and threw on a plain, navy blue top that hung limply from me. I walked out to Mandy who was waiting patiently.

"Well?" I asked.

"NO!" Mandy said with a sour look on her face. "It makes you look frumpy. You are beautiful, don't be afraid to show off a little!" she scolded. Then her eyes wandered to the paint splotches near my right knee. "And Violet, try clothes *without paint!*" I rolled my eyes, even let out an irritated growling sound, spun around, and marched back into my room.

Each time I returned to the kitchen, I got a similar reaction from Mandy, "...too frumpy...too baggy...too sloppy!" With my last outfit,

Mandy exclaimed, "Violet, Honey, you are going on a *date!* You're not going to hang out in the living room with Dex. I know you hate dressing up, and I know you don't like feeling uncomfortable, but you should put *some* effort in." I could tell that Mandy's emotions were hovering somewhere between frustration and sympathy over my obvious lack of experience with this situation. She took a deep breath and said, "V, remember when we went to dinner in the city for Grandma's birthday, you looked beautiful without even trying. Think along those lines." I was grateful for the hint.

I nodded to Mandy, but said nothing as I turned back and went to my room. Once in there, I searched through my closet until I found a pair of faded blue jeans, with some worn spots around the knees. Though jeans like these were in high demand, and sold for a small fortune, my artfully distressed jeans were authentic, worn out by over-wear and yard work. They fit snugly, perfectly, showing off the curves that I often tried to hide.

I paired the jeans with my favorite shirt: a fitted black, deep scoop-neck that dipped down in the back, revealing my shoulders and sat slightly cropped, just above my waist. The shirt fit snugly, but wasn't tight. It complimented my figure and the jeans. I avoided the mirror and clomped out of my room, looking and feeling impatient and uncomfortable. Mandy was back behind the newspaper.

I cleared my throat loudly to get her attention, as if she hadn't heard the thunderous steps I had taken to get to the kitchen. "So, how do I look now?" I asked impatiently, arms folded tightly in front of me, my foot tapping and the air moving quickly and forcefully in and out of my nose.

Mandy's face lit up. "That's it! That's the perfect outfit. You look absolutely beautiful." Mandy gushed while I turned red and rolled my eyes. Secretly though, I knew she was right. The outfit had felt right the second I put it on.

"Thanks," I mumbled.

"Luca is going to just... well, let's just say, I hope you listened *very carefully* when we talked the other day." I gave another eye roll, and my cheeks turned even redder as I remembered the kiss in my studio again. I was momentarily lost in that thought when I realized Mandy was still talking.

"Violet? Are you listening to me?"

"Uh...yeah, yes. What?" I said, a little embarrassed having been caught daydreaming.

"I *said,* Luca is a very nice guy, who is lucky to have you," she beamed. Pride and motherly love dripped from her every word. "It's too bad your dad isn't here. He'd be overwhelmed by you, and he would like Luca. But..."

I hated when she did this. Every now and then Mandy would bring up my father. She had never spoken ill of him while I was younger, but as the years went on, and he distanced himself further and further from me, Mandy became less restrained with her anger. She couldn't understand how he could move on with his life and leave such an important part of it behind. I had tried to explain to her so many times that I was okay with it, and that we had just grown apart, but it still bothered Mandy that, "he doesn't want to know you...see you every day...we had our problems, but taking it out on you is just unforgivable." I had told her over and over to let it go, and she had. He rarely came up anymore.

"Okay, Mandy! Enough. Let's not bring the Jorge baggage out on top of everything else."

"What *else* is there?" she asked.

"OOPS!" I reminded myself that Mandy didn't know anything else was going on.

"I just meant...you know, my *budding romance...*er...that's all." I stumbled over my words as Mandy eyed me suspiciously. After a long moment, Mandy seemed to shrug it off.

"I'm off to bed. I'm not going in till seven tonight, so I can get a few good hours in," she said, standing and stretching, already in her pajamas.

"Well, goodnight then," I said.

"Goodnight," Mandy yawned and left the kitchen.

"Hey, where's Dex?" I asked before Mandy had reached her bedroom. I realized I didn't hear him anywhere.

"Oh, he went to the library about an hour ago," she called back to me sleepily.

I thought this was kind of strange, not that he went to the library—he loved the library—but having gotten up that early on a Saturday morning...that was odd. But, I didn't think any more about it and went to my room to throw on some painting clothes so I could spend a little time on my Luca painting. I still could not think of a name for it. I knew the name was going to have to be perfect, and really capture the essence of the painting, and since it wasn't complete yet, I decided to wait until it was finished to name it.

I spent a few hours in the studio, losing track of time, as usual. When I noticed the sun was no longer coming in the windows, I looked at my phone, and panicked. *"I'm LATE!"* I dropped everything and ran into the house. I hurled myself through the back door, leaving the screen door flapping behind me. I sprinted through the house, past Dexter, who was now on the couch flipping through the channels.

"Whoa, what's up?" he asked, though he didn't really sound that interested.

"Can't talk, REALLY late!" I said in a blur as I slammed the bathroom door. I was undressed and in the shower before the door latch clicked. I quickly towel-dried my hair, deciding a ponytail was my best bet at this point. I slipped on my robe, towel on head and ran for my room. I looked at my phone again. *"2:45. I can do this,"* I reassured myself.

I first chose some of my nicest undergarments, convincing myself that it was all part of the feeling good about myself that

Mandy had encouraged. I reminded myself that Luca and I really needed to take our physical relationship more slowly. I grabbed the clothes that were laid out on my bed and slipped them on quickly, twisting and adjusting to get everything in just the right place. Then there was the shoe dilemma. Mandy and I hadn't really discussed shoes, and I certainly couldn't wake my mother for that. Right? No, definitely not.

I opened my closet and peered at my shoe rack, mentally narrowing it down to three pairs, all black: low-top Allstars, chunky ankle boots with a zipper up the inside, or shiny, dressy shoes with multiple straps, pointy toes, and impossible heels. I decided the sneakers would make Mandy sad, and I couldn't even remember why I even owned the strappy black ones, so I chose the boots. They'd compliment the jeans, they were comfortable, and they didn't make me feel like a different person.

Now it was back into the bathroom to fix my hair, and even dab on a little makeup. Just enough to make me look like I wasn't wearing any. No matter how little I put on, I still felt like I was wearing too much, remembering the recent make-up fiasco. So I took tissues and cotton balls to blot away the majority of it. I was about to look in the mirror when my scalp began to tingle. *"He's almost here!"*

I wasn't sure why I was suddenly so nervous; Luca did not intimidate me, and I felt more at ease with him than anyone I'd ever met. I decided it was both the idea of a surprise, which I normally did not like, but which made me more excited than usual, and maybe the pressure of what might happen, physically, between us. Again, the previous evening's encounter came flooding back into my mind, sending my pulse soaring. I knew Luca would never pressure me into anything that I wasn't ready for. I was actually more concerned about my own desires and how far *I* would allow things to go.

When I was with Luca, all fear left me. But, a piece of me, a piece that was trying very hard to be heard, knew that I wasn't ready for sex. It was a frightening thought—being that vulnerable at the hands of someone else, regardless of how perfect that person was.

I put it out of my mind and dashed into my room again to accessorize. I chose simple silver hoop earrings my grandma had given me that would be seen nicely with my hair up and my favorite necklace, a thin silver strand that held a small crystal wrapped in silver. I rubbed a little perfume on my inner wrists and behind my ears. Well, I hoped it was a little. I could hardly smell it myself as I had always had a very weak and limited sense of smell. I took a strong whiff of my arm, and was able to capture just a wisp of the sweet smell.

Then my heart jumped when I heard Luca's tires roll smoothly into my driveway and come to a stop. I heard the car door open and close and his even footsteps as they landed on each of the stepping-stones leading to the front porch. I heard the knocker bang three times. *"Please let Dexter be nice!"* I said to myself. I could hear Dexter walking slowly—too slowly—to the door.

He opened it and greeted Luca with a colorless, "What's up?" and then nothing. I imagined Luca had nodded a greeting because I heard two sets of steps move into the living room where one person, Dexter, plopped onto the couch. I guessed Luca was just standing there, waiting, which made me move more quickly. I grabbed my bag, my phone, and remembering what Luca had said, a t-shirt. I took a deep breath and headed into the living room.

Luca obviously knew I was coming because he turned to see me before I had even made it into his line of sight. And when I did, his eyes grew wider than ever. He blinked a few times and swallowed hard. My reaction to his reaction was my usual scarlet cheeks. I wanted to laugh, thinking I was glad I'd removed the blush I'd put on earlier. Then Luca spoke. "Wow! I don't know what to say. You look..."

"Incredible!" Dexter finished Luca's sentence for him. Luca's reaction had made Dexter look my way.

"Uh...yeah, I was going to say 'beautiful,' but 'incredible' definitely works," Luca agreed, never taking his eyes off of me, although all of a sudden his voice had an edge to it that I couldn't quite place.

"You look really nice too," I complimented Luca. In fact, he looked more than nice. He looked a little incredible himself. His hair was as careless as ever, thick black curls tumbling over his forehead, skimming his long eyelashes, and his eyes had their familiar, captivating depth, but he looked different out of his shorts and t-shirt.

Tonight he wore jeans, faded and worn, like mine. They fit as if they were made just for his body. He had on a close-fitting, short-sleeved, blue button-up that accentuated his solid frame. Though he wore it untucked, and I could see a white t-shirt sticking out from underneath, I noticed how much older he looked and even more handsome than I imagined he could. I wondered if I looked older in his eyes as well.

"Thanks," he replied to my compliment.

I steadied myself with a quick breath and took Luca's hand. I was still amazed by how easy it was to just reach out and take his hand. Touching him was so easy. Too easy, I reminded myself. This made my fears rush back. I told myself that just because we looked older didn't mean we were older or ready to take the next life-changing step in our still-new relationship. Simultaneously, the feel of Luca's hand wrapped around mine also made me feel more calm.

"Ready?" I asked him.

"Where are you two beautiful people going?" Dexter asked. I knew he was using sarcasm to hide sadness.

"I don't know," I answered. "Apparently it's a surprise that only Luca and *Mandy* know about." I glared at Luca, feigning anger.

Ignoring Dexter, Luca said, "I had to tell her. It was the right thing to do. Are you mad?"

"A little, but I'll get over it. At least she was able to help me choose my outfit," I said, holding my free arm out to my side like a model.

"Remind me to thank her later," he said with a sly smile, and I could have sworn he shifted his eyes to Dexter and glared almost imperceptibly, but I caught it.

"What was that?" I wondered.

"A surprise huh? How *romantic,"* Dexter said with the same veiled sarcasm as his previous comment.

"Let's go already!" I said.

"Bye," Dexter said flatly.

"See ya," Luca replied icily, turning away. This time I was sure I wasn't imagining things. I couldn't help but think that Luca was angry about something. He definitely didn't sound like his usual cool, collected self.

"Bye, Dex, see you later," I said.

18

Luca and I left the house and were driving when I finally asked, "So what was *that* back there with Dexter?" I tried to make my voice sound confused, not confrontational, but Luca's attitude toward Dexter had bothered me.

Luca didn't look at me, but shifted around in his seat, glancing into his mirrors, trying to look busy. He knew I wouldn't let it go without a response though. That's when I knew I definitely hadn't imagined anything. "What was what?" he asked, failing at being nonchalant.

"Well, you're usually really nice to Dex—even when he's a jerk—and I'm not saying he doesn't totally deserve it, and maybe I just imagined it, but you sounded...I don't know..." I was looking for the right words "*Like a jerk!*" is what I wanted to say, but didn't. "You sounded...not as *friendly* as usual."

Luca sighed, only adding further confirmation to what I thought.

"What's wrong?" I asked.

"It's just...ugh." He didn't seem to want to say whatever he was thinking.

I touched his free hand to let him know that he could tell me anything. "It's okay, you can tell me," I assured him. "Whatever it is."

"I'm embarrassed to say it, but his *ogling* you pissed me off, made me...I don't know...*jealous*!" he said, a touch of the anger I'd heard in the house returning to his voice. With that I did something I probably shouldn't have done, but it just came out. I laughed, but quickly covered my mouth.

"You're laughing! I don't think it's funny, Violet."

I quickly sobered. "Sorry. I'm not laughing at you." He cut his eyes at me. He obviously didn't believe me. "Really, I'm not, I swear. It's just that the whole idea of it makes me laugh."

"Why? What do you mean?" he sounded confused.

"Well, first of all, the idea of anyone being jealous over *me*—it's funny—" I explained. Luca began to protest but I cut him off quickly. "And the fact that it's Dexter...I mean...really?" I had to stifle a new round of chuckles that were threatening.

"First of all, you are seriously hot, and I am sure Dexter and I are not the only ones who think that." I rolled my eyes and flushed pink. He wasn't finished.

"And as far as Dexter is concerned, he's a guy. You may think of him as a *brother*, and I know you've been friends since you were little, which sometimes freaks me out too, by the way—it's like you can finish each other's sentences—it's unsettling if you're *the new guy*..." he was rambling and though his words sounded ridiculous to me, it was kind of cute, endearing even. Luca jealous of Dexter. It was just weird. "Anyway, he's a guy that obviously worships you, and I don't need to be able to read his mind to know what he was thinking when he saw you back there. If it was anything even close to what I was thinking—" he trailed off. We sat in silence for a minute.

"Uh...wow," was all I could get out at first.

"Yeah," he sighed.

This was completely new to me. Even in the short time Luca and I had been together, I had gotten used to *him* being there for *me,* comforting me, not the other way around. I was in the hot seat now, and I had to find comforting words. After all, a relationship is about two people, and I was more than willing to do my share.

"Luca, you can't change how Dex feels about me, and believe me, I would if I could. And yeah, Dexter and I know each other so well, it's scary, but he's not you. He'll never be you." I reached for his free hand again. "Remember that every second you and I spend together *hurts* him. I know he can be an ass, but he *is* trying, in his own strange way, he's trying. So can you please try too, or try again?"

He didn't say anything for a minute, but when he did, his tone had eased. "Yes. And you're right. I'm sorry. I was being unfair," he admitted sheepishly. "If I were Dexter, I don't know if I could handle seeing you with someone else." He brought my hand up to his mouth and kissed it. "It won't happen again."

I took his hand in my two and said, "Don't worry about it, you're only human." I smiled as he met my eyes.

The tension gone, I decided it was time for a change of subject to get our first real date back on track. I was dying to know where he was taking me. "So, where are we going?"

"Not yet," he answered. I squirmed and set my mouth in a line. I crossed my arms like a petulant child having a silent tantrum.

"I promise, you'll know soon enough. Just be patient." He put on a fake fatherly voice and spoke to me like I *was* a child.

"Fine, I'll try," I said.

"Good," he replied, sounding a little triumphant

I could see the direction we were headed in, and it confirmed what I had suspected all along, that we were going into New York City. I could hardly contain my excitement. I hadn't been there in months, and that had been for my grandma's birthday. I loved New York. The restaurants, the culture, but most of all, I loved the fact that no one was a freak in New York. It was a place where even Violet Arena could fit in.

"You know, when I was little, Mandy and my grandmother used to take me into the city all the time. We would go to The Met, eat lunch, and sometimes even go to a play. It was so great," I told Luca, letting him know that I had figured out a small part of his plan.

"So, you think you know what I have planned for you, huh?" he asked teasingly.

"Well, obviously we are going to the city, but what are we doing there?"

"Not yet! Man, you are impatient! You really don't like surprises, do you?" Luca said, his tone light and teasing.

"No. Sorry. But will I find out soon?"

"Yes."

We drove on, listening to music and chatting, careful to keep the topics light. It was still bright out as we neared the city and the skyline came into view.

"I'm glad there isn't a lot of traffic, so we can get to the surprise faster," I said.

"Yeah, I was going to get train tickets, but since we are going to get back so late, I figured a car would be our best bet."

"Late, huh?"

Instead of acknowledging my question, Luca said, "I hope you like Italian food."

"I love it!" I answered.

"Good. One of my dad's cousins from Italy opened a restaurant, and I was hoping we could go there for dinner," he explained.

"That sounds really great," I smiled.

"But first, we have somewhere else to go." Luca said with a sneaky grin. Before I knew it, the Guggenheim was in our view. I loved the Guggenheim! It housed the best collection of modern art in the world, and I'd only been there a few times. Luca drove until he found a parking garage. We parked, got out, and walked in the warm late afternoon sun. We crossed several streets until we were standing in the shadow of the architectural behemoth.

"It's an amazing building, isn't it?" I asked him.

"Yeah, but inside is something I think you are going to love even more," he explained. I was about to burst with anticipation until I saw the banner: "PICASSO: THE SCULPTOR, MAR 13-AUGUST 7." I couldn't say anything, so I just pulled him toward me and kissed him.

"Let's go!" he said, breaking free and yanking me eagerly to the door, too excited to merely walk like the mature young adults we resembled. Once inside, Luca, always considerate, bought us tickets and paid for an audio tour. We walked through the entire museum, spiraling up from the narrow bottom to the wide top, taking in all of the precious works of art. I was in my version of Heaven. Luca said he liked how artists could make art out of anything and was envious of how inspired they were.

"It's intimidating the way some people, like you, can express yourselves," he admitted.

"Oh, so I intimidate you, huh?" I asked playfully as I curled into Luca's arms in front of a sculpture appropriately entitled, *The Kiss.* Luca's face turned serious before he answered,

"Every minute that I'm with you." I was speechless. He had disarmed me while I had been attempting humor.

"Let's go see Picasso!" I finally said, mock-punching his arm.

"Lead the way."

I led him to the special exhibit where I lost myself in the beauty and raw emotion of each sculpture. Picasso was best known for his paintings, but his sculpture was equally powerful and intriguing. I could have stayed there forever, but I knew we had to get going. As we left, I squeezed Luca's hand and said, "Thank you."

"My pleasure," he smiled. "Dinner?"

"Absolutely."

We arrived at the restaurant a little after seven, and there was a line out the door. "We'll never get in," I said, a bit disappointed.

"I know the owners, remember?" He took my hand and led me

past the dozen or so people lined up outside. When we reached the door, Luca surprised me by speaking Italian to the maître d who promptly put his hand on Luca's shoulder and motioned for him to follow. Luca pulled me along with him as the waiting patrons glared and whispered.

You speak Italian? I asked silently, my eyes open wide.

Just a little. My dad's family was from Italy, so he's always spoken a little Italian to me.

Impressive, I commented. Another layer of Luca revealed to me. So far, each layer intrigued me more than the last. I wondered what other surprises he had in store.

We sat at a cozy little table in the back corner of the dimly lit restaurant. Soft guitar music strummed in the background, and light flickered off the plastered walls. I couldn't stop looking as the candle on the table illuminated the contours of Luca's face. "This place is beautiful," I said. He smiled.

"So, do you speak Spanish?" he asked after we ordered drinks and an appetizer.

"A little. My dad is an only child and both of his parents passed away before I was born, so I haven't actually been around Spanish-speakers much, but Mandy speaks some and has always tried to keep me practicing. I've taken three years in school, so I'm okay, not fluent though." *"You have to actually talk to people,"* I wanted to add, but thought better of it.

"I do give all of my paintings Spanish names, though."

"That's really cool."

"What about your poetry?" I asked.

"What about it?" He looked up, and for once, I saw a little tiny crack in his cool, collected demeanor. It only made him more attractive.

"Does any of your Italian ever make an appearance?" I continued.

"No, not really." His response and lack of elaboration let me know that his writing might be his weakness.

"So...when do I get to read some more?" I asked. I had only read the one poem he sent me weeks earlier that made my knees weak. I had committed it to memory.

"Whenever you'd like," he replied, seeming to regain his usual confidence.

"How 'bout now." I wasn't sure why I pressed him, but something in me wanted to hear one of his poems. He instantly looked uncomfortable again.

"Sorry. I didn't mean to put you on the spot. It's ridiculous of me to think that you just have poems memorized and want to spout them ou—"

She is a beautiful contradiction;
Dark and bright,
Shadow and light.

She is unrivaled talent
making the world come alive
swirling colors into reality.

She is unfathomable beauty,
within and without,
She humbles me.

The words, spoken silently, directly into my brain, my heart, my soul, left me speechless.

"That was...it was..." I couldn't continue. Tears welled up and caught in my throat.

Just then the waiter came over with our appetizer. I sat unmoving for a minute, trying to pull the tears back in. The waiter was gone, but I still couldn't speak

"I just wrote that one last night," he said quietly. "Well, that version of it anyway. It's been written and rewritten a dozen times since..." he trailed off and for the first time ever, Luca was the one blushing. It was faint, and maybe no one else would have noticed, but I did.

I found my voice. "It's beautiful."

"Because it's about you." Another one of his catch-Violet-off guard comments that worked like a charm.

I fought the tears again, this time by gulping large sips of water, hoping the cool liquid would steady me. It did, a bit. I saw now why my painting had affected Luca the way it did. Poetry, just like a painting, could be light and fluffy or deep and drenched in emotion.

I decided that if we didn't start eating, we might never get to it, so I stuck my fork into a piece of tomato and a slab of mozzarella dripping in balsamic vinegar, and moved them to my plate. I cut them and took a small bite.

When the rest of our food arrived, we ate and talked some more. Two hours slipped by seamlessly, never the awkward pauses or uncomfortable silences that I thought were supposed to be a part of new romances and first dates—even if this was only a first date in the formal sense. Luca and I had been in sync from the day we connected, and in some ways, as we found out in conversation after conversation, we had been in sync most of our lives.

"So, Picasso?" Luca asked.

"What about him?"

"You've never really told me why he's your favorite."

"Well, I guess it's his creativity and rebelliousness," I explained. "I mean, he started out as this incredibly talented, but *traditional* artist, and then he moved to Paris and *found himself*, made his own rules, redefined what art could be. And he was so passionate. He seemed to always paint his emotions. He even expressed his political views in his work. I mean, I don't love the way he treated women, so he definitely wasn't perfect..." I rambled on, talking in between bites of food. When I looked at Luca, he was staring at me, mouth opened slightly. My cheeks flushed.

"What?"

"I guess it was more of an answer than I expected."

"Oh, sorry," I said shyly.

"No, no, don't be sorry. I mean, I am seriously impressed. Beautiful and brilliant."

"Alright, enough. Stop complimenting me already!" I teased. I loved it, but it was not something I thought I would ever get used to.

"You'd better get used to it, Violet. I told you before, I am going to compliment you and stare at you, and say sappy, mushy things to you whether you like it or not," he teased back, but I knew he meant it.

Sufficiently stuffed and blissfully content, I reached over and put my hands on top of Luca's while we waited for the check. "This has been the best date I have ever been on," I told him,
then added jokingly, "Well, it's actually the ONLY date I've ever been on, but it has been perfect."

"Well, it's not over yet," he said, then looked at his watch. "It's only nine-thirty. You aren't going to turn into a pumpkin or anything, are you?" he laughed. I smiled, but in my mind I could not imagine what else Luca could possibly have planned. Picasso, a romantic dinner, what else was there?

"I hope you don't mind some *after dinner music,*" he said.

"Um...no, not at all," I said. "What kind of music?" I asked.

"You'll see," he replied.

Luca paid the bill and we left the restaurant. "Do you mind if we take a cab from here? We've got a seriously good spot, and I don't think we'll get that lucky again?" he asked.

"No, a cab is fine," I said, and Luca hailed one just a few feet from the restaurant.

We got into the cab, and he gave the driver an address that meant nothing to me. We drove for twenty minutes until we pulled up in front of an unappealing squat building. The facade was all black with barred windows that were also blacked out. A neon sign blinked the word "grind." I gulped and stared wide-eyed at this seedy hole in the wall. Luca read my apprehension and sent a thought, *Trust me,* and squeezed my hand.

He paid the driver and led me out of the car. I allowed myself to be pulled along, trusting that Luca knew what he was doing. After all, since the night had been perfect so far, I couldn't imagine he'd put me in danger or take me somewhere I wouldn't like.

There were several small groups of teenagers milling around outside. I didn't like being around large groups of people, but this crowd looked more like me than the majority of kids at my school. They were, for the most part, dressed in jeans and dark colors, a few had piercings and tattoos. I was grateful for Luca's t-shirt advice. I changed effortlessly in the cab, having learned the ancient female art of changing into a second shirt while magically removing the first shirt. Since I now didn't feel overdressed, and Luca held my hand tightly, I was more at ease than was usual for me.

There was music pulsating from inside. I put all the obvious clues together and determined that we were probably going to see a band, but what band? Luca pulled me inside where a security guard scanned his phone, and we were each stamped with an invisible mark on our hands. Once inside, I noticed right away that the music actually hurt my ears. It was so loud, and my hearing was so acute, that the music seemed to be ricocheting around inside my head. I worked hard to focus around the sound, pushing it to the back of my mind. Thankfully, it seemed to work.

Is the music bothering you? I asked Luca, seeing his eyes squinting like he was in some discomfort. Telepathy came in very handy when, even with supersonic hearing, it was impossible to hear someone even a few inches away.

Yeah. It hurts!

Think around it. Just try to tune it out, I instructed. I waited a moment while he worked out his dilemma, the mental strain showing on his face

That's better. How did you figure that out?

I've noticed lately how I can focus on many different things, pushing some to the back of my mind and pulling some forward. It's very convenient, I explained confidently. *So who are we here to see...hear?*

Do you remember the day we were driving to Lake Morgan? Luca continued silently.

Of course. I smiled at him.

Well, you mentioned that you liked 'some obscure band' called Max, and I read that they were playing here, and...

My eyes grew wide. *Max! Max is playing* here? *Tonight? Now?*

Luca nodded, and I threw my arms around him. Shortly after, the music began. Max took the stage and played a two-hour set. I had thought I was the only person who knew their music and loved it. But here I was in a room full of people who were jumping up and down, and singing along to *my* favorite band. At first I was apprehensive, so used to being reserved and quiet, but as the music picked up and the crowd roared, I was swept up. I lost my inhibitions and joined them, jumping, singing...letting go. Luca was right beside me the whole time. Every time I looked at him he seemed to be watching me, just like he had in the museum.

When the band left the stage, Luca and I left the club hand in hand and hopped into a passing cab, tired and exhilarated. I leaned my head on Luca's shoulder, my eyes closed, a peaceful smile on my face. I put my hand on my bag and felt the shape of my phone. Panic took hold of me. I grabbed the phone and looked at the time. "OH GOD, MANDY IS GOING TO FREAK OUT! IT'S AFTER ONE!"

"Don't worry Violet, Mandy knows what time we'll be home, and I texted her from the club," he assured me as he put my head back to his shoulder and stroked my hair, so that I could resume my dizzying bliss. I reached my arm around the front of him and gave him a squeeze. When we got to his car, Luca had to wake me up. I shook and sleepily moved myself out of one car and into another, exhausted, but happier than ever.

Luca drove home while I dozed in and out. When we arrived at my house, he opened my door, unhooked my seatbelt and he actually *carried* me to the door. "I'm fine," I slurred over and over, "Put me down, I can walk."

"I've got you, don't worry Lois," he joked. I smiled at our private Superman joke, but kept my eyes closed. Luca rang the doorbell and Dexter opened it a little too quickly.

"Is she...drunk?" I heard Dexter ask through my haze of exhaustion. Luca laughed enough for me to stir.

"No, just really tired," he clarified. "I'm just going to bring her to her room." Luca waited for Dexter to move out of the way. Dexter stood frozen for a moment, not letting Luca by. Obviously, Luca was tired too and not in the mood for Dexter's *great protector* act. "*Excuse* me," Luca said sharply. This pulled me from my sleepy state. Dexter was eyeing Luca, but finally stepped out of the way. "Thank you," Luca said curtly. He then carried me to my room and sat me down on the edge of my bed. He tried to disentangle my arms from his neck, but I refused to let go.

"Violet, it's really late. I should go," he whispered close to my ear. His warm breath was like a jolt of caffeine that awakened every nerve ending in my body. I forgot all about trying to convince myself to be good with Luca.

"No," I mumbled. "Stay a little while, please," I murmured into his ear. This was enough to convince him.

"Okay, but just for a few minutes," he said as he made himself more comfortable beside me. I nuzzled into his chest, and he put his arm around me. I couldn't take the closeness any longer. In the dark, quiet of my room, I leaned over and began to kiss him slowly, but with a depth and purpose that grew by the second.

He returned my advances, and I slid so that my back was propped against the wall. Luca moved with me. Our hands moved in synchronization with our lips, caressing, stroking. Luca smoothed my hair, then his hands continued until they ran down the length of my back. My skin burned from his touch, and my brain ceased to work properly.

My hands were around his waist when, with a complete absence of thought or logic, I slid them under his shirt, stroking his sides and sliding my hands up and down his back, from his shoulder blades to his waist. My hands touching his bare skin did something to Luca. His kisses became more forceful. His lips left mine and moved down the side of my jawline. He slowly kissed a line around my neck and along my collarbone, each kiss soft as a whisper, but capable of sending shock waves through my entire being.

Then his lips were back to mine. He slid his hands under *my* shirt now and grasped my waist gently. I understood why he had reacted the way he did when I touched the bare skin of his back. I was completely sure that I would combust right there on the spot. He moved his palms slowly around the small of my back and then one hand trailed up the contours of my spine. When his hand reached my bra strap, it froze, he froze. It was like an off switch had been flipped. And I knew why. We had reached a point where a decision had to be made, and I was grateful that Luca made it for us.

Luca gently forced me from him and pushed his forehead into mine. Our hands stayed exactly where they had stopped, his on my back, mine on his waist. We panted heavily. After a long moment, Luca moved his hands and removed mine from his waist, holding them in his lap. I stayed very still, trying to compose myself. I didn't know what to say. Apparently neither did Luca, or like me, he was still trying to calm himself, or both.

"Ummm," he managed to say, and swallowed, breath still heavy. My eyes were open and looking at Luca's flushed face in the dark room. I couldn't help but smile. His eyes remained closed.

"I know," I said in reply. I knew exactly what he meant. We were headed down a certain path, one neither of us was familiar with.

One neither of us was sure we were ready for, regardless of our feelings for one another.

Then Luca opened his eyes to find mine staring at him. He took my face in his hands. "I...I'm...sorry!" he whispered in the dark, looking lost for words.

"Why? Please don't be. I don't know what just happened there, my body kind of *took over.* Sorry," I said shyly.

"No apologies necessary...are you...*okay?"* he asked, now looking a little concerned.

"I've never been better actually...little *frustrated* at the moment..." I smiled. "Frustrated" was an understatement. I felt like a race car that had been driven at full speed into a brick wall, engine still revving. "but...good, very, very good," I assured him. He laughed quietly, obviously understanding my frustration.

"We should probably talk about that, huh? You know...*the talk?"* he clarified.

"Oh yeah, we definitely need to, but not right now...?" I told him. I didn't want to ruin the moment by analyzing it, and it was at least three in the morning.

"Okay, I should definitely go before *the talk* becomes obsolete." He laughed gently, but I knew he wasn't really joking. He was right.

"Will I see you tomorrow?" I asked, though it sounded more like pleading.

"Of course," he said. Then he brushed his lips against mine one last time and started for the door.

"Luca," I stopped him.

"Yeah?" he asked from the doorway, his figure illuminated by the light that framed the doorway.

"Thank you. This was, without a doubt, the best night of my entire life." I wanted him to know this before he left.

"I'm glad," was his simple response before he turned to leave.

I got up, put on my pajamas, and flopped back into bed. I drifted off to sleep feeling a little lonely without Luca's arms wrapped around me. I thought I dreamed of him telling me he loved me.

19

Later that day—much later—I awoke to the bustle of Mandy moving around the house. I looked at my new alarm clock. The large red numbers, 1:11, assaulted my vision. I still couldn't get used to it. I had pretended to despise my little pink princess clock with the chimes and syrupy sweet princess voice telling me when it was time to get up, but now I missed it. This new one felt all wrong in my room, even if it did have the uncanny ability to make me look at it on double digits, just like the princess one had, just like almost every other clock I had ever looked at. I shrugged and tried to channel Luca, anxious to talk to him after our amazing night. It wasn't difficult, I simply directed a thought to him, *Luca, are you there?*

Yeah...just got up a little while ago, he answered almost immediately.

Me too.

I meant to ask you about Dexter when you left last night. I hope he kept his mouth shut with Mandy, I thought to him. I knew Dexter would invent his own version of what went on behind my closed door.

I'm sure he did. He was cool to me when I left. He didn't really say anything, just kind of nodded a goodbye. I doubt his goal is to get you in trouble.

You're probably right. I think he was a little weirded-out by...you being in my room though. I hope he knows that nothing happened, I said wearily knowing full well that so much had happened.

Nothing, huh? he joked.

I know it wasn't 'nothing', I conceded. There was something else I wanted to say to him because even though I didn't regret one second of the episode in my room, I felt like maybe Luca might get the wrong idea about me. After all, I had rather quickly gone from being reclusive, unsocial, barely-speaking Violet, to being Violet who can't get enough of Luca. *Um, Luca?*

Yeah?

About last night. I...That's not me, I swear. I've never...and I was very...

His tone was comforting when he interrupted me, *I know that. I should have been better behaved and left you in your room.*

I wouldn't have let you, I joked, though I wasn't sure it was actually the truth. I could feel his laughter ripple through me like it was my own, his now-familiar luminescent blue light brightening.

So what do we do now? he asked. This was such a loaded question, and a difficult one to answer. When I was with Luca, I couldn't reason, and I didn't want to. It was only at a distance, a distance I despised, when I could think clearly through whether or not I was ready for sex. A physical relationship was new to me, but so was an emotional one, and sex was such a big step. And even though my body was definitely ready, and fighting me every time Luca and I were near one another, it had only been just over a month since our first kiss, since my first kiss *ever* (well, besides Dexter's despicable display). I surmised that waiting was probably the best thing to do.

I guess we wait till we're totally ready. Because I'm ready, but not ready, ya know?

Yeah, I do. But I know that when you're ready, I'll be here waiting. I honestly can't wait to be with you. His usual blatant honesty, while disarming, made me smile wide.

Does that mean that you've never...either? I couldn't even say, "sex."

Nope. I've barely dated, let alone... He didn't finish the thought. Even though I was pretty sure of what his answer was going to be, a sense of deep relief flowed through me when he confirmed it.

Good. Neither of us said anything for a couple of minutes.

What are you up to today? Luca finally asked, changing the subject.

Well, considering it's so late, probably nothing much except studying. I have my English final tomorrow. How about you?

I guess I should study too, but I'd rather fly or throw boulders or do anything that does not involve studying or being away from you, he said with laughter.

You can come over and study with Dex and me. I mean we have the same finals, essentially.

You sure?

Of course.

Okay, see you in about an hour?

Sure.

I loped into the kitchen, my fuzzy elephant slippers sliding across the carpet, my old polka-dotted robe hanging from my body, dragging the belt like a tail.

"Hey, Mandy," I yawned as I began gathering the items needed for a bowl of cereal.

"Hi, Honey. It's so late, even for you," she commented.

"Late night. Sorry," I said, sitting at the table pouring myself some cereal.

"It's okay. Luca texted me," Mandy told me, "Did you have fun?" I could tell she was dying for details. I stalled, not quite ready to divulge them.

"So, I assume by the lack of preparation that we are *not* doing Sunday dinner tonight?" I asked, though I knew they weren't. Mandy had told me that the day before. I just wanted to talk about anything else.

"No. Remember I told you I had plans?" Mandy reminded me.

"Oh yeah, what are you doing tonight...meeting?" I asked.

"Er...no, I have a date...with Gerry," she answered. Then she got up and began flitting around the kitchen, trying to look busy and distracted. I wasn't about to let her off the hook, but then I thought if Mandy could pry, so could I.

"You and Gerry again, huh?" I asked, eyeing my mother with a teasing grin.

"Yeah, I figure, why not?" Mandy stopped what she was doing and looked at me. "I mean, he's a nice guy and you like him, right?"

"Oh yeah, Mandy. Gerry's great. I always wondered why you guys hadn't hooked up a long time ago," I told her honestly. I felt bad for my mother. For most of my childhood, Mandy had been careful to keep any relationships she'd had, if she'd had any at all, away from me. Finally, when I was thirteen, my mother sat me down and explained that she might decide to go on a date one day and asked me how I felt about that. I had told her to go for it. Mandy had smiled and hugged me, thanking me for being so understanding. She went on a few dates after that, but to my knowledge, that was all. No boyfriends, no relationships. If they had existed, Mandy was a master of illusion.

When Gerry came along, and I actually *liked* him, I'd hoped they would get serious, but that never seemed to materialize. Now that I was with Luca, I couldn't understand how Mandy had denied herself for so long. Maybe she hadn't met anyone who made her feel the way Luca made me feel. This thought made me so sad for Mandy and even more full of guilt to think that she had gone nearly thirteen years without that kind of connection.

There was probably some underlying fear and self-consciousness about getting into a relationship again, maybe even some leftover feelings for my dad, but I knew that, for the most part, Mandy had sacrificed her own happiness for me. She had been determined to give me stability and consistency. And now, as

I studied my mother moving around the kitchen, trying to avoid talking about her relationship, I knew how Mandy must feel all the times when I shut her out. I suddenly felt compelled to divulge the details of my date.

"Mandy, the date was the most perfect night of my life!" I blurted out. Mandy stopped abruptly and moved back to the table. She slid into a chair across from me, eager to hear more. "He took me to a Picasso sculpture exhibit at the Guggenheim!" I couldn't have hidden my enthusiasm if I tried. "Then dinner at his cousin's Italian restaurant...*he speaks Italian*!"

"Italian...sexy!" Mandy commented. That made me blush, particularly because she was so right.

"Then we went to see my favorite band play at some club." I knew as I retold even a few of the previous night's events, it would be difficult to keep my face from lighting up. I could tell by Mandy's face that I was right. "It was truly an amazing night," I said

"It sounds like it," she said with a smile.

"Well, Luca will be over in about a half hour to study, I better go make myself presentable," I said, placing my bowl in the sink and putting away the cereal and milk.

"Seeing him again?" Mandy asked, the edge of motherly concern coming out with no subtlety at all.

"Do we have to do this again?" I whined. I was really not in the mood to have yet another conversation about how fast Luca and I had become serious and how I needed to be careful about jumping into situations I may not be ready for. After all, didn't Luca and I just have this conversation? Of course, Mandy didn't know that.

"I just think you two are rushing into things. There's something to be said for being apart *a little bit*, that's all," Mandy explained, the concern still evident.

"I didn't see him Friday night!" I said defensively, sounding like a bratty child instead of an adult who wanted to be respected and taken seriously. "And besides, all *THREE* of us will be studying," I clarified defiantly.

"Fine Violet, I just don't want you having to make a decision you aren't ready to make yet," she said so calmly that it made my blood pressure skyrocket.

"WE ARE *NOT* HAVING SEX!" I yelled.

"Whose not having sex?" Dexter asked flippantly as he came into the kitchen, obviously having overheard the increasingly loud conversation between mother and daughter.

"Me! That's who!" I said angrily as I stormed out of the kitchen. I briefly worried if Dexter would mention the night before. I heard his footsteps coming fast behind me.

"V! Wait up!" Dexter called, catching up to me and putting his hand on my shoulder. I stopped but didn't turn to look at him.

"What!?" I asked, still fuming.

"It's just...last night...did...?" Dexter couldn't even get the question out.

Now I turned around, my eyes like daggers. "Not that it's ANY of your business, but Luca and I did NOT have sex last night!" I said in a strained whisper through gritted teeth.

"Oh...well...I'm...sorry," he said quietly, looking down now. "Not about you not having sex, I'm glad about that actually. I'm sorry about making you—" he stopped.

I cut off his nonsensical rambling, "*WHEN* we do, don't hold your breath waiting for me to fill you in on the details!" I spun away from him, marched into my room, and slammed the door. I knew I had to cancel the study date. Luca would be disappointed, so was I, but I felt like having him over now would be even worse.

Luca? There was a pause.

Yeah?

Are you on your way?

Not yet, why?

I have to cancel. I'm sorry. Even the voice in my head shook with anger and sadness.

Why? What's wrong?

My mother and Dexter are conspiring against me...us.

What do you mean? He laughed a little.

Well, Mandy keeps trying to talk to me about sex and Dexter keeps sticking his nose where it doesn't belong!

Oh. Did Dexter say something to Mandy about me being in your room last night? he asked.

No. She just thinks we are spending too much time together and Dexter was curious *about our* activities *last night,* I explained.

Well, I don't agree with Mandy, but I respect her. She's just being your mom. I mean my parents said something similar to me too. That's why I can't wait for you to come to dinner Tuesday, so they can meet you and see for themselves why I always want to be with you, he teased. My stomach lurched at the reminder of Tuesday's dinner.

Okay, well then I guess I should study. I'll talk to you before bed tonight, and I'll see in the morning...usual time? I asked.

Of course.

Bye.

I spent the rest of the day sulking and painting. Not studying.

20

We had planned on Luca dropping Dexter and me off at home after school on Tuesday and then Luca returning to pick me up later for dinner at his house. In theory it all sounded great. I would spend the evening at Luca's house, have dinner with his parents, and let them get to know me. The thing about theories was that they weren't always correct, which is why they were theories and not facts. I imagined a few different scenarios, and all of them ended badly.

First, I couldn't imagine what I'd talk to Luca's parents about, and I was sure that my inability to stimulate them with conversation would make them dislike me, and then they would not want Luca to spend so much time with me.

Another possibility was that they knew who Mandy was, or at the very least, would find out about her *hobbies*, decide I was a freak like my mother, and strongly discourage Luca from spending time with me. No matter what, it didn't seem like there was a good way for this to go. But maybe, just *maybe*, since Luca was a wonderful, caring, compassionate person, the apple hadn't fallen far from the tree, and since he liked me so much, maybe his parents would too. It sounded too good to be true.

Though I tried to hide it and stay positive, Luca knew I was nervous and consequently had spent all of Monday and Tuesday trying to reassure me that I would get along great with his parents and that they would love me. I thought I had kept my fear well-hidden, but who was I kidding? Luca knew me well already, and when you shared brain-space with someone, from time to time, you got a chance to nose around a little inside their head and noticed some of the thoughts and feelings that lurked in the shadows. I had to admit there had been times when our connection was *open* that I had occasionally taken a peek into what was going on in Luca's mind.

I tried not to linger too long or snoop too much, but I had learned a little about him. For example, I knew that my self-deprecation upset him even if he didn't say it, and I knew that he was nervous about dinner with his parents too, but not for the same reasons I was. He was concerned about whether or not *I* would like *them*. So, I tried very hard to stay upbeat and positive about the dinner.

As planned, Luca dropped Dexter and me off at home. Just a quick kiss and he was pulling out of the driveway again. He'd be back in two hours, and I needed to get ready. I was actually happy that Mandy was home so she could assist me in choosing an outfit yet again. I knew she was eating this up. She had waited nearly seventeen years to share these moments with me, and I think she had begun to wonder if they'd ever happen.

When I got in, she looked at me and immediately assessed my mood. "Violet, stop looking like you are about to attend your execution!" she said.

I just sighed and rolled my eyes while I walked to my room, leaving Mandy and Dexter to exchange "hellos" and talk about their respective days, but I quickly returned to the living room. She and I both knew that I needed help.

"Okay. What do I wear to this dinner?" I asked, skipping the greetings. I had no time for small talk.

"Well, what are you having?" Mandy asked.

"I have no idea!" I shrieked, exasperated. "I didn't request a menu!" I added, too sarcastically. "I'm sorry. Sorry. I'm just nervous." I breathed deeply. "I don't know what we're having."

"Okay. Well, is anyone else coming?" she asked. I tried to keep my cool even though I was tired of the questions.

Another breath. "Not that I know of. I'm pretty sure *I'm* the guest of honor," I sighed.

"Violet, what is the big deal? You're going to someone's house to consume food, not apply for a job!" Dexter finally said, clearly annoyed. I'm sure his annoyance had more to do with Luca and me than it had to do with my handling of this dinner.

"Dexter. It *is* a big deal to Violet. She's never met Luca's parents, and well, meeting your boyfriend's parents is intimidating," she explained. Hearing her say "boyfriend" made me cringe. I felt like a gooey, love-sick character in some sappy teen romance movie. I suddenly regretted asking Mandy for help, but there was no getting out of it now.

"Whatever," he sighed and left the room.

"Ignore Dexter," Mandy said once he was out of earshot.

"I'm trying to! Can you please just help me?" I pleaded.

"Of course. It sounds pretty casual, and I am sure Luca has told you a lot about his parents, what they are like. From what he's told me, they seem pretty laid back, not formal or uptight." I had to admit, she was probably right about Luca's parents. I was sure I shouldn't expect anything over the top.

"Okay, jeans?" I asked. I needed more.

"Maybe not. Something casual but nice, no t-shirts, something like... maybe the blue dress. I love that one, and it looks great on you." She'd actually made a good suggestion. I didn't love dresses, but I actually felt good in that one.

"That sounds good actually," I admitted.

"Shoes?" I wasn't finished.

"How about those brown sandal-thingies...you know, the ones that kind of come up your ankle...?"

"I guess I could wear them." I hated those shoes. Mandy bought them for me because they were "in style" and she had "seen so many girls wearing them." Apparently she didn't know me as well as I thought. "Maybe I'll wear my black sandals...what do you think?" Nothing wrong with a counter-suggestion.

"Those sound fine," she conceded.

"Okay, so I guess I'll go get ready then," I said as I began to walk away. However, I knew I owed my mother more than that, so I stopped and walked back to her. I could see the shock on her face as I bent down and gave her a gentle hug. "Thanks, Mom," I said quietly, and I really did mean it. She squeezed me back much harder, like she'd never let me go.

"You're welcome, Ollie." I could hear a slight shaking in her voice. I knew she was crying a little. She hadn't called me Ollie in years. That was my nickname when I was a little girl. Suddenly, I was very glad that I had included her in this. I let go. We let go. I walked to the bathroom to shower.

Luca arrived on time. A tornado whirled in my abdomen. My hands shook slightly as he took one and walked me to the car. "You look beautiful," he said.

"Thank you."

Then, we were on our way. There was no turning back. "Are you seriously nervous?" he asked. My stiff body language gave me away.

"A little," I conceded.

"I wish you wouldn't be. It's going to be fine." He added silently, *They're going to love you.*

I hope so.

We pulled into the driveway I remembered from the day of the car accident. The house was a split ranch style with brick on the foundation and cedar shingles that covered the rest of the house. The landscaping was sparse, with only a few low, thick green shrubs spaced evenly along the brick. There were two large pots of red flowers at the base of the stairs that led to the front porch. It was so different from my house. I was concentrating so hard on the house's facade that Luca had to practically pull me out of the car and up the stairs. I took several deep breaths, counting as I exhaled so that I could calm down.

If you run out of things to talk about, you can always amaze them by moving the furniture with your mind, he said to me as we were just about to step through the door.

I don't think redecorating will get them to like me, I replied dryly.

His attempt to calm me with humor worked like a charm, and I was smiling as we entered the house. Immediately upon entering, we were faced with two sets of stairs, one going up, the other down. I could hear voices coming from the upstairs, which is where Luca was taking me. Still holding my hand, we left a small landing with shiny hardwood floors and proceeded into a big, bright kitchen where a dark-haired woman was standing at a small island in the center, chopping something and talking on the phone. She looked up at us as we entered, a huge welcoming smile across her face.

"Gotta go. Luca's home...okay, bye," and she hung up the phone. She almost threw down her knife and bounded toward us. My hand grasped Luca's more firmly. As I tried to smile without looking frightened— I'm not sure if I accomplished that— she stuck out her hand, forcing me to let go of Luca's. As she shook my hand, she grasped our interlocked hands with her free hand. I was unprepared for this enthusiastic welcome.

"Hi, I'm Gina!" I was immediately surprised by how little Luca resembled her. Though they both had dark hair, hers was tightly curled and had some red tones in it. Her eyes, which were more narrow than his large, wide ones, were a golden brown and stood out against her light brown skin. She was a bit shorter than me with a thicker frame than Luca.

"Mom, this is Violet," Luca said.

"Hi," I said shyly, but I was proud of myself for looking her in the eyes instead of at my shoes.

"Come in. Come in," she said as she ushered us into the kitchen.

She went back to her chopping, but looked up frequently to continue our conversation.

"Luca has said such wonderful things about you, and you two have been spending so much time together…" I could tell this was her subtle mom-way of letting me know that she too was *interested* in why Luca and I were suddenly inseparable. "...so, of course, we wanted to meet you." She smiled. Her smile was warm and sincere like Luca's, and I briefly felt a little more at ease and a little less like I was a suspect in a crime, but I prepared myself anyway, in case the mood shifted.

"My husband will be in here in a sec, he's on the phone," she explained. I nodded. Of course she didn't know that I had already guessed that because I could hear her husband on the phone from the moment I entered the house. To be polite, I tuned out his conversation. I stood there, mute for a minute, wondering what else there was for me to say.

"Luca says you are a very talented artist," she said in a way that made me think she was asking a question.

"Well, I paint and sketch, but Luca is a little biased, I think." I looked at Luca shyly and smiled. He rolled his eyes. His mother seemed to be watching our exchanges very carefully, scrutinizing, like she was looking for physical evidence of some hold I might have over him.

"Luca showed us that sketch you gave him, and it is absolutely beautiful," she gushed.

"Thank you," I replied, my cheeks giving away my embarrassment. *You showed them?* I thought to him. He took my hand back into his as a reply. This did not escape his mother's watchful eye either.

I remembered the sketch I had reluctantly given Luca one afternoon when he asked/begged me. It was a sketch I'd done of him in pastels while he was lying in the hammock in my backyard. It was simple, just him reclining in a hammock, one leg out, hanging over the side, his eyes closed, one hand limply on his stomach, the other behind his head. The lighting was perfect. The sun, which was beginning to set, threw diffused light on the whole scene, with narrow rays coming through the leaves, falling all over Luca.

I captured the very edges of the trees and a piece of my studio in the distance. And because it was of him, it was anything but simple. The subject of any piece of artwork can make even the most mundane scene extraordinary, and this sketch was proof of that. But I was embarrassed because it was very personal, and I was sure that my deep feelings for her son came through in the sketch.

I heard footsteps coming toward us, and I guessed it was Luca's father. I turned my head in the direction of the kitchen's entrance, anticipating his arrival. When he walked in, I was taken aback by how much Luca favored him. He was a handsome man, slightly taller than Luca, but with the same wavy, dark hair, albeit sprinkled with strands of gray. His facial features were that of Luca's, but older, with thin creases around his eyes and mouth. They shared the same wide eyes, though his were hazel, not black like Luca's and mine. They were similarly built too, lean, but not thin, sturdy, but not too broad.

"You must be Violet?" he asked with Luca's smile, and I liked him instantly.

"Yes," I replied, this time with a little more confidence and my hand extended in greeting.

"I'm Anthony."

"It's nice to meet you," I said honestly. Everything about Luca's father made me feel at ease because he reminded me so much of Luca. It wasn't that I didn't like Luca's mother; she was pleasant and friendly. It was just that she seemed a little more suspicious of me than his father did.

"I hope everybody is hungry!" Gina said.

"Can I help you with something?" I asked, remembering my

manners.

"If you and Luca could set the table, Anthony and I will get the rest finished up," she responded.

"Sure."

While Luca and I set the table and his parents finished preparing dinner, they continued to ask me questions...nothing too personal or invasive, thankfully.

"So, you are a vegetarian too?" his mother asked

"Yes," I answered. What more was there to say?

"Because of your beliefs?" she asked.

"Um well actually, meat doesn't agree with me, but even if it did, I don't know that I'd eat it," I explained.

"That's so strange that you and Luca both have a problem digesting meat. Isn't it Anthony?" I couldn't tell if she was really surprised, or if she was saying something else. Luca's dad just shrugged.

"Did you have a good time in the city the other night?" his father asked. Of course his parents would know that he had taken me to the city. The question just caught me off guard.

"Um, I had an amazing time. It was the nicest thing anyone has ever done for me." My confession surprised even me. I deciphered by his mother's look of surprise that Luca hadn't really revealed all the details of our date.

"Oh...that's good," she responded. But his father just smiled, which made me smile too.

Dinner was served. It was delicious, but I was too nervous to eat much.

"The food is delicious, Mrs. Verone," I complimented.

"Thank you, and please call me Gina," she said. I nodded. Somehow it was easier to call my own mother by her first name than Luca's.

Conversation was light, mostly about school, and my art, a little about Mandy, what she did for a living, my dad—nothing deeper than the basics.

"Do you like dogs, Violet?" Gina asked.

"I love them, but my mother is allergic, so we haven't ever had one," I explained.

"That's too bad."

"Yeah, I have wanted a dog my entire life. Once when I was about ten, I found a little stray, and brought it home. Of course my mom is so compassionate, she wanted to keep it. Unfortunately, after about half an hour, her eyes were nearly swollen shut, and she was jamming an epi-pen into her leg." Everyone laughed at the story, including me. I was feeling more comfortable than I ever thought I could.

"Well, if you ever want to come to the shelter, we always need extra hands. Then you can get all that dog love out of your system," Gina offered.

"I'd love to!" I said enthusiastically. "I'll help anyway that I can."

"Luca has worked there since he was little. He's great with the dogs." I smiled and nodded. Of course he was. Who wouldn't love him?

After dinner, we all cleaned up and Luca asked if I wanted to see his room.

"Yeah, sure," I said, trying to sound casual, though the prospect of being in his room made my stomach churn even if his parents were just above us in the kitchen. He led me down the double flight of stairs. We turned right at the bottom, and he opened the door to his bedroom.

"Well, this is it," he said as he let me in.

I didn't answer. Instead, I walked into the middle of the room, looking all around. Luca said nothing, giving me time to soak it all in. The room was dimly lit with a floor lamp in the far corner and a small lamp on the desk in another corner. Because it was a downstairs room, the ceiling was low and there was a high window that I assumed let in very little light. The bed pressed against the wall to the right of the door had a headboard with bookshelves brimming over with books.

In fact, there were books stacked haphazardly on every surface of the room. I glanced at a few titles and was amazed at how varied the selection was: *Walden and Other Transcendental Writings, Harry Potter and the Order of the Phoenix,* and several other novels.

"You have a *wide* variety of books! I thought my tastes were all over the place," I finally said. He just nodded. "I love it," I told him. "And of course I am a huge Harry Potter fan!"

"I know," he said simply. He came behind me and put his arms around me, "I told you, we were made for each other," he said quietly into my ear. I smiled because I knew he was right. And though his whispered words caused goosebumps to rise up on my skin, I freed myself from his embrace and continued to wander through this space that was his. Above his bed was the Picasso print I got him when we were at the Guggenheim. I stopped abruptly when I saw his sketch...my sketch...hanging above his desk. He'd put it in a frame, making it look so *official*. He saw me looking at it.

I hope you like the frame, he thought to me.

My eyes were wet. *It's perfect,* I said. I turned away from it and continued my survey.

Then I went over to a bookshelf that lined the wall opposite the bed. Again, a seemingly random collection of books filled each shelf. I was skimming titles when one caught my eye, *The Twelfth Planet*. I kept reading. He had all the books in that series. I knew these books all too well, though I had never dared open one up. Mandy had this series and read and quoted them like they were sacred religious texts.

I knew from her that the books dealt with theories about extraterrestrial intervention in human development. I swallowed hard and continued looking. To my surprise, I saw other titles that

I knew from Mandy. I was in shock, frozen in front of the bookshelf. Luca came up behind me and put his hands on my shoulders. When I didn't respond to his touch, he spoke to me silently.

Violet? Violet, what's wrong?

"Did you know?" I asked, trying to control the oncoming avalanche of emotions that was rumbling.

"Did I know what?" he asked, obviously confused.

I pointed to the bookshelf, unable to speak or even think rationally. He looked at the books I was referring to, and suddenly his expression changed. He dropped his eyes.

"Oh," he whispered.

"Oh? You mean you *did* know?" I almost screeched. In the span of thirty seconds, my whole world, a world I was barely even used to yet, was unraveling. My inner voice spoke to me, yelled to me, flinging questions that I couldn't deflect, *"How much did he know about Mandy already? Did he target me? Does he know more than he's telling me?"*

I could hardly even concentrate on Luca, who was now sounding more and more concerned.

"Violet! Please listen to me. I don't know what you mean by, 'did I know?'" I still couldn't look at him. He stepped around and in front of me. His voice had a different sound now. I detected anger, and it surprised me. It was enough to silence my inner voice and force me to look at him. His voice may have hinted at anger, but his eyes were full of anguish.

"Now listen!" he repeated a little louder and more harshly. "These books—," he gestured to the books I had pointed to, "—are something I have had an interest in since I was a little kid. Aliens...UFO's...that stuff has always been interesting to me." He paused now, gauging my reaction. My jaw clenched, and my brows furrowed, but I decided that I owed him the opportunity to explain.

"I wasn't trying to hide anything from you, I've told you how much I like science fiction. I just didn't talk much about this because I know how it bothers you, and I completely respect that." He stopped. I couldn't figure out if he was trying to gather his thoughts to say something else, or if he was giving me an opportunity to respond. After a minute of silence, I realized he must have been waiting for me. I had calmed a bit, started thinking rationally, allowing my feelings for Luca to override my inner voice. I also began to realize that everything he was saying was making sense.

"So, obviously you'd heard the rumors about me...about Mandy..." I wasn't really asking. I knew he had, everyone had. But, he nodded with humility. "And this...*interest* of yours...it's purely coincidental?" Now I was asking the real question.

"Of course, Violet," he said, though it sounded more like a plea for forgiveness. This time I nodded, confirming the information for myself. "Violet, I don't know what to say. I know it all seems too *coincidental* for you. but I am telling you, I was interested in this, reading these books, long before I moved here and met you," he promised. "I read Henry David Thoreau too because I love the outdoors and nature, but that doesn't mean I'm going to abandon society and run off to live in the woods," he reasoned. Another great point.

I looked into his eyes through the glassy tears that had begun to fill my own. I was searching for some sign that he was lying to me, trying to save himself, but I couldn't find anything but sincerity. "I believe you," I said matter-of-factly because it was absolutely true.

"Good," he said as he took a cautious step closer to me, almost as if he were asking my permission to reach out to me. This is when it hit me...how ridiculous and unforgivable my behavior was. From the moment we had first spoken, touching Luca had been so easy, always right, never awkward. He was kind and gentle, generous and understanding, and here I was vilifying him for having an interest in something that I didn't like. Now I felt terrible. The tears came.

Apparently my crying was more than he could stand. *Please don't cry. I'll throw them away.* If he was trying to make me feel worse, it was working. I grabbed onto him, sniffling and sobbing little whimpers into his chest, and shaking my head trying to tell him, "No, that's not it," but unable to get the words out. He held me tightly until my sobs began to subside.

Finally I was at least able to form a thought and pass it along to him. *I'm sorry. I am so sorry. Please forgive me.* He pushed me away from him and held me at arm's length. I couldn't decipher the look on his face.

"Forgive you...? You didn't do anything wrong. I should've been more sensitive...or given you more warning. I know how hard it's been for you. I'm the one who is sorry for having upset you so much." I couldn't stand to see the pain on his face as he blamed himself.

"Stop. Please stop." I finally found my voice. I took a deep breath, freed one of my arms and wiped the mostly dried tears away with the palm of my hand. "Look, this isn't your fault. These are my issues, and I have to deal with them." I led him over to the edge of his bed where I sat and pulled him down next to me. "I have been through years of torture because of my mother, but that isn't your fault or even hers really. I am going to have to get over it," I said firmly. Then my voice softened, and I knew exactly what I wanted to say, what I had to say. "Luca," I paused.

"Yes?" he whispered.

"I never, ever even imagined I could be *this way* with anyone, especially you. More than that, I never imagined anyone would ever want to be with me this way. You are always telling me that I am amazing, but it's you...you are the one who is amazing. You are considerate and accepting and generous and..." he silenced me with a kiss. It was gentle and tender...and filled with forgiveness. Eventually, he pulled back, and moved my hair behind my ear.

"I appreciate that you are saying all these nice things about me, but the truth is, it's easy for me to be all those things with you, it isn't a conscious thing I am doing. I love you, Violet," he confessed.

I blinked. *"He said it! He actually said it!"* He didn't say it like he was expecting a response, but in a way that told me it didn't matter whether or not I said it back, just as long as I knew that was how he felt. Of course I loved him too, I just hadn't ever said those words to anyone before, aside from my mother and grandmother, and now the meaning was so different.

"I know you do," I said, and it was true, I knew he loved me more than I knew anything. "I love you too," I replied, holding his gaze, knowing that I had to say it without looking away.

"Well, now that's out of the way..." he smiled. I couldn't help but smile back. "We'd better go upstairs before they come looking for us," he said.

"Is there a bathroom down here? I need to clean myself up," I said, knowing my face was probably still red from crying.

"Sure...right down the hall on the left. It's mine, so if it's kind of...gross, sorry."

"That's okay," I laughed. "I live with Dexter, remember?" And I went to wash up.

Luca led me back upstairs where I talked with his parents some more, now feeling a bit more confident. We had dessert, and then it was time for Luca to take me home.

"Violet, we are so glad to have met you. Please don't be a stranger. You're welcome here whenever you'd like, and at the shelter," Gina said.

"Thank you. Dinner was great, and it was so nice to finally meet you," I said.

"Violet, take care, and I hope we see you again soon," his father said.

"Thanks, you too," I said as Luca led me out the front door. We walked silently to the car. Luca let me in the passenger side then slid into his seat.

"I told you they'd love you!" he said.

"I don't know...your mom dropped a lot of 'you're spending too much time together' hints," I said.

"She's just being a mom...Mandy does the same to me, remember?" he reminded me.

"Yeah, you're probably right," I admitted. We drove for a few minutes, just listening to music.

"Can you believe there's only a week of school left?" he asked me.

"No! It's been an *eventful* year, to say the least," I said.

He grabbed my hand. "It's been a great year," he said as he pulled my hand and brushed his lips across my fingers.

"So, any big plans for the summer?" he asked.

"Well, I'm going to paint and read, and maybe spend some time with my boyfriend," I said teasingly.

"Oh, what a lucky guy." He played along. "Seriously though, have you ever been camping?"

"Camping? Me? No," I answered as if the idea was absolutely ridiculous.

"Well, I'd like to change that. Can I take you camping this summer?" he asked eagerly.

The thought of sleeping on the hard ground while animals made noises was unappealing to me, but spending time with Luca was very appealing. "Er, sure. Will your family care if I tag along?" I asked.

"Well no, of course not, but I was thinking that maybe just you and I could go, or we could bring Dexter," he said.

"Oh," I answered. *"Oh!"* I answered again when I caught onto what he was saying.

"No, no...I didn't mean, I wasn't implying that we...you know..." he said, looking embarrassed. "I only meant that we could do some flying, or just hike...I could help you understand why I enjoy camping," he clarified.

"Oh…sorry," I tried to recover, though now my face was a deep shade of scarlet. "Um...that sounds fun. Dexter hates the outdoors, but he has been begging to see us "in action," I said, subtly letting him know that it might be a good idea for Dexter to come along.

"Sure," he replied. "I'll plan it, and we can go sometime in the next couple of weeks. How does that sound?"

"Good," I said. I'd have a couple of weeks to prepare myself for this.

We pulled into my driveway and kissed goodnight in his car before he walked me to the front door. He leaned in for one more kiss and thought, *I love you.*

I love you too, Luca, I replied. Then I went into the house.

The moment I walked in, Mandy was ready to assault me with questions about my dinner with his family. "Soooo....Are his parents nice? Did you have fun? What did you have...?" The questions went on and on. I gave her the overall gist of it. "Yes, his parents are nice. We had raviolis. I had fun. His mom said I could work at the shelter."

"I'm so glad, Violet. And you know what? You're different. You look different."

I looked at her in surprise. I did *feel* different, but I didn't think it showed on my face. "What do you mean?" I asked, eager to know what she saw.

"Oh I don't know exactly. It's like you're...happier. You look happy," she said. "Luca's good for you," she added. No words she could have said could have been better than those. Her acceptance of Luca and her understanding of my feelings for him were paramount.

"Thanks. I told you so." I smiled a sarcastic smile. "By the way, how was the date with Gerry?" I asked. I felt it only right to take an interest in her life too. And she looked happier herself.

"It was really good," she said dreamily, her cheeks reddening.

Mandy was swooning over Gerry! It was about time.

"Mandy, you are blushing!" I laughed.

"I am not, Violet!" she protested, but her smile gave her away.

"So does this mean you and Gerry are finally going to *get together?"*

"Goodnight, Violet." She hugged me and told me it was time for bed, a statement with which I agreed completely even if she was completely avoiding my question.

"Goodnight, Mandy."

"Oh Violet, Dexter is out on the patio, can you please tell him it's getting late?" she asked. Although I thought she was really just making an excuse for me to talk to Dexter.

"Sure," I said as I went toward the single French door that led out to the patio from the kitchen. As I approached him, I couldn't help but smile. He looked so peaceful reclined on the long lawn chair, earbuds in, eyes fixed on a book. He didn't hear or see me coming, so I surprised him. I crept slowly behind him, staying out of sight and then grabbed him by the shoulders quickly. He let out a scream, a chain of profanity, and nearly jumped out of the chair. By the time he turned around to see who had spooked him, I was bent over laughing.

"Really freaking funny, V!" he said, trying to sound angry. But I could hear the playfulness in his voice.

"Sorry," I laughed. "I couldn't help myself!" It was true, I hadn't done anything like that to Dexter in a while and it felt good to joke with him.

"So, how was 'meeting the parents?'" he asked, making air quotes with his fingers and ignoring my laughter.

"It was good." Then I told him about what happened in Luca's room, not the "I love you" part or the kissing part, but the book part. I had to tell someone besides Luca, and in the past it would have always been Dexter, so I figured, why shouldn't it be now?

According to him, we were still the best of friends and he was going to be supportive.

"Dex, you know Luca reads a lot of those books Mandy reads," I just said it, no preface, nothing, just put it out there, seeing if it would register a reaction.

"Really? That's cool." he said first, but then added, "So, you freaked out when you found out, right?" I couldn't help but smirk. Ugh, he knew me so well!

"A little," I sighed with a half-hearted smile.

"So you think he believes in all that stuff too?" I knew Dexter had read the books and was skeptical. It was at that moment that I realized that I hadn't really stopped to contemplate Luca's beliefs. I didn't know what he thought. Also, at the time, in his room, there were other, more pressing matters to deal with than whether or not he agreed with the theories presented in them.

I answered honestly, "I don't know Dex, he knows my...*feelings*, and we don't talk about that."

"But, when you saw the books, didn't you ask?"

"No. I told you, I freaked out and then we *dealt* with that..." I explained vaguely. I didn't want to say any more. He waited to speak.

"Well V, you're going to have to find out eventually right?" he asked pointedly. "I mean Mandy *is* your mother, so that aspect of your world isn't going away anytime soon..." he pointed out.

Leave it to Dexter to always make me think about the things I don't want to think about. I knew he was right, of course. It's just that I had pushed that topic so far away from me that I wasn't even sure what my own beliefs were. So, how could I ask Luca what he thought? If I did, a conversation about the whole topic would be inevitable.

"I'm tired. It's time for bed. Goodnight, Dex." He and I both knew I was completely avoiding his question.

"Goodnight, Violet," he sighed, "And you might want to stop being so damn selfish, by the way. That guy really likes you, and you aren't being fair," he added before going inside, leaving me standing alone in the backyard facing the truth of his words.

I stood still on the patio for a moment, breathing in the cool, damp night air and clearing my head before I went to bed. I just wanted to remember the best parts of the evening, like meeting the people who made Luca who he was and seeing his room, and of course, Luca telling me he loved me. It sort of worked. I was able to push the unpleasant topic of my conversation with Dexter aside and think about Luca, escaping reality just a little while longer. The problem was, the more I thought about Luca, the more I knew Dexter was right.

That night as I lay in bed, I envisioned a new painting that I was eager to get started on.

21

The last week of school dragged on. Finals ended and there wasn't much left to do before graduation. Mandy actually let me and Dexter stay home and Luca, Dexter, and I spent the day in the city, just walking through the park, eating, and checking out a few museums. Luca and Dexter were getting along better and better, and I felt more able to be Luca's girlfriend while Dexter was around.

When the week finally ended, we were all ready to get to graduation and get the summer started. Luca still hadn't said a word to me about the book incident at his house, and I still hadn't taken Dexter's advice and asked him his beliefs. But, I knew it would have to be discussed eventually. Like Dexter said, it was, "inevitable."

The day finally arrived. Graduation. Even if we were only going to the local college, I was getting away from Lake Hansen High School once and for all. No more looks or comments. And no more Stephanie Baker. She was, thankfully, headed to some big state school down South. North Carolina or Georgia. Who cared? Wherever it was, it was hundreds of miles away. And even better, Luca and Dexter were sticking around too. We had two more years to decide where we went next. That gave us a lot of time. Who knew what the next few years would hold? I was content and confident that Luca would still be in my life.

During our first weekend of freedom, Luca and I spent time at Nature Park, walking through the maze, using our telepathy and sensory powers...*practicing*. For me it was just as amazing as it had been the first time. It never got old or boring. But, I still wouldn't—couldn't—tell Dexter about those powers. It was just too personal, and I wanted to keep it between Luca and me.

I started volunteering at the dog shelter. I even dragged Dexter there a few times, though he'd gotten a job at the library and started taking summer classes at the community college, so he wasn't around as often.

I also spent a lot of time at Luca's house. His parents had me over for dinner often and some nights we'd just hang out in his basement and watch movies or play video games. I wasn't ever able to get Dexter there though. I guess it was just a bit too much for him. I, on the other hand, was beginning to feel very comfortable there.

Luca and I also spent many afternoons in the clearing or at the lake near the clearing. I always brought my sketchpad and pastels, and Luca always brought a book and a notebook. We had to be prepared in case anyone else happened to be in the clearing, and we couldn't fly or hurl giant rocks. This was fine with me. Any time I spent with Luca was perfect, and being at my new favorite place was just a bonus.

One particularly warm day when we got to the clearing, there were several hikers cutting across, so we decided to spend a little time sketching and writing back at the lake. There was a small boat in the water with a solitary fisherman, but besides him and the distant hikers who were crisscrossing the woods, there was no one else around. Luca sat back, knees up, and read while I sat cross-legged in the grass, sketching.

Try as I might to capture the beauty of the majestic trees that encircled the lake or the sunlight playing on the tips of the long, golden grass and shimmering water, I was always compelled to sketch Luca. I had memorized the soft, smooth lines of his face and could almost draw them from memory, though I preferred to have an excuse to stare at him for long periods of time.

At first my drawings embarrassed Luca, and he protested, telling me to use my "limitless talents" to capture the pure, unique beauty of the clearing. But when he realized how much I enjoyed drawing him, he gave up his protests and let me sketch without guilt. Even he had to admit that the sketches were some of the most beautiful I'd ever done, capturing his essence completely.

As I sketched Luca reading, I realized it must be extremely warm because I was actually feeling a bit uncomfortable from the heat. Generally, the heat or cold didn't bother me much, and it was only in extremes that my body reacted to the temperature. Luca was much the same, so we realized that was yet another *gift*. However, today the heat was strong, and I wished I had worn a lighter shirt, maybe a tank top.

As I thought this, Luca reached back and grabbed his own shirt, yanked it over the front of his head, balled it up, and lay back on it, using it as a pillow. My breath stopped, and I let out the slightest gasp that I hoped Luca didn't hear. I had little experience with unclothed men, and here was...*my* man, half-naked, lying in the clearing. I looked around to see if anyone else was marveling at his body.

By now the few hikers that had crossed our path were out of sight. Luca and I were alone. I laughed nervously when the scene reminded me of a page out of some cheesy romance novel. Of course the novel probably wasn't the science fiction version that Luca and I would have to be a part of. He propped up on his elbows and said, "What's so funny?" I tried to compose my face and act naturally, showing no signs of my racing heart and speeding pulse. I was glad the heat had already turned my cheeks pink so he wouldn't notice the blush.

"Um...nothing....nothing," I chirped too quickly

"O...kay." He eyed me strangely. "Hey are you warm?" he asked.

"Uh...yeah." I suppressed a smile. "It must be the heat wave...you know, climate change, extreme temperatures." I paused and then asked, before I realized the words had come out of my mouth, "I guess you are too?" and gestured to his bare chest with my head.

"Oh, yeah," he said. I swallowed. This was almost more than I could handle.

"Why, am I turning you on?" He was joking, of course, but my mouth dropped open and I began to stutter, though no actual words came out. Luca caught on that his joke might not have been so funny. He tried to play it off.

"You can take yours off too...then we'd be even, and equally...you know...*distracted.*" He smiled.

"Very funny," I scowled. "I think I'll be okay," I answered snidely.

He sat all the way up and started to put his shirt back on when I stopped him. "NO!" I yelled. "Leave it off...please," I said, embarrassed by my enthusiasm. "Uh...it's a good change...for the sketches." I was doing a terrible job of covering up my eagerness.

"Okay...whatever you say," he said, and lay back down. "Just try to control yourself," he added with a silent chuckle to himself, but he knew I could hear it.

I rolled my eyes and continued sketching, grateful that once again he had said exactly the right thing to make me feel better and lighten the mood. But the frightening fact was that I didn't know just how long I could control myself.

The mood was peaceful. I was still sketching and Luca was still being beautiful and reading when I had to go and ruin it. "Luca, I need to ask you something," I began.

"Sure, anything," he answered as he propped himself back up, and I moved over to sit beside him, hyper-aware of the fact that his shirt was still balled-up behind him.

I rushed right in, barely pausing to breathe for fear that I would lose my nerve.

"Okay...remember that night in your room, the first time I came for dinner, the book thing...my...reaction?"

"Yeah," he said. Now he sat up straighter, looking concerned.

"Well, I just wondered...since we've never really talked about it, and it's been such a big part of my life...uh...um, where do you stand on the whole alien issue?" I blurted out.

He took a deep breath and seemed to be deliberating.

"What is it?" I asked. I was panicked. I viewed his pause as a definite negative sign.

"I just...I know you hate talking about this..." he responded.

"I know, but I...it's important that we clear the air...that I know where you stand...I'm not going to be angry or freak out, I promise," I added with the most reassuring smile I could muster.

"Promise?" he questioned. I knew by his reaction that I was in for an answer I didn't necessarily want to hear. I braced myself.

"Well, I think there's life out there," he said casually. "In fact, I am pretty convinced of it..." He paused and looked at me nervously, probably checking to see if I was going to keep my word. For my part I used every shred of self-control to keep my face from contorting, determined to keep my promise. I must have done well because he continued slowly, as if he were a doctor delivering tragic news.

He cleared his throat before saying, "I've never seen UFOs or anything, Violet, but... I guess I'm a *believer,*" he stated. "And those books—they aren't necessarily science fiction or bogus theories to me—" He scanned my face, trying to determine whether he'd said too much. Since I truly couldn't speak, I did the only thing I could do, I thought, *Thank you for being honest with me.*

That is *what you wanted, right? The truth?* I could hear the anxiety in his thoughts, and it made me feel horrible. I couldn't be upset with him for doing what he always did: giving me *exactly* what I asked for. That's one of the things I loved about Luca, the way he could be the most gentle human being I had ever known, always ready to protect me, but also not side-step anything, and not lie to me.

"Are you…are *we* okay?" he asked out loud.

"Yes, we're fine." I forced a smile. I hoped my body language didn't hint at the ball of anxiety that had gathered in the pit of my stomach.

Luca put his arm around me, and I leaned into him. We just sat that way for a long time, not speaking. Luca finally said, "You know, you've never actually told me what you think about Mandy's friends and experiences. I know you hate the topic, but since we are being honest..." This was something I had barely allowed myself to contemplate. I didn't even know where I stood, but I had to give him an answer.

"Fair enough," I began. "As you are well aware by now, my mother is not shy about her *beliefs* and *experiences*. The problem is, it's always been so in-my-face that I have felt suffocated by it. So, I never let myself really think about whether or not it was all real," I explained.

"I can understand that," he said.

"So, you want to know if I *believe?* That's tough. The truth is, probably, but I don't want to," I said simply. I had never said these words out loud. Never imagined that I could form an actual opinion on the matter. I imagined that when I did someday, I would feel lighter, like I had unburdened a very heavy load. But I didn't. I felt like I had just ripped off a scab to expose a painfully deep gash. I let out a long, deep breath.

Luca put his arm around me again. "Sorry, I shouldn't have pushed you."

"No, it's okay. It really is. Why shouldn't you get to ask the same questions I ask of you? I mean, what gives me the right to have so many rules and barriers?"

"Well, it's done. I asked. You answered. That's it." He smiled and hugged me. But he and I both knew that was not the end of it. It was something that was going to come back to haunt us. We just didn't know when. I had a feeling it was going to be sooner rather than later.

***

We drove back to my house in peaceful silence. When we pulled into the driveway, I felt like I had to say something to ease Luca's conscience and put this behind us, at least for now. "You know I love you, right?" I told him.

"I know," he said with a smile, and I knew he did, that was never in doubt, but I swear I could see something else deep inside, something sad.

"Come on, let's go in." I took his hand and led him inside.

The TV was on and Dexter was in the kitchen. I guessed he was cooking because I heard things banging and slamming, and Dexter couldn't make a bowl of cereal without sounding like he was preparing a five-course meal. "Hey Dex!" I called out to him. Luca had taken a seat on the couch, and I snuggled in next to him, letting him know even further that what happened at the lake was forgotten.

"Hi," he called back. "You want some—" He came out of the kitchen, "Oh, hey Luca, I didn't know you were here," he said looking a little dejected but also like he was getting used to feeling dejected. "Uh...do either of you want some pizza? I'm just heating some up."

"I'm good," Luca replied, "but thanks."

"No thanks, not hungry," I told him. He disappeared into the kitchen.

Then Luca surprised me a little. "Hey Dexter?" he called. Luca talked to Dexter nearly every day, but it was rarely more than small talk and beyond "Hi", he didn't really *talk* to Dexter unless Dexter initiated the conversation. And given Dexter's frequent changes in temperament, this was probably the best approach. So, I couldn't begin to guess what Luca was going to say.

Dexter came out from the kitchen, obviously as surprised as I was. "Yeah?"

"I told Violet I wanted to take her camping, and I thought maybe you'd like to come too. You know, see some cool stuff?" I looked at him, stunned. First of all, this was news to me. I mean, he'd mentioned it before school got out, but we hadn't talked about it since. Secondly, it was *camping.* Also, after my reaction to him shirtless by the lake, I wasn't sure being alone in the woods in a tent was a good idea, even with Dexter there. I spoke up.

"Uh, Luca, are you sure that's a good idea...I mean...we don't even know if Mandy will say yes..." I stumbled over my words.

"No, it's fine. You two go camping. I hate nature anyway!" he growled and stormed out. Dexter had obviously misinterpreted my response to mean that I didn't want him there. Given my growing lack of self-control, in a way, he couldn't have been more wrong.

I rolled my eyes at his sensitivity, but I followed after him. "Dex," I said gently when I went into the kitchen, "You're wrong. It has nothing to do with me not wanting you there. I just...I don't know. I guess I don't... oh hell, I am afraid to be in the woods at night!" Dexter began to laugh. I heard a little bit of laughter from the living room too. My face flamed from embarrassment. What I said wasn't a complete lie. I really wasn't excited about all the animals and bugs and sounds that I believed came with the woods at night.

"What's so funny?" I asked defensively.

"You don't want to go camping because you're afraid? You? Super-strength, super-vision? What are you afraid of?" He was still chuckling.

"I don't know." It did seem ridiculous now. "Animals, bugs, you know..." I said weakly.

"I think we'll be okay, and besides, isn't *Loverboy* out there some great outdoorsman or something?" he added sarcastically.

"Yes, *Luca* does camp and hike and stuff. I know, it's stupid, so are we gonna go?" I asked.

"Sure."

"But I thought you 'hate nature.'" I dropped my voice to poorly imitate him.

"Are you gonna fly?" he asked.

"Yes!" I groaned with an eye roll.

He smiled curiously, "Then I can learn to freaking love nature." I rolled my eyes again.

"We do have one *small* obstacle," I reminded him.

"What?" he asked.

"Mandy." I said. "I could lie and tell her we are going with Luca's family..."

"You could...but..."

"But what?"

"You get cell service there right?"

"Yeah, why?" I couldn't see where he was going with this.

"If she can get in touch with you, and I am going with you like we are the happy-go-lucky three musketeers...then I doubt Mandy will have a problem with it. Do you? Also, you're eighteen and you're starting college in a few weeks."

I remembered why I loved Dexter so much, and I did love him, just not in the way he hoped. I was so taken by my feelings for him that I leaned forward, planted a kiss on his cheek and flung my arms around him. "That's why you're the best." But when I looked at him, I instantly regretted my enthusiasm. His face had turned scarlet, and his jaw was clenched. I was only inches from him, with my arms still awkwardly around his neck when Luca came around the corner. I knew he'd heard our very innocent conversation, but his face looked puzzled when he saw me close to Dexter and Dexter flaming red.

"Is everything...okay?" he asked a little more darkly than I was used to. I realized what he must be thinking.

Dexter turned instantly back to the counter and busied himself while he mumbled, "Fine."

I decided it was best to simply ignore the weird tension. "Luca, everything is fine. I convinced Dexter to go camping, and then he made me realize that Mandy will definitely let us go if she knows he's coming."

"Of course she will," he replied with a twinge of *something* in his voice.

"Why don't we go out on the patio?" I took his hand and led him out.

"I have to go actually. I'll call you later though." He kissed my cheek and turned to go. I stood there dumb-struck for a second. It wasn't until he was walking out the front door that I woke up.

Dexter turned to me. "What the hell just happened?"

"I...I don't know," I said, but I knew. It was the same thing that had happened the night of our first date. "I think Luca might be *jealous*!" I said.

Dexter was trying very hard not to smile, "Really?" He wasn't trying hard enough!

"Wipe that stupid gloating, smug smile off your face! You know that kiss ON YOUR CHEEK was not what Luca thinks it was!"

He got serious. "I know."

I heard Luca getting into his car, and I screamed *WAIT!* directly to his brain. I heard the car door open then close, so I bolted out the front door.

I sprinted to his car and nearly ripped the driver's side door off before I regained control of my strength. I stood outside the car while Luca sat in the driver's seat.

"You didn't see what you think you saw, Luca," I pleaded. "You *know* that!"

"So what *was* that in there with Dexter?" He motioned his head toward the house.

He still didn't look at me.

"That was me giving Dexter a kiss on the cheek," I said matter-of-factly.

"Your brother?" he said sourly.

"Luca, are you kidding me? We've been through this already," I almost shouted. I was a little angry about what I figured Luca was thinking. I thought I'd made my feelings for Dexter clear to both Luca *and* Dexter.

"I have NEVER tried to hide mine and Dexter's friendship from you. He has been my best friend since we were eight. For all intents and purposes, he *is* my brother,"

"I *know,* but just because you feel that way doesn't mean he does." He was pouting now, and I didn't like it.

"I know that. Don't you think I know that! I just keep hurting him and hurting him, even when I am not trying to. All of this..." I motioned in the air around me, "... has hurt him because not only is he not my best friend anymore, but every time we are all together, I know it hurts him, even when he doesn't say anything."

This seemed to strike a nerve, "What do you mean he's not your best friend anymore," he asked.

I softened a little. "Luca, you've got to know that *you* are my best friend. I love Dexter, but not the way I love you, and I do love you. You're the one I share my thoughts and fears and *time* with." I paused. "I can't even believe you are making me say this!" I was angry.

He closed his eyes and put his head down on the steering wheel. "You're right Violet. You are so right. I promised you on our first date that I wouldn't do this again. It's not fair to you or Dexter. I'm being an insensitive jerk."

"Well...yeah." I smiled and ran my fingers through his hair. He picked his head up and looked at me that way—into me.

"Luca, I can't keep justifying my friendship with Dexter *and* reassuring you." I wasn't giving him an ultimatum; I just wanted him to know that it hurt when he acted like that. "You have to promise to talk to me about what's bothering you, like you always do about everything else and to not freak out."

"I promise, I will never do that again. I just saw you two so close together and his face was all red and…it made me crazy." He bent his head into the steering wheel again.

I reached down and took one of his hands and led him out of the car. He kept his head hung low, not looking at me. I put my hand on his cheek and gently lifted his face to look at me. "It's okay." I assured him softly.

"Okay." He nodded, but he still looked embarrassed.

I reached up with my other hand and cupped his face in my hands. "If I ever saw another girl come near you, I would probably flip out and go *super-Violet* on her, so I guess I can forgive you," I said with a smile.

He brightened a bit, even smiled a little. "Thanks, but I can promise you that will NEVER happen." He leaned toward me now and hugged me. Then he released me from his embrace just enough to press me against the car and kiss me with a passion and intensity that further convinced me.

At some point Luca must have realized the time because he pulled away without warning. "I really have to go. I promised my mom I'd fill in at the shelter." He sounded disappointed.

"It's okay," I replied, still only inches from him

"Ah, I'm sure I could make up some excuse—" He leaned in again and kissed me, but I kept my composure.

"No, Luca," I said around his lips, "you have to go. Now is not the time to go making your mom hate me," I reminded him. "Not with our camping trip right around the corner." He backed away and sighed.

"Speaking of which, when is the big trip?" I asked. I wasn't sure if the camping idea had been shelved.

"Well, I am working at the shelter this week Wednesday,

Thursday and Friday. You're working Thursday and Friday, right?"

"Of course." I had been volunteering a few days a week. Gina asked me if I wanted to work there as in an actual job once my semester started because I was so good with the dogs, and I accepted. She and I got along great and I was enjoying getting to know her, so I wanted to remain in her good graces.

"How about Monday and Tuesday?" he asked. "Fewer people will be camping during the week."

"Are you still okay with Dexter coming?"

"Absolutely. This is my problem, and I am going to have to get over it myself," he assured me.

"Are your parents okay with this?" I asked. I thought about how much I liked his mom, but knew how protective she could be.

"Yeah. I made sure they knew Dexter was coming though," he smiled.

"Hmmm," was my reply. We were always on the same wavelength.

"I guess you should go so your parents don't think I've kidnapped you. I want your mom to keep liking me, and not just because I clean up after the dogs."

"I don't think you have to worry about that. I told you, they love you. My dad talks about you all the time."

That made me smile. I loved Mr. Verone. "Good."

"Call me later," he said.

"Of course," he leaned in for another kiss. "I love you."

"Me too," he replied and reluctantly walked away.

When I got back into the house, I found Dexter stretched out on the couch flipping channels. He looked up at me and then back to the TV.

"Um...Luca wanted to apologize for being a jerk," I said.

"Okay," he said snottily.

"Dex, cut him some slack. I think if anyone could understand what he's feeling, it would be you."

The overwhelming honesty of my comment seemed to cut deeply. He sighed and looked at me, almost the same way Luca looked at me, but with a twinge of sadness that made me hurt for him. "I can," was all he said. He looked at me for a few more seconds and turned back to the TV like he'd come out of a brief trance.

22

Dexter had been hounding me since school ended, begging to see what Luca and I had been practicing, so I figured the camping trip would be a good way to give us some time to show our powers and answer any of Dexter's questions. Even with good reasons for going, I was still apprehensive.

For one, I enjoyed sleeping *indoors*, preferably in a bed. For another, I was a little afraid of what might happen between Luca and me together, overnight. I knew how little self-control I had around him, and it had been getting worse. That was partly why I was glad Luca had thought of bringing Dexter. Maybe he had the same idea, or maybe he just wanted to show me that he respected how important Dexter was to me.

And of course, Dexter had been right: Mandy agreed to the camping trip easily, but with her *stipulations*. Dexter and Luca would share a tent (that was the main stipulation).

On the following Monday afternoon, Dexter and I loaded all of our gear into Luca's car. Mandy had gone to bed already, but not before giving me yet another lecture about my lack of experience and the importance of being sensitive to Dexter's feelings. I grudgingly reassured her that I would not do anything stupid and reminded her that Dexter was going to be there, and I reiterated the fact that I wouldn't hurt Dexter like that. Ironically, while packing, Dexter asked, "So, are you really planning on sleeping all alone in a tent while me and *Loverboy* are all cozy in our tent?

"Yes, Dexter, that's exactly what I have planned," I said, though inside I was reeling at the thought of sleeping alone in a tent in the woods. I told myself that even if Luca did sleep in the same tent with me, I could control myself. It would be purely for comfort and safety. Besides, we had agreed to wait a little longer. Of course that had been after our first date, and now we had waited a *little* while longer. Who was I kidding? If Luca and I were alone in a tent, I would have a *very* hard time controlling myself. Two tents were a good idea.

***

"Everybody ready?" Luca asked as we piled into the car. The three of us together in Luca's car was becoming a very regular occurrence.

"Yup," replied Dexter indifferently.

"Do we have everything?" I asked, still a little nervous about my first camping trip.

"Two tents, three sleeping bags, water, flashlights, food..." Luca rattled off a list as he put the car in reverse and backed out of my driveway. "Violet, I camp all the time."

"Did you remember to bring marshmallows?" I asked excitedly.

"Yes, Violet. I could never forget the marshmallows to *memorialize* your first ever camping trip," Luca said, rolling his eyes.

"Good," I said curtly.

Dexter already had his earbuds in and seemed as if he might be asleep any minute. Because of his childhood, Dexter had the uncanny gift of being able to fall asleep basically anywhere, under any circumstances. Thunderstorms and jackhammers were no match for his sleeping ability.

Luca could barely contain his excitement. "You're gonna have fun, I promise."

Are you sure you don't mind Dexter tagging along? I asked silently, just in case Dexter wasn't asleep. I had asked Luca this question, in some form, several times over the previous week. Each time his reply was the same.

Of course not. I think it's a good idea to let him really see what we can do. Again he sounded very excited. I think he was looking forward to an audience. I, on the other hand, was not thrilled about showing off my powers.

The ride was as beautiful as it always was, perhaps even more so with the sun making its initial preparations for setting and turning the leaves of the trees into more shades of gold and golden-green than I had ever seen. There was little talk in the car, just the radio playing quietly. My thoughts were about the next thirty-six hours. I wondered what Dexter's reactions would be and hoped he wouldn't look at me too differently after he saw me flying through the air.

As usual, we parked in the pull-off. The stopping of the car woke Dexter from his slumber. He yawned and stretched. "Are we here already?" he asked through a yawn.

"We were only in the car for half an hour!" I laughed. "We are sort of there, but not quite. That was the easy part," I joked. "You still have about a forty-five minute hike, at least." And then I realized just how much harder the hike would be for Dexter than it was for Luca and me. It worried me a bit, considering Dexter's general inactivity. "You think you'll be okay, Dex?" I asked.

"I'll be fine, Violet. Besides, if I get tired, you can just carry me on your back." He smiled. The funny part of his comment was the truth of it.

"Yeah..." I responded, "I actually could."

Dexter's eyes widened at me for just a second as he took in that fact. After he'd digested the information, he shook it off and looked like himself again before he said, "I'll be fine."

The hike was not as relaxing as it usually was with Dexter complaining and groaning the whole way. I found it funny how little he saw of the beauty and serenity of the surroundings as he growled about the dirt and the wet and his aches and pains. Despite his complaints, we made it to the (thankfully) empty clearing shortly before sundown.

Luca dropped his pack and went back into the trees for some firewood, then proceeded to build a fire like an expert outdoorsman. The acrid smell of the burning wood was exactly the smell I had always associated with camping.

We put up the small, pop-up tents, one for Dexter and Luca and one for me. As the sun dipped lower and lower into the sky and darkness got closer, sleeping alone in one of those thin, nylon tents with all the strange, unidentifiable sounds of the woods at night became less and less appealing. And with my hearing, there were even more sounds. I pushed the anxiety aside and sat with Luca and Dexter around the campfire, eating, talking, and laughing.

Then I went into my tent and slipped into my soft, comfortable flannel pajama pants, long-sleeved tee, and hooded sweatshirt. These were my favorite, most comfortable clothes, and since temperature wasn't much of an issue, it didn't matter that they were all wrong for the summer evening. Dexter noticed this as I came out of my tent.

"V, aren't you going to like, sweat to death? It's July. It's like seventy degrees tonight," he asked.

"No...besides, it gets chilly up here at night. Right, Luca?" I looked at Luca for some sign of what I should say.

You don't want to tell him? he asked me silently. I took a deep breath and turned back to Dexter.

"Dex, the truth is...unless it's really hot, like *really* hot, or really, really, really cold, although I can't remember it ever being cold enough—" I trailed off for a moment as I realized that the extreme heat had bothered me, but the cold, even when it had been absolutely frigid outside, seemed to have little effect on me. Even as a kid, Mandy would bundle me up in the winter, and I'd always incur her wrath when I came home unbuttoned with no scarf or mittens. I suppose I actually only wore sweaters and coats out of habit or comfort.

"Yes?" Dexter asked, jolting me from my thoughts.

"Sorry...anyway, I...we...don't really feel the temperature variations the same way you do." I bit my lip as I allowed what I'd just told Dexter to sink in. This only took a second.

"Wow. Cool. That comes in handy, huh?" He smiled a little, but he didn't seem shocked or anything. "So, the flying, the kick-ass strength, the tough skin, and you are impervious to heat and cold. Anything else?"

I froze. What should I say? I didn't want to lie to Dexter, but I wasn't ready to reveal everything. Luca must've seen the panic on my face because he answered for me. "We can hear really well, but you know that one too—I think Violet is better at that than me—and our eyesight is sharp and not affected much by low light." He had told him more than Dexter had asked but still didn't reveal the telepathy.

"So, right now, it's dark and I can't see past where the fire light goes, but you can?" Dexter looked at me.

I nodded. "I mean it's not like I can see for miles, it's just that the lack of light doesn't make it too much harder for me to see," I tried to explain. I realized how difficult it was to understand if you weren't actually experiencing it.

He just nodded. "So, is that all?" he asked. He reacted so nonchalantly that I wondered whether he had rehearsed his reactions so as not to appear too freaked out as he witnessed the things I was going to reveal to him.

"All?" I screeched. "That's not enough?"

"No, it's not that. It's just...it seems like you keep adding on, so I just wondered..." he laughed but trailed off.

"Actually, there's one other thing," Luca said. My eyes grew wide, and I screamed, *NO!* into his brain, but he ignored me. Dexter sat up straighter. "We have a kind of telekinesis."

"Oh thank god!" I thought to myself. I'd forgotten he didn't know that. I couldn't even keep track of my own powers! Luca looked at me and smiled while I glared at him. He had scared me on purpose, for his own amusement. He was lucky I loved him or else he might not have been forgiven.

"You mean like you can move things with your mind?!" Dexter was eager now. He was almost as excited as when he learned we could fly.

"I thought it was just metal," I explained. "Like pipes and spoons. But then I picked up some plastic pieces of my broken clock, so I guess it isn't only metal, although I think the connection to metal is stronger."

Dexter looked at me curiously and then something clicked. "I knew it! I knew something weird happened with that car accident!" he shouted.

"Yeah well, I reacted out of instinct. I didn't even know I could do that until the pipes just rolled to the side instead of through our windshield." I recalled the events with crystal clear accuracy. I was lost in thought for a moment until I felt Luca's hand rubbing my back gently. I gave him a quick smile. After that Dexter didn't ask any more questions.

We ate more. Then we talked more. We stuck to lighter subjects for the rest of the night.

"Well, I'm going to bed," Dexter said after he'd stuffed himself. "I assume we have a busy day tomorrow?" he asked with an expectant smile that matched the eagerness in his voice.

"Aren't you going to roast marshmallows with us?" I asked.

"No, I'm beat. Besides, I'm not really a roast-marshmallows kind of guy." He stood and stretched and then headed into his tent.

Luca turned to me, holding a bag of big, fluffy white marshmallows, "So, let's eat some marshmallows."

I knew it was silly to be so excited over such an activity, but I thought it was the quintessential camping experience, especially since I couldn't really roast a hot dog on a stick. I pulled a soft marshmallow out of the bag and stuck it on the end of a sharpened stick. Then I held it high above the fire. I wasn't sure what was supposed to happen. Nothing happened.

"You're not doing it right," Luca corrected, laughing. "Some people like to hold it further away and toast it really slowly, but not me. You've got to let it catch fire for a second and then blow the fire out," he explained. "Watch," he instructed as he took the stick from my hand. He stuck my marshmallow directly into the flames and then pulled it back. It looked like the flaming arrow of some medieval warrior. He quickly blew out the flame. Now there was an unappetizing, charred, blackened mass clinging to the end of the stick.

"I'm supposed to *eat* that?" I asked with my nose scrunched disapprovingly.

"Trust me, it's delicious."

I closed my eyes and opened my mouth. Luca stuck the whole marshmallow right in. It filled my entire mouth, and I felt ridiculous trying to keep it all inside. Luca was enjoying himself immensely. As the marshmallow's charred exterior gave way to the gooey sweet interior, my face changed.

"Mmmm. This is SOOO good!" I mumbled with a marshmallow-stuffed mouth.

"Told you."

I gorged myself on marshmallows until I thought I was going to throw up.

"Okay, enough. I'm going to be sick," I finally said.

Luca laughed, "Yeah, I think you might have...overdone it."

I nodded in agreement. While we were laughing about my marshmallow over-indulgence, I told Luca, "You don't think you're off the hook for the telekinesis thing, do you?"

He looked at me with an angelic, "Who me?" face. "I don't know *what* you're talking about," he said innocently.

"Mm, hmm?" I eyed him accusingly.

"What?" He tried very hard to suppress a smile, but it didn't work.

"You will pay for that one," I warned, trying, but failing, at being firm and serious.

"Are you going to punish me?" he asked. The joking was now gone. It had been replaced by something very different. It was flirty, seductive even.

My stomach twisted and I couldn't answer him. He used my silence as an opportunity to lean in and kiss me. It was perfect. A beautiful summer night, crackling fire, warm breeze... The kissing went on a while—a long while. I was snuggled in Luca's lap, enjoying the closeness, and thinking how nice it was that we were alone when I heard a loud snore. Dexter! I pulled away. We weren't alone. "I think I should go to bed. It has to be really late, and we do have a busy day tomorrow. Trust me, Dexter is not going to let us rest," I told him.

"Yeah, I guess so," he said, sounding disappointed. But he didn't release me. "Violet, are you sure you are going to be okay in there alone?" he asked. I was certain he was asking something more. I wanted to say, "No, please come sleep in there with me, I'll be good." But I didn't. I couldn't. Because I'd be lying.

"Um...yeah...yes, I'll be fine," I said apprehensively, trying to convince myself more than Luca. I knew he saw right through my facade. He was simply waiting for me to say the word and he'd volunteer to sleep in my tent. "I'm going to bed. I'm fine. Goodnight." I leaned over and kissed him quickly, afraid to let the kiss go on too long.

"Goodnight," he sighed, "I love you."

I turned and smiled. No matter how many times he said that

to me, my heart squeezed and my breath caught. "Love you too." Luca waited for me to get into my tent before going into his own.

I slid into my sleeping bag, but couldn't get comfortable. I lay there, rigid and unmoving. Every unidentifiable sound seemed like it was just outside the tent and made me increasingly more anxious. There was no light, and my eyes widened either in response to the lack of light or from fear.

After a little while, I began to relax, taking deep breaths and coaxing the tension out of my body a little at a time. The sounds became less threatening, and I had finally settled myself enough to close my eyes and at least think about trying to sleep. My mind was starting to go when, in the distance, I heard a "Snap!" I gasped, but quickly covered my mouth.

Of course, Luca had heard my frightened cry and was in my tent before I even realized what was going on. "Are you okay?" he asked, worry saturating his tone.

"Uh...yeah..." I hesitated. "No, not really," I finally admitted. "There are so many noises, and I know it's immature and ridiculous to be afraid of them, but...I heard a snap," I whined. Then Luca laid down beside me.

"It's okay," he whispered into my ear. This whispering cleared my mind of whatever had been scaring me, and now a new fear gripped me. I was afraid that I was never letting him out of that tent, and I was afraid of what that might mean. But my biggest fear was that I didn't really care.

My need for him materialized and began to grow. His whispered comfort then became a kiss on my neck, just below my ear. Soft, familiar lips pressed gently against my skin, sending vibrations through me. This kiss turned into several that trailed down my neck and back up my chin, searching for my mouth. When his lips found mine, his kisses were gentle at first. Then, as hands moved through hair and breath grew hot, the kisses intensified.

My need had grown bigger than the tent, bigger than my entire being. Luca stopped kissing me, but only long enough to work his way into my sleeping bag with me. Our lips moved even more fiercely together, and his body pressed against mine with a closeness that I didn't think was humanly possible, but which also didn't feel like enough. Luca moved so that he leaned over me, using his arms to prop himself up. He then brought his head down and kissed my forehead, my nose, my lips, my chin, trailing down my neck. When my sweatshirt and t-shirt impeded his advances, I reacted out of instinct, not pausing to think of the implications of my move, but squirming out of them as quickly and efficiently as I could, though it was difficult with both of us in a single sleeping bag. With my shirts out of the way, Luca continued to kiss my neck, his hands moving everywhere.

My body took over without the use or need of my mind. I grabbed at his shirt until it was over his head and out of my way. He wrapped his arms tightly around me, gathering me up to him. Every place where our skin touched sent vibrations of electricity through my body, and I wondered if Luca was feeling the same thing. But his soft moans as my mouth found his ear, his throat, his chest, and my hands explored his body, let me know he was, and it enticed me even further.

The experience was filled with impossible contradictions. Though my body was supposedly impervious to hot and cold, I felt the heat in the sleeping bag and the heat that burned violently inside of me. My body trembled, not out of cold or fear, but out of my need for Luca. My mind was both empty of coherent thoughts and filled completely with Luca. His hands and lips caressed me gently and ferociously.

Breathing was difficult, but not in any way that was uncomfortable. I felt like I didn't need air. I only needed Luca. I knew that the situation was reaching a point of no turning back. This was further than we had ever taken our physical relationship.

This thought registered with me, but was then pushed aside by the feel of Luca's skin on mine. Out of sheer instinct, I reached down and grabbed the button on his shorts. He stopped and grabbed my hand.

"Violet, are you *absolutely* sure? I know we said we would wait. And Dexter..." Luca asked in a husky whisper. I knew all I had to do was say the word and he would stop. I was sure of it. This was why I loved him so much. He was always more concerned about my happiness than his own. And I did love him, which was why everything seemed so right. I looked up at his beautiful, kind face, eyes so full of love, and then to his bare chest and was suddenly very grateful that I had a superpower that made me able to see in the dark.

"I am beyond sure, Luca. Dexter has his earbuds in and he sleeps like the dead. There's nothing I want more right now than you," I told him, no trace of hesitation or reluctance in my voice. Those two things didn't exist. I tried to remember what reasons we might have had for wanting to postpone this, but not a single one came to mind.

"But, if you don't want to..." He didn't answer in words, but instead, he moved my hand back to where it had been before his pause. We both hesitated at the idea of what came next.

"Don't worry, I came...prepared," he breathed into my ear.

I found this funny. "Oh really. Was this your plan all along? Lure me into the woods and—" I said with a quiet giggle.

"No plan, just..." he struggled for words. I realized I'd made him feel self-conscious.

"I'm sorry Luca, I was being funny...well, apparently not very. It's okay, I appreciate that you cared enough to think about it. I actually came...*prepared* too. I have been prepared for a while now," I admitted and reached one arm out of the sleeping bag to grab a small zippered pouch near my head.

Then Luca laughed, a little too loudly. We both heard Dexter stir momentarily. I tossed the pouch, threw my hand over Luca's mouth and thought, *Shhhhh.* He laughed silently under the pressure of my hand. I couldn't help myself and laughed too. When I let go, he said silently, *So, who said we can't read each other's minds?*

That was enough talking for me. I abruptly cut off all of Luca's thoughts by pressing my lips to his and plunging willingly into the unknown.

I slept peacefully in Luca's arms the rest of the night, and not one sound from the *wild* outdoors got through to me. As the sun began to make an appearance, I opened my eyes to convince myself that I wasn't dreaming, and to my satisfaction saw nothing but Luca and the inside of the small tent that cocooned us snuggly. My head was on Luca's bare chest and I closed my eyes once again, so filled with pure joy and satisfaction that moving seemed like a chore. Then I heard a loud snore and remembered Dexter's existence in the other tent.

My eyes sprang open and a small, surprised sound escaped my lips. This startled Luca who then opened his eyes and blinked several times as the early morning light assaulted him. He knew exactly where he was though. He tightened his grasp on me. "What's wrong?"

"Dexter," I whispered. "I don't want him to know, not yet."

He smiled a relieved smile. "I'll get back in there before he wakes up."

"Thank you," I said as I laid my head back onto his chest. He kissed my hair and pulled me close. I had never felt such security and peace in my life.

A few minutes later Luca reminded me that he should get back to his tent.

"Oh right," I said. He unzipped the side of the sleeping bag and slid out, leaving me still mostly unclothed, lying dreamily on my pillow. I looked up at him, kneeling in the low tent, shirtless, buttoning his shorts. I smiled wide.

"What?" he asked.

"I'm just...*admiring* you. Is that okay?" I asked playfully.

"Oh. Well, admire away," he joked back. "I'd like to do some admiring too." He leaned down and peeked into the sleeping bag, as I fought him off weakly, trying to control my giggles.

"All right, just go already!" I said in a loud whisper. He threw on his shirt and kissed me tenderly and too long to convince me that he was serious about leaving. Before I allowed myself to get swept up in his kisses, I pushed him away and said, "GO!"

Love you, he thought to me.

You too, I replied. And then I was left alone in the tent to remember the previous night. I truly had not planned on what happened. I would have never invited Dexter if I had. But like everything with Luca had been so far, it was just *right.* And I wasn't sorry. There was no regret, no *morning after* remorse. I was glad, though, that I had prepared myself, knowing that my own self-control was weakening, and wanting to do the right thing when the inevitable happened. At least Mandy would be proud of me for that, though I had no intention of sharing this experience with my mother.

I replayed every detail of the night. The shroud of darkness had made it all seem surreal. But my heart and mind told me it was completely real. It was the first time for both of us, so there were no expectations to encumber us. It wasn't as easy as it seemed in movies. And yes, it hurt a little at first.

The pain was replaced with a completely new feeling, a warmth and completeness I had never known before. There was pleasure and happiness, pure desire and so much love. I didn't need to read his mind, there was no doubt about how Luca felt about me. And my love for him was close to uncontainable. It was so powerful that it was almost tangible. It seemed to have mass and take up space. The previous night had only solidified that love and proved to me what I had known almost since the first time we'd spoken: we were meant for one another.

I had heard girls at school talking, gossiping, “airing their dirty laundry,” as Mandy would say, about what they did and who they did it with. In some twisted way, I used to think that maybe I was jealous of a guy wanting them like that, but now I wondered how anyone would want to give absolutely all of themselves to someone for anything less than love.

23

I heard Dexter's booming voice, "I came to see some flying!" he yelled. I could make out his shape outside my tent.

"I'll be right there, Mr. Patience!" I called back. I scrambled to get dressed, brush my hair and teeth, and wash my face. All of this was accomplished using a small bowl of water. I felt like a real camper! When I thought I was presentable enough, I lumbered out of the tent, happy to be able to stand fully upright. I stretched and yawned, looking around. "Where's Luca?" I asked when I didn't see him in the open tent.

"Loverboy said he'd be right back," Dexter said sarcastically. "He was already up when I got up, so…did you sleep okay?" he asked. "No psycho-animal attacks in the middle of the night?"

"Funny!" I said sourly. I was getting *very* uncomfortable with this conversation. "How did you sleep?"

"Great. Put some music on, and I was in dreamland all night. It wasn't much different than when I used to sleep on your bedroom floor." He looked at me with a grin. "Remember?"

I relaxed. My secret safe. "How could I *not* remember? Just think, we used to be happy to sleep on the floor...weird," I mused.

Just then, Luca came walking back toward us. I may have imagined it, but he looked even more beautiful. He looked at me and said, "Good morning, Beautiful."

"Good morning," Dexter replied before I could say anything. "And enough with the nicknames already." Luca and I laughed at Dexter's little joke. I knew that humor had always been Dexter's way of coping, and I was glad he was at least coping.

"I believe I am the beautiful one he was referring to," I chided, cutting my eyes at Dexter.

"Yes you are," Luca affirmed as he leaned over to give me a quick kiss and a wink.

"Alright, enough with the love-fest already, let's see some cool stuff!" Dexter interrupted our moment, but both Luca and I laughed again.

"Okay, what do you want to see first?" Luca asked him.

"Oh, uh, I don't know. Let's see..." Dexter said sarcastically. "Oh yeah...FLYING! Duh! What could be better than that!?" Luca and I exchanged a secret smile.

I can think of something, Luca said to me only. I rolled my eyes.

"You sure you don't want to start small and build up to that? I don't want you to be disappointed when I toss a huge tree limb from one end of the clearing to the other," I joked.

"No, the fly—wait—can you *do* that?" he asked, a look of total astonishment on his face.

"Absolutely," I said nonchalantly, though truthfully I could probably only make it halfway across the clearing.

"Okay, so it's early, there shouldn't be anyone hiking yet, but we should still be careful," Luca said to both Dexter and me. I nodded in agreement.

"How about over by the tree line?" I pointed in the distance, to the far side of the clearing where the trails got much more difficult and there were always fewer hikers.

"Let's go," he smiled. Dexter was already moving. I had never seen him so motivated to do anything. It made me smile. Luca and I easily caught up.

When we got to our destination, I wasn't sure how to start, what to do. It felt awkward. Luca was ready.

"Okay Dexter, I hope it's all you expected." Luca took my hand

and for some reason, I felt compelled to close my eyes. Slowly, we began to rise. We were only a few feet off the ground when I realized something was wrong. At first I thought Dexter's widened eyes were simply a reaction to seeing me and Luca hovering above the ground. But when his look turned to one of panic, I knew it was more than that. I settled back down to the ground and his face was one of surprise.

"Dexter? Dex, what's wrong?" I asked him.

"Uh...Ummm. I..." He was unable to get anything intelligible out.

"I know at first it's a little weird..." Luca was trying to help, but Dexter had gone mute.

"Yeah Dex, you should have seen me the first time it happened." Nothing was working. "Okay well, maybe that's enough for tod—" I was saying when Dexter cut me off.

"NO! NO! You…you don't get it!" he yelled.

"Get what?" Luca and I asked simultaneously. Dexter was scaring me.

"You were gone," he said. Luca and I exchanged bewildered glances. I shrugged at him, and he raised his eyebrows at me.

"We only lifted a few feet off the—"

"NO! YOU. WERE. GONE! You disappeared." He was close to hysterics.

"Disappeared? What the hell are you talking about, Dexter? We never left this spot," I said with a nervous laugh. I was getting freaked out.

He grabbed my arms. "Violet! When you went… or right before, I'm not sure which, you disappeared from your feet up. Just vanished."

"But...but..." It was my turn to be hysterical.

"Dexter, I could see Violet. Are you sure?" Luca was trying to sound calm, but I could hear a strain in his voice.

"Luca, you were gone too," he explained. He was calming now. "Look!" He pulled out his phone because, of course, he'd recorded us. Sure enough, as we began to lift, we disappeared.

No one spoke for a couple of minutes. Each of us seemed to be processing this new piece of information. It was Dexter who broke the silence. "So you think if you carried me, I would disappear too?" Luca and I both looked at him in astonishment. What we saw was Dexter grinning with an excited gleam in his eyes. Apparently he had processed everything and determined that disappearing or not, mine and Luca's flying capabilities were still amazing and he wanted to be part of it.

"Dexter, you can't be serious?" I asked. "We just disappeared before your eyes and you want to be a part of that?"

"Hell yeah!" he said enthusiastically. At this I could do nothing but laugh. *This* was Dexter. Not the awe-struck mute from a few minutes before.

"O...kay," I said reluctantly. "Let's try." I was beyond reluctant to A, *carry* Dexter and B, take him into some disappearing act that I wasn't even sure how I performed.

"So, will you carry me?" Dexter asked. Of course it would be me and not Luca. That would be even weirder.

"Uh...yeah," I agreed. But the more I thought about it, the more I realized I probably didn't have to carry him. As he approached me, I held my hand up, "Wait."

"Come on V, I know carrying me is weird, but—"

"No, that's not it."

"What is it, Violet?" Luca asked curiously

"Well, maybe...God this is gonna sound really weird..." Now I didn't want to say my theory out loud.

"Go ahead," Luca encouraged.

"Alright. Well, I was just thinking that Dexter said he saw me disappear from my feet up. So, maybe our flying is more like a...I don't know..." I searched for the right words, "...like a bubble or something that engulfs us and lifts us up." Dexter and Luca were rapt. They nodded at me in unison.

"That sounds really...possible, Violet. And maybe we control it with our minds like the other stuff," Luca added.

"Yeah," Dexter agreed. His face told me he'd agree with anything at that moment.

"So," I felt a little more confidence building in me now, "Maybe if you just stand next to me, or hold my hand or something, I can just... *put* you in the bubble with me," I explained.

"If you don't want to carry me, all you had to do was say so," Dexter whined. I was about to tell him where to go when I saw his familiar sarcastic smile, so I just rolled my eyes.

"Do you think I'm right, Luca?" I asked. I suddenly wasn't so sure of my theory.

"I do," he said.

"But wait," Dexter interjected. "Didn't you say that you weren't sure how you flew, so how are you going to include me if you don't know how you're doing it?" *Damn.* Leave it to Dexter to find the first hole in my theory.

"I don't think it matters." Luca to the rescue! "Like all of our powers, flying just kind of happens, so maybe we don't have to really *think* about it. You know what I mean?" I did. But, Dexter didn't.

"Whatever, let's give it a shot. What's the worst that can happen, you have to carry me?" Dexter was really enjoying himself. I ignored him.

"Okay, so Dexter, come stand next to me and hold my hand."

"Gladly," he said with a smug smile.

"Or not!" I glanced at Luca, but his green-eyed monster was in check.

"Sorry. Okay, I'll be good," Dexter promised.

"Okay, so come hold my hand, and we'll just do the same thing we did before," I commanded.

Dexter stood next to me and took my hand. I wasn't surprised that his was a little clammy. I knew that Dexter liked to pretend everything was funny, but in the shadow of his first flight, he was nervous. I gave his hand a light squeeze. When he looked over at me, I smiled. "Let's go," I said and looked at Luca. He smiled and nodded. Within seconds, we were airborne. We were *all* airborne.

"Oh. My. God!" Dexter shouted. I looked at his face and it made me smile wide. We were about ten feet off the ground. To be holding someone's hand was kind of awkward because we were still in the same position we'd started in, standing, but without any ground beneath us. The few times Luca and I had practiced flying, we had *assumed the position*, turning our bodies so that we looked like superheroes. I turned to see Luca doing just that.

I instinctively knew I shouldn't let go of Dexter's hand, but if we were really in some sort of bubble, maybe his body would behave just as mine and Luca's did. So I said to Dexter, "If we are going to fly, let's do it right." While I maintained a hold of his hand, I thought about turning both his body and mine so that we appeared to be lying down. It worked! It was almost as if my mind controlled whatever was in my bubble with me. It was incredible.

Dexter's loud, "Whoohooo!" let me know that he felt the same.

No matter how many times I flew, it was never *not* amazing. But I remembered the first time I did it purposely, when Luca and I had come to this same place and experienced it together. So, I knew what Dexter was feeling. The exhilaration, the freedom, and even the fear. Because I knew that there was still fear behind all of the amazing stuff. I knew because I still felt it each time.

There was that idea in the back of my mind, "*How can I be flying? How is this possible?*" So, even when I was up there, I kept thinking that at any time, I'd just drop out of the sky because I knew that people couldn't just fly. Period. But, here we were...in the air, flying. Then I heard Luca.

"Dexter looks like he's having a good time," he laughed.

"Ya think?" I answered.

"What?" Asked Dexter, coming out of his awe for a moment.

"Oh, I was talking to Luca," I told him. That's when things got weird...well, *weirder.*

Dexter looked all around. "Oh I forgot about him, where is he? I didn't hear him."

I looked where Dexter was looking, which was right at Luca. "Dex, he's right there." I pointed with my free hand. "You can't see him, can you?" It was a rhetorical question. I knew that he obviously could not see Luca. Just because Dexter was with me didn't mean that he had the same abilities I did.

He shook his head. He didn't seem too bothered by this fact, so I decided not to be either.

Dexter can't hear me, huh? Luca asked. But like me, he knew the answer.

Nope, or see you, I answered. Then I smiled, *but he really doesn't care.* Luca laughed and we continued to fly higher and faster. As we flew I continued thinking about my theory and how I'd been right so far, so I decided to try something. "Dex, I'm gonna let go of your hand okay?"

"Huh? What?"

"Trust me. I think you're safe in here," I assured him, gesturing to the air around us.

"Okay," he said, but he sounded unsure. Slowly I released his hand. For an instant, I lost my faith in my own theory and I was sure I made a mistake and he was going to drop out of the sky. So I concentrated extra hard on keeping him inside of a bubble that I wasn't sure even existed. Then the unthinkable happened.

Dexter instantly began to plummet to the jagged, rocky ground a hundred feet below. There wasn't enough time to panic, only to scream. I swooped down, Superman-style, and grabbed his hand. It was enough to bring him safely back in.

Once our initial shock wore off, I turned to Dexter. "Oh my God, Dex, are you okay? I'm so sorry," I whined. Dexter laughed loudly.

"You saved my life!" he yelled.

"I almost ended it Dexter!" I countered.

"Oh, yeah, well, whatever. Forget it. I'm alive."

"Maybe we should get down," I suggested.

"NO! Not yet, please." He was determined to stay in the air.

Luca finally interrupted, *Everybody okay?*

Yeah, fine. I'm just freaked out. I think we should get him on solid ground.

Dexter looks just fine to me, Luca pointed out. I rolled my eyes at him.

Whose side are you on anyway? I asked.

He just laughed and flew ahead of us.

Dexter didn't know I was talking to Luca, but when he saw me look ahead, he must have figured that Luca had gone ahead of us. "Are you letting him win?" Dexter teased, "Let's race him." I just rolled my eyes in response.

"Unless you think you can't beat him. He's probably pretty fast," he goaded. I swallowed my anxiety, gripped Dexter's hand so firmly I saw him wince, and took off after Luca.

When we finally put our feet back on the ground, there was a permanent smile plastered on Dexter's face, and he didn't once stop looking at me. His look was more than admiration. It was reverence, and it made me feel awkward.

"Violet, I don't know what to say," Dexter said.

"Don't say anything," I tried to stave off his gushing. It didn't work.

"That was amazing!" he finally said, but then added, "No, it was beyond amazing. It was freaking...unbelievable!" He was almost shouting as he said this. I felt bad about initially trying to stop him from enjoying the experience, but it was my own fear and anxiety.

"When I was over in the woods, I saw some hikers, and I heard a few more a little ways off, so I guess we are done with flying for the day," Luca said when he could tell Dexter was about to ask for another round.

"Damn!" Dexter whined. He got all droopy and appeared to actually be pouting.

"I was thinking maybe we could go for a swim in the lake. What do you think?" Luca asked.

"So that's it? That's all for today?" Dexter sounded so dejected.

"Get over it, Dex. Now that we know a little more about how it works, we probably don't need to come all the way up here to practice." I explained.

His face lit up. "You mean we can do that anywhere because no one can see?!" It wasn't really a question.

Uh-oh. "Well, not *anywhere*. I mean, I think people would notice if you and Luca and I just, you know, disappeared," I explained, not wanting him to treat my powers like a carnival ride.

"True, but it does open up more possibilities!"

"So, swimming?" Luca asked again.

"Yeah, I could go for a swim," Dexter said. "I'm sure Violet's not going in though unless there's a pool somewhere out here," he smirked.

"Haha," I said dryly. "For your information, I actually went into the lake…once."

"For exactly forty-five seconds," Luca teased. Damn! They were forming an alliance.

I had to defend myself. "It was cold and slimy and something touched my leg!"

"Okay, it was not cold, and it was not *slimy*, and fish do *live* in the lake," Luca continued.

"Whatever, I don't feel like swimming anyway, but don't let me stop you two. I can just draw," I countered.

"Sounds good, let's go," Dexter said.

We packed up all of our gear and headed back down the mountain. Dexter had a much easier time descending, and after what he'd experienced, his step seemed lighter, springier. Something else was different too. I couldn't quite place it, but he seemed happier. It was great to see him and Luca getting along so well. I smiled thinking that maybe, just maybe, we'd finally navigated that chasm in our relationship.

We passed several hikers on the way down, but when we reached the lake there were far fewer people around. I quickly propped myself up against some of our gear while Dexter stripped to his boxers, and ran full-force off the small dock that stretched out onto the water. There was a brief scream after his big splash when he realized how frigid the water was. I was laughing until I took my eyes from the water and saw Luca getting undressed. I know it had only been hours since I had seen even more of him, but the sight of him pulling his shirt over his head still made my breath catch and my heart flutter.

"Would you please just hurry up and get in the water!" I teased.

He looked at me with playful seductiveness. *If Dexter weren't here...* he thought to me with a quick raising of his eyebrows. I just rolled my eyes and shook my head in mock annoyance. Gratefully, he opted to leave his shorts on. Luca bent down and kissed me before transforming into a five year old and racing headlong off the dock to join Dexter.

For the next couple of hours Luca and Dexter alternately swam, read, and ate while I sketched. It was truly amazing how well they were getting along. Dexter's attitude toward Luca had done a complete turn-around.

Here and there people would pass by on their way to the trails. A few even stopped to take a quick dip in the lake. But it was a big lake, so other than that, it was a quiet, peaceful afternoon.

Luca had just finished enjoying what he'd promised would be his final swim and was thumbing through a book, and Dexter was still in the water, when two hikers came up the trail that led to the lake from the parking lot and pull-off, and the mood suddenly shifted. They walked slowly, and something about them just wasn't sitting right with me. I couldn't explain it, but I didn't like how I felt. I looked up as they moved slowly past us. Luca and I were sitting cross-legged about ten yards from the dock. I didn't need to look up again to know they were backtracking and coming closer to us; I could hear their footfalls, as could Luca.

"Hi," said a man standing over us, only a few feet away. He looked to be in his early forties, tall, and he was sweating. He was dressed from head to toe in *real,* hiking gear. He reminded me of an ad for outdoor equipment—khaki shorts, green khaki, short-sleeved button-up shirt, and khaki vest with multiple pockets and a green, broad-brimmed hat with a string under his chin to keep it securely on his head. His boots looked brand new and his small backpack was clean and unscathed.

"Hello," Luca said apprehensively. I did not greet him. I simply looked up with what I imagined was a suspicious glare. The man's smile faltered just a bit.

Then he cleared his throat and continued. "We're a little lost," he said, nodding in the direction of his companion, another man, a bit younger and shorter who seemed to be trying to look at me and Luca without us knowing it. He wasn't doing a good job. Something about the way he studied me made me uneasy. He too was dressed in crisp, clean hiking gear.

"We heard there was a nice clearing nearby, and we've crisscrossed this path several times, but we can't seem to find it. Do you know how to get there?" he asked. I thought it strange that the man claimed to be lost when they were only a short distance into the trail from the pull-off. It was nearly impossible to get lost on this well-worn stretch of path. Besides that, I hadn't seen *or heard* them crossing the trail once. Of course, these two had no idea what good hearing and vision Luca and I had. As usual, Luca's thinking was in line with mine.

"No, sorry," Luca replied. I looked at him conspiratorially, knowing precisely why he had lied.

"Do you come here a lot? We've never been, but we were told the trails around this lake are spectacular."

"No, we don't really hike. We just come to the lake," Luca replied flatly. I hoped the men didn't notice our pile of gear a few feet away that would give away our lie.

"Well, thanks anyway, I hope we find it," replied the man.

"Yeah, good luck," Luca said and casually continued reading his book.

The two hikers disappeared onto the main trail leading away from the lake, back toward the road. It was strange that they hadn't continued on the trail into the woods.

That was weird, I said silently, just in case there was *any* possible way they could hear me.

Oh yeah, he replied.

Is that why you lied about the clearing?

Yeah. I mean, did you notice how new and clean their clothes were? Pretty weird for two people who have supposedly been hiking for a while, he answered.

I thought the same thing, I told him. *What do you think was really going on?* I asked. *I mean, do you think they were here for... us, or just...* I didn't know how to finish my question. I couldn't shake the feeling that they were absolutely there for us. Panic set in. Luca must have sensed my anxiety.

I really don't know, Violet. I was thankful that he respected me enough to not lie just to appease me. *Maybe we should just call it a day.* I nodded in agreement. I called out to Dexter and waved him in. He dragged himself to the shore.

"What's up with you two? Who were those guys you were talking to?" he asked when he saw the solemn expressions we wore.

"Not sure," I answered as truthfully as possible. "Can we go, and we'll talk in the car?"

Dexter looked confused and concerned. "Yeah, okay," he said. He got dressed and helped us grab our things. We quickly set off for the car.

There were two other cars at the pull out besides ours, one that had obviously been there for a while, and one that had arrived more recently. I could actually hear the engine cooling—ticking and sizzling—so I knew it had only been there for a few minutes. I curiously peeked into the windows while Luca and Dexter loaded our things into the back of the car. I gasped and nearly jumped when I saw what was inside.

"Oh my god!" I said. Dexter and Luca were at my side in seconds.

"What V?" Dexter asked, his voice thick with concern.

I pointed inside the car. "Look in the back."

Luca did as I said. "Damn!"

Dexter had a look too. "Yeah so? Bags. What's the big deal?"

It was a big deal because the bags were from an outdoor outfitters. There were also some tags for clothing lying on the back seat. I knew this must belong to the mysterious hikers. Instinctively, I looked around to see if anyone was watching us.

Luca had connected the dots and like me, began craning his neck in all directions.

Do you hear the car too? It hasn't been here very long, I told him silently.

You are really in tune with your hearing, aren't you? he asked, briefly turning his attention to me. We had realized that my hearing was more acute than his or that I was more in tune to my hearing capabilities than he was with his. We had batted around a few potential reasons, but I was convinced it was from the years of solitude that left me listening, always on the outside.

This is weird Luca, I don't like it, I said.

"Yeah," he agreed out loud. "Let's go," he reiterated.

"Yeah what?" Dexter asked. I guess we'd forgotten about him and that he didn't know about our silent communication.

"Dex, we need to go. We'll talk in the car," I said nervously. Dexter sighed. I knew he hated being on the outside of whatever was going on. I hated that he was being left out, but at that moment my fear and paranoia were more important than his hurt feelings.

We hopped in Luca's car and took off. Dexter just looked confused, but Luca and I were both nervous, though neither of us was sure exactly what we had to be nervous about. After a few minutes, Dexter obviously couldn't hold it in any longer, "What the hell is going on, Violet?"

In response to his question, or ignoring it all together, I asked the question that I was most afraid of knowing the answer to, the question that had been begging to be asked, "Luca, do you think they...*know*?" My voice was almost a whisper, as if I were trying to hide the question from someone.

"I can't say for sure, but it seems like they were looking for *something*...or someone. I just don't know if it was us," he said with an edge to his voice that confirmed that he was more nervous than he was letting on.

And then I said what my now panicked, paranoid mind was thinking, "I think they know."

"*Know?* Like know about you two and the super stuff?!" Dexter said in horror. I nodded, tears threatening.

"Okay Violet, let's not jump to conclusions. Those guys could've just been some weird guys from the city trying to play *outdoorsmen* for the day...you know, brand new hiking gear, no idea what they're doing..." Luca said, but he sounded like he was trying to convince the both of us, not just me.

"But how do you explain the car still making noise and the fact that they said they were crisscrossing the woods, when we CLEARLY would have heard them?" I was growing more anxious by the second.

"I guess I can't," he shrugged. "We can't worry about it though...we can't live in fear," he added.

"But it *is* scary," I stated, though I know it came out as a question. "To think that there could be people out there who know about us...it's unnerving...what does that even mean...how could they know?" We had no answers, so we just sat quietly.

"Do you remember the first time you took me to the clearing?" I asked.

"Sure," Luca replied with the faintest hint of a smile. How could he even think like that at a time like this? I ignored it.

"When we were...in the woods, after..." I couldn't believe *I* was doing it now. I was thinking of that amazing kiss, letting it flood my mind when we were potentially being found out. I shook my head to clear it. "Anyway, remember we saw the hiker behind the tree?" I could see him really thinking now.

"Yeah, but..."

I cut him off, "What if he saw us, Luca?" I asked quietly.

"Saw what? Who?" Dexter chimed in. I had all but forgotten he was in the car.

"When Violet and I flew together the first time, we *may have* seen a hiker, and we thought there was a remote possibility that he saw us," Luca answered.

"Yeah but we normal people can't see you, remember?" Dexter reminded us.

"You're normal?" I joked to ease my own tension. It helped because we all at least smiled.

"That's beside the point. The point is, no one else could see you unless they..." he stopped. I turned to look at him.

"Unless what?" I pressed.

"Unless they are like us." Luca answered flatly. We sat in stunned silence, letting that remote possibility sink in.

"Or saw you disappear," Dexter offered. "It's pretty freaky on this side of it."

My mind reeled. Our conversation was on the edge, the brink of *why* and *how* and inching toward opening an explosion of questions that we had no answers to. And despite all my previous attempts to avoid it all together, I was compelled to ask Luca, "Do you think there are more of us?" I knew it was a possibility. It seemed too odd that we were two anomalies, with the same abilities that just happened to find one another.

I regarded this as both a blessing and a curse. A blessing because it made me feel less alone and less freakish, comforted by the fact that there might actually be other people out there that had the same abilities as we have, could relate to what Luca and I were going through. It could be a curse though if it could make us more visible.

"I've always suspected...I mean we have talked about it..." he reminded me of one of the first lengthy conversations we ever had about our powers, the day of the car accident when he and I went for pizza. I did remember. Back then I was still trying to figure out what was going on, so the thought of *others* was intriguing, but way more than I could have handled at the time.

"Well, first of all, we don't know that that's the case...we don't have any proof. And if they did know about us...or are like us..." We all let that just hang there, no one willing to complete the sentence.

I caught sight of Dexter's expression in the backseat through the visor mirror. He seemed to be in deep thought. Then he asked, "So, what do we do now?"

"*We?*" I countered, eyebrows raised. I couldn't help but smile. Dexter's loyalty was unflinching. Even Luca smiled.

"Yeah, I'm all in, Violet. You should know that!" He sounded a little disappointed in me.

"I know," I replied with a sigh.

"I guess we just have to keep a close eye out for anyone acting suspiciously around us, following us..." Luca said.

"Do you think they'll follow us?" I asked fearfully, glancing over my shoulder to search the back window. Dexter did the same.

"I don't know, but if they *do* know anything about us, they would fear us—our strength," Luca said reassuringly. "Unless they are like us, in which case, maybe they are just trying to find answers," he added. How could he be so calm?

"Yeah. What if they are...*like you*...and they are interested in finding others too...it's not like they are just gonna walk up and say, 'hey do you guys have super powers?'"

"Dexter's right," Luca said sheepishly under my glare.

An interesting theory, definitely. It made sense. They wouldn't want to come right out and ask us if we had superpowers just in case they were wrong. This made me feel better for about a minute. But then I found the hole in this theory. I was suddenly very sure that they were not like me and Luca.

I shared it with Luca only. *Let's say there are more of us...don't you think that we'd be able to sense them or maybe receive thoughts from them...Like, maybe they'd test us by trying to send us thoughts or something.*

He considered my argument for a minute. *Maybe we can only hear each other*, he countered.

Maybe, I said, but I was doubtful. What I really believed was that we were not alone, and if we were not alone, then the others would be able to communicate with us in similar ways as we communicated with one another. But I didn't tell Luca this. In fact, we stopped talking about the hikers completely. All the way home, I continually turned around to look behind us.

24

When we pulled into the driveway, I was pretty sure that Luca was thinking about the strange hikers and the potential implications just as much as I was. He came around and opened my door. At this point in our relationship, I simply waited for him to open it rather than going through the charade of trying to open it myself.

Dexter was already out of the car and grabbing stuff from the trunk. "Later Luca, we'll talk," he said conspiratorially. I shot a look at both him and Luca, but Dexter ignored me.

"Yeah, later," Luca said.

"What was all that about?" I asked. "You two are best friends now or something?" I asked, sounding a little more like a snotty child than I'd intended.

"Maybe. He is without a best friend these days," Luca teased.

I rolled my eyes. "That's not funny," I protested. "But, I am glad you guys are friends now. Things feel...*different*, don't they?" I wondered if he sensed the difference in Dexter too.

"Yeah, they do," he said in agreement.

"You're coming in, right?" I asked expectantly. I just didn't want to let him go yet. I was still feeling really freaked out and didn't want him to leave yet.

"As long as you want me," he said with a wicked smile that made me forget the hikers and the questions lingering over us and made me only remember our amazing night together.

I kissed him gently in response. He embraced me tightly, and whispered in my ear, “We're going to be fine. I wouldn't let anyone near you.” I knew I had been right. He was still worrying about what happened with the hikers even if he appeared to be his usual calm, collected self.

I know, I told him. *That's why I love you.*

***

Mandy was in her room getting ready for work when we came in. Dexter had already made himself a snack and was resting comfortably on the couch. “You survived,” Mandy teased when Luca and I came in.

“Funny, Mandy!” I said, a little embarrassed by how everyone had expected me to just lose it out in the woods at night.

“I was actually talking about you, Dexter,” she said with a laugh.

“They were both great, Mandy. You would have been very proud of them,” Luca said.

"Thanks," Dexter and I both said sourly, while Luca smiled.

"I still can't believe you both slept all alone in the woods!" Mandy laughed.

I tried to keep my face from reddening, and I noticed Luca suddenly became very interested in whatever Dexter was watching on TV. I hoped Mandy's super-mothering skills and keen sense of *everything* didn't pick up on our behavior. I tried to react accordingly. I rolled my eyes and turned away to bring my things into my room.

When I came out, Mandy was just about ready to leave. “Honey, you look tired. You should try to get to bed early,” she said to me. I knew she was hinting at the fact that Luca and I probably needed a time-out.

“I will Mandy,” I promised when she leaned over and kissed the top of my head before repeating the action with Dexter *and Luca!* He looked at me sideways and smiled. I buried my face in my hands.

"Kill me now!"

"See you tomorrow. Oh and Luca, ask your mom if she wants me to bring anything for the cook-out." Mandy said, reminding me that Luca's parents had invited us all over for a family meet and greet. *"Oh no!"*

"I told her about your carrot cake, and she was hoping you might make that...I was hoping actually," he said shyly, looking so much like a little boy, it made me smile.

Mandy giggled. "Of course I will make it," and she ruffled his hair. "Bye guys."

Once she'd gone, Dexter said to Luca, "I guess she likes you." To my utter astonishment, there wasn't even a hint of jealousy in his voice. Luca smiled and then snuggled in closer to me on the couch.

"So, are we done talking about the weird stuff that happened today or what?" Dexter blurted out, just when my brain had finally begun to settle.

"Yeah Dex, I think we're done for today." I was done. Luca was disappointed, I could tell, but he didn't push the issue, and I appreciated that.

"Okay, whatever," Dexter sighed. He was never letting this go.

"Actually, I really need to go," Luca said. "My dad texted me when you were in the kitchen and he sort of *hinted* that maybe I've been gone long enough."

"Man, your parents and Mandy are gonna get along great!" Dexter laughed.

I walked Luca out, kissed him goodnight, and watched him drive away. Even though I knew I could talk to him whenever I wanted to, and I knew I would see him the next day, I felt a little pang of sadness when he left.

I returned to the house, wandered into the living room, and plopped down on the couch. Looking around, I felt both exhausted from our camping trip, and all that came with it, and restless in my thoughts. I was deciding if I should paint or just zone out in front of the TV. That's when I noticed what Dexter was watching. "Why are you watching this with the old antenna?"

"Wi-Fi is out again and my phone is charging" he explained through mouthfuls of chips.

"There's not even a cloud in the sky. When are they gonna fix this stuff?" I asked. Dropped cell calls and unpredictable Wi-Fi were not the end of the world, but it was annoying.

Then, out of nowhere, "V, can I ask you something and you have to promise not to get mad?"

I was reluctant. I did *not* want to talk about the hikers, but I agreed. "O...kay."

He hesitated before speaking, and then his face did something that I knew all too well—it turned pink. *"Uh oh!"* I thought, not sure what to expect.

"Did you and Luca... *you know*...last night?" He raised his eyebrows in case I didn't know what "you know" meant.

My face dropped. A flood of emotions washed through me: anger, disbelief, shock, more anger. *"Oh my god! Oh my god! Oh my god! How could he know? He was sleeping. Wasn't he sleeping?"* My mind began to replay the previous night, trying to find something, some noise that Dexter made that might indicate that he was awake. Of course I couldn't think of anything.

I turned around and pretended to be folding the blue throw that was draped over the arm of the chair where I was sitting. All I could do was stammer out the first thing that came to my mind. "Wh...wh...what are you talking about? Luca slept in a tent with you last night," I barely got out. I was a terrible liar, and if my bright red face didn't give me away, my stumbling words would. Besides, this was Dexter, and I could never lie to him whether I wanted to or not.

"V, I know Luca left the tent. I wasn't sure how long he'd been gone, but then I heard him come back in, and it was sort of getting light out so, I knew he'd been with you for a while," he explained. I listened for the anger and resentment, the jealousy and pain, but it wasn't there.

I got up and started milling around the living room, unable to stay in one place and unable to look at Dexter. I knew I was going to end up telling him the truth, and that scared me to death. I took a breath and continued.

"I was finally falling asleep, you know, getting used to the sounds, when I heard some kind of snapping noise," I said barely above a whisper, feeling the need to give him all the information. "I screamed and covered my mouth really fast, but not fast enough because in about ten seconds Luca was in my tent." Dexter laughed a little which made me pause in wonder. I thought maybe I could just end it at that.

Dexter had other ideas. "So, that's it huh? He just came in and scared the monsters away, and you guys fell asleep?" Was he trying to torture me?

"Well, uh...kind of," I answered evasively.

"Kind of? Either that's what happened or it's not," Dexter pried.

Guilt began to surge in me. So I did what I do when I feel bad, I got angry. "Why is this your business?" I asked defensively, almost shouting.

"It's not," he said and unpaused his movie.

I was fuming. I crossed my arms over my chest and stomped into my room, slamming the door with super-human force, shaking the entire house. Sleeping with Luca was the most amazing experience of my entire life, and Dexter was ruining it. I took out my sketch book and called Luca.

Hi Violet, I wasn't expecting to hear from you already. What's up? Miss me already? Luca asked with a laugh. I let the shimmering blue light fill my head and wash away my anger.

I just wanted to say hi, I explained.

I don't believe you, what's wrong?

"Damn!" I thought only to myself. *"I can't hide anything from anybody!"*

Dexter knows, I said.

Knows? Knows what?

I didn't answer. I knew if I stayed silent long enough, he'd get it. He did.

Oh.

Yeah, I replied. Another long pause.

Are you sorry? he asked.

NO! I mean I wish Dexter hadn't been there, but no, I have absolutely no regrets, I assured him. It was true. I was angry and felt guilty, but I was not sorry.

Good because that would make me sad. Last night was... he paused, *even better than flying.*

It definitely was. I smiled at the memory of it.

So was he really pissed off? Luca asked.

Nope.

No? What did he say? I could hear the surprise in his voice.

He just asked if we did. He said he knew you weren't in the tent for a long time, I explained.

What did you tell him?

I told him that it was not his business, which is basically an admission of guilt.

But he wasn't angry?

No. I stopped and thought about Dexter's reaction. In retrospect, I had been the only irrational one in the room. *It was weird actually.*

Then Luca asked me a question I didn't want to answer. *So what are you going to do now?*

I don't know! I whined.

I think you should talk to him. If he wasn't mad, maybe he just wants to talk to you…like friends.

I groaned. I didn't know if Luca could hear that or not.

Listen Violet, if he knew all along, think about how good things were on the camping trip. He was really cool with me and seemed happier than I've ever seen him, Luca reasoned. He made a lot of sense.

You're right as usual. I'll talk to him.

I love you, he said.

Love you too.

As I was about to get up to talk to Dexter, there was a knock at my door. I guess Dexter and I were still more in sync than I thought. "Come in," I said, trying to remove the anger that still lingered in my voice.

He opened the door and stood in the doorway, seemingly afraid to cross the threshold and sustain my wrath. "It's okay," I told him, "I'm done being mad at you." He smiled a little but still entered cautiously.

"I wanted to apologize." Those weren't the words I expected to hear. I expected some humility, but not an apology.

"I freaked out. Why are you apologizing?" I sighed.

"Because, you're right, it's not my business." He paused as if he was trying to form his words carefully. "It's just that there was a time when you would've told me when important stuff happened to you. Even when your powers started, I had to find out by accident."

And there was the guilt again. "Dex, you know why I didn't tell you about the powers...and as far as stuff between me and Luca, I didn't think that was a subject you wanted to hear about."

"I know. But, the truth is, even if I do have some...*unresolved* feelings..." he smiled, "well, that's my problem and we've been more than just friends forever, so I guess I want you to be able to still tell me stuff," he admitted.

"Are you sure?" I asked, still skeptical. The old Dexter would say all these mature things, then throw everything in my face when he felt hurt. He seemed different though. I was beginning to believe this new version of Dexter.

"Yes, Violet. I am not going to freak out. I promise," he said.

"You are different, aren't you? Luca and I both noticed it while we were camping," I admitted.

"Yeah. I don't really know what changed, but I guess I had a kind of epiphany."

"Big word," I teased, but then more seriously I added, "What was this epiphany about?"

"Well, first I realized that I was a much happier person when you and I were friends—real friends—and even if I can't just switch off my other feelings, I can behave better and remember that I care a lot about you being happy."

"*WOW!*" I thought to myself. I couldn't believe he was saying these things! "That's very..." I searched for the right words, "...mature and kind and *Dexter-ish* of you," I chuckled. He laughed too.

"I don't know how 'Dexter-ish' it is, but it should be," he admitted.

"It's the Dexter I used to know," I reassured him. Dexter had always been kind to me anyway, and Mandy, even if he hated the rest of the world.

"Well thanks. I think you give me more credit than I deserve, but I'll take it," he said. "So, wanna talk...like friends?" He was serious.

I was still apprehensive. "You're sure? You want to hear it? Whatever it is?" I asked, bracing for the change in his face that might give away his true feelings. It never came.

"Yes! I'm sure!" he said, feigning irritation.

I let out a long breath, preparing myself to say the words out loud. "Yes, we *did*," I said awkwardly. He and I both knew what I was referring to. I studied his face, still waiting for it. Again, it didn't come.

"Whoa! You slut!" But he was laughing, not insulting me. This was my Dexter. I laughed with him. Although he wasn't getting off the hook that easily.

"Hey! You can't say that to me!" I jokingly protested. Then his laughter subsided and his face was serious again. *"Oh no! Here it comes!"*

"So, are you okay? I mean, I know for you this is a really big, huge deal." He really did care!

"I really am. I'm better than okay. I have never felt so...content and loved." I had to tone down my gushing. Even if Dexter was sincere, I didn't want to stick the knife in *and* give it a twist. He didn't say anything for a minute, and I was afraid I had said too much.

"Well, I'm glad at least that it was a good experience for you. A lot of girls don't get that, right?" he said and then added, "and, I'm glad it was Luca, because I thought I cared about you, but that's the other thing I realized during the trip, that guy *seriously* loves you. He's got it bad." Dexter smiled.

"I know." I wrinkled my nose and added, "me too." Somehow this was more embarrassing and intimate than talking about the sex part.

Then Dexter did the most uncharacteristically, un-Dexter-y thing, he sat on the edge of my bed next to me and hugged me. This was not an, "I love you, but you don't love me," hug. This was a true, "I love you like my friend, my sister," kind of hug, so I did the only thing that felt right, I hugged him right back with everything that I had in me. Then I started to cry like a baby. I was sniffling and slobbering into his shoulder. I could almost hear his eyes rolling. He didn't push me away, but he kept holding me.

"Okay Violet, this is a good thing, stop crying."

I pulled away, and said through the snuffles and whimpers and tears, "That's why I'm crying. I am so happy. Everything finally feels normal again…well, sort of."

When I looked at him, he didn't even try to hide the tears that had welled up in his eyes too. Then I was crying into his shoulder again. We held each other for a few long minutes, reclaiming our bond and our friendship.

Eventually, we separated and talked a little more. He admitted how much he liked Luca even though at first he wanted nothing more than to hate his guts. I explained to him how that's just not possible with Luca because there's nothing to hate. He grudgingly agreed.

"He likes you too, you know. Really. Not just for me. I mean it was important to him that you two got along for my sake, but he genuinely likes you," I explained.

"I know he does. That's weird," he laughed. "Nobody likes me." He laughed again.

"You're wrong, and you know it. I mean if you're talking about the 'cretins' at our school, then you're probably right." I laughed now. "But people who know you, people who mean something, we love you."

His shoulders shook once like he was laughing, but the laugh barely touched his face. "Thanks," he said. "Look, I'm tired. All the physical activity from today has exhausted my lazy ass. I'm going to bed."

He got up to go, but then turned around with a wicked smile on his face. "*You* should be damn near dead from your lack of sleep *and* excessive physical activity!" he teased.

I jumped up and punched him in his arm, really hard. Too hard. He almost crumpled to the ground. I grabbed him and held him up. I didn't want to laugh, but he was, and I couldn't help myself.

"I am so sorry Dex!" I said between my laughter.

"No you're not!" he argued through his own laughter. "You are a superhero AND a super-*bitch*!"

That got him another punch, but this time a more controlled one that wouldn't send him to the floor. When we were finally done laughing, he said, "Goodnight V." Just like the good old days.

"Goodnight Dex, and sorry again." I don't think I sounded very apologetic.

"Ah it's just another one of those things I'll have to get used to." He smiled one last time and left, closing my door behind him. I let out the longest sigh ever. I couldn't believe what had just happened. Dexter and I were friends again AND he knew I slept with Luca. Could I really be this lucky?

After I got ready for bed, I told Luca everything that transpired between Dexter and me. I told him about Dexter's admission to liking him, and that I actually told Dexter about *us.*

How did he take that part?

He said he was glad it was a 'good experience' and glad that it was with you because he... I felt embarrassed saying the next part.

Because why? Luca pressed.

Because he could see how much you love me, I finally said.

He's right.

I know. A long pause.

So, a 'good experience' huh? Sounds like a trip to a museum or community service. I could hear his laughter.

Those were his words, not mine, I said.

We haven't really talked about it since it happened. What are your words? he asked.

My thoughts about the night before were like my paint pallet after I'd been painting all day. The swirl of color was beautiful but indescribable because it was nearly impossible to separate out the individual colors. My emotions were the same, a blur of love, desire and pleasure. It was difficult to sort them out into a coherent statement.

Last night was... my words were failing me because there were none strong enough to describe our first time together.

Perfect? he answered for me.

More. I felt...I feel...whole.

When he finally responded, it was one of his classic, bare-all, Luca statements that made my tears swell. *I've known for a long time that I loved you, but I didn't know how much until last night.*

I didn't know anyone could love me as much as you showed me you do, I replied.

Then Luca lightened the mood by adding, *Maybe next time I can try even harder*. Though I giggled, my stomach knotted as I thought about "next time."

We'll see, I said. *Goodnight Luca.*

Goodnight Violet.

That night, no strange mother, no bullies, no weird hikers, no freakish superpowers, nothing could ruin the complete bliss I felt as I drifted to sleep knowing that at least for that moment, everything in my life was perfect.

25

A few days later, I pulled my bike into the driveway after having gone to get some paint, and I got a surprise when I felt Luca's presence and saw Luca's car. He'd told me that he had to work at the shelter, and I wasn't going to see him until that night. I almost skipped inside. As I got closer to the door, I started to hear Luca and Dexter talking. This elevated my happiness. I loved knowing that Luca and Dexter were really becoming friends. That was until I caught a fragment of their conversation and lingered outside to hear a little more.

"So, you don't think she'll go for it?" This was Dexter.

"No, and I don't want to push her. This whole thing is a lot for her to handle with Mandy's history and..." I was glad Luca was at least being sensitive to my feelings.

"Jesus Christ! She has to get over that someday. Okay, Mandy believes she was abducted by aliens and isn't afraid to say it! So. What?!" My anger almost made me burst through the door. Almost. I had enough restraint to know that I should keep listening. I wanted to hear Luca defend me.

"She will Dexter. It's been hard for her. You know that." That was my Luca.

"But dude, you've got to *want* to know? Don't you?" I was beginning to wonder who was more interested in finding answers, Luca or Dexter.

"Of course I do, but I can't force her," Luca explained.

"Who said to force *her?* Can't you find out? Didn't you say that she told you it was cool if you researched and checked into stuff?"

"Yeah, and I have a little, but I think she was humoring me." Luca gave a little laugh. Did he really think I was just humoring him, that I would freak out if he looked into our *situation?* Then a more horrifying thought occurred to me: Was I humoring him? How would I react if he found some substantial evidence or wanted to really talk about what was happening to us? I should have gone right in, stopped sneaking around and eavesdropping, but I didn't. I kept listening.

"Look, some of this stuff we found is pretty credible. I mean that stuff I found about the sightings and then that guy, he's like some kind of underground guru!" Dexter said, and I heard the rustling of paper. "*We! We! They were working together? Since when had Luca and Dexter become a 'we?'*" I knew I couldn't stand much more. I was going to give Luca a chance to respond, and then I would let them have it!

"I know. I really want to go check that guy out, it's only like two hours from here, but I can't lie to her and I also can't make her come with me. I don't want this to come between us." My anger toward Luca subsided a little as he displayed his loyalty.

"You got it bad!" Dexter laughed. My anger returned! "Lucky for you, V has it just as bad. She is gonna get mad, but she'll get over it. She loves you so much...it's... it's sickening actually." He laughed again. Was this all just a big joke to him? I wanted to go in there and use my super-strength to show him just how mad I was. Until that moment, I had found Dexter's persistence endearing, but now I wanted him to shut up and leave Luca alone, but he wasn't finished pushing his pointy nose where it clearly didn't belong.

"Luca, let's be honest here, you and me, and I think even V, we *know* what's going on, we just need to verify some stuff and get the evidence we need to be sure."

"I don't know. I guess I do wish she would at least entertain the thought..." No, not Luca too!

"Maybe if you and I figure it all out, and then kind of present it to her together, she can't deny it. She'll have to face it." Dexter was becoming more selfish by the second. He wanted all of this for himself, not for me. I hoped Luca would see that.

"Maybe, but I think it might just make her more angry," Luca said. At least he could still see reason.

"Well, it's up to you. If it were me..." That was it. I lost it. I launched myself through the front door and right at Dexter. I stopped inches from his face.

"IT'S NOT UP TO YOU!" I screamed.

"V—what—where—?" He stumbled over his words. Luca was already on his feet and by my side. My anger, his anxiety and Dexter's shock and fear made for a toxic environment.

"Shut up Dexter, just shut the hell up!" I was still shouting. Luca gently but firmly grabbed my arm.

"Violet," he said soothingly, "calm down. Please." I didn't respond. I knew if I turned and looked in his eyes, I would be done, and I wanted to finish this. I wrenched my arm away from him and inched closer to Dexter. I began poking him in the chest, forcing him to back up.

"You think my superpowers are so 'bad ass'? You want to see how destructive I can be? Stephanie Baker isn't the only one who can piss me off enough to use them! Especially when you completely betray me and start thinking about your own crap and what *you* want to know! Forget about me, the one who is actually dealing with it!" I had never been so violent and threatening in my life. I was frightening myself. Luca was there again. This time his voice was louder, more forceful.

"Enough Violet. You're going to feel bad if you hurt him," he said. He was right. I knew it. His words mixed with my own fear made me stop and think about what I was doing. Then my rage turned to tears. I turned to Luca.

"How could you?" I asked him. Suddenly I felt so alone and betrayed.

"Violet, I—" he tried to explain, but I didn't let him.

"Luca, I know I've asked a lot, but you went behind my back and..." I looked to Dexter, "...conspired against me!" I cried.

"No one was conspiring, Violet," Luca said quietly.

"Violet, why don't you just get over it already! Stop crying like a damn baby because your mommy embarrassed you. You think you're the only one whose parents aren't the people you wish they were? You think you're the only one whose life hasn't turned out the way you planned?" Dexter was coming at me now. "Grow the hell up, Violet!" he yelled then paused. In a much calmer tone he added, "Maybe if you would just deal with what's going on, you could be a stronger person for it. I'm tired of always being strong for both of us."

Then he turned away from me. I thought he was done, but he still had one last thing to say. He turned back to me. "You say you love Luca so much. If that's true, why don't you stop forcing him to prove he loves you by denying him what he really wants to know...the truth."

Dexter's words were like punches in the gut. I actually clutched my abdomen with one hand while I reached for the stability of the wall with the other. Everything he said was one hundred percent true. And the truth hurt, especially since I was completely unprepared to face it because even though I knew it was true, it didn't instantly eradicate the feelings of hurt and betrayal. Instead it joined with those feelings and made me even more irrational.

"Violet? Violet are you..." Luca's voice seemed far away, like it had to fight its way through the thoughts swarming through my overwhelmed brain. "I'm sorry. I shouldn't have—" he didn't finish. He sounded strange, almost scared. But at that moment I was still selfish Violet, betrayed Violet, irrational Violet. I wanted to wallow in self-pity and pain. So, I reacted poorly. Again.

"I don't want to hear it right now," I cried through the tears that were flowing in thick streams down my face.

"Just let me explain," he pleaded.

"Not now!" I said. "You lied, and you and Dexter—" I didn't have to finish. He knew what I meant. You and Dexter conspired against me. You and Dexter kept me in the dark. You and Dexter betrayed me.

"Please Violet, I didn't mean to lie and Dexter, he just helped me research a little. That's all, I swear..." I thought I heard tears in his voice, but I couldn't look at him to confirm.

Then I whispered words to Luca that I never thought I'd say, and which I regretted as soon as they'd left my mouth, "I think you should go."

He didn't protest. "Okay. If that's what you want." Before walking away he said, "I love you."

I listened to his footsteps trudge to the door. I heard the door squeak open. There was a pause, and I imagined he'd stopped to look back and see if I'd come to my senses. I hadn't. My stubbornness wouldn't allow it. Then I listened as the door closed and Luca got into his car and left. I could hear his car until it turned onto Fleming Avenue and blended in with the rest of the traffic.

And I was left alone with my depleting anger and the many truths I was still unwilling to face.

I swallowed my pride long enough to answer him when he thought, *I love you, Violet* before he went to sleep.

I love you too, I replied, unable to say or think anything else.

I cried myself to sleep, in agony over the way I had left things with Luca. So when I woke up the next morning, I decided I had to try to make things right. Admittedly, I was still pretty angry with Dexter. It was easier to stay mad at him, but I justified it by telling myself that he was being selfish and not really thinking about me. Even if some of the things he'd said were accurate, he went about all of it the wrong way, trying to lure Luca to his side. It was simple. It felt like he was against me, and I had never felt that before. So, it would take some time for me to forgive him.

I quickly got dressed and headed to Luca's on my bike. I had to apologize in person. When I got there, his car wasn't in the driveway, and I hadn't felt his presence. Maybe he had gone to run an errand or skate or work at the shelter. I went to the door. Though I was nervous about what I had to do, I was comfortable enough now to go to the door and talk to his parents. I had even had lunch with Gina once when Luca was working, and I went over to borrow a book.

I rang the doorbell. Gina answered with a big smile. "Violet, what a surprise!" She leaned over and hugged me.

"Is Luca here?" I asked, trying to keep my tone sunny and light.

"No, sorry sweetie," she said with a frown. "He left this morning. He's going hiking up near the Catskills for the day. I thought you'd be with him," she added suspiciously.

I didn't want Gina to see that this had come as a huge blow, so I recovered as best as I could, "Oh...I forgot it was today. I just...I couldn't go...I um...I had stuff to do today. But thanks."

When I got back home, I tore through the front door, nearly ripping it from the hinges, my super-strength an afterthought. Anger pulsed through me. No, not anger exactly, or not the anger I originally believed it to be. I had thought I was angry with Luca. But, deep down, I knew my anger was just that irrational rage that isn't ever really directed *toward* anyone in particular. I was just completely enraged at the situation, at the ridiculousness of it all, and at the complete and total helplessness I felt.

I knew I was being unfair. Hadn't I been the one who told Luca that he should keep looking for answers if he felt the need to? I suppose if I was being truthful, I had sort of envisioned he'd say something like, "I don't need to know anything else Violet. I have you and blah, blah, blah…" or something equally romantic and ridiculous! I was clearly delusional. And selfish. Who wouldn't want to know? Well, besides me? And even I couldn't lie and say that I wasn't remotely *interested* because I was. But, I was more frightened of what I'd find out. Or which parts of my own theories would be confirmed.

I was so wrapped up in my anger that even with my unparalleled eyesight, I didn't notice Mandy on the couch when I came in. I hurled my backpack to the floor, where it slid to a stop against the wall, creating a small indentation near the baseboard and rattling the entire entryway.

"Could you be careful not to break the entire house?" Mandy's calm, almost playful voice stopped me like I'd hit a brick wall.

"I…I…" I stammered, unable to form a sentence. I hadn't expected her to be home. Normally at this time she was at work, and since I hadn't seen her car in the driveway, I was doubly surprised. The sudden shock of seeing her startled me out of my angry state and left me standing dumbly, my chest heaving as my breaths came heavily, a byproduct of the temper tantrum I'd been having. "What are you…why aren't you at work?" I asked. "I—I didn't see your car."

"I gave away my shift to Anne," she said. "You remember Anne? The nice woman who gave me that old bench for the backyard," she added without much of a pause, leaving me no room to respond with anything more than a nod while she hurried into her next sentence. "She needs the money," she quickly added, sounding almost like she had rehearsed her words. It was obvious that she was trying to sound like there was nothing out of the ordinary, but it wasn't working. Besides, Mandy and I both knew that she never, ever, gave away a shift. She never took a sick day.

In fact, a few years back she had the flu and Dexter and I both begged her to stay home because she looked so bad. We even hid the keys! But, she dragged herself into work. Her supervisor took one look at her and sent her home. She had the next two days off, willed herself to get better, and returned to her regular schedule. "And my car is getting fixed *again!* It hasn't been the same since the accident, I may have to consider a new one, but I really don't want to spend the mon—"

I cut off her rambling. "Yeah right," I said, finally able to get a word in. "You've never given up a shift, and you know it," I continued forcefully, the anger that had waned now returned because my mother was lying to me. "What's really going on?" I asked directly. Then I looked right into her bright green eyes, and saw nothing but love and concern. This softened me, but my tone let her know I was not taking any more weak excuses.

She looked away from me for a second and forced out a long, deep breath, seeming to prepare herself for what she was about to say. I waited, not patiently, but I waited, tapping my foot, arms crossed, breath coming in short, exasperated puffs from my flaring nostrils.

"Okay Violet, I stayed home because we need to talk," she said with a sigh. I got the feeling she wasn't exactly thrilled about whatever it was she had to say to me. I cringed at the thought of what it might be. She couldn't *know* anything, could she?

"About what?" I asked defensively. I was trying to play it off, but I came out sounding like a snotty kid.

"Violet, where's Luca?" she asked in a tone Mandy rarely ever used.

I was dumb-struck again. My mouth opened and closed a few times, but nothing came out. I imagined I must look like a fish out of water, gasping for air.

"And Dexter?" she continued without letting me answer her first question.

I looked around. Where *was* Dexter? I let my super-hearing range out around me, listening for his familiar sounds, and those subtle ones I had come to learn with the onset of my powers: the muffled music of his earbuds, the tapping of his hand on his thigh, his slightly rattly breathing due to mild allergies. I heard nothing.

So, Dexter wasn't home? So what? He could just be working or avoiding me (which was a good idea considering the fact that I wanted to tear him to shreds and was one of only two people I knew who could do it, literally).

"Luca is...he's...he's not here!" I spit out. Saying these words brought tears to my eyes and new anger because crying in front of anyone, particularly Mandy, was not something I did. And I had already done it once in front of Luca. Twice in one day was unacceptable. But I kept on. "I thought Dexter was here, but frankly I don't care where the hell he is!" That was the truth.

"Violet, I know you are angry with both of them right now, and though you don't want to admit it, I think you know where they are, even if you don't want to tell me," she said softly. "The real question is, why aren't you with them?

My mind reeled. "What? How? *They*? *Them*! Dexter and Luca were together?" They *had* conspired against me. My rage reached a point that I didn't recognize. Red tinged the corners of my vision. My face burned. My jaw clenched and unclenched of its own accord. Every muscle in me tightened. I felt like a piece of elastic stretched to the breaking point.

Mandy got up from her comfortable position on the couch, a position that hadn't shifted much from the moment I walked in. She glided over to where I stood like a pressure cooker, ready to blow. Hesitantly, she touched my arm, and when she did, that feather-light touch might as well have been a jackhammer. My defenses fell, crumbling around me. I stood before her, shattered.

She pulled me into her arms and squeezed me harder than she had since I was six years old, and I lost it. A jagged torrent of tears and indecipherable sounds and snot poured out from the core of me. She held me for a long time. At some point we moved to the couch, but I don't remember it happening. I do remember her stroking my hair and whispering that everything would be okay. I didn't believe her. How could anything ever be okay again?

Eventually the tears began to slow as the fatigue of crying set in. My breath steadied a bit, and my mind began to clear. She pulled away from me and looked at my swollen, red face. She smiled. "Can we do this now?" she asked. She wasn't pressing me; she was kind and spoke softly. I knew what she meant. She wanted to know if I was ready for it, whatever "this" was. The anger and fear and pain that had exploded from me like a volcanic eruption had mellowed. I was as ready as I ever could be for what she had to say. I slowly slipped out of her arms and sat up a little straighter. I took a shaky breath, wiped the dried up tears from my face with the back of my sleeve and nodded. But before she could begin, I said something to her that needed to be said.

"I'm sorry, Mom," I mumbled in a whisper.

She smiled a big, sad smile, her eyes now filled with tears. "Oh Violet. My beautiful, amazing Violet, you don't have to apologize for having emotions. It's what makes you human." Then her face changed almost imperceptibly. But I saw it when she said the word "human." It was as if she had said something she hadn't meant to say. She blinked once and recovered her smile, thinking I hadn't noticed. I wished I hadn't.

I cleared my throat, "So, you wanted to talk?" I wanted this over with. I had started thinking about Luca and how badly I needed to tell him I loved him and that I was sorry. I didn't know if I was out of telepathic range, but it didn't matter. What I had to say had to be said in person, out loud.

"Violet, I don't know the specifics, but for a long time now I have suspected that something is going on with you, something I can't quite understand. Do you know what I mean?" she asked. I had to say something. But how much? What should I tell her? If I said too much, I ran the risk of hearing her theories which were potentially closer to the truth than I was ready to admit.

"Yes," was my answer.

"And Luca knows too. Right? Maybe he even has something to do with it?"

"Yes," I decided to stick to as many one-word answers as possible to avoid saying too much.

"Violet, I said that I have known your whole life that you were *different*. I don't just mean your personality or your amazing artistic ability. I mean, you. Are. Different," she emphasized these last words to let me know that she was, to a greater extent than I realized, wise to what was going on. She continued, "I think I've known something since you were little, and you never really got hurt. Hell, you were pulling yourself up in your crib at three months old. That's not normal."

I looked down. Her last statement sliced through me like a blade. She wasn't done. "And then that thing with Carol at the car accident. Violet I know you didn't get her out like you said. Men twice your size couldn't budge her door, and the steering column was pushed forward." I looked up at her. She really had known for a long time. I felt a rush of panic and anxiety. My breath started coming faster. Mandy reached out and rubbed my back.

"I'm not saying this to upset you. I just want you to know that I love you, no matter who you are and I want you to know that you don't have to go through this alone."

I responded on instinct. "I'm not alone. I haven't been. I have Luca. And Dexter." But after I said it I thought about the argument Luca and I had and my anger toward him and Dexter and the tears threatened to return.

"Violet, Luca and Dexter love you so much, and so do I. Stop pushing us away just because you don't want to deal with the truth," she commanded gently.

"What do I do Mandy? I'm not even sure what's going on. *What* I am!" I shouted.

She didn't even hesitate, "I think you know exactly what you are," she said directly.

"That's what I'm afraid of!" I screamed and the tears came back.

Again Mandy held me for a long time. When I eventually started to feel a little more sane, there were so many thoughts racing through my mind, but I couldn't stop to pay attention to any single one until Mandy said the one thing that could focus my attention. "Violet, Honey, we have a lot to talk about, and you have a lot to think about, but the most important thing right this second is for you to go to Luca." She quickly added, "And Dexter."

I quickly raised my head. "Luca," I whispered. "I have to find him," I said desperately, replaying my tirade from the day before. I had behaved so poorly, so irrationally.

"Then go," she insisted. "I assume you know *how* to get to him?" she asked as if once again she was letting me know that she knew more than she was telling me. I had to ignore that for now. I had to get to Luca. Nothing else mattered. I nodded, stood up, shook off my scattered thoughts, and left through the back door.

I didn't know if Mandy followed me, and truthfully, at this point, it didn't really matter. For all I knew, she was aware of my flying abilities. Even if she wasn't, Mandy was tough, always expecting the unexpected, so watching me disappear might throw her for a second, but she'd deal with it. Still, I went to the most secluded spot that I could find in the backyard. I automatically tuned into Luca, let my thoughts go to him and focus only on him, and when I did, I could sense him. I knew I could find him. Then, I took off.

26

As I surged through the air, it was as if there were a rope attaching me to Luca, leading me right to him. As long as I stayed focused on finding him, I knew I would get there. When I was very close to Luca, I knew he would know I was looking for him.

I came over a bank of trees and spotted Luca's car. It was pulled over on the side of a road that seemed to be nearly deserted. I knew he was aware that I had come because he looked up to where I was still hovering, using his hand to shield his eyes from the sun. He smiled reassuringly, and I knew things would be okay. I looked around to make sure no one was around to see me suddenly appear out of nowhere when I landed. I set myself down gently behind a giant oak tree that was only a few yards from the car.

All I had thought about was getting to Luca and saying I was sorry, but now that I was there, my stomach twisted and flipped and my mind was blank. Luca didn't give me time to walk to him. He raced over to me and had me in his arms in seconds.

"Please don't hate me, Violet," he pleaded into my hair. "I wasn't running *away* from you. I'm running toward something...something I *need* to know." There was silence. I couldn't answer him. Hate him? *Hate* him? What could he mean?

"Violet?!" he spoke urgently and held me back so that he could look at me. He kept his hands gently on the tops of my shoulders. "Please talk to me...just don't hate me...please...I love you. I was stupid." I registered that the last few words came out almost like a whimper.

It took me a second to realize that he was pleading with me. Did he actually believe that I could feel anything at all but total and unconditional love for him? Of course he did. I had behaved so childishly...so selfishly. Now I was saturated with guilt. I had to answer him, and relieve his pain, but I was so ashamed that I couldn't even look at him. So I looked at my shoes and said what had to be said.

"I could NEVER, NEVER hate you. Do you understand? The thought..." I had to pause and get the anger I felt for myself in check "I mean, to think that I actually let you conceive that I could have anything but love for you is...is..." Though my words began to shake and my eyes welled with tears, I had to look up at him. It would be an even bigger crime not to look him in the eye to say this. "...it's sickening. I am ashamed of myself," I said with conviction.

He reached his hand to my cheek and wiped away a tear that rolled down. My anger swelled. I did not want him to feel sorry for me. I wanted him to be angry with me and tell me I *was* selfish. But, this was Luca, and this was why I loved him. Because I knew that he loved me the same way I loved him. Unconditionally. I reached up and wiped my teary eyes with the back of my sleeve. He stood there patiently, waiting for me to get myself together. I swallowed hard. I had more to say before he tried to say anything nice to me.

"I know it isn't fair that I tried to hold you back from learning the truth," I admitted. "A small piece of me—a *very small* piece—is curious too." His eyebrows jumped up slightly. "Luca, I have never been more sorry. Never."

His look of astonishment said everything. He definitely had not been prepared for my submission. Anger, yes, but acquiescence, absolutely not.

"Why are you apologizing? *I* lied. *I* left. *I* went behind your back. I even enlisted Dexter as an ally," his voice was filled with remorse.

"Luca! Stop!" I said more loudly and forcefully than I had planned. I just couldn't continue to let him berate himself. "Okay, the Dexter thing was low, and I am not going to say that the lying didn't hurt." This admission made him wince. I had to recover quickly. "BUT..." I added with force and then softened, taking his right hand into both of mine. "...but, I didn't exactly give you a choice, did I? I was completely thick-headed and irrational. I have been all along," I admitted with an attempt at a smile. "It was not fair of me to ever ask you not to investigate—to turn against the curiosity of human nature." I had to pause as Mandy's words and my reaction to them came flooding back to me. Luca took my pause as a sign that I wanted a response of some kind.

"So, you aren't mad?" he asked timidly, eyeing me suspiciously.

"Not at you, no," I answered.

"But?"

"I *am* mad...at the situation. But, that's something *I* have to deal with. And I'm trying," I answered as honestly as I could.

"I know you are Violet, but you aren't dealing with this alone. *We* will deal with it. I love you. I hope you still believe that." He cupped my face in his hands.

"I know that. Of course I do," I responded and allowed him to swallow me in his embrace.

We stayed that way for a minute. I could have stayed that way forever. Nothing felt better or more right than being in Luca's arms, his strong hands stroking my hair, his warm breath washing over my neck. However, I had come all this way for more than just a reconciliation, though that was the most important part. I surprised him when I abruptly pulled away and said, "So, don't *we* have somewhere important we need to be?"

"*We*?" he asked.

"Yes. I told you, I want to know too."

"Are you sure? I mean I don't even know how credible this

source is...Dexter found him—" He stopped suddenly, obviously waiting for my reaction to Dexter being in on this whole scheme. I think I surprised him again by not reacting the way he expected.

"Luca, credible source or not, I think I am ready to accept what I am...what we are." He gaped at me.

"Luca?" I searched his eyes for some sign of what he was thinking. "Are you alright?" I asked.

He blinked a few times then answered. "Uh yeah I think...I think so." Then there was another pause. "You...what do you mean you know '*what we are?*'" he asked. "You don't..." he couldn't finish.

"Luca. I'm not stupid. I put the pieces together so long ago. I just wouldn't let myself believe it was true. You can't tell me you don't think the same thing?"

"You know I do. I just can't believe you're saying this."

"Yeah well, it's a new me," I said wryly.

"What brought on this change?" he asked.

"I don't know. I guess I just realized that you can't fight fate, and if I have to be *this*," I surveyed myself, "at least I'm *this* with you." He smiled and held me to him again.

We were ready for a subject change, at least for a little while. Like Mandy said, we'd have plenty of time to deal with the details later. "So, where is Dexter anyway?" I looked around. I knew he had to be close by.

"I think he's being nice and letting us make up," Luca explained. "We are making up, aren't we?" he asked shyly. I answered him by reaching up, wrapping my arms around his neck and kissing him fiercely. A few minutes later, while Luca and I continued to make up, I heard Dexter's unmistakable dragging footsteps approaching. I released Luca, and he walked in the direction of Dexter's footsteps.

I leaned back on the heels of my hands on the hood of Luca's car, feigning indignation. Then Dexter appeared from behind the warehouse closest to us. He hung his head and wore the sheepish look of a child who has just told an unbelievable lie. He didn't look up as he continued to approach. I couldn't stand it. I had to end his misery.

I wiped the mock anger from my face and replaced it with genuine forgiveness. I stood up and walked over to meet him. Without giving him time to react, I grabbed him in an embrace and squeezed. For a fraction of a second he was too stunned to move, but then he relented and placed his arms awkwardly around my back, hugging me like we were long lost friends that had been parted for too long. And that's exactly what we were. When we separated, I looked up at him and smiled, letting him know that all was forgiven. He smiled back. He understood. Dexter always understood.

"Dex, I owe you an even bigger apology than I owe Luca. Everything you said was exactly right."

"V, just stop, we both said a lot of stupid stuff we didn't mean," he protested.

"No, I have to say this to you. I owe you this."

"You don't owe me anything, V."

"I do. You were right. I always let you fight my battles for me, and I was weak. *I* was the one being selfish. Yeah, my life hasn't turned out the way I would have planned, but so what? Whose does? Besides, in a lot of ways, it's turned out better. Okay, I have weird abilities, and I am probably not exactly...*human,"* I sucked in a short breath. I hadn't ever said that part out loud, and it startled me. Dexter's eyes snapped open wide, and he shook his head in disbelief. I heard Luca take a quick breath. I continued, "but I have the most loyal, accepting friend anyone could ask for."

I turned to address Luca. "And I have you. I know you say we were attracted to each other before we realized we were...well, whatever we are, but the truth is, if we hadn't *connected,* who knows? I can assure you that I would have never acted on my feelings, and if you had acted on yours, I probably would have just ignored you or thought you were joking." I snorted a little humorless laugh while Luca shook his head as if to say that I was wrong. But I wasn't wrong.

"So, I know I have not behaved well. I've been childish and irrational and selfish, and I am very, very sorry, to both of you," I said, hopefully closing the lid on the old Violet, and making way for a new, stronger, more rational version of myself.

"You are totally and completely forgiven," Dexter said. Then he ruffled my hair and took a few steps away, giving Luca a chance to forgive me too. As he stepped in front of me, I looked up at him apologetically, but with a new sense of determination.

"You already know how I feel. I don't think you have anything to be forgiven for, but if it will make you happy, I formally forgive you," he said and then took a silly, over-exaggerated bow.

"Stop it," I laughed. "Get up." I pulled him up to standing and rolled my eyes at him, but we were both laughing.

Dexter wandered back over, and the three of us stood in silence for a minute, unsure of our next move. I knew that Luca and Dexter were waiting for me, so I would have to be the one to initiate whatever came next. "Okay, so let's go." I loaded my voice with as much enthusiasm as possible. That put the two of them in motion. Dexter got in the back on the driver's side, and Luca didn't miss a beat. He was at my door before I could get there. I smiled. Things were going to be fine. He opened my door, and before I climbed in, I reached up on my toes and gave him the quickest kiss. He smiled as I ducked into the car.

Dexter was reading directions from his phone. "So, we need to go about twelve more miles down this road," he said as he craned his neck from the back seat. He pointed straight ahead to where the warehouses ended and the desolate two-lane road continued. "Then it says we go west on Ogden for like fifteen minutes. It shouldn't be too far." I looked to where he was pointing. The sun was almost finished setting, leaving the sky a beautiful blazing, orangey-pink, growing gradually darker as my eyes followed it upward.

"So, where are we anyway?" I asked.

"Um...we're somewhere between Ogden and Milton," Luca answered.

"Basically the middle of nowhere," Dexter added.

I was amazed. "But that's like fifty miles from Lake Hansen!"

"Yeah, so?" Dexter commented.

"Dexter, you know how I got here," I reminded him.

"You...NO WAY!" His face was pure excitement. "No way you flew all the way here!?"

I nodded and smiled smugly, though I was just as shocked as he was. I never felt like I was going that fast or far. I didn't even know I was capable of going that far!

"But, how?" he asked again. I guess I had never stopped to think about how unbelievable all of this was to someone *on the outside*.

I looked at Luca. He also looked eager to hear my answer.

"I really don't know." I paused to think. "I mean once I made the mental connection..." Uh-oh. I'd said too much. Dexter's face said it all. Luca and I had never told him about the telepathy or the fact that we could *find* each other. "Dexter, I'm sorry. We should have told you. It's just..." I didn't know what to say.

"It's okay, V. I get it. And a few months, or weeks, ago, it probably would have destroyed me. But, you know it's all good." Then he got excited again, "So, tell me about it. Can you like, read each other's minds or what? I mean I know you can't read mine because there have been times you would have been way more pissed at me, maybe even like literally, threw me out of the house," he laughed.

I felt instant relief. Luca, who hadn't let go of my hand since he'd gotten into the car, gave it a squeeze. *Phew!* he thought to me. I looked at him and smiled.

"Hey, no fair! I am RIGHT here!" Dexter growled, noticing our exchange.

"Whoops. Sorry," I said.

"So, are you going to answer my question or what?" he pressed, anxious and demanding.

We are *going to talk about your flight later, right?* Luca thought to me, while keeping his eyes on the road.

I didn't answer with a thought, just a quick sideways glance. I knew he saw me because he narrowed his eyes and arched one eyebrow.

Giving nothing away of our brief communication, Luca responded to Dexter.

"Well, we can't actually *read* each other's minds like you're thinking," he explained.

"Yeah, we kind of direct thoughts to one another and...well, we can find one another, like I found you and Luca today. Like some kind of homing device. Like GPS," I tried to explain. It was a lot harder than I'd imagined it would be.

"So, you can't just take a look inside each other's minds whenever you feel like it...no eavesdropping?" he asked eagerly.

"That's not entirely true." Luca eyed me cautiously. My eyes widened a bit. He was probably referring to the fact that when we used this internal homing device, it sort of left an *open channel* into our thoughts. So, I knew he was basically apologizing to me for *taking a peek* while I was looking for him. I smiled to let him know it was alright. After all, I knew the risks when I set out to find him, and at this point, there was nothing I wouldn't share willingly anyway. So, it really didn't matter. I hoped my face could convey all of that.

"What do you mean?" Dexter asked urgently.

"What Luca means is that at certain times, like when I was actively searching for him, my mind was *open*—meaning he could basically see inside if he *chose* to." I stressed the last two words, and I kept my eyes on Luca while I said them. Dexter seemed to understand what I meant. He couldn't hide his struggle: should he press me for more information (which he was clearly dying to do), or should he let it go, and let me off the hook?

Dexter wasn't so tormented. He had only one goal: get more information.

"Okay, so when she was looking for us, did you know right away? Is that why you pulled over?" he asked Luca.

"Probably not immediately, but pretty quickly I'd bet. I can't explain it well, but I felt her *presence* in my mind," he explained. "I have gotten so used to what it feels like to have her thoughts come to me." He smiled as if he were remembering something, then kept going, now directing his explanation to me, "But I knew it wasn't a thought because I didn't see the light."

"The *what*?" Dexter asked, perplexed.

"Oh, well when we channel our thoughts, we each have a color that accompanies the thoughts themselves. It's like a shimmering light, sort of...," Luca paused, "this is hard, um..." He looked to me for help. I had been thinking about what Luca said, about knowing that I was coming. It brought up so many questions. But I decided to help him out first.

"Dex. It's like when I hear a thought from Luca, I hear it almost like you would hear any external sound, but I also hear it like it's my own thought. Then, along with it, my brain sort of fills with a silvery-blue light." I think I explained it effectively because I looked back and Dexter was slowly nodding his head, a look of deep-thought etched across his face.

"I think I get it. What color is your light?"

"Purple," Luca answered for me. "Like...violet," he

smiled.

"Hmm. So, when you knew Violet was coming for us, did you tell her where we were? Is that how she found us...you?" Dexter asked Luca.

"No," Luca and I answered in unison. Then only Luca said, "But I pulled over when I knew she was close by so it would be easier for her to get to us."

"Uh...I thought maybe it would be better if...if I didn't say anything." He turned to me now. "I kind of saw a little of what happened with Mandy, or at least I saw what you were thinking about." He paused. "And I wasn't sure if you were ready to hear from me." I swallowed and bit my lip as I felt the pink rising in my cheeks. I worried about what he might have seen or heard. He moved his eyes back to the road. Dexter sat back in his seat and had already put his earbuds in to give us privacy.

"I promise I wasn't prying. I felt you in here..." He pointed to his temple, "...and I just wanted to make sure you were okay. I knew you weren't sending me a thought so I assumed you weren't ready to talk."

"Thanks. You were right," I sighed, relieved that he had left me to my thoughts.

"Can I ask you something?" he asked after a moment of silence.

"Of course."

"Are you okay? I mean I know that whatever went on with you and Mandy, it made you upset."

I let out a long breath before answering. I had been so fixated on finding Luca that I hadn't thought much about the things that Mandy said to me.

"Hang on," I said with a finger up. I reached back and popped out one of Dexter's earbuds. "Dex, I want you to hear this."

"Uh, okay." He looked surprised, but elated.

"Mandy knows. I don't know what or how much, but she's not

completely in the dark, that's for sure. She alluded to knowing I was 'different' and that I had to 'find out who I was.'" I looked directly into Dexter's eyes. The benefit of knowing someone as well as I knew Dexter, is knowing when they were lying.

"I swear, Violet, I didn't say anything. She asked what was up and I told her you and Luca were fighting about him wanting to go somewhere you didn't want him to go." He was so defensive, and I decided, so innocent.

"I believe you Dexter. I'm at a loss. I guess we'll have to deal with all that later. Right now we have to get where we're going and deal with something else," I said with a note of dread.

We drove along silently for a few minutes, each lost in one thought or another. Dexter broke the silence. "So Violet, you never did explain how you got here!" Luca and I laughed, but I knew he would demand an answer.

"I told you, I flew," I said, trying to sound nonchalant (which is impossible when you're talking about having actually *flown* somewhere).

"Yeah I know, but I didn't know you could go that far." Now Luca's eyes were on me expectantly too.

"I don't know. While I was flying, I had no idea how long I was up there or how fast I was going." I bit my lip. Luca and Dexter were both looking at me like I was on fire. It made me uncomfortable, but I continued. "Well, I chalk it up to determination, I guess. I *had* to get here. And we've never really tested how fast or how far." I explained. Although inside I was just as curious as they were. There were questions, tons and tons of questions. I stared out the window as we drove toward the answers.

27

We had been on a desolate stretch of road for a while when Dexter spoke up, "According to this, it should be like five more minutes up the road on the right." He studied his phone, "Damn it!"

"What?" I spun around to see what was wrong.

"Damn service went out again!"

"This is getting ridiculous. It's like every other day, and if I can't get through to Mandy, she'll freak," I explained.

"You texted her after you got to us, right?" Luca asked me.

"Yeah. I told her not to expect us until the morning, at least. She said, 'ok be safe,' so I guess she's okay with that," I said. But it was all too weird. Mandy was okay with us being gone all night. I guess whatever she assumed we were dealing with would supersede any of her fears about Luca and I being alone together.

"Well, it doesn't matter now. It should be right up here, where that pond is." Dexter gestured in the direction of what looked like the entry of a driveway.

Luca put on his turn signal and made a right turn. I gasped at what I saw. I had imagined that a reclusive *extraterrestrial guru* would live in some stereotypically weird house, almost a shack, dilapidated with random items scattered around, like a junkyard. But this place was amazing. It was like something out of a fairy tale. It was small, but elegant. There was a lot of very natural-looking wood and glass, almost like a log cabin and a cottage were somehow fused together. It seemed to fit right into the landscape. "Are you sure this is it?" I asked. This could *not* be it.

"That's what the directions said. My phone's back and I just checked again." Dexter was also staring at the house in awe.

"This place is amazing," Luca said as he pulled the car up the driveway and put it in park.

"So we just go up to the door and say, 'could you tell us what you know about aliens?'" I asked, now feeling more apprehensive than ever.

"Yeah, I talked to the guy online and then on the phone, and he was cool with us coming after I kind of explained the situation." As Dexter said this, my eyes shot open wide.

"You told him?" I yelled. "What if he's like some psycho or like those hiker guys?" I continued.

"Violet, calm down!" he yelled back. "I would never tell someone *your* secret," he said, his voice lower. I breathed a relieved sigh.

"Sorry," though I didn't sound apologetic. "You said you explained the situation, so I just assumed..."

"Well, you assumed wrong," he said, now obviously pissed off.

"What did you tell him, Dexter?" Luca asked much more calmly than I had.

"I told him that I was really interested in all that stuff and that I thought I might be a...whatever you are," he admitted.

"You said it was you?" I was shocked. "That's just as dangerous, Dex."

"It's gonna be fine, V, trust me, I have a really good feeling about this," he said confidently. I guess at this point I didn't have much choice.

"I hope you're right," was all I could say to him.

"I trust Dexter," Luca said, though I wasn't sure if he was just trying to assure me, or if he was telling me the truth. Either way, it didn't matter; we were sitting in this guy's driveway, a few yards away from someone who may be able to shed some light on what was happening to us. I saw some movement behind the big picture window in front. I couldn't make out anything definite from the glare and the tint, but I assumed whoever it was, was aware of our arrival and wondering why we hadn't gotten out of the car yet.

Ready? Luca asked me silently.

I took his hand in response. "Let's get this over with," I said with all the enthusiasm I could find.

We spilled out of the car and moved silently to the front door. The long pathway leading to the door was almost as beautiful as the house. It was covered in a canopy of ancient trees. Like the Japanese garden at Nature Park, there was a footpath of tiny pebbles that crunched when my feet landed on them, no matter how softly I stepped. A pair of rough-hewn wooden benches lined one side of the path while low, lush vegetation bordered the house. There were dim lights embedded in the ground all along the path. I couldn't help but look all around me while I moved hand-in-hand with Luca. If our purpose for being there had been different, it might have even been romantic.

When we reached the very large wooden door, I took a deep breath as Dexter grasped the heavy iron knocker and banged three times against the metal plate behind it. I could hear footsteps coming toward the door, and in those last seconds before it opened, my mind flipped through a thousand mental images I had of who might be on the other side. For some reason, it settled on Comic Book Guy from *The Simpsons*. I was glad because just before the door swung open, I had to suppress a smile, lightening my mood and easing my anxiety, if only for a fraction of a second.

Then the door opened, and the man who stood before us was nothing, I mean *nothing,* like what I would have *ever* imagined!

This man who greeted us was not a middle-aged, overweight, wild-haired loon, but a very normal-looking, *very* attractive, young man with a warm smile and friendly eyes that told us instantly that he was glad to see us. He had shaggy, sand-colored hair and bright eyes. His skin was bronzed from the sun like someone who spent a lot of time outdoors.

"Hi, Mr. Austen?" Dexter asked as he stuck out his hand.

"Yes. You are Dexter?" he asked in reply as he firmly shook Dexter's hand, studying him all the while.

"Yeah, I'm Dexter Schultz and these are my friends, Violet and Luca." Dexter motioned to the two of us standing beside him. When Mr. Austen looked at me and Luca with the same scrutiny as he had Dexter, his eyes grew wide, like he was surprised by something he saw. He quickly composed his face back into the friendly, welcoming look he wore when he opened the door, and stuck out his hand. But by this time, my face had flushed pink.

"Luca, Violet. It's nice to meet both of you." He shook our hands warmly. "Come on in, I'll get you something to drink and we can talk." He showed us into the front entryway which was seriously amazing.

The floor was slate, but not squares set in neat, geometric patterns, but natural, rough shapes. Each piece looked as if it had been sliced right off of the side of a mountain and thrown down onto the floor of this magnificent house. The walls, where there wasn't a large pane of glass, were honey-colored wood, also looking unfinished and finished at the same time with knot-holes and grain. It was the most beautiful place I'd ever seen.

"Your house is...amazing," I said to Mr. Austen.

"Thanks. I love it too. Built it myself. Took me three years," he said proudly as he looked all around at his handiwork.

"You did this yourself?" Luca asked in amazement.

"Well, I had a little help here and there, but, yeah I did most of it on my own," he smiled.

We all stood in the wide open living room, which seemed to be the main space of the house. I looked up and saw a loft above us, and wondered what that room was used for. Mr. Austen jolted me from my daydreams about living in a house just like it someday. "So, you are here to find out some information, right?" he asked, without taking his eyes off of me and Luca.

"Uh, yeah. We have questions about...extraterrestrial experimentation on humans," Dexter said as easily as if he were asking him what kind of wood he used to build the house.

At that, Mr. Austen's eyes left me and Luca. He nodded at Dexter. "How 'bout I get us some coffee and we sit out on the back deck?" he asked. We all nodded in agreement and followed him to the back of the house where two glass panels seemed to just open up and become the outside. "Make yourselves comfortable and I'll get those drinks," he said.

The three of us walked out to the well-lit deck and found seats. Luca, who hadn't said much since we arrived, sat very close to me —protectively close. Maybe he had also noticed the way Mr. Austen had stared at us, or maybe he had noticed me staring at Mr. Austen. Either way, it was clear that he was making an effort to show that he and I were together. A few minutes later, Mr. Austen came out with a tray of mugs which he placed on the table.

"Mr. Austen—" Dexter began.

"Please, call me Eli," he interrupted.

Luca got right to the point, "Eli, we need to know what you know and how you know it." Dexter and I both shot Luca a surprising look, and then I thought to him, *Relax, Luca, you're going to scare him.* I squeezed Luca's hand again to reassure him. He breathed slowly and I felt his hand relax a bit.

Sorry, he thought to me. I heard Dexter sigh. Now that he knew about the telepathy, he knew what to look for. He rolled his eyes at me.

Eli raised his eyebrows for just a second, probably surprised by

Luca's candor. He quickly recovered, flowing right into his answer. "Well, those are two very different things. And I guess I would like to know a little bit more about why I should tell you," he countered. He didn't seem like he was trying to be rude, just cautious. I understood his reservations. Here were three strange teenagers who had sought him out and showed up at his door one night, asking for answers. He had reason to be cautious.

I wanted to smooth things over before our visit became pointless. "Mr. Aus—sorry, Eli, I know us being here is strange, and I totally understand your caution...it's been the way I have lived my entire life, but I'm just gonna come clean and tell you...I think I'm not completely human." I took a deep breath so that I would be able to continue, ignoring the feeling like I had just been punched in the stomach. "If you can help to clarify any part of what's going on for me, I would be very appreciative."

All eyes were on me, and all mouths hung open. They and I could not believe what I had just said. What had I just said? Had I just told a stranger that I might not be completely human?

"I...I...I don't know wha—are you saying you are a...a real...*hybrid*?" Eli finally stammered. "*Hybrid*?" Until that second, I hadn't had a word for it. Hybrid. Part human, part...what?

"Both of us, actually," Luca spoke up, clearing his throat and putting his arm firmly around my shoulders again. Eli just sat there blinking. After a few minutes of silence, he found his voice.

"It's just that until now, you've been a...a theory, a remote possibility," he said, his eyes wide and watery with excitement and possibility.

"I'm not absolutely sure that we are...what *you* think we are, but there's a very strong possibility," I explained.

"I noticed the tone to your skin and your slightly larger than normal black eyes..." Eli explained. "Of course, that doesn't exactly prove anything. Is there anything else that makes you believe that you're a hybrid?" Eli looked at me. I looked at Dexter pleading with him to not say anything until I decided what I should say.

Luca, what should we say? I asked silently. He didn't answer me, instead he answered Eli.

"We have certain...abilities," Luca said without elaborating. I shot him a cautious look.

"Like?" Eli asked.

"We're really strong and— and our skin is very thick," I said in a rush, "Not impenetrable, but thick."

Eli responded with, "Hmm." As his brow furrowed and his lips pursed together tightly in thought.

Then I did something so shocking, there was no turning back, I disappeared. Well, actually I levitated, but to Eli (and Dexter), I had vanished. With no warning to anyone I just began to lift up from my seated position. I allowed myself to get about five feet up and then just stopped, hovering in mid-air. The silence was profound. From my invisible perch above them, I watched Eli's eyes open wide. Luca was the only one who could see me. I nodded to him, and I knew he understood because I heard him ask, "Yeah, so can you help us?"

Without taking his eyes off the spot where I had been, he responded, "I think I can." Then he looked at Luca and smiled.

"Good," Luca replied. Then I slowly brought myself back down and reappeared

"For a very long time now, decades, and in some cultures, centuries, there have been people who have believed that extraterrestrial life forms visited Earth and *altered* the human species," Eli began to explain after the initial shock of my disappearing act had worn off.

"Is that what the missing link stuff is all about?" I interjected, remembering that torturous day in biology, not so long ago.

"Some think so," he continued. "Like I said, the beliefs vary from culture to culture; some specific ones prevail in the *ET community*. Some believe that modern man was already well on his way to developing, and the aliens simply *enhanced* him and sped up the process, presenting themselves as gods to the new species, and helping him develop more...depth or intelligence. Others believe that extraterrestrials have participated in a wide variety of *activities* on our planet from mining operations to exploration, to genetic experimentation—the results of which would be hybrids," he said nodding toward me and Luca.

"And then there are some who believe it goes back even further —that humans as we know them would not exist in their current form at all if these ETs hadn't seriously altered some prehistoric species that were far from current humans, and that they may have initially even been created as a slave labor force that developed beyond what the ETs had anticipated."

We all sat there absorbing this information. "The first and last of these theories supposes that all humans are, therefore, infused to some degree with alien DNA, some more than others depending on where your origins lie."

"So what do you believe?" Luca asked.

Eli laughed. Just a quick chuckle. "Well, I guess I lean toward the first and second. I think extraterrestrials probably did visit early man and then came back for many different reasons over the course of our history," he said. I saw Dexter nod in agreement.

"And what about...*us*? Where do we fit into all this?" I asked in a whisper. Even though I had spent most of my life living with Mandy's theories, it had always felt *not real*, or at the very least, *very, very far away.* Now it was real and close. Too real. Too close.

"Good question," he said, then paused before going on. "Like I said before, hybrids like you, are something that many of us in the *community* have believed existed, but with no real proof. And to what extent others may exist, no one really knows." He paused,

"I would guess you are both about seventeen or eighteen?" he asked.

"Eighteen this past May," I answered.

"May," Luca confirmed.

"So that means you would have been conceived...during the time of the mass sightings," he clarified. The thought of when I had been *conceived* was not something I ever really thought about, and didn't really ever want to. Eli continued, "We believe at that time, the ETs impregnated women on our planet with embryos that were composed of both human and alien DNA."

I was beyond words. If I hadn't been sitting down, I would have needed to. This information confirmed everything Mandy had ever said about the abduction, the experimentation... *It's all real Luca, isn't it?* I thought to him. He looked at me and nodded. Eli caught this and looked at us puzzled.

"We can communicate telepathically," I said flatly.

"Just another perk," Dexter said dryly

"Unbelievable!" Eli whispered.

"Yup," I agreed unenthusiastically.

"So can you tell us anything else?" Luca asked Eli.

"What do you want to know?"

"How do you know all this? How does 'the community' know all this? And who they?" Dexter asked.

"Like I said before, some cultures have been telling stories about ETs for centuries, and there has been *underground* research on this stuff for decades. It's only recently that some of these researchers have begun to go public. Of course, they are shunned by the mainstream and labeled as lunatics. And the community is a generic term that describes some tightly and some loosely affiliated groups of these researchers and enthusiasts."

Leave it to Dexter to ask the question everyone else is thinking but no one has the nerve to ask, "So how did you get involved in this stuff? You seem pretty normal." I covered my face with my hand,

Luca fought back a smile, and thankfully, Eli laughed.

"Thanks Dexter. I think I'm pretty normal," he responded lightly, but then continued with his explanation. "Well, I was an archaeology student when I was first introduced to these theories. My goal was to become the one who found the definitive answer to human origins. I had a professor in graduate school, Dr. Anderson Gideon, whom I respected and admired. He was as well-known for his odd demeanor, as much as he was known for his work in the field. He was like many very intelligent people—a little eccentric. That's what I liked about him. His classes were never dull, and his research trips were awesome. But, he was fired because he wrote a controversial book, under a pseudonym.

"In it, he put forth the theory that humans had been *helped* in their development. He had done extensive research, cited ancient texts, poured through centuries of stories and histories from ancient cultures."

Luca cut in, "I think I might have read it, was it *The Making of Man*?" he asked.

"That's it," Eli confirmed with a smile that told Luca he was impressed. I looked at Luca, remembering the first time I had been in his room and his seen collection of books.

Eli continued, "As you can guess, the scientific community scoffed at it. He was eventually found to be the author, he lost credibility, was ridiculed, and eventually fired. I didn't jump to defend him. In fact, I was shocked. I thought he'd lost his mind, and I wanted nothing to do with him. After all, my career hadn't even begun yet and associating myself with him would have been a death sentence." He paused, and I sensed a bit of shame still left in him.

"Then one day, I came across the book in a used book store. On a whim, I picked it up and began to read. Before I knew it, I found myself captivated by it. It all seemed to make so much sense. Of course, I maintained some skepticism. So when I was done, I did a little research of my own, checked his sources, his references. I found that everything he had written was basically true, and in the end, I agreed whole-heartedly with his theories," he explained. I couldn't help wondering if one of the books on our shelves at home was by Professor Gideon.

"So what did you do?" Dexter asked, his face eager.

"I did what I thought was right...I found him, and the community. I continued his research, and began some of my own, while trying to maintain anonymity."

This made me want to ask a question, "Are you ashamed of your beliefs? Is that why you want to be anonymous?" I could understand not wanting to put a spotlight on these particular beliefs.

Eli smiled at me, "No, not ashamed, just...realistic. I know what the mainstream scientific community thinks, or at least what they aren't willing to admit, and so in order to maintain some sort of respectful reputation, I have kept my name out of it. Professor Gideon said that since his reputation was already destroyed, we would just attribute the research and findings to him. This way, I could stay up to date on what mainstream archaeology was finding."

When he said it, it sounded so simple. Almost normal. I yawned. I was physically and mentally depleted. I had a million more questions, and I'm sure Luca and Dexter did too, but their faces told me they were as exhausted as I was.

You okay? Luca asked.

Yeah, just so tired. Can we be done for tonight? Please, I pleaded.

He didn't answer me directly, instead he spoke to all of us. "I can't speak for everyone but myself Violet, but we've had a really long day, and I think we are going to call it a night. If it's okay with you, we'll come back tomorrow when we've had a chance to process all of this and sleep," he said as he got up.

"Of course," Eli said. "But, there aren't any hotels for...well, there really aren't any hotels."

"That's okay, I brought camping gear for me and Dexter. We can make room for Violet." Luca put his arm around me and pulled me toward him.

"Great, camping with you two again," Dexter mumbled sarcastically.

"Don't be ridiculous," Eli interjected. "Stay here. It's already late. By the time you find a decent site, get your tents up, it'll be morning," he argued. "I have plenty of room. You are welcome to it."

He was so sincere, I would have felt bad for saying no, and I was so exhausted. This time I spoke for everyone, "Are you sure? We don't want to impose."

"No imposition. I promise." I don't know why I trusted him, I just did. I guess this was one of those rare moments where I saw the good in a person and proved I was Mandy's daughter.

Violet, are you sure? We don't know this guy, Luca asked me.

Luca, he's harmless, we're exhausted...Oh yeah, and we have superpowers, remember? I replied.

"Okay, if you don't mind," Luca answered.

"There's a spare room off the kitchen, and then there's the couch," Eli told us.

"My favorite," Dexter said flatly. Eli raised an eyebrow.

"We'll take the room if that's okay with you Dex?" Luca said.

"Oh yeah, that's fine." More sarcasm. As if Luca and I could even fathom having sex in a stranger's house—a stranger who basically just confirmed that Luca and I were half-alien hybrids. I don't think so.

"I don't care where I sleep, I just need to sleep!" I finally said, having lost all patience.

Eli showed Luca and me to a small guest room where there was a wooden bed that matched the nature theme of the rest of the house. It looked as if it had been carved into the room. Huge windows created almost one wall of the room. They were covered with opaque shades that fit each window perfectly. Eli showed us how to use a remote control to raise and lower them.

Off to the side of the room was a small bathroom with a shower that was also completely glass, only this glass was thickly frosted. "Feel free to shower. There are towels under the sink," Eli said before wishing us goodnight.

I texted Mandy to let her know we were safe and told her I'd call her in the morning. Luca and I got ready for bed. He had brought a few extra t-shirts and boxers, so at least I had something to change into to sleep. It wasn't however until Luca came into the room wearing a pair of boxers and nothing else that I realized that he and I were about to spend the night together for only the second time ever. Though I knew without any doubt that nothing would happen, my stomach still began to do little flips and dips at the sight of him. Luca took one look at me in his too big t-shirt and smiled.

"What?" I asked, turning pink.

"Nothing. You just...you look cute."

"Cute?" I asked, shaking my head.

"Yeah, cute," he said, climbing into the bed. "Come on, it's late. Let's get some sleep." He motioned for me to join him. I slowly peeled back the covers and got in next to him. He clicked off the bedside light, and we lay there in the dark, breathing and thinking.

Luca always seemed to know my emotions even better than I did. Of course he knew that the day and night had drained me. So, I was relieved when he slid closer to me and pulled me into his arms. I felt my whole body relax. *I am so proud of you. I love you,* he said silently, and kissed my cheek.

I turned slightly and kissed him on his lips. *I love you too.* I snuggled into him more deeply and fell asleep.

28

I woke up at the first sign of sunlight. I should have slept longer. I needed to sleep longer. But I was in a strange place physically and mentally, therefore, I was awake. Luca was still asleep, and I didn't have the heart to wake him, so I got up, slipped on my jeans and intended to go out to the back porch. I was intercepted by Eli in the kitchen. I must have been groggy from lack of sleep not to have heard him, so seeing him startled me, and I gave a little gasp

"Good morning, Violet." He looked up from making coffee and smiled at me warmly. I was still having trouble reconciling this attractive, young guy with the UFO-loving weirdo I had expected.

"Uh...good morning. Sorry, I was just gonna go out to the porch. I didn't mean to disturb you," I said.

"You're not. I'm just making coffee. Luca and Dexter still sleeping?" he asked.

"Yeah, Dexter can sleep anywhere, under any circumstances, and Luca camps a lot, so I guess he's used to sleeping in strange places...not that your house is strange...I just meant—"

"Relax, Violet. I know what you meant," he laughed. "Want some coffee?"

"No thanks."

"How about tea?" he countered.

"Tea would be great, thank you."

I waited silently in the kitchen, not sure what to say. After a few minutes, Eli handed me a steaming cup of tea. I nodded and smiled as thanks.

"Mind if I join you? I had some things to ask you last night that I never had a chance to," he asked eagerly

"Sure," I answered with trepidation.

"If you'd rather not talk about it..."

"No, it's out there now, so we might as well talk about it," I shrugged. He led me out to the amazing back porch, only now I could truly see just how breathtaking it was. The porch sat at least fifteen feet off the ground and provided a spectacular view of the woods that ringed the backyard.

"I would love to paint from here," I said without even thinking, breathing in the fresh, clean morning air.

"You're an artist?" Eli asked with real interest.

"Depends who you ask, I guess." I smiled weakly, never taking my eyes off the scenery. I didn't like talking about myself, but Eli didn't know that. "So what did you want to ask me?" I turned to look at him.

"Well, have you always had these abilities?"

"No. Yes. Some of them, I guess. I didn't really know I had them, but once they started to make themselves known, they just sort of...grew exponentially. And then I started to remember things from when I was little, like not getting cuts and scrapes when Dexter was loaded with them," I explained. The faster I could answer these questions, the better.

"You must have thought you were going crazy?" he laughed.

"You can't even imagine," I replied, vividly remembering the day my powers exploded in the bathroom at school.

"No, I can't," he said sadly. "I bet it's been hard to hide them, huh?"

I gave a humorless laugh, "Yeah, you aren't the only one leading a double life." He nodded in understanding.

"So, do you teach somewhere? At a university? I didn't know if one was nearby." I was trying to change the subject and fish for information at the same time. I mean, how could he afford to live all the way out here in this unbelievable house? I'm no contractor, but I know houses like this, whether they are small or not, cost a lot.

"I did very briefly, but I have sort of *dropped out* of the mainstream over the last couple of years, choosing to focus more on the ET stuff."

"No offense, but I can't imagine the UFO business pays very much. Believe me I know, my mother has been *involved* for years," I said with an eye roll.

"Really? So you are familiar with a lot of what we talked about then?"

"No, not really. I have avoided it like the plague. Her lifestyle has made me a social outcast," I groused.

"Understood."

We stood there quietly, looking out over the deck. Then he said, "I have also written a couple of books."

"Like Dr. Gideon's?" I asked, wondering if Mandy or Luca had read his too.

"No actually, I write science fiction novels," he admitted.

"Really?" I looked at him with surprise. I was very interested now. Sci-fi is not my favorite genre, but it was still really cool to be in the presence of a real author. "What have you written?"

"Have you heard of the *New Earth* series?"

"Um, actually yeah, I have." I had seen a display in a bookstore the week before. "Haven't read them though, sorry," I admitted sheepishly. "Kind of *living* through a sci-fi book right now, so reading about it..."

"It's all right." He was smiling again. He was easy to talk to and so genuine. "They've gotten pretty popular. It's a little surreal actually. But I can definitely see why a science fiction book wouldn't exactly be an *escape* for you." His face showed an understanding that I appreciated.

"Yeah," I agreed.

"Could you do me a favor?" he asked.

"Um...yeah, sure." I said apprehensively.

"Could you keep the book thing to yourself? I mean, I write under a pseudonym. Of course, if you want to tell Luca and Dexter —it's just that I'd rather not have other people finding me. Fans can be...intrusive."

How could I say no? This guy had been so welcoming and helpful. Keeping his secret was the least I could do. Besides, who else would I tell? All of my friends? "Of course," I said.

"Thanks."

More silence until something occurred to me, "Isn't the *New Earth* series about aliens taking over Earth or something?"

"Something like that. Actually, knowing what I do now, my books are a little *less* science fiction than I thought." He smiled and raised his eyebrows. More silence. When I looked over to Eli, he was looking at me strangely. Too intensely. It made me self-conscious, so I looked away again and slung my hair over my reddening face. I guess he noticed.

"Sorry, I wasn't trying to make you uncomfortable, it's just, you are *very* interesting."

We stood silently again. I was looking for an easy excuse to leave the porch now, get back to Luca, but Eli wasn't done.

"I just mean...I always wondered what a hybrid—if they existed —might look like, be like, and you aren't at all what I expected," he explained. And even though there was nothing overtly wrong with the words he used, something in his tone, or the way he looked at me made me feel uneasy.

"Neither is Luca," he quickly tacked on. Maybe I was just imagining things. I am someone, some*thing* he didn't even know existed, so maybe that's why he was acting so strangely.

"Oh, well, thanks...," I mumbled. His explanation didn't make me feel any better.

"Sorry, that sounded...weird. I didn't mean for it to. Forget I said it," he pleaded. Now he looked uncomfortable.

"It's okay," I said with my head turned back to the woods.

He cleared his throat, "So about what I wanted to talk—ask —you..." He apparently realized that he'd said more than I was comfortable with and abruptly changed the subject.

"Yes?"

"Why, or how did you disappear last night?"

"Huh, that's a big question." I took a breath, "Well, until recently, I actually didn't know I *could* disappear." I continued explaining to him about how Luca and I showed Dexter how we flew and how we had figured out that we actually disappear when we fly. I also told him that Luca and I could see and hear each other just fine, but that Dexter hadn't been able to see us. The entire time I spoke, he just shook his head in amazement, his eyes widening.

"It's just unbelievable," he kept repeating. "I mean lately with the interruptions, I thought maybe... I just can't beli—"

"Interruptions?" I asked.

"The cell phone and satellite stuff. We've believed it was *them,* maybe coming closer to our planet or purposely interfering with our technology. We aren't quite sure why or exactly what it means, but some think it's significant."

Could all these dropped calls and TV problems really be the result of aliens? "I never considered anything like that," I admitted.

"I know it's a lot, but can I ask you something else?" He had a new look of curiosity on his face.

"Sure, why not."

"Do you make a habit of looking at the clock at double digits?" I raised my eyebrows at his seemingly random question.

"Yeah, I...actually do, why?" How could he have guessed something like that?

"Many of us believe that this is a way that *they* might *check in* on hybrids or even abductees," he explained. "That you are kind of pre-programmed to look at the clock at those odd times. Like a tracking device of sorts."

My face fell. No way! No way! I suddenly felt like I was some sort of robot. I grasped the railing tightly and instinctively looked up to the sky, imagining some unseen beings watching my every move. I felt violated. Could this be real?

"Are you okay?" he asked, following my eyes upward.

"I don't know. This is...I was only able to even admit this all to myself *yesterday*...I mean, I have suspected for months, but no way would I let it be a real possibility. And now you basically confirm my worst nightmare: that I am some half-human, half-alien hybrid freak. And then you tell me that I may have been, *am being* watched or *tracked*. It's unnerving and scary, and...it really sucks!" I was close to tears.

He came up and put his hand on my shoulder. "I'm sorry, Violet. All these years I have been excited at the possibility of your existence, I never really thought about how it would actually affect you." He moved a step closer. I liked Eli, but I didn't want him to comfort me. I wanted Luca. So I sobered up and sniffed back my tears.

"I'm okay. I'm...I'll be fine." I felt some inexplicable need to remind him that I was with Luca. "I guess it's a good thing that I have Luca to go through this with. And Dexter."

He immediately removed his hand and stepped back, apparently sensing the change in my demeanor. "You are lucky. They are obviously two very loyal guys," he said.

"They are." I paused. "In fact, I should go see if they're up. I think I heard Dexter." Without giving him a chance to respond, I quickly left the deck and made my way to Luca.

Dexter was still sound asleep on the couch, earbuds in, mouth hanging open. It made me smile to see him. Over the previous few months, there had been times when I thought Dexter and I were okay, but then something would happen to change things again. But now, ironically, in the midst of pure abnormality, everything felt *normal* again

When I got to the guest room, Luca was still asleep. I could look at him sleeping peacefully forever. Who was I kidding? I could look at him doing absolutely *anything* forever. He was still in the same position he was in when I got out of bed, his already unruly hair splayed out over his forehead and across the pillow. Looking at him, I thought about how he'd react to Eli's apparent interest in me. I also wondered if Eli would show the same interest in Luca as he had in me.

I walked over and sat on the edge of the bed. I gently trailed my fingers through his hair, wanting to wake him but not startle him. He began to stir, and his eyes fluttered open. I could tell he had a brief second of not knowing where he was, but he quickly recovered and turned toward me with a smile. "What are you doing up?" he asked.

"I've been up for a while—talking to Eli," I told him.

"Oh," he said curtly, turning his eyes from me to the ceiling.

"What's wrong?" I asked, though I had already guessed. Luca was jealous. Of course this wasn't something I necessarily minded. Sometimes it was kind of endearing, but other times, like now, it was not.

"Ugghhh!" he growled, "It's just...I'm probably being paranoid and you don't want to hear it."

"Paranoid about what?" I scrunched my nose.

"The way he looked at you—I just didn't like it."

"Oh," I answered simply.

"Aren't you going to call me crazy or say that I am being

ridiculous?"

"You are. It *is* ridiculous. He's a nice guy and he's been really helpful and hospitable," I explained. I don't lie to Luca. Ever. But, it seemed unnecessary to make him angry over something I was pretty sure was a misunderstanding.

"I know, it's just...I don't know what I'm saying...forget it," he said. He shook his head, sat up and ran his hand through his hair.

"I think Eli is just...intense. I mean he just met *hybrids* he had only imagined could exist. It would be like...like...finding out the Easter Bunny is real. It's a lot to take in, ya know?" I smiled. "I don't think it's quite sunk in for me," I said. This seemed to make Luca forget Eli. He looked at me and immediately took my hands.

"Violet, I'm sorry. You're right. I mean, we just found out some unbelievable stuff. And you...you just, are you okay with all of this?" His concern was evident and genuine. "I mean after everything, you are surprisingly...*not* freaking out."

I chuckled once. "*Not* freaking out is subjective," I said, "I guess I kind of figured it out anyway, so hearing it confirmed was sort of...anticlimactic." I laughed again. I couldn't believe I had reached a point where I could actually joke about this. "So, I'm fine," I told him, and for the first time, I believed it.

"See, I told you you're amazing," he said simply, leaning forward to kiss me.

"Yeah well, Eli told me some other stuff too. I'll tell you and Dexter later, but I think we should get going soon. Mandy is going to worry even more if we are too late. Gina too, I'm sure."

It wasn't that I didn't want to tell him anything else, I just felt like we had accomplished our goal and now it was time to leave.

He looked at me curiously, like he really wanted me to tell him whatever else it was that I knew. But, he dealt with waiting. "Okay.

Is Dexter up yet?"

"No, not yet. I'll go get him."

Luca stood up and stretched, and I made the mistake of looking at him before I had a chance to turn around. Him in his boxers and nothing else. I couldn't help but stare. I didn't want to help it. I walked over to him and wrapped my arms around him. "You *never* have to worry about anybody else coming between us," I reached up and kissed him in such a way that let him know I meant it. "Believe me now?"

"I don't know," he joked. "You might have to try a little harder to convince me," he whispered into my ear and kissed me again.

We were still kissing when I heard someone clear his throat. "Do you two ever stop?" Came a familiarly sarcastic voice.

"Shut up Dexter!" I growled with an eye roll and a smile.

"Seriously, is this really the time and place for a love fest?" he replied. I had to laugh. He looked ridiculous with his hair sticking up all over and sleep lines across his cheek.

"We were just saying that it was about time we got going," I told him.

"Yeah that's exactly what it looked like you were telling him." He was laying on the sarcasm extra thick. As usual, I ignored him. Just like a child, this usually made him stop. It worked perfectly. "You sure you want to go? Don't you have more questions or something?"

"Not really. I mean, Eli basically answered the questions we had," Luca answered.

"Yeah, but he probably knows a lot of other cool stuff," Dexter whined. He wasn't done probing Eli, but Luca and I were.

"Maybe," I said.

Dexter must have realized that I was truly done because he changed his tone. "All right, let's go. I guess I can always talk to him online," he pouted.

"Thanks Dex," I smiled. "You two get dressed," I commanded. "I will get all our stuff together, and then we can all say goodbye."

Luca left for the bathroom, and I assumed Dexter went back to the living room to get his clothes. I stayed behind in the guest room, making sure I got all the things we brought and made the bed. A few minutes later, we were all in the living room, ready to go. Eli stayed out of our way. I wasn't sure where he was, but he wasn't in the house, and when I concentrated, I could hear someone banging something around outside. I assumed it was him. As we were about to leave, I heard him trudging up the steps, and then he came striding in from the back porch.

"Leaving already?" he asked.

"Uh yeah, we have to get back, but thanks a lot for letting us stay and helping us out," Dexter said as he walked over to Eli and stuck his hand out. His behavior was nothing short of hero-worship. Eli had obviously made quite an impression on him.

Eli then looked at Luca and me with a strange urgency in his eyes. "Violet, Luca, I need to tell you something very important," he said gravely. "I didn't want to scare you last night, especially before I was sure that you were what you claimed to be." His tone, the look on his face...I was suddenly frightened.

"What is it?" Luca demanded.

"Sit please," he offered, gesturing to the couch, but none of us moved an inch.

"Just tell us," Luca demanded.

"Okay. Well, there are *other* people who believe that you exist. They too are part of the community, but they've been on the fringe for years," he explained. I couldn't help but imagine what kind of people were on the fringe of a UFO community. The thought was unsettling.

Eli continued, "They...they believed you existed, even more so than others of us. But they're... how shall I put this?

Disgruntled."

"What does that mean? They're pissed off at ETs?" Dexter asked.

"I guess you could say that. They are people—abductees and the like—who believe that their *experiences* ruined their lives, ruined relationships, etc. I guess you could say that they suffer from a sort of post-traumatic stress disorder. They are depressed and angry and generally...'pissed off,'" he explained, quoting Dexter. My thoughts instantly turned to Marilyn. No one embodied this description more.

"So, what does that mean for us?" Luca asked. I wondered the same thing.

"Well, they are sure you exist and they are determined to find you, perhaps expose you, and maybe, ultimately, get rid of you," he said solemnly. "We refer to them as *Hybrid Hunters*," he added.

Immediately, my mind started to flip through the last several months, searching for a moment when Luca and I could have been exposed. It took only seconds before I thought to him, *The hikers!*

He looked at me in a way I couldn't quite read. It was as if he was trying to fight his own fear, mask it for my sake. He wasn't quite succeeding. *Violet, we've talked about...don't worry...*He couldn't even finish his thought.

Dexter was talking to Eli. My mind was so preoccupied, I couldn't even focus on what they were saying while Luca and I were communicating. I hoped Dexter didn't say anything to Eli about the hikers. I just wanted to be able to think about it before we talked to someone outside of our little *community* of three. It wasn't that I didn't trust Eli, but knowing that these people might be out there, actively looking for us, made me suspicious of everyone.

"...much do you think they know?" I caught the end of Dexter's question.

"They suspect like the rest of us, but some of them claim that...they were actually carrying hybrid babies, and they had miscarriages and they are now sterile."

I gasped before I could stop myself.

Everyone looked at me. "Our mothers, Luca." It was only after I'd said it that I realized it had been out loud.

"What about them?" Eli asked eagerly.

"After they had us, they were both unable to have kids again," Luca explained.

Eli nodded sadly.

"So do you think it's true...some of these *disgruntled* abductees, do you think they miscarried hybrids?" Dexter turned back to Eli. There was more concern in his voice than I had heard in a while. He had been completely immersed in knowing the origins of mine and Luca's powers that he often forgot that we were actually having to live with them.

"Luca and Violet are living proof that human women have given birth to hybrid children, so it stands to reason that some of these women could have miscarried...maybe their bodies were unable to accept the hybrid or maybe they just miscarried. Whatever the reason, some of these women were emotionally scarred."

"Not all the women who are Hybrid Hunters could have been impregnated, and what about the guys?" I asked, trying to get more information about the hikers.

"Like I said, some are people who claim to have been abducted. Some say they were experimented on. There are even a few who say their spouses were abducted and it changed them so profoundly that their relationships ended," Eli explained further. I knew someone just like that!

"Like I said, pissed off," Dexter simplified it for all of us.

"I guess it doesn't really matter why they're pissed, it just matters that they are and that they want to find us," Luca said. After he said it, he squeezed my hand. Dexter and Eli nodded in agreement.

"So where does that leave us?" I asked. "How worried do we need to be?"

"I wouldn't be too worried," Eli said calmly, "I mean no one else knows, right?" he asked.

We all shook our heads, but I thought of Mandy and what she probably knew. "Be careful online." He looked at Dexter, remembering how they had initially communicated. "They phish for information."

"Okay," Dexter agreed.

"Be careful about using some of your powers where *anyone* can see, obviously," he told me and Luca.

"And Violet," he spoke only to me now. I listened intently. "You said your mom is heavily involved, so be careful. Chances are she associates with people in the Hybrid Hunter movement."

Marilyn, I thought to Luca. He looked up at me solemnly.

"Wouldn't she know? Mandy would never associate with people like th—" Dexter said defensively, but was cut off by Eli.

"Don't be so sure. They like to hide so they can find out as much as possible. Does your mother know about you?" he asked. I didn't know what to say. Dexter shot me a quick look that let me know he was against telling Eli. Dexter always protected Mandy first. Luca said *No* to me instantly.

"I don't think so. Like I told you earlier, I have kept my distance from that aspect of her life," I reminded him of our conversation

"That's good. You should be safe."

"We will be," Luca said reassuringly, his arm tight around me. I believed him. He would always protect me even if I could protect myself just fine. But it was frightening not knowing if, when, or how they might come at us.

"You can contact me at any time. And my door is always open to you if you need a place to go that's out of the way," he said.

We thanked him, shook his hand, and picked up our stuff. Luca and I, hand in hand, with Dexter loping along beside us, headed out filled with more knowledge than we had ever imagined existed.

29

As the ride home began, we were all very quiet, even Dexter. I knew my mind was swimming with "what-ifs" and "oh my gods." When I had left Mandy less than twenty-four hours before, after having an emotional catharsis, I had been willing to accept what seemed like the inevitable. And I did accept it. I didn't like it, and could never see myself embracing it, but I did accept it, which I considered a huge step.

Eli had clarified so much and answered questions I hadn't even thought of asking. I was a hybrid, half human, half—what? Alien seemed like too broad a term. Where were they from? Why did they create hybrids like me and Luca? Where were the others? There had to be others, of that I was certain. But, there were questions upon questions.

It was what I was thinking about, and I was sure it was what Luca and Dexter were thinking about. Luca hadn't let go of my hand since we'd left. He looked straight ahead, occasionally looking over at me with a tight smile. I was certain his mind was on the Hybrid Hunters. Even though the thought of them freaked me out, it was almost too much to take in. I had only just allowed myself to accept what I was, so the thought of some group of people who wanted to confirm my existence and then potentially end it, was just too much. So my mind did the only thing it could do to keep me sane, it blocked them out. I only wished Luca could do the same.

I love you, I thought to him. He looked at me curiously.

What? I asked, confused by his look.

Nothing. It's just, what was that for? he asked.

It was for...nothing. I just felt like telling you. You look stressed, I explained.

He smiled. This time his smile was wider and more genuine. *I'm okay,* he thought to me.

You'd better be. I leaned against his arm. I hoped I'd helped him. He spent so much time helping me, it was my turn. Then it occurred to me that something had shifted in our relationship. I wasn't sure when in the course of the previous twenty-four hours it had happened, but it had. All of a sudden, I wasn't the frightened girl who hid from the truth. I was stronger and smarter and more confident. I was ready to stop being someone who needed constant protection from reality.

Two very long hours later, we arrived back in my driveway. Without warning, a knot formed in my stomach. It wasn't until I saw Mandy's little car sitting in the driveway that I remembered the conversation she and I had the day before—a lifetime before. Had it really only been a day? One single day changed everything. Dexter stirred in the back seat.

"We're home already?" he asked rhetorically, rubbing the sleep from his eyes. How could anyone sleep that much?

"Come on, let's get everything from the trunk," Luca said as he got out of the car. Dexter was already at the back of the car, unloading our things. I still hadn't moved. Luca sat back in his seat. "What's wrong, Violet?" he asked softly, taking my hand and looking concerned.

"I...I don't know what to say to Mandy," I answered simply. He nodded.

"Do you think she'll ask?"

"Probably not. She's too nice. She'll want to give me time. But then I will just be prolonging her pain. She deserves to know," I said. "She *is* my mother."

"Violet, we just went through a lot. Mandy is smart. She'll take one look at you and realize you aren't ready to talk about it. And I know that you'll be ready soon. She'll wait. She loves you." I knew that everything he said was the absolute truth. He continued, "And if she knows about you, she knows about me too, right?" he asked though he knew the answer. I nodded.

"So, you aren't going in there alone. You'll never be alone if you don't want to be. So let's go in there together. Okay?"

"Okay," I said quietly but with a weak smile. I got out of the car and slowly made my way to the trunk to help Dexter carry the supplies.

"It's gonna be okay, V," Dexter said without warning. He made me remember how well he knew me and how easily he could read me.

"I know, Dex. Thanks," I said. "Let's get this over with."

All three of us shuffled into the house, laden with sleeping bags, backpacks, and coolers. I could hear Mandy in the kitchen washing dishes. As soon as the front door closed behind us, she went silent. The water continued to run but she had obviously stopped moving.

I knew Luca heard her too. He set down the bag he'd been carrying and squeezed my arm. *Just relax. It's going to be great.*

"Mandy?" I called out, trying to make my voice sound as normal as possible.

"In here," she replied. "Be right out." I detected the strain in her voice as well, and there was something comforting in knowing she was nervous too. No matter how big a part of her life the UFO stuff was, it wouldn't be easy to learn that your daughter is a human-alien hybrid, implanted in your body without your consent. It was then that her lifetime of pure and utter devotion to me was overwhelming to consider. At that moment, I loved my mother more than I ever had before.

We moved into the living room, depositing our things in a pile on the floor. For a minute we stood around awkwardly, not sure what to do. Then Dexter shed his shoes, plopped onto the couch, remote-in-hand, and brought the TV to life. Luca made a comment about what was on, and he too sat on the couch, paying attention to the TV. He was determined to stay and lend me his support until I was willing to let him go.

The water turned off, and I knew Mandy would be in the living room in seconds. I wasn't sure exactly what I was afraid of, but fear seized me in the pit of my stomach. At Eli's house, the reality was far away. Now we were back to the real world, our world, and a big part of that world was about to be in front of me, desperate for answers.

Mandy rounded the corner, dish towel in her hands, drying the suds from them. At the same time as I did, Luca and Dexter looked up at her. She looked at them first, "Hi guys. Good trip?" she asked.

They both nodded, but neither actually spoke. Then she turned to me. "Hi Mandy," I said sheepishly.

"Hi," she said with a wide smile as she glided over to where I sat on the loveseat and sat next to me. "So...are you okay?" she asked.

I wasn't sure what I wanted to say. I knew I didn't have it in me to tell her everything—not yet, maybe not ever—but I knew I had to say something to comfort her. Her stress level was probably rivaling mine.

"Well, I found *them*." I nodded in the direction of Dexter and Luca who had made themselves practically invisible. But, no matter how quiet they were being, Dexter and Luca were paying attention.

"I'm so glad," she said to me, but then she addressed Luca. "Luca?"

He turned his attention to her. "Yes?" She didn't answer him right away, instead she leaned over and grabbed him in an embrace. He was startled but reciprocated the hug. I sat back smiling, knowing we would all be okay eventually. When she let him out of the embrace, she kept a hold of his arms.

"Thank you, Luca. I know I gave you both a hard time about getting so serious, so quickly. Thank you for caring about Violet and being there for her."

"You don't ever have to thank me for that," he said seriously. "And you're her mother, you're supposed to worry. My mom has done the same. But, I love Violet and I will always be here for her." He was talking to her, but he was looking at me. We were all smiles and hugs, but I knew there were more questions to come.

"And Dexter?" He reluctantly looked to Mandy as she called him. Dexter was not one for gooey compliments, but he couldn't resist Mandy. "Thank you, too. You are the best friend, the best brother, and the best *son* anyone could ever ask for." She knew getting up and hugging him was out of the question, especially since at the word 'son,' his eyes became glassy and he widened them slightly in the universal gesture of attempting to not cry. He had to force himself not to turn back to the TV. In fact, just after he nodded his response to Mandy, he did snap his head back to the direction of the TV, pretending to be engrossed in whatever was on it. Mandy and I shared a smile, both knowing that Dexter had appreciated what she said.

We sat without speaking for several minutes. Then Mandy asked me the question I had dreaded, the question I wasn't sure I had an answer to, "So Violet, besides Luca and Dexter, did you find what you were looking for?" All eyes were suddenly on me.

Instead of grasping for some pseudo-answer, the perfect words found their way into my mind and out of my mouth, "Let's just say, I know who I am."

"And who is that?"

I grinned, "I'm Violet Arena…the girl whose mother believes in aliens."

It was Mandy's turn to shed tears. She laughed and cried and hugged me tightly.

Violet, you are so much more, Luca thought to me. And I knew he was right.

EPILOGUE

Summer was halfway over and life at home was settling into something more comfortable than it had been in a long time. Luca became an almost-permanent fixture in our little family, even spending time with Dexter when I was painting.

Besides spending as much time as possible with Luca, I also spent more time with Mandy. She never brought up my *condition*, waiting patiently until I wanted to talk about it. The problem was, for me, there wasn't really anything to talk about. I am a hybrid, half-human, half-whatever. End of story. Knowing this, acknowledging it, didn't seem to warrant endless discussion. Even Luca and I rarely brought it up unless Dexter asked us to perform some great feat like opening the pickle jar that no one else seemed to be able to budge or listening for the ice cream truck so he could go out to get his cone at the last possible second. He begged us to take him flying again, but we decided it was too soon with the potentially dangerous Hybrid Hunters out there.

Mandy, Dexter, and I went to Luca's house for a cookout. Though I had dreaded it almost as much as I had dreaded facing what I was, it turned out great. Gina and Mandy hit it off, and an unlikely friendship developed between Mr. Verone and Dexter.

Mostly, I spent time immersed in my art. I sketched Luca, decorating the walls of my studio and my room with his form. One evening, Luca was over, playing some video game with Dexter while I painted when the calm and peace I had finally found was disrupted once more. I thought that my earlier realizations had changed everything more than anything else ever could. Oh how wrong I was.

Luca crept quietly into my studio while I had my music blaring. I was so into what I was doing that I didn't even know he was in there until he snuck up behind me and put his arms around my waist, snuggling his nose into the back of my neck. I was startled for a moment, jumping at his touch. But it only took me a second to realize it was him, so I leaned my back into his chest and let his lips trail down the side of my neck.

"Mmmm," I sighed. "Are you and Dexter all done playing?" I tried to tease, but my voice came out breathy and quiet.

"For now," he whispered in between kisses. "I don't want to bother you. You seemed very into what you were painting, which is incredible, by the way." When he said the last words, his head tilted up and away from my neck. He was now focused, I knew, on the painting in front of me. The one I had begun shortly after we returned from Eli's.

It was a self-portrait of sorts, with my face in the foreground, half-obscured in a translucent shadow, behind which the faintest image of a *gray* could be seen (only to those really looking). Behind me was another partially shadowed figure, Luca, also half-obscured in shadow. Surrounding the images were swirls of color that almost seemed to be pulsating with movement.

His arms slipped from my waist, and he moved to stand beside me, taking in all of my unfinished piece. "This is it, isn't it?" He looked at me. I nodded with a half-smile. We both knew what "it" meant. *The* painting. My masterpiece. "Violet, this is beautiful," he gushed. "It's so...so different." I smiled, not because of the flattery, though that was still something for me to get used to. I smiled because I knew he *understood*, really understood what this painting said, what it meant for me.

Aceptacion, I told him, *Acceptance*, not wanting to spoil the moment with spoken words. Without taking his eyes from the painting, he grabbed my hand and gave it the supportive squeeze I had become accustomed to.

We stood that way for a few minutes, just quietly looking at the painting, holding hands, when something strange happened. At once, as if we had to, our eyes both looked to the little digital clock I kept on a shelf in the corner. 11:11 p.m.

For a moment I thought Luca was sending me a thought, as the familiar silvery blue light began to fill my mind. I waited for the words, the thought, but nothing happened. It was when I turned to look at Luca questioningly that he turned to me with the same confused look on his face. I opened my mouth to ask him what was going on, but before I could get the words out, his eyes grew wide, and I knew why.

A new light had appeared in my brain, and I could only assume it had appeared in his, as well. But it was not just one light, but a spectrum of what seemed like hundreds, maybe even thousands of lights, of so many variations of so many colors, it was impossible to give each a name. Almost as quickly as they appeared, they were accompanied by sound. It began as a sort of buzzing jumble, like the rise and fall of a swarm of bees.

Then the din began to take on a more definite quality, to morph into what sounded like words, with different, distinct voices. There were just so many of them that it was nearly impossible to differentiate between them. Occasionally, I would catch an isolated word, and I could swear I heard different languages, maybe a French word, something that sounded like Arabic and Chinese. In an instant, it all made sense to me.

Luca's hand was gripping mine so tightly, I knew he was seeing and hearing the same things. I had always been able to carry on a conversation out loud with someone else at the same time that Luca and I were having one telepathically. But with all the colors and sounds reverberating through my very full brain, I wasn't sure if that would be the case, but I had to try.

"Luca?" I asked. His eyes had been closed tightly, his forehead crinkled in concentration. At the sound of his name, he opened his eyes wide. "Luca, you know what this is." It wasn't a question. He nodded solemnly.

"It's *them,*" he answered in a nearly inaudible whisper.

"*All* of them," I confirmed.

"Violet, what's happening?" he asked me. This was the first time, since we'd met (with the exception of when I'd caught up with him and Dexter before we went to see Eli) that he looked scared—really scared. And I wasn't. I'm not sure why I wasn't afraid, but I wasn't. If anything, I sort of felt a sense of peace—Luca and I really weren't alone.

Hello. A voice cut into my thoughts, overpowering the cacophony of sound. I knew all the others heard it too because suddenly the chattering stopped. Ceased. All at once. Without any warning, I gasped. This new voice had no color.

The new voice continued. *By now you have all become aware of what you are,* it said in an almost robotic voice, like a computer speaking. A flat, generic male voice with neither inflection nor emotion. Luca and I tensed, waiting for more. *We are your creators. We created you almost nineteen years ago and have been monitoring you.*

Then nothing. I assumed that all the others, their points of light still present in my mind, were also processing this information, wondering what would happen now. Then a new voice—brilliant orange, quiet and shaky.

Why? it asked simply.

We assume you are asking why you were created. Our mission was to find life beyond our planet. Then we were to experiment on and improve that life, the same computerized voice explained.

A long silence ensued. Then...

The clocks. Are they part of this? asked a silvery pink, high-pitched voice.

We have used the clocks to track you. Well, that explained a lot. It was just as Eli had said, and it felt a little creepy.

A new voice, male, opaque gray, less shaky, but more defiant asked, *How were we* created*?* He said "created" like it disgusted him, like it was profanity. I completely understood.

For thousands of your years, we have been experimenting with your species. In stages, we incrementally altered your DNA to aid in your evolutionary progress. Your species has contained increasingly larger traces of our species' genetic material. Nineteen years ago, it was decided you were ready for the full-hybrid phase. We found DNA strains that would be most compatible with the hybridization process.

What does that mean? I looked up, shocked. It was Luca's voice.

We took DNA from your male parent, spliced it with our own genetic material and implanted this new embryo into your female parent.

That means, genetically, we are not our mother's children? My brain formed the question before I even had time to process what I was asking.

That is partially correct. There is a minute amount of DNA from your female parent. Just enough to accept the hybrid embryo. That is all the time we have been allotted before your technology detects our presence. We will contact you again.

As quickly as they'd come, the lights disappeared, and Luca and I were alone in my studio.

Without one word or sound or breath, he pulled me into his arms. I clung to him, digging my fingertips into his back, and as a single tear slid down my cheek, I whispered the only word that could escape my lips, "Mandy."

ACKNOWLEDGEMENT

There are so many people to thank who made this book possible. The biggest thank you goes to my husband, who always made sure I had the time and space to write and who listened to every idea and every possible revision. I am grateful to my daughters who inspired and encouraged me and also accepted that sometimes mom was just going to have to lock herself away and write! I am equally grateful to my beta readers over the years: Ed Scanlan, Mark Griffin, and Koni McKinney, to name a few. I am also appreciative for the helpful editing of Erin Young and her attention to detail. My dear friends who have listened and advised (Kate, Megan, Noell, Anne, Bridgette), you're the best! Another special shout-out to Koni McKinney who took my idea for a cover design and used her creativity and flair to make it happen. I also want to thank *Ancient Aliens* for the inspiration!

ABOUT THE AUTHOR

Adria Accomando

Adria is an author, mother, wife, and teacher. Besides fiction, she writes and performs poetry. In her free time, when she isn't writing, she loves to be with her family, travel, read, and spend time outdoors. Adria has lived up and down the east coast but currently lives in Virginia with her family.

Made in the USA
Las Vegas, NV
16 September 2024

95386549R00229